11/17

STILLHOUSE
LAKE

OTHER TITLES BY RACHEL CAINE

The Great Library

Weather Warden

Outcast Season

Revivalist

Working Stiff
Two Weeks' Notice
Terminated

Red Letter Days

Devil's Bargain
Devil's Due

Stand-Alone Titles

Prince of Shadows

STILLHOUSE
LAKE

RACHEL
CAINE

THOMAS & MERCER

Text copyright © 2017 Rachel Caine LLC

Published by Thomas & Mercer, Seattle

www.apub.com

Amazon, the Amazon logo, and Thomas & Mercer are trademarks of Amazon.com, Inc., or its affiliates.

ISBN-13: 9781477848661
ISBN-10: 1477848665

Cover design by Shasti O'Leary-Soudant

Printed in the United States of America

To Lucienne, who immediately believed.

PROLOGUE

GINA ROYAL
Wichita, Kansas

Gina never asked about the garage.

That thought would keep her awake every night for years after, pulsing hot against her eyelids. *I should have asked. Should have known.* But she'd never asked, she didn't know, and in the end, that was what destroyed her.

She normally would have been home at three in the afternoon, but her husband had called to say he had an emergency at work and she'd have to fetch Brady and Lily from school. It was no bother, really—there was still plenty of time to finish up in the house before starting dinner. He'd been so lovely and apologetic about having to disrupt her schedule. Mel really could be the best, most charming man, and she was going to make it up to him; she'd already decided that. She'd cook his favorite dish for dinner: liver and onions, served with a nice pinot noir she already had out on the counter. Then a family night, a movie on the couch with the kids. Maybe that new superhero movie the kids were clamoring to see, though Mel was careful about what they watched. Lily would curl into Gina's side, a warm bundle, and Brady would end up sprawled across his dad's lap with his head up on the arm of the sofa. Only bendable kids could be comfortable like that, but it was Mel's favorite thing in the world, family time. Well. His second-favorite, after his woodworking. Gina hoped that he wouldn't make an excuse to go out and tinker around in his workshop this evening.

Normal life. Comfortable life. Not perfect, of course. Nobody had a perfect marriage, did they? But Gina was satisfied, at least most of the time.

She'd been gone from the house for only half an hour, just long enough to race to school, pick up the kids, and hurry home. Her first thought as she turned the corner and saw the flashing lights on her block was *Oh God, what if someone's house is on fire?* She was properly horrified at the idea, but in the next, selfish second, she thought, *Dinner's going to be so late.* It was petty but exasperating.

The street was completely blocked off. She counted three police cars behind the barricade, their flashing light bars bathing the nearly identical ranch houses in blood red and bruise blue. An ambulance and a fire truck crouched farther down the street, apparently idle.

"Mom?" That was seven-year-old Brady, who was in the back seat. "Mom, what's happening? Is that *our house*?" He sounded thrilled. "Is it on *fire*?"

Gina slowed the car to a crawl and tried to take in the scene: a churned-up lawn, a flattened bed of irises, crushed bushes. The battered corpse of a mailbox lay half in the gutter.

Their mailbox. *Their* lawn. *Their* house.

At the end of that trail of destruction was a maroon SUV, engine still hissing steam. It was embedded halfway into the front-facing brick wall of their garage—*Mel's workshop*—and leaned drunkenly on a pile of debris that had once been part of their solid brick home. She'd always imagined their house as being so firm, so solid, so *normal*. The vomited pile of bricks and broken Sheetrock looked obscene. It looked vulnerable.

She imagined the SUV's path as it jumped the curb, took out the mailbox, slalomed the yard, and crashed into the garage. As she did, her foot finally hit the brake of her own vehicle, hard enough that she felt the jolt all the way through her spine.

"Mom!" Brady yelled, almost in her ear, and she instinctively put out a hand to hush him. In the passenger seat, ten-year-old Lily had yanked her earbuds out and leaned forward. Her lips parted as she saw the damage at their house, but she didn't say anything. Her eyes were huge with shock.

"Sorry," Gina said, hardly aware of what she was saying. "Something's wrong, baby. Lily? Are you okay?"

"What's happening?" Lily asked.

"Are you okay?"

"I'm fine! What's happening?"

Gina didn't answer. Her attention was pulled back to the house. She felt strangely raw and exposed, looking at the damage. Her home always seemed so safe to her, such a fortress, and now it was breached. Security had proved a lie, no stronger than bricks and wood and drywall.

Neighbors had poured out onto the street to gawk and gossip, which made it all so much worse. Even old Mrs. Millson, the retired schoolteacher who rarely left her house. She was the neighborhood gossip and rumormonger, never shy about speculating on the private lives of everyone within her line of sight. She wore a faded housecoat and leaned heavily on a walker, and her day nurse stood beside her. They both looked fascinated.

A policeman approached Gina's vehicle, and she quickly rolled down her window and gave him an apologetic smile.

"Officer," she said. "That's my house there, the one that the SUV crashed into. Can I park here? I need to look over the damage and call my husband. This is just *awful!* I hope the driver wasn't hurt too badly . . . Was he drunk? This corner can be dangerous."

3

The officer's expression went from blank to hard-focused as she spoke, and she didn't understand why, not at all, but knew it wasn't good. "This is your house?"

"Yes, it is."

"What's your name?"

"Royal. Gina Royal. Officer—"

He took a step back and rested his hand on the butt of his gun. "Turn your engine off, ma'am," he said as he signaled to another cop, who came at a jog. "Get the detective. Go!"

Gina wet her lips. "Officer, maybe you didn't understand—"

"Ma'am, turn your engine off *now*." It was a harsh order this time. She shifted the vehicle into park and turned the key. The motor spun down to silence, and she could hear the buzz of conversation from the curious onlookers gathering on the far sidewalk. "Keep both hands on the wheel. No sudden moves. Are there any weapons in the van with you?"

"No, of course there aren't. Sir, I have my kids in here!"

He didn't take his hand off his gun, and she felt a surge of anger. *This is ridiculous. They have us mixed up with someone else. I haven't done anything!*

"Ma'am, I'm going to ask you again: Do you have any weapons?" The raw edge to his voice derailed her outrage and replaced it with cold panic. For a second she couldn't speak.

She finally managed to say, "No! I don't have any weapons. Nothing."

"What's wrong, Mom?" Brady asked, his voice sharp with alarm. "Why is the policeman so mad at us?"

"Nothing's wrong, baby. Everything's going to be just fine." *Keep your hands on the wheel, hands on the wheel . . .* She was desperate to hug her son but didn't dare. She could see that Brady didn't believe the false warmth of her voice. She didn't believe it herself. "Just sit right here, okay? Don't move. Both of you, *don't move*."

Lily was staring at the officer outside the car. "Is he going to shoot us, Mom? Is he going to shoot?" Because they'd all seen videos, hadn't they, of people shot to death, innocent people who'd made the wrong move, said the wrong thing, been in the wrong place at the wrong time. And she imagined it happening, vividly . . . her kids dying and her unable to do a thing to stop it. A bright flash of light, screams, darkness.

"Of course he's not going to shoot you! Baby, please *don't move!*" She turned back to the policeman and said, "Officer, please, you're scaring them. I have no idea what this is about!"

A woman with a gold police badge hanging around her neck walked past the barricade, past the officer, and right up to Gina's window. She had a tired face and bleak, dark eyes, and she took in the situation at a glance. "Mrs. Royal? Gina Royal?"

"Yes, ma'am."

"You're the wife of Melvin Royal?" He hated to be called Melvin. Only ever Mel, but it didn't seem like a time to tell the woman that, so Gina just nodded in response. "My name is Detective Salazar. I'd like you to step out of the vehicle, please. Keep both hands in view."

"My kids—"

"They can stay where they are for now. We'll take care of them. Please step out."

"What in God's name is wrong? That's *our* house. This is crazy. We're the *victims* here!" Fear—for herself, for her kids—made her irrational, and she heard a strange tone in her voice that surprised her. She sounded unhinged, like one of those clueless people on the news who always made her feel both pity and contempt. *I'd never sound like that in a crisis.* How often had she thought that? But she did. She sounded exactly like them. Panic fluttered like a trapped moth in her chest, and she couldn't seem to keep her breathing steady. It was all too much, too fast.

"A victim. Sure you are." The detective opened her door. "Step out." No *please* this time. The officer who'd called the detective stepped away, and his hand was still on his gun, and *why*, why were they treating her like this, like a criminal? *This is just a mistake. All a terrible, stupid mistake!* Out of instinct, she reached for her purse, but Salazar immediately took it and handed it to the patrol officer. "Hands on the hood, Mrs. Royal."

"Why? I don't understand what's—"

Detective Salazar didn't give her a chance to finish. She spun Gina around and shoved her forward against the car. Gina broke her fall with outstretched hands on the hot metal of the hood. It was like touching a stove burner, but she didn't dare pull away. She felt dazed. This was a *mistake*. Some terrible *mistake*, and in another minute they'd apologize and she would graciously forgive them for being so rude, and they'd laugh and she'd invite them in for iced tea . . . she might have some of those lemon cookies left, if Mel hadn't eaten the rest; he really loved his lemon cookies . . .

She gasped when Salazar's hands slid impersonally over areas that she had *no right to touch*. Gina tried to resist, but the detective shoved her back in place with real force. "Mrs. Royal! Don't make this worse! Listen to me. You are under arrest. You have the right to remain silent—"

"I'm *what*? That's *my house*! That car drove *into my house*!" Her son and daughter could see this humiliation, right in front of them. Her neighbors all stared. Some had cell phones out. They were taking pictures. Video. Uploading this horrible violation to the Internet so bored people around the world could mock her, and it wouldn't matter later that it was all a mistake, would it? The Internet was forever. She was always warning Lily about that.

Salazar continued to talk, telling her about rights that she couldn't possibly comprehend in that moment, and Gina didn't resist as the detective pinned her hands behind her back. She just didn't know how to even begin.

The metal of the handcuffs felt like a cold slap on her damp skin, and Gina fought a strange, high buzzing in her head. She felt sweat rolling down her face and neck, but everything seemed separated from her. Distant. *This isn't happening. This can't be happening. I'll call Mel. Mel will sort this out, and we'll all have a good laugh later.* She could not comprehend how she'd gone in a minute or two from normal life to . . . to this.

Brady was yelling and trying to get out of the car, but the policeman kept him inside. Lily seemed too stunned and scared to move. Gina looked toward them and said in a surprisingly rational voice, "Brady. Lily. It's okay—please don't be afraid. It'll be okay. Just do what they tell you. I'm all right. This is all just a mistake, okay? It's going to be all right." Salazar's hand was painfully tight on her upper arm, and Gina turned her head toward the detective. "Please. Please, whatever you think I did, *I didn't do it!* Please make sure my kids are okay!"

"I will," Salazar said, unexpectedly kind. "But you need to come with me, Gina."

"Is it—do you think I did this? Drove this thing into our house? I didn't! I'm not drunk, if you think—" She stopped, because she could see a man sitting on a cot by the ambulance, breathing oxygen. A paramedic was treating him for a wound to the scalp, and a police officer hovered nearby. "Is that him? Is that the driver? Is he *drunk?*"

"Yes," Salazar said. "Total accident, if you call drunk driving an accident. He hit early happy hour, made a wrong turn—says he was trying to make it back to the freeway—and took the corner too fast. Ended up with his front end inside your garage."

"But—" Gina was utterly lost now. Completely, horribly at sea. "But if you have *him*, why are you—"

"You ever go into your garage, Mrs. Royal?"

"I—no. No, my husband turned it into a workshop. We put cabinets over the door from the kitchen; he goes into it from a side door."

"So the door at the back doesn't go up? You don't park in it anymore?"

"No, he took the motor out, you have to go in through the side door. We have a covered carport, so I don't need—look, what is this? What is going on?"

Salazar gave her a look. It wasn't angry now; it was almost apologetic. Almost. "I'm going to show you something, and I need you to explain it to me, okay?"

She walked Gina around the barricade, up the sidewalk where black tire marks veered and careened in muddy ditches through the yard, all the way up to where the rear of the SUV stuck obscenely out of a jumble of red bricks and debris. This wall must have held a pegboard with Melvin's tools. She saw a bent saw mixed in with the chalky drywall dust and for a second could only think, *He's going to be so upset, I don't know how to tell him about any of this.* Mel loved his workshop. It was his sanctuary.

Then Salazar said, "I'd like you to explain her."

She pointed.

Gina looked up, past the hood of the SUV, and saw the life-size naked doll hanging from a winch hook in the center of the garage. For a bizarre instant, she nearly laughed at the utter inappropriateness of it. It dangled there from a wire noose around its neck, loose arms and legs, not even doll-perfect in proportions, a flawed thing, strangely discolored . . . And why would anyone paint a doll's face that hideous purple black, flay off pieces of the skin, make the eyes red and bulbous and staring, the tongue protruding from swollen lips . . .

And that was when she had one single, awful realization.

It's not a doll.

And against all her best intentions, she began to scream and couldn't stop.

1

GWEN PROCTOR
FOUR YEARS LATER
Stillhouse Lake, Tennessee

"Begin."

I take a deep breath that reeks of burned gunpowder and old sweat, set my stance, focus, and pull the trigger. I keep my body balanced for the shock. Some people blink involuntarily with every shot; I've discovered that I simply don't. It isn't training, just biology, but it makes me feel that much more in control. I'm grateful for the edge.

The heavy, powerful .357 roars and bucks, sending familiar shocks through me, but I'm not focused on the noise or the kick. Only the target at the end of the range. If noise distracted me, the constant din of other shooters—men, women, and even a few teens at the other stations—would have already spoiled my aim. The steady roar of gunfire, even through the thick muffle of ear protection, sounds like a particularly violent, constant storm.

I finish firing, release the cylinder, remove the empty shells, and set the gun on the range rest with the wheel still open, muzzle pointed downrange. Then I remove my eye protection and put the glasses down. "Done."

From behind me, the range instructor says, "Step back, please." I do. He picks up and examines my weapon, nods, and hits the switch to bring the target forward. "Your safety's excellent." He has his voice pitched loudly to be heard over the noise and the barrier of hearing protection we both wear. It's already a little hoarse; he spends most of his day shouting.

"Here's hoping my accuracy is, too," I yell back.

But I already know it is. I can see it before the paper target is half-way back on the glide. Empty holes fluttering, all in the tight red ring.

"Center mass," the instructor says, giving me a thumbs-up. "That's a letter-perfect pass. Good job, Ms. Proctor."

"Thank you for making it so painless," I say in turn. He steps back and gives me space, and I close the cylinder and replace the weapon in its zipped bag. Safe.

"We'll get your scores in to the state office, and you should get your carry permit in no time." The instructor is a young man with a tight burr haircut, former military. He has a soft, blurred accent that, though Southern, doesn't have the sharper lilt of Tennessee . . . Georgia, I think. Nice young man, at least ten years below the age I'd ever consider dating. If I dated. He's unfailingly polite. I am *Ms. Proctor*, always.

He shakes hands with me, and I grin back. "See you next time, Javi." Privilege of my age and gender. I get to use his first name. I said *Mr. Esparza* for the first solid month, until he gently corrected me.

"Next time—" Something catches his attention, and his easy calm shifts to sudden alertness. His focus goes down the line, and he bellows out, "Cease fire! Cease fire!"

I feel a sweep of adrenaline ping every nerve, and I go very still, assessing, but this isn't about me. Raggedly, all the percussive noise of the range dies, and people pull their weapons down, elbows in, while he walks down four stalls. There's a burly man there with a semiauto pistol. Javi orders him to clear the firearm and step away.

"What'd I do?" the man asks in a belligerent tone. I pick up my bag, nerves still jangling, and head for the door, though I do it slowly. I realize the man hasn't done as Javi instructed; instead, he's chosen to get defensive. Not a good idea. Javi's face goes stiff, and his body language changes with it.

"Clear that weapon and place it on the shelf, sir. Now."

"Ain't no call for this. I know what I'm doing! Been shooting for years!"

"Sir, I saw you turn your loaded weapon in the direction of another shooter. You know the rules. Always point the muzzle downrange. *Now clear it and put it down.* If you don't follow my instructions, I will remove you from the range and the police will be called. Do you understand?"

Smiling, calm Javier Esparza is now someone else entirely, and the force of his command blasts through the room like a stun grenade. The offending shooter fumbles at his gun, gets the clip out, and throws it and the weapon down on the counter. I notice the muzzle still isn't pointed downrange.

Javi's voice has gone clear and soft now. "Sir, I said clear your weapon."

"I did!"

"Step back."

As the man stares, Javi reaches for the gun, ejects the last cartridge from the slide, and sets the bullet down on the counter beside the clip. "That's how people get killed. If you can't learn how to properly clear a weapon, you need to find another range," he says. "If you don't know how to obey a range instructor's orders, find another range. In fact, you might want to just find another range. You endanger yourself and everybody here when you ignore safety rules, do you understand?"

The man's face turns a puffy, unhealthy red, and he balls his fists.

Javi puts the gun back down exactly the way it had been when he picked it up, turns it downrange, and then pointedly turns it to lie on its other side. "Ejection port goes up, sir." He steps back and locks eyes with the man. Javi's wearing jeans and a blue polo shirt, and the shooter is wearing a camo shirt and old army-surplus uniform pants, but it's clear as day which one is the soldier. "I think you're done for the day, Mr. Getts. Never shoot angry."

I've never seen a man so clearly on the edge of either outright, unthinking violence or a massive heart attack. His hand twitches, and I can see him wondering how fast he can get to his gun, load it, and start to fire. There's a heavy, sick weight to the air, and I find my hand moving the zipper slowly down on the bag I'm holding, my mind calculating the steps—just as he is—to preparing my gun to fire. I'm fast. Faster than him.

Javier isn't armed.

The tension shatters as one of the other people standing frozen at a shooting station takes a single step out, halfway between me and the angry guy. He's smaller than both Javi and the red-faced man, and he has sandy-blond hair that might have been close-cropped once but is growing out to fan his ears now. Lithe, not muscular. I've seen him around but don't know his name.

"Hey now, mister, let's just gear this back," he says in an accent that doesn't sound like Tennessee to me but comes from somewhere more in the Midwest. Folksy. It's a calm, quiet sort of voice, seductively reasonable. "The range master's just doing his job, all right? And he's right. You start shooting angry, never know what could happen."

It's amazing, watching the rage drain out of Getts, as if someone has kicked a plug loose in him. He takes a couple of deep breaths, color fading back to something like normal, and nods stiffly. "Shit," he says. "Guess I got a little ruffled there. Won't happen again."

The other man nods back and returns to his shooting window, avoiding everyone's curious looks. He starts checking over his own pistol, which is oriented the correct way, downrange.

"Mr. Getts, let's talk outside," Javier says, which is polite and correct, but Carl's face twists up again, and I see a vein pulse in his temple. He starts to protest and then senses the weight of eyes on him, all the other shooters waiting in silence, watching. He steps back into the booth and angrily begins shoving his kit into a bag. "Fucking power-hungry wetback," he mutters, then stalks toward the door. I pull in a breath, but Javi lays a friendly hand on my shoulder as the door slams behind him.

"Funny how that asshole listens to the white guy before the range master," I say. All of us in here are white, with the exception of Javier. Tennessee has no shortage of people of color, but you'd never know it from the makeup of the people on the firing line.

"Carl's a jackass, and I didn't want him in here anyway," Javi says.

"Doesn't matter. You can't let him talk to you that way," I say, because I want to slam a fist into Carl's teeth. I know it wouldn't go well. I still want to do it.

"He can talk any way he wants. Blessings of living in a free country." Javi sounds pleasant, still. "Doesn't mean no consequences, ma'am. He'll be getting a letter banning him from the range. Not because of what he said, but I don't trust him to be responsible around other shooters. Not only are we entitled to turn people away for unsafe and aggressive behavior, we're required to." He smiles a little. A grim, cold little smile. "And if he wants to have a word with me in the parking lot sometime later, fine. We can do that."

"He might bring his beer buddies."

"That'll be fun."

"So, who was the guy that stepped up?" I jerk my head toward the man; he's already got his hearing protection on again. I'm curious, because he's not a usual range rat, or at least not during the times I tend to shoot.

"Sam Cade." Javi shrugs. "He's okay. New guy. Kinda surprised he did that. Most people wouldn't."

I hold out my hand. He shakes it. "Thank you, sir. You run a tight range."

"I owe it to everybody who comes here. Be safe out there," he says, then turns back to the waiting shooters. He breaks out his drill sergeant voice again. "Range is clear! Commence fire!"

I duck out as the thunder of bullets rattles again. The run-in between Javi and the other man has shaved a little off my good mood, but I still feel vastly elated as I leave my hearing protection on the rack outside. *Fully certified.* I've been thinking about it for a very long time, cautious, unsure about whether or not I dared to put my name on official records. I'd always had guns, but it had been a risk, carrying without a license. I finally felt settled well enough here that I could take the leap.

My phone buzzes as I unlock the car, and I nearly fumble it as I open up the back to place my gear inside. "Hello?"

"Mrs. Proctor?"

"*Ms.* Proctor," I automatically correct, then glance at the caller ID. I have to suppress a groan. School administration office. It's a number with which I am already depressingly familiar.

"I'm sorry to tell you that your daughter, Atlanta—"

"Is in trouble," I finish for the woman on the other end. "So I guess this must be Tuesday." I lift the panel on the floor. Beneath, there's a lockbox, big enough for the gun bag, and I put it in and slam the box shut, then pull the carpet back over to conceal it.

The woman on the other end of the call makes a disapproving sound, low in her throat. Her voice rises a notch. "It's not funny, Mrs. Proctor. The principal is going to need you to come in to have a serious discussion. This is the fourth incident in three months, and it's simply not acceptable behavior for a girl of Lanny's age!"

Lanny is fourteen, a perfectly predictable age to be acting out, but I don't say that. I just ask, "What happened?" as I walk to the front of the Jeep and climb in. I have to leave the door open a moment to let the suffocating heat bleed out; I hadn't managed to score one of the shady spots in the range's narrow parking lot.

"The principal would much rather discuss it in person. Your daughter will need to be picked up from the office. She's been suspended from classes for a week."

"A *week*? What did she do?"

"As I said, the principal would prefer to talk face-to-face. Half an hour?"

Half an hour doesn't give me time to take a shower and get rid of the smell of the range, but maybe that's for the best. Having a gunpowder perfume probably wouldn't hurt me in this particular situation. "Fine," I say. "I'll be there."

I say it calmly. Most mothers, I think, would have been angry and upset, but in the great history of disasters in my life, this hardly deserves a raised eyebrow.

As soon as I hang up, my phone buzzes with a text, and I figure it will be Lanny, trying to get her side of the story out fast before I hear the less charitable official version.

It isn't Lanny, though, and as I crank up the Jeep, I see my son's name glowing on the screen. *Connor.* I swipe and read the text, which is terse and to the point: Lanny in fight. 1. It takes me a second to translate that last bit, but of course the number one equals *won*. I can't decide whether he's proud or frantic: proud that his sister held her own, or frantic that it might get them booted out of school again. It's a valid fear. This past year has been a brief, fragile peace between unpacking boxes and packing them again, and I don't want it to end so soon, either. The kids deserve a little peace, and a sense of stability and safety. Connor already has anxiety issues. Lanny acts out on a regular basis.

None of us is whole anymore. I try not to blame myself for that, but it's hard.

It damn sure isn't *their* fault.

I text back a quick reply and put the Jeep in reverse. I've changed vehicles frequently over the past few years, from necessity, but this one . . . I love this one. I bought it cheap for cash on Craigslist, a quick and anonymous purchase, and it's just the right thing for the steep, woody terrain around the lake, and the hills that stretch up toward misty blue mountains.

The Jeep is a fighter. It's seen hard times. The transmission needs work, the steering's a little off. But scars and all, it has survived, and it still keeps rolling.

The symbolism isn't lost on me.

It bucks a little as I steer down the steep hill, passing through cool pine shade and into blazing noonday sun again. The shooting range sits on an overlook, and as I turn onto the road that leads down, the lake slips gradually into view. Light shatters and scatters on the ripples and shifts of the deep blue-green water. Stillhouse Lake is a hidden gem. Used to be an expensive gated community, but with the financial crunch, the community's funds cratered, and the gates now stand permanently open, the guardhouse at the entrance empty except for spiders and the occasional raccoon. Still, the illusion of wealth lingers here: a scattering of high, fancy houses, though many of the other dwellings are more along the lines of smaller cabins now. There are boaters on the water, but it's far from crowded even in today's fine weather. The dark pines scratch at the sky as I speed past them down the narrow road, and the sense of finally being *right* strikes me again.

I haven't found many places in the past few years that felt even a little safe, and certainly none that felt like . . . like home. But this place—the lake, the hills, the pines, the half-wild remoteness—eases the part of me that never really relaxes anymore. The first time I'd seen it,

I'd thought, *This is the place.* I put no stock in past lives, but it felt like recognition. Acceptance. Destiny.

Damn it, Lanny, I don't want to have to leave this behind so soon because you can't learn to blend. Don't do this to us.

Gwen Proctor is the fourth identity I've had since leaving Wichita. Gina Royal lies dead in the past; I'm not that woman anymore. In fact, I can hardly recognize her now, that weak creature who'd submitted, pretended, smoothed over every ripple of trouble that rose.

Who'd aided and abetted, however unconsciously.

Gina's long dead, and I don't mourn her. I feel so distant that I wouldn't recognize the old me if I passed her on the street. I'm glad I've escaped a hell I had hardly even recognized when I was burning in it. Glad that I've pulled the kids out, too.

And they, too, have reinvented themselves—even if they've been forced to. I've let them pick their own names each time we had to move on, though I've had to regretfully reject some of the more creative efforts. This time they are Connor and Atlanta—Lanny, for short. We almost never slip up and use our birth names anymore. *Our prisoner names,* Lanny calls them. She isn't wrong, though I loathe that my kids have to think of their early lives this way now. That they have to hate their father. He deserves that, of course, but they don't.

Choosing their own names is all the control I can give my children as I drag them town to town, school to school, putting distance and time between us and the horrors of the past. It isn't enough. Can never be enough. Kids need security, stability, and I haven't been able to give them any of that. I don't even know if I ever *can* give them that.

But I've kept them safe from the wolves, at least: the most basic and important job of a parent, to keep her offspring from being eaten by predators.

Even the ones I can't see.

The road glides me around the lake, past the cutoff to our house. Not *the* house, as I usually think of such things, but finally *our* house.

I've grown attached. That isn't long-term smart, but I can't help it; I'm tired of running, of temporary rented addresses and new fake names and new imperfect lies. I had an opportunity: I'd been given a heads-up about this place and scored the house for cash at an incredibly poorly attended bankruptcy auction a year ago. Some financed-to-the-hilt family had built it as their rustic dream getaway, then abandoned it to squatters, and the place had been a wreck. Together, the kids and I had cleaned it, repaired it, and made it into our own. We'd painted the walls in our own colors—bold ones, in Connor's room at least. *That,* I thought, *is a sure sign we're making it a real home: no more beige walls and rental-property bland carpets. We are here. We are* staying.

Our house, best of all, has a built-in safe room. For the sake of Connor's enthusiasm, I call it our Zombie Apocalypse Bugout Shelter, and we've fixed it up with zombie-fighting gear and signs that read **No Zombie Parking, Trespassers Will Be Dismembered.**

I wince and try not to think too deeply about that. I hope—and I know it's a vain hope, really—that all Connor knows about death and dismemberment comes from watching TV shows and films. He says he doesn't remember much from the old days, when he was Brady . . . or at least, that's what he tells me when I ask. He never went back to school in Wichita after that day, so the schoolyard bullies had no chance to scream the story at him. He and Lanny went into the custody of my mother out in Maine, in a remote and peaceful place. She'd kept her computer locked up in a cabinet and used it only sparingly. The kids hadn't found out much during that year and a half; they'd been kept away from magazines and newspapers, and the only TV in the house had been under my mother's strict control.

Still, I know the kids have found ways to dig up at least some of the details about what their father did. I would have, in their place.

It's possible that Connor's current zombie apocalypse obsession is his cryptic way of working things out.

Lanny's the one I really worry about. She was old enough to remember a lot . . . The accident. The arrests. The trials. The hushed and hurried conversations my mother must have had on the phone with friends and enemies and strangers.

Lanny must remember the hate mail that poured into my mom's mailbox.

But what I worry about most is how she remembers her father, because like it or not, *believe* it or not, he had been a good father to his kids, and they had loved him with their entire hearts.

He'd never been that man, not really. Being a good father was just a mask he'd worn to hide the monster underneath. But that didn't mean the kids have forgotten how it felt to be loved by Melvin Royal. Without meaning to, I remember how warm he could seem, how *safe*. When he gave his attention, he gave it completely. He'd loved them, and me, and it had felt real.

But it couldn't have been real. Not considering what he was. I must not have known the difference, and it makes me sick when I realize all that I got wrong.

I slow the Jeep as another big vehicle swings around a sharp curve ahead—the Johansens. They are car-proud people; the SUV's black finish glints perfection, and there isn't even a fine film of dust. So much for off-roading. I wave, and the older couple wave back.

I'd made a point of meeting our closest neighbors the first week we moved in, because it seemed like a good precaution to assess them early for threats, or as possible resources in an emergency. I don't count the Johansens as either. They are just . . . there. *Most people just take up space anyway.* The whisper comes and goes in my head, and it frightens me, because I hate remembering Melvin Royal's voice. That was nothing he'd ever said at home, ever said to me, but I'd seen the video of him saying it at the trial. He'd said it utterly casually about the women he'd torn apart.

19

Mel infected me like a virus, and I have an unhealthy surety deep down that I'll never get completely well again.

It takes a solid fifteen minutes to navigate the steep road down to the main highway, which slips in ribbon waves through the trees. Trees thin, grow shorter and sparser, and then the Jeep rolls past the rustic, sun-blighted sign that announces Norton. The top right corner of the sign is obliterated by a cluster of shotgun pellet strikes. Of course. It wouldn't be the country if drunks weren't shooting signs.

Norton's a typical small Southern town, with old family establishments clinging on grimly next to repurposed antique stores, everyone hanging by a fragile economic thread. Chain outfits are slowly taking over. Old Navy. Starbucks. The yellow-arch scourge of McDonald's.

The school is a single complex of three buildings built in a tight little triangle, with a shared space for athletic and arts between. I check in with the single guard on duty—armed, as is customary around here, with a handgun—in his little shack, and score a faded visitor pass before proceeding.

The lunch bell has already sounded, and all over the grounds young people eat, laugh, and engage in flirting, bullying, teasing. Normal life. Lanny won't be among them, and if I know my son, Connor won't be, either. I have to use the intercom to state my name and business before the secretary buzzes me inside, where the smell of stale sneakers, Pine-Sol, and cafeteria food hits me in a familiar puff.

Funny how all schools smell the same. I'm instantly thirteen again, and guilty of something.

As I walk into the junior high's administration office, I find Connor slouched in one of the hard-plastic chairs, staring at his shoes.

Called it.

He looks up when the door opens, and I see the relief spread over his sun-browned face. "It wasn't her fault," he says, before I can even say hello. "Mom, it *wasn't.*" He's an earnest eleven now, and his sister is fourteen—tough ages even at the best of times. He looks pale and shaken and worried, which bothers me. I can see that he's been biting his fingernails again. His index finger is bleeding. His voice seems hoarse, as if he's been crying, though his eyes look clear enough. *He needs more counseling,* I think, but counseling means more in-depth records, and records mean complications we can't afford, not yet. But if he really needs it, if I see signs he's regressing to the state he was in three years ago . . . I'll risk it. Even if that means we are found, and the cycle of names and addresses starts all over again.

"It's going to be okay," I say, and then I draw him into a hug. He lets me, which is unusual, but there are no witnesses here. Even so, he feels tense and solid in my arms, and I let him go quicker than I intended. "You should go on to lunch. I'll take care of your sister now."

"I will," he says. "But I couldn't—" He doesn't finish, but I understand. *I couldn't leave her alone,* he means. One thing about my kids: they stick together. Always, even while they bicker and fight. They haven't let each other down since the day of *The Event.* That's how I try to think of it, in capitals and italics: *The Event,* like it's a scary movie, something removed from our lives that we can forget. Fictional and distant.

Sometimes, it even helps.

"Go on," I tell him gently. "We'll see you tonight."

Connor goes, though not without a glance back over his shoulder. I'm biased, maybe, but I think he's a handsome kid—sparkling amber eyes, brown hair that needs a trim. A sharp, clever face. He's made some friends here at Norton Junior High, which is a relief. They share typical eleven-year-old interests in video games and movies and TV shows and books, and if they're a little nerdy, it's a good kind of nerdy, the kind that comes from rabid enthusiasm and imagination.

Lanny's a bigger problem.

Much bigger.

I take in a deep breath, let it out, and knock on Principal Anne Wilson's door. When I enter, I find Lanny in a chair against the wall. I recognize the cross-armed, head-down posture. Silent, passive resistance.

My daughter has on baggy black pants with chains and straps, and a torn, faded Ramones T-shirt she must have stolen out of my closet. She's let her newly dyed black hair fall loose and ragged around her face. The studded bracelets and dog collar look shiny and sharp. Like the pants, they're new.

"Ms. Proctor," the principal says, motioning me to the padded guest chair in front of the desk. Lanny has one of the hard-plastic ones off to the side—the chair of shame, presumably, worn shiny by dozens, if not hundreds, of militant little asses. "I think you already see part of the problem. I thought we agreed that Atlanta wouldn't wear these kinds of clothes to school anymore. We have a dress code that we have to enforce. I don't like it any more than you do, believe me."

Principal Wilson is a middle-aged African American woman with natural hair and comfortable layers of fat; she's not a bad person, and she isn't making this some kind of moral crusade. She has rules to follow, and Lanny? Well. My daughter isn't good with rules. Or boundaries.

"Goth kids aren't violent assholes," Lanny mutters. "That's some bullshit propaganda, you know."

"Atlanta!" Principal Wilson says sharply. "Language! And I'm speaking to your mother."

Lanny doesn't look up, but I can well imagine the epic eye roll under that curtain of black hair.

I force a smile. "This isn't what she had on when she left this morning. I'm sorry about this."

"Well, *I'm* not sorry," Lanny says. "It's fucking ridiculous that they can tell me what to wear! What is this, Catholic school?"

Principal Wilson's expression doesn't change. "Also, obviously, there is her attitude."

"You're talking about me like I'm not even here! Like I'm not a person!" Lanny says, raising her head. "I can show you some *attitude*."

The shock of seeing her face makes me flinch before I can control it. Pale makeup, heavy black eyeliner, corpse-blue lipstick. Skull earrings.

For a moment I can't breathe, because her face morphs from my daughter's to something else, someone else, someone dangling from a thick cable noose, limp hair sticky around her head, eyes bulging, what skin she had left that same shade . . .

Put it in the box. Lock it up. You can't go there. I know damned well Lanny has done this deliberately, and our eyes meet, challenge, hold. She has an eerie ability to find and push my buttons. She got it from her father. I see him in the shape of her eyes, in the tilt of her head.

And that scares me.

"And," Principal Wilson continues, "there's the fight."

I don't look away from my daughter. "Are you hurt?"

Lanny shows me her right fist and raw knuckles. *Ouch.* She has a shadow of a smirk on her blue lips. "You should see the other girl."

"The other girl," Principal Wilson says, "has a black eye. She also has parents who are the type to have lawyers on speed dial."

We both ignore her, and I nod for Lanny to continue. "She slapped me first, Mom," Lanny says. "Hard. *After* she shoved me. She said I was looking at her stupid boyfriend, which I wasn't—he's gross, and anyway, he was looking at *me*. Not my fault."

"Where's the other girl?" I look at Principal Wilson. "Why isn't she here?"

"She was picked up by her parents half an hour ago and taken home. Dahlia Brown is an A student who swears she did nothing to bring it on. She has witnesses to back her up."

There are always witnesses in junior high, and they always say what their friends want them to say. Surely Principal Wilson knows that. She also knows that Lanny is the new kid, the one who doesn't fit in. That's because my daughter has taken up the goth lifestyle in part as a control mechanism: pushing others away before she can be pushed. That, and in some strange way, she's dealing with the secret horror show that is her childhood.

"I didn't start it," Lanny says, and I believe her. I'll probably be the only one. "I *hate* this fucking school."

I believe that, too.

I turn my attention back to the woman at the desk. "So you're suspending Lanny, but not this other girl, is that right?"

"I really have no option. Between the dress code violation, the fight, and her attitude about the whole incident . . ." Wilson waits, clearly anticipating the argument to come, but I just nod.

"Okay. Does she have her schoolwork?"

Hard to miss the relief that slips over the principal's face, that this parent who reeks of gunpowder isn't going to make a scene. "Yes. I made sure she does. She can come back to classes next week."

"Come on, Lanny," I say, rising. "We'll talk about this at home."

"Mom, I didn't—"

"At home."

Lanny lets out a sigh, grabs her backpack, and slouches out of the office with her dyed-black hair hiding her expression, which surely isn't pleasant.

"Just a moment, please. I'm going to need specific assurances before I let Atlanta back in classes," Wilson says. "We have a no-tolerance policy, and I'm bending it because I know you're a good person and want her to fit in here. But this is the last chance, Mrs. Proctor. The very last chance. I'm so sorry."

"Please don't call me that," I say. "Ms. Proctor will do. Has since the 1970s, I believe." I rise and offer her my hand. Hers is a moderate handshake, businesslike, nothing more. These days, I count merely businesslike as a positive. "We'll talk next week."

Outside, Lanny has chosen the very same chair her brother used; it's probably still warm from his body heat. Do they mean to do it, or is it just instinct? Are they getting *too* close? Have my paranoia and constant vigilance made them like this?

I draw in a breath and let it go. The last thing I want to do is over-analyze the kids. They've had enough of that.

"Come on," I say. "Let's kick it, as the kids say."

Lanny looks cross. "Ugh. We really don't." She hesitates and looks down at her boots. "You're not mad?"

"Oh, I'm furious. I'm planning to eat all my feelings at Kathy's Kakes. And you're going to eat them with me. Like it or not."

Lanny's reached the age where being enthusiastic about anything, even skipping school to eat ridiculously butter-loaded cake, isn't cool, so she just shrugs. "Whatever. As long as I get out of here."

"Do I even want to ask where you got all this stuff you're wearing?"

"What stuff?"

"Really, kid? That's how you're rolling with it?"

Lanny rolls her eyes. "It's just *clothes*. I'm pretty sure every girl wears clothes to school."

"Surprisingly few want to join Marilyn Manson's backup band."

"Marilyn who?"

"Thanks for making me feel like a crone. Did you order all this online?"

"So what if I did?"

"You didn't use my credit cards, did you? You know how dangerous that is."

"I'm not an idiot. I saved up and bought a preload, just like you taught me. I had it sent to the PO box in Boston and remailed. Twice."

That eases a dark, anxious knot in my chest, and I nod. "Okay then. Let's discuss it over calories."

We don't discuss anything, really. The cake slices are huge, and delicious, and homemade, and there's no point being mad while eating them. Kathy's Kakes is popular, and there are people all around us enjoying the treats. A dad with three little ones is rubbernecking on his phone, and the kids are taking advantage of his inattention to dump cupcake crumbs everywhere and paint their faces with vivid blue icing.

In the corner there's a studious young woman with a tablet computer; as she twists to plug it in, I see a tattoo on her shoulder beneath her tank top. Something colorful. An older couple sits at what looks like formal tea, with fancy china and a round cake tower crammed with tiny bites on the table between them. I wonder if having tea requires you to look like it bores you to death.

Even Lanny eases her attitude by the time we finish eating, and with her corpse-dark lipstick rubbed away, she almost looks normal as we talk, cautiously, about the cake, about the weekend, about books. It isn't until we're on the road, grinding gears back up the trail to Stillhouse Lake, that I am forced to spoil things. "Lanny—look. You're a smart girl. You know if you stand out like this, pictures will get taken and passed around, and you'll get posted on social media. We can't have that."

"Since when is my life a *we* problem, Mom? Oh, wait. I remember. Since *ever*."

I'd done my absolute best to shield my kids from the worst of the horrors that had followed *The Event*, and so had my mother in her turn when I'd been tried as an accessory. I hoped that whatever Lanny remembered, or had learned, it was a shallow trickle instead of the toxic flood I'd been submerged in. My mother had been forced to tell Lanny and Connor—Lily and Brady then—that their father was a murderer, that he was going to trial and then to prison. That he'd killed multiple young women. She hadn't told them the details, and I didn't want the kids to know them. But that was then, and I know I can't keep the worst of it from Lanny for much longer. Fourteen is far too young to comprehend the depravity of Melvin Royal.

"We all have to keep a low profile," I say. "You know this, Lanny. It's for our safety. You understand, don't you?"

"Sure," she says, pointedly looking away. "Because they're always looking for us. These mythical strangers you're so afraid of."

"They aren't—" I take in a breath and remind myself, again, that an argument does neither of us good. "We live by the rules for a reason."

"Your rules. Your reasons." She rests her head against the Jeep's seat, as if too bored to hold it up anymore. "You know, if I go goth, nobody will recognize me anyway. They just look at the makeup, not the face."

Lanny has a clever point. "Maybe not, but here in Norton, it'll get you expelled."

"Homeschooling is still a thing, isn't it?"

And it would have been an easy answer, too. I'd considered it seriously, many times, but the paperwork took ages, and until recently we'd always been on the move. Besides, I want my kids to be socialized. To be part of the normal world. They've had too much unnatural crap in their lives already.

"Maybe there's a compromise," I say. "Mrs. Wilson doesn't object to the hair. Maybe tone down the makeup, lose the accessories, don't go full black on the clothes. You can still be weird. Just not *weird*."

She momentarily brightens. "Can I finally get an Instagram account, then? And a real phone instead of these stupid flip things?"

"Don't push it."

"Mom. You keep saying you want me to be normal. *Everybody* has social media. I mean, even *Principal Wilson* has a lame-ass Facebook page full of stupid cat pictures and weird memes. And she has a Twitter account!"

"Well, you're an antiestablishment rebel; work with that. Be different by refusing to follow the trend."

That wasn't flying, and she gave me a disgusted look. "So you want me to be a complete social leper. Great. There's such a thing as an anonymous *handle*, you know. Doesn't have to be my name on it. I swear, I'll make sure nobody knows who I am."

"No. Because about two seconds after you open an account, it'll be full of selfies. Location tagged." The toughest thing in this image-obsessed day and age was trying to keep the kids' images off the Internet. There are eyes always searching for us, and those eyes never close. They don't even blink.

"God, you're such a pain in the ass," Lanny mutters. She hunches in on herself to stare out the window at the lake. "And of course we have to live at the ass-crack of nowhere because you're so paranoid. Unless you plan on packing us up and moving us to someplace even more redneck."

I let the paranoid part slide past, because it's true. "You don't think the ass-crack of nowhere is beautiful?"

Lanny says nothing. At least she doesn't have a smart comeback, which is a minor victory. I take every victory I can get these days.

I steer into the gravel driveway and bounce the Jeep up the hill to the cabin, and Lanny is out the passenger side before I've even pulled the parking brake. "The alarm's set!" I shout after her.

"Duh! Isn't it always?"

Lanny's already inside, and I hear the rapid tones of the six-digit code being punched. The interior door slams before I can hear the all-clear signal, but Lanny never gets it wrong. Connor does, sometimes, because he's not as careful about it—always thinking of something else. Funny how the two of them have changed places in four years. Connor's now the one with the rich interior life, always reading, while Lanny lives with her armor bolted proudly on the outside, begging for trouble.

"You're on laundry duty!" I say as I enter after Lanny, who, of course, is already slamming her bedroom door. Emphatically. "And we're going to have to talk about this sooner or later! You know that!"

The surly silence behind the door disagrees. It doesn't matter. I never give up when it's important. Lanny knows that better than anyone.

I reset the alarm and then take a moment to put my stuff away, stash everything in its proper place. I like to have order, so that I never have to waste a moment in an emergency. Sometimes I turn the lights out and run crisis drills. *There's a fire in the hall. What's your escape route? Where are your weapons?* I know it's obsessive and unhealthy.

It's also practical as hell.

I mentally rehearse what I'd do if an intruder broke in the garage door. *Grab knife from block. Rush forward to block him in the door. Stab stab stab. While he's reeling, slice the tendons at the ankles. Down.*

Always, in my rehearsals, it's Mel coming for us—Mel, looking exactly the same as he had in the trial, wearing a charcoal-gray suit his lawyer had bought, with a blue silk tie and pocket square that matched his denim-colored eyes. He looks like a well-dressed, normal man, and the disguise is *perfect.*

I hadn't been in the crowd at his court appearance, where everyone reported he'd looked like a perfectly innocent man; I'd been locked up, awaiting my own trial. But a photographer had captured him at just the right moment as he turned and looked at the crowd, the victims' families. He still *looked* the same, but his eyes had gone flat and soulless, and seeing that picture had given me the eerie feeling that something cold and alien was inside of that body, staring out. That creature hadn't felt the need to hide anymore.

When I imagine Mel coming for us, that's what's staring out of his face.

Exercise done, I make sure all the doors are locked. Connor has his own code, and when he comes home, I'll listen for the tones and the reset. I can tell if it's wrong, or if he forgets. The key fob to set the whole system to alert and ring in the Norton Police Department is constantly with me in my pocket. My first action in any emergency.

I sit down at the computer in the bedroom I've made my office. It's a smallish room, with a narrow closet that holds winter clothes and supplies, and it's dominated by a battered, magnificent rolltop desk I rescued from an antiques shop my first day in Norton. The date penciled on the drawer puts it at 1902. It's heavier than my car, and someone had used it as a workbench at some point, but it's so large that it comfortably holds computer, keyboard, and mouse, plus a small printer.

I enter my passcode and hit the target to start the search algorithm running. This is a relatively new computer, bought fresh when I got to

Stillhouse Lake, but it's been customized with all manner of black-hat goodies by a hacker who goes by the name Absalom.

In the days and weeks and months after Mel's trial, while I sat in jail and endured my own legal torment, Absalom had been one of a huge baying pack of online abusers to go after me, analyzing every aspect of my life for hints of guilt.

After I was acquitted, though, the firestorm *really* started.

He'd unearthed every detail of my life and made it available online. He'd organized troll armies to relentlessly attack me, my friends, my neighbors. He'd found even my most distant relatives and doxed their addresses. He'd hounded the two cousins that Mel still had living and driven one of them to the brink of suicide.

But he'd drawn the line when the trolls he pushed in my direction went after my kids instead.

I'd gotten a remarkable message from him just after that hideous campaign started, a heartfelt e-mail that talked about his own childhood traumas, his own pain, and how he'd pursued me to banish his own demons. The train he'd started couldn't be stopped; the crusade had taken on a life of its own. But he wanted to help me, and what was more, he *could* help me.

By that time we'd been on the run out of Wichita, desperate and uncertain, and having him offer a hand? That had been the turning point. That had been the moment I'd retaken control of my life, with Absalom's help.

Absalom isn't my friend. We don't chat, and I suspect he still hates me on some level. But he helps. He builds false identities. He finds me safe havens. He does what he can to control the constant online harassment. When I get a new computer, he images it from backups he keeps in a secure cloud, so I don't lose data. He writes the custom search algorithms that allow me to keep track of the Sicko Patrol.

For this favor, of course, I pay him money. No need to be pals. We keep it strictly business.

While the search is running, I make a cup of hot tea with honey and sip it with my eyes shut, gathering myself for the challenge. I always keep certain things within reach as I do this: A loaded gun. My cell phone, ready to speed-dial Absalom if there's an issue. And last but not least, a plastic garbage bag into which I can throw up, if necessary.

Because this, *this* thing: this is hard. It's like sticking my head into a blast furnace, a writhing fury of mindless hatred and vile fury, and I am always shaken and scorched when I back away.

But it has to be done. Daily.

I feel the tension spiral down from my head, slithering like a cold serpent along my spine, my shoulders, and coiling heavily in my stomach. I'm never fully prepared when the search results come back, but today, as ever, I try to be calm, observant, distanced.

There are fourteen pages of results. The top link is new; someone's opened a thread on Reddit, and now the gruesome descriptions, speculations, and howls for justice are ginning up again. I grit my teeth and click the link.

Where's Melvin's Little Helper these days? Would love to pay that church lady hypocrite bitch a visit. They like to call me *church lady* because our family had been a member of one of the larger Baptist churches in Wichita, though Mel was spotty on attendance. I'd usually been there with the kids. There are plenty of ironic pictures posted on that theme—split screens of me and the kids at church, crime scene photos of the dead woman in the garage.

On Sunday mornings, Mel had usually excused himself by saying he had things to do in the workshop.

Things to do. I have to close my eyes for a moment, because there's a hidden monster's joke in those words. He'd never thought of the women he'd tortured and murdered as people. He thought of them as objects. Things.

I open my eyes, take a breath, and move on to the next link.

Hope Gina and her kids get raped and ripped and hung up like meat so people can spit on them. Mutilating Mel don't deserve a family. That one's accompanied by a crime scene photo of someone else's kids shot and dumped in a ditch. The callous hypocrisy is breathtaking. This troll is exploiting someone else's personal horror to make his point about mine. He doesn't care about children.

He cares about revenge.

I run through the rest in a sickening rush.

You see his daughter? Lily? I'd bump that til its cold.

Burn them alive and put em out with piss.

I got an idea, find some working outhouse and drown the kids in shit. Then send her directions on where to find them.

How can we make her suffer? Suggestions? Anybody got eyes on the bitch?

On and on and on. I leave Reddit, go to Twitter, find more threats, more hate, more vitriol—just in concise, 140-character bites. Then the blogs. 8chan. The true crime message boards. The websites that are shrines to Mel's crimes.

On the message boards and websites, the deaths of innocent young women are casual drive-by entertainment. Historical information. At least those armchair detectives aren't very threatening; Mel's family is just a footnote to the real story for them. They're not dedicated to our destruction.

The ones who are more interested in *us*, in Melvin Royal's missing family . . . those are the ones who could be dangerous.

And there are hundreds, maybe thousands of them—all competing to outdo one another with terrible new ways to *punish* me and the kids. *My kids.* It's a sick horror show, devoid of even a shred of conscience. None of them recognize that they're talking about people, real people who can be hurt. Who bleed. Who can be murdered. Or if they do recognize that, they absolutely don't give a shit.

There are some, an unnerving skim of this unholy broth, who are true, cold sociopaths.

I print it all out, highlight usernames and handles, and begin cross-referencing in the database I keep. Most of the names on the list are old hands at this; they have, for whatever reasons, fixated on us. Some are newer, zealous acolytes who've just stumbled on Mel's crimes and are looking to exact some retribution "for the victims," but it's really got nothing at all to do with Mel's victims. I rarely see any of their names mentioned. To this particular crop of vigilantes, the victims didn't matter alive, and they don't matter now. It's an excuse to let their vilest impulses out to play. These trolls are no different from Mel in many ways—except that unlike him, they probably won't act on those impulses.

Probably.

But then, that's why I keep the gun sitting next to me, to remind me that if they do, if they dare come near my kids, they'll pay the price. I will not let anyone hurt them ever again.

I pause in reading, because whoever the psychopath is behind the handle *fuckemall2hell*, he's stumbled over a careless piece of court paperwork that has one of our older addresses. He's publicly posted the street address, looped in victims' families, called reporters, sent out downloadable posters that have our pictures on them, with the words MISSING: HAVE YOU SEEN THESE PEOPLE? It's a tactic these savages have adopted recently, trying to play on genuine humanity and concern. He's preying on the better instincts of people to rat us out so that predators can reach us more easily.

I'm more worried for the innocent people now living at that address he's distributed, though. They might not have any idea what's coming. I send an anonymous e-mail to the detective in the area—a grudging ally—to let him know the address is being passed around again, and I hope for the best. Hope that the family living in that house doesn't wake up to packages of rancid meat and dead animals nailed to their door, to a flood of torture porn, to terrifying threats in their inboxes and mailboxes and on their phones and at their work. I clearly remember the shock of discovering the flood of abuse being leveled at my empty house, even though I was safely in jail and the kids had been spirited away to Maine.

If the current residents have kids, I pray they aren't targeted. Mine were. Signs on telephone poles. Their pictures sent to pornographers as models. There are no limits for the hate. It's free-floating, a toxic cloud of moral outrage and mob mentality, and it doesn't care who it hurts. Only that it does.

The address that this particular troll has uncovered is a dead end; it can't lead him to our door, or our new names. There are at least eight broken trails between where he points and where I now sit, but that doesn't comfort me. I've gotten good at this out of sheer necessity, but I'm not *them*. I don't have the same rancid drive. All I want to do is survive—and keep my kids as safe as I can.

I finish checking, shake the stress out of my arms and hands, drink the cold tea, and stand up to pace the office. I want to hold on to the gun as I do, but that's a terrible idea. Unsafe and paranoid. I stare at the quiet gleam of it, the safety it promises, though I know that's a lie, too, as much a lie as any Mel ever told me. Guns don't keep anyone safe. They only equal the playing field.

"Mom?"

A voice from the doorway, and I turn too quickly, heart hammering, glad that I don't have the gun now because surprising me is a bad idea, and it's Connor standing there, book bag dragging at his right hand. He doesn't seem to notice that he's startled me, or he's so used to it he doesn't care.

"Is Lanny okay?" he asks me, and I force a smile and nod.

"Yes, sweetie, she's fine. How was school?" I am only half listening, because I'm thinking that I didn't hear him come in, didn't hear the code, didn't hear the reset. I'd been too deep in concentration. Dangerous. I should be more aware.

He doesn't answer the question anyway. He gestures at the computer. "Did you finish the Sicko Patrol?"

It catches me by surprise. I say, "Where did you hear that?" But I answer my own question. "Lanny?"

He shrugs. "You're looking for stalkers, right?"

"Right."

"Everybody gets mean stuff on the Internet, Mom. You shouldn't take it so seriously. Just ignore them. They'll go away."

That, I think, is a maddening thing to say on so many levels. As if the Internet is a fantasy world, inhabited by imaginary people. As if we're *ordinary people* in the first place. And most of all, it's such a young *male* thing to say, this automatic assumption of safety. Women, even girls of Lanny's age, don't think that way. Parents don't. Older people don't. It reveals a certain blind, entitled ignorance to how dangerous the world really is.

It occurs to me, a little sickly, that I've helped him form that attitude because of how I've insulated him. Protected him. But what else can I do? Constantly terrify him? That can't help.

"Thanks for the opinion I didn't ask for," I tell him. "But I'm all right with doing this." I sort the papers and file them. I've always kept both electronic and paper records; in my experience, the police are more comfortable with paper. It feels like proof to them in a way that data on a screen doesn't. In an emergency, we might not be able to pull data in time, anyway.

"Sicko Patrol completed," I say, then shut and lock the file drawer. I drop the key in my pocket. It's attached to the alarm fob, and it's never out of my possession. I don't want Connor or Lanny to go through those files. Not ever. Lanny has a laptop of her own now, but I have strict parental controls enabled. Not only does it not give her the results, but I'll be alerted—and have been—when she tries to search keywords about her father, the murders, or anything related to it.

I can't risk giving Connor a computer quite yet, but the pressure to give him online access is growing at an impressive rate.

Lanny flings her door open and flits past the office, dodging Connor on her way down the hall. She's still wearing her goth pants and Ramones T-shirt, black hair fluttering in the breeze. Heading to the kitchen, I guess, for her typical afternoon snack of rice cakes and energy drink. Connor stares after her. He doesn't look surprised. Just resigned. "All the sisters in the world, and mine has to dress like somebody out of *The Nightmare Before Christmas*," he says. "She's trying to make herself not as pretty, you know."

It's a surprising insight from a kid his age. I blink, and it strikes me hard that beneath her oversize pants and shaggy hair and corpse makeup, Lanny is pretty. Growing into her bones, turning tall and hinting at curves. As a mom, I always think of her as beautiful, but now others will, too. The edgy style keeps people at a distance and changes the standards by which she will be judged.

That's clever and heartbreaking at the same time.

Connor turns and heads off to his room.

"Wait! Connor! Did you reset the alarm?"

"Of course," he calls back without stopping. His door closes with finality, but no force. Lanny returns with her rice cakes and energy drink and flops into the small chair in the corner of my office. She puts the energy drink down and gives me a mock salute.

"All present and correct, Master Sergeant," she says. Then she slumps at an angle functionally impossible for anyone over twenty-five. "I've been thinking. I want to get a job."

"No."

"I can help with the money."

"No. Your job is to be in school." I have to bite my lip to keep from complaining that my daughter used to like school. *Lily Royal* had liked school. She'd been in drama class and a programming club. But *Lanny* couldn't stand out. Couldn't have interests that made her special. Couldn't make friends and tell them anything approaching the truth. No surprise it made school hell for her.

"This girl you got into the fight with," I say. "You understand it can't happen? Why you can't get into these things?"

"I *didn't* get into it. She started it. What, you want me to lose? Get the shit beat out of me? I thought you were all about self-defense!"

"I want you to walk away."

"Oh, sure, *you* would. That's all you do, walk away. Oh, I'm sorry. I mean *run*."

There's nothing quite as scorching as a teenager's contempt. It has a breathless sting, and it lingers for a very long time. I try not to let her see she's scored points, but I don't trust myself to speak. I pick up the teacup and head for the kitchen, the comfort of running water to rinse away the dregs. She follows, but not to hit at me again. I can tell by the way she's hanging back that she regrets having said it and isn't quite sure how to take it back. Or even if she wants to.

As I put the teacup and saucer in the dishwasher, she says, "I was thinking of going out for a run . . . ?"

"Not alone you don't," I say, which is automatic, and then I realize she was counting on it. A nonapology apology. I hate even giving up the control of letting them ride the school bus, but venturing out on their own around the lake? No. "We'll go together. I'll change."

I change into leggings and a loose T-shirt over a sports bra, heavy socks, good running shoes. When I come out, Lanny is stretching lithely. She has on a red sports bra, no shirt, and black leggings with harlequin patterns down the sides. I just look at her until she sighs, grabs a T-shirt, and pulls it on.

"Nobody else runs in T-shirts," she grumbles at me.

I say, "I'm going to want that Ramones shirt back. It's a classic. And I'll bet you can't name a single song."

"'I Wanna Be Sedated,'" Lanny immediately shoots back. I don't respond. Lily had been medicated a lot, that first half year after *The Event*. She hadn't been able to sleep for days, and when she finally had fallen into a restless doze, she'd woken up screaming, crying for her mother. The mother who was in prison. "Unless you'd prefer 'We're a Happy Family'?"

I say nothing, because her song choices are completely on point. I turn off the alarm, open the door, and call for Connor to reset it. He grunts from somewhere down the hall, and I have to hope he means yes.

Lanny rabbits ahead, but I catch up at the end of the gravel drive, and we head east on the road at a good, loose lope. It's a perfect time of day, with the air warm, the sun low and friendly, the lake calm and dotted with boats. Other joggers pass us heading the other direction, and I open up the pace, Lanny pulling easily up. Neighbors wave at us from porches. *So friendly.* I wave back, but it's all surface, this trust. I know if these good people knew who I really was, knew whom I'd married, they'd be just like our old neighbors . . . distrustful, disgusted, afraid to be anywhere near us. And maybe they'd be right to be afraid. Melvin Royal casts a long, dark shadow.

We're halfway around the lake before Lanny, gasping, calls a halt to lean against a swaying pine. I'm not winded yet, but my calf muscles are burning and the points of my hips ache, and I stretch and keep up a light in-place jog while my daughter catches her breath. "You okay?" I ask. Lanny gives me a filthy look. "That's a yes?"

"Sure," Lanny says. "Whatever. Why do we have to make this so Olympic-level?"

"You know why."

Lanny looks away. "Same reason you signed me up with that Krav Maga freak last year."

"I thought you liked Krav Maga."

She shrugs, still studying some fronds down by her shoes. "I don't like thinking I need it."

"Neither do I, baby. But we have to face facts. There are dangers out there, and we need to be ready. You're old enough to get that."

Lanny straightens up. "Okay. Guess I'm ready. Try not to run me lame this time, Terminator Mom."

That's hard for me. While I was still Gina, but after *The Event*, I'd taken up running, and it had been grueling and exhausting until I built up my strength. Now, when I stop holding myself back, I run like I feel breath on my neck, as if I'm running for my life. It's not healthy or safe, and I'm well aware that driving myself that hard is a form of self-punishment, and also an expression of the fear I live with every day.

I forget, despite my best efforts. I'm not even aware of Lanny falling back, gasping, limping, until I'm around a curve and realize that I'm running alone in the shadow of the pines. Not even sure where I lost her.

I end up stretching against a tree and, finally, perching on a handy old boulder as I wait. I see her in the distance, walking slowly, limping a bit, and I feel a surge of guilt. *What kind of a mother am I, running a kid into the ground like that?*

That sixth sense I've developed suddenly drenches me in adrenaline, and I straighten up and turn my head.

Someone's there.

I catch sight of a person standing in the shadows of the pines, and my nerves—never calm—go tight. I slide off the boulder and into a ready stance, and I face the shadow head-on. "Who is it?"

He gives me a dry, nervous laugh and shuffles out. It's an old man, skin like dark, dry paper, gray whiskers, gray curls tight against his scalp. Even his ears droop. He leans heavily on a cane. "Sorry, miss. Wasn't meaning to worry you. I was just looking at the boats. Always like the lines of them. Never was much of a sailor, though. I spent my time on dry land." He wears an old jacket with military patches on it . . . artillery patches. Not World War II, but Korea, Vietnam, one of those less clear-cut conflicts. "I'm Ezekiel Claremont, live right over there up the hill. Been here since half forever. Everybody this side of the lake calls me Easy."

I'm ashamed for assuming the worst, and I advance and offer my hand. He has a firm, dry grip, but his bones feel fragile beneath it. "Hi, Easy. I'm Gwen. We live up over there, near the Johansens."

"Aw, yeah, you're some new folks. Nice to meet you. Sorry I haven't been up that way, but I don't do as much walking these days. Still healing up since I broke my hip six months back. Don't get old, young lady—it's a pain in the ass." He turns as Lanny lurches to a stop a few feet away and braces herself, bent over with her hands on her thighs. "Hello. You okay, there?"

"Fine," Lanny gasps. "Peachy. Hi."

I don't *quite* laugh. "This is my daughter, Atlanta. Everybody calls her Lanny. Lanny, this is Mr. Claremont. Easy, for short."

"Atlanta? I was born in Atlanta. Fine city, full of life and culture. Miss it sometimes." Mr. Claremont nods decisively to Lanny, who returns the gesture after a guarded look at me. "Well, I'd better get myself on home. Takes me a while to get up that hill. My daughter keeps after me to sell my place and move somewhere easier to get around, but I'm not ready to give up this view just yet. You know what I mean?"

I do. "You going to be okay?" I ask, because I can see his house, and it's an impressive distance uphill for a man with a bad hip and a cane.

"Fine, fine, thank you. I'm old, not decrepit. Not yet. Besides, the doctor says it's good for me." He laughs. "What's good for you never *feels* good, my experience."

"Boy, is that true," Lanny agrees. "Nice to meet you, Mr. Claremont."

"Easy," he says, starting his way up the hill. "You run safe, now!"

"We will," I say, then turn a sweaty grin on my daughter. "Race you the rest of the way."

"Come *on*! I'm practically dead here!"

"Lanny."

"I'll walk, thanks. You run if you want."

"I was kidding."

"Oh."

2

We've almost made it home again when my phone pings with a text message. It's an anonymous number, and hackles immediately go stiff at the back of my neck. I come to a stop and step off the road. Lanny gleefully jogs on by.

I swipe and open. It's from Absalom; it has his cryptic little text signature as the first character: Å. Then, **Are you anywhere near Missoula?**

He never asks exactly where we are, and I never tell. I type back, **Why?**

Somebody's posted a thing. Looks like they got it wrong. I'll try to head off and divert. Bad for whoever they're tagging. CYÅ.

That was Absalom's standard signoff, and sure enough, no more pings arrive. I assume he uses disposable phones, just as I do; his number changes every month like clockwork, always unrecognizable, though his symbol usage is totally consistent. I can't afford that many burners, so mine stays the same for six months at a time, the kids' phones for a year. A little stability in an unstable world.

The second that someone gets close, though, I burn everything—phones, e-mail accounts, everything. If there's a second close call around our location, Absalom notifies me, and we pack up and go. That's been our routine for the past few years now. It sucks, but we're used to it.

We *have* to be used to it.

I realize I'm looking forward to receiving that treasured concealed carry permit in the mail with an almost physical hunger. I'm not one of those jackasses who feel the need to strap an AR15 to their back to pick up groceries; those people live in a dystopian fantasy where they're the heroes in a world full of threats. I understand them, in a way. They feel powerless, in a world full of uncertainty. But it's still a fantasy.

I live in the real world, where I know that the only thing that stands between me and a thriving, violent, *organized* bunch of angry men could be the sidearm I carry. I don't need or want to advertise that fact. I don't *want* to use it. But I'm ready and willing.

I'm fully committed to our survival.

Lanny's celebrating wildly up ahead, and I let her have her victory. We stop at the mailbox for the day's haul of mostly junk mail. Lanny's stopped limping by now, charley horse smoothed away, but she continues to pace as I sort through the envelopes. I'm just a couple in when I realize that someone's walking toward us down the road, and I feel my body shift into a balanced stance, a different state of alertness.

It's the man from the gun range, the one who'd de-escalated Carl Getts from murder to general mayhem. *Sam.* I'm surprised to see him here, on foot. Have I ever glimpsed him around here before? Maybe at a distance. He looks vaguely familiar in this context. I must have seen him out walking or jogging, like so many others.

He continues walking in our direction, hands in his pockets, headphones in. When he sees me watching him, he gives me a vague wave and nod and keeps walking right past us, heading the opposite of the route we took around the lake. I keep my attention fixed on him until he goes over the slight rise that branches off to the upper homes—the Johansens', a little above ours, then Officer Graham's place—and he disappears. Just taking a walk. But where is he coming from?

It's probably obsessive that I feel I need to know.

As we enter the house, I turn to enter the alarm code. My fingers touch the keypad before I realize that I don't need to enter the code, because the alarm isn't beeping.

It isn't on.

I freeze, standing in the doorway, blocking my daughter's way in. She tries to push past, and I give her a fierce, wild look and put my finger to my lips, then point to the keypad.

Her face, pink from the exercise and sun, goes tense, and she steps back, and back again. I keep an extra set of car keys in the potted plant just inside the door, and now I scoop them out and toss them to her as I mouth, *"Go!"*

She doesn't hesitate. I've trained her well. She turns and runs for the Jeep, and I shut and lock the front door behind me. Whatever's inside, I want to keep it focused on me. I put the mail on the closest flat surface, careful not to make much noise, and the house lays itself out for me, all my options running fast through my mind.

It's only four steps to the small gun safe under the couch. I kneel down and press my thumb to the lock, and the door springs open with a small, metallic click. I pull out the Sig Sauer. It's my favorite and most reliable weapon. I know it's loaded and ready, one in the chamber, and I keep my pulse slow and my finger off the trigger as I move quietly across to the kitchen, the hallway, down.

I hear the Jeep start up and pull away with a hiss of tires on gravel. *Good girl.* She knows to keep driving for five minutes and, if I don't give her the all-clear, to call the police, then head for our rendezvous point almost fifty miles away and dig up a geocached stash of money and fresh IDs. If she has to, she can disappear without us.

I swallow hard, because now I'm alone with the fear that something terrible has happened to my son.

I'm drawing close to my bedroom. When I steal a look inside, I see nothing out of order. It's just as I left it, down to the shoes tumbled carelessly in the corner.

Lanny's bedroom is next on the same side, across from the main bathroom that we share. For an awful moment I think someone's ransacked her room, but then I realize that I never checked it before heading out to the range this morning, and she'd left the bed unmade, discarded clothes slumped over half the floor.

Connor. The pulse in my temples throbs faster, and all my self-control can't slow it down. *Please, God, no, don't take my baby, don't.*

His door is shut. He's put up a KEEP OUT, ZOMBIE INSIDE sign, but when I carefully, slowly try the handle I realize that it isn't locked. I have two choices: enter fast or slow.

I enter fast, banging the door open, gun coming up in a smooth arc as I brace myself with a shoulder against the rebounding wood, and I scare my son half to death with the whole production.

He's lying on his bed, headphones on and music audible from where I stand, but the percussive bang of the door against the wall brings him bolt upright, clawing the headphones off. He yells when he sees the gun, and I instantly lower it, but not before I see blind terror in his eyes.

It's gone in a second, replaced by boiling fury. "*Jesus*, Mom! What the hell?"

"I'm sorry," I say. My pulse is hammering perversely much faster now, responding to the adrenaline dumped into my bloodstream by the shock. My hands are shaking. I put the weapon down carefully on his dresser, ejection port up, barrel pointed away from both of us. Range rules. "Honey, I'm sorry. I thought—" I don't want to say it out loud. I manage to drag in a trembling breath and sink down to a crouch, hands pressed to my forehead. "Oh God. You just forgot to turn it on when we left."

I hear the music shut off in midscream, the headphones clatter to the floor. The bed creaks as Connor sits on the edge of it, looking at me. I risk a glance at him, finally. My eyes feel red and hot, though I'm not crying. I haven't in a long time.

"The alarm? I forgot to turn it on?" He sighs and bends forward, as if he has a sore stomach. "Mom. You've got to stop going off the rails; you're going to kill one of us, you know that? We're out here in the middle of nowhere—nobody else even locks their doors!"

I don't answer. He's right, of course. I *have* overreacted, and not for the first time. I have pointed a loaded gun at my child. His anger is understandable, and so is his defensiveness.

But he hasn't seen the pictures I get when I go through the Sicko Patrol postings.

It's a hobby of a particular subset of online stalkers. Some of them are very good at Photoshop. They take gruesome crime scene photos and graft our faces onto victims. They alter images on child pornography so I see my daughter and son brutalized in unimaginable ways.

The one that haunts me, and I know will always haunt me, is the image of a young boy Connor's age mutilated and left lying in a tangle of blood-soaked sheets in his own bed. That one popped up recently with a caption: *God's justice for murderers.*

It's right that Connor's angry at me. It's fine that he feels unfairly blamed and hemmed in by stupid, unnecessary, paranoid rules. I can't help that. I must defend him from very real monsters.

But I can't explain that to him. I don't want to have to show him that world, the reality that runs like a black river underneath this one. I want him to stay in the world where a boy can collect comics and put fantasy posters on his walls and dress up like a zombie for Halloween.

I say nothing. I stand up, when my legs are capable, and pick up the gun. I walk out and shut the door quietly behind me.

Through it, my son yells, "Wait until I tell Social Services!" I think he's joking. I hope.

I walk to the gun safe, put the Sig back in, and lock it away before I call my daughter and tell her to come home. I reset the alarm as I do. Habit.

I've just finished the call when I pick up the mail and carry it to the kitchen. I badly need water; my mouth has a dry, metallic taste like old blood. As I'm drinking, I sort through the circulars, charity pleas, local business mailings. I pause on something that doesn't belong: a manila envelope with my name and address printed on the outside and a postmark from Willow Creek, Oregon. That's my last remailing service. So whatever's inside has followed a long, broken trail to reach me.

I don't touch it. I open a drawer and take out a pair of blue nitrile gloves. I slip them on before I carefully, neatly slit open the top of the envelope and pull out the other one, business-size, that sits within it.

I recognize the return address in a flash and drop that envelope unopened to the counter. It isn't a conscious decision, no more than if I'd realized I was holding a live cockroach.

The letter is from El Dorado, the prison where Mel is held waiting for his execution day. It's been a long wait, and the lawyers tell me it'll be at least ten years before his appeals are exhausted. And Kansas hasn't carried out an execution for more than twenty years. So who knows when his sentence will finally be imposed. Until it is, he sits and thinks. He thinks a lot about me.

And he writes letters. There's a pattern to them that I've figured out, and that is why I don't immediately touch this one.

I stare at the envelope for a long time, and it catches me by surprise when I hear the front door open and the alarm starts beeping. Lanny's fast fingers cancel and reset.

I don't move from where I am, as if the envelope might attack if I don't stare it down.

Lanny puts the keys in the potted plant and walks past me to open the fridge and pull out a bottled water, which she cracks and gulps thirstily before saying, "So, let me guess. Brain-dead Connor forgot to turn on the alarm. Again. Did you shoot him?"

I don't answer. I don't move. From the corner of my eye, I'm aware she's staring at me, and that her body language shifts as she realizes what's going on.

Before I can guess what she's planning, my daughter grabs the envelope off the counter.

"No!" I turn on her, but it's too late; she's already sliding a black-painted fingernail under the flap and ripping it open, revealing pale paper inside. I reach out to snatch it away. She steps back, agile and angry.

"Does he write to me, too? To Connor?" she asks me. "Do you get these a lot? You said *he never wrote!*" I hear the betrayal in her voice, and I hate it.

"Lanny, give me the letter. Please." I try to sound authoritative and calm, but inside I am drowning in dread.

She focuses on my hands, sweating inside the blue gloves. "Jesus, Mom. He's already in jail. You don't have to preserve any damn evidence."

"Please."

She drops the torn envelope and unfolds the paper.

"Please don't," I whisper, defeated. Sick.

Mel has a schedule. He'll send two letters that are perfectly, wonderfully the *old* Mel I married: kind, sweet, funny, thoughtful, concerned. They will show exactly the man he pretended to be, down to the last, loving declaration. He doesn't protest his innocence, because he knows he can't do that; the evidence was never in doubt. But he can, and does, write about his feelings for me and the children. His love and care and concern.

Two times out of three.

But this is the third letter.

I see the exact moment when all her illusions are ripped away, when she spots the monster in those carefully inked words. I see her hands tremble, like the needle of a seismograph signaling an earthquake. I see the numb, scared look in her eyes.

And I can't bear it.

I take the paper from her suddenly unresisting hand, fold it shut, and drop it on the counter. Then I put my arms around her. She's stiff for a moment, and then she melts against me, face hot against mine, fine little shakes convulsing her body like wild current.

"Shh," I tell her, and stroke her black hair as if she's six years old, a child scared of the dark. "Shh, baby. It's okay."

She shakes her head, pulls away, and walks to her room. She closes the door.

I look at the folded paper and feel a surge of hate so strong that it nearly tears me apart. *How dare you,* I think to the man who's written those words, who's done that to my child. *How dare you, you fucking bastard.*

I don't read what Melvin Royal has written to me. I know what it says, because I've read it before. This is the letter where the mask comes off, and he talks about how I've disappointed him, taken his children away and poisoned them against him. He describes what he'll do to me if he ever has a chance. He's inventive. Descriptive. Repellently direct.

Then, as if he hasn't threatened to brutally murder me, he switches gears and asks how the kids are doing. Says he loves them. And of course he does, because in his mind, they're just reflections of himself. Not real people in their own right. If he meets them now, recognizes they're not the little plastic dolls he loved before . . . they'll become *other*. Potential victims, like me.

I put the letter back in the envelope, pick up a pencil, mark the date on it, and put the envelope back in the larger remailing service packaging. I feel better once that's done, as if I've disposed of a bomb. Tomorrow I'll send the entire package back, marked NO SUCH ADDRESS, and the remailing service will have preexisting instructions to FedEx it to the Kansas Bureau of Investigation agent in charge of Melvin's case. So far, the KBI hasn't been able to figure out how he gets those letters past the prison's normal screening process. I still hold out hope.

Lanny is wrong about why I put on the gloves. It isn't to preserve evidence. I wear them for the same reason doctors do: to prevent infection.

Melvin Royal is a contagious, fatal disease.

◆ ◆ ◆

The rest of the day is deceptively quiet. Connor says nothing about the incident in his bedroom; Lanny says nothing, period. The two of them boot up a video game, and while they're at it, my time is my own. I make dinner, like a normal mother. We eat in silence.

The next day, Lanny stays locked in her room, since she's banned from the classroom. I decide not to interfere; I can hear her binge-watching a TV show. Connor's off to school. It itches at me to have him go alone to the bus stop, and I watch from the window until he climbs on board. It would irritate him beyond measure if I actually walked him there and waited.

When he returns that afternoon on the bus, I step out to greet him but cover it by pretending to poke around in the small flower garden at the front of the house, as if his arrival is completely incidental. He gets off the bus, heavily burdened by his backpack, and two other boys pile off after. The three of them talk, and for a second I worry about bullies, but they seem friendly. The strangers are both blond, one about Connor's age and one a year or two older. The older one is alarmingly tall and broad, but he gives Connor a friendly wave and grin, and I watch the two of them jog off to take the trail to the left. They certainly don't belong to the Johansens, who are an older couple with grown kids who've visited them exactly once since

I've been here. No, they must be Officer Graham's kids. Graham is a uniformed member of the Norton police force. Unlike me, Graham's family is Old Tennessee; from what I've heard, he's the last of several generations of solid country people who had property here at the lake well before it ever turned into the playground of the wealthy. I still need to drop by, introduce myself, assess the man, and try to start a quiet alliance. I might need law enforcement on my side at some point. I've tried a couple of times but gotten no answer at the door. That's understandable. Cops work odd hours.

"Hey, kid. How was school?" I ask Connor as he trudges past me. I pat the soil I disturbed more firmly back around a spray of blooms.

"Fine," he says, without enthusiasm. "I've got a paper due tomorrow."

"On what?"

He hitches his backpack into a more comfortable position. "Biology. It's okay. I've got it."

"Do you want me to read it when you're done?"

"I'm okay."

He goes inside, and I stand up to rub the dirt from my palms. I worry about him, of course. Worry about the scare I gave him (and myself) yesterday. Worry about whether or not he needs more counseling. He's turned into such a quiet, introverted kid, and it scares me as much as Lanny's outbursts. I don't know what he's thinking most of the time, and every once in a while I see a look, a tilt of his head, that reminds me so strongly of his father that I go cold inside, waiting to see that monster look out of his eyes . . . but I've never seen it. I don't believe that evil is inherited.

I can't.

I make a pizza for dinner, and we've all eaten and are watching a movie together when the doorbell rings, followed by a loud, brisk knock. It makes my throat seize up, and I come off the couch in one convulsive leap. Lanny starts to get up, and I urgently motion her back, silently gesturing for her and Connor to go down the hall.

They look at each other.

The knock bangs again, louder. It sounds impatient. I think about the gun in its safe under the couch, but then I slowly ease the curtain back and peek outside.

Police. There is a uniformed officer on our front porch, and the old feeling of anxiety threatens to drown me for a moment. I'm Gina Royal again. I'm back on our old Wichita street, my hands cuffed behind my back, looking at the handiwork of my husband. Listening to myself scream.

Stop, I tell myself, then let the word ring through my body like Javi's cease-fire command at the gun range.

I disarm the alarm and open the door, not allowing myself to think about what could happen next.

A big, pale policeman is standing there, sharply dressed and creased and polished. He's a foot taller than I am and broad in the shoulders, and he has that wary, unreadable look I'm so familiar with. Comes standard-issue with badges.

I smile at him despite the wail of panic going on inside me. "Officer. How can I help you?"

"Hi, Ms. Proctor, right? Sorry to drop in like this. My son told me your boy lost this on the bus today. I figured I'd return it." He hands over a small silver flip phone. Connor's, I recognize it instantly. I color-code the kids' phones, so they don't mix them up and I can tell at a glance which is which. I feel a flash of anger at my son for being careless, and then one of real fear. Losing a phone means losing our tight control of information, though the only numbers he has programmed in are to his friends here, to me, and to Lanny. Still. It's a breach in our wall. A lapse of attention.

I don't say anything in a timely fashion, not even *thank you*, and Officer Graham shifts a little. He has a strong-boned face, clear brown eyes, and an awkward little smile. "I've been meaning to stop over and say hello. But look, if this is a bad time—"

"No, no, of course not, I'm sorry, I—I mean, thank you for returning this." Lanny has reached forward and paused the movie by now, and I step aside to let him come in. As he does, I shut the door and, by sheer reflex, rearm the system. "Can I offer you some refreshment? It's Officer Graham, right?"

"Lancel Graham, yes, ma'am. Lance, if we're not being fancy." He has a solid, old-school Tennessee accent, the kind that comes from never venturing far from your doorstep. "If you've got some iced tea, that'd go down nice."

"Of course. Sweet tea?"

"Is there any other kind?" He has his hat off immediately and self-consciously rubs his head, disordering his hair. "Sounds wonderful. I've had a long, thirsty day."

I'm not used to liking someone instinctively, and he seems to be working hard to charm me. It puts me on my guard. He's going out of his way to be polite, respectful, and he has a way of carrying himself that minimizes his broad frame and muscles. Probably damn good at his job. There's a certain timbre in his voice; he can probably talk down an angry suspect without laying a finger on anyone. I don't trust snake charmers . . . but I like the easy smile he gives my kids. That goes a long way.

It occurs to me then that I should be damn grateful that it's a *cop* who's brought back this phone. It's password-protected, of course, but in the wrong hands, knowledgeable hands, it could have done damage. "Thanks so much for returning Connor's phone," I say as I pour Officer Graham iced tea from a pitcher in the fridge. "I swear, he's never lost it before. I'm glad your son found it and knew who it belonged to."

"I'm sorry, Mom," my son says from the couch. He sounds subdued and anxious. "I didn't mean to lose it. I didn't know it was gone!"

Most tweens, I think, would miss their phone if parted from it for thirty seconds, but my kids are forced to live in an alien world, one where they can't use their phones for much beyond the basics. No such thing as smartphones, to them. Of the two of the kids, I'd have said Connor was more into the tech; he had buddies, geeky buddies, who texted him, at least. Lanny was . . . less social.

"It's okay," I tell him and mean it, because, *God*, I'd busted on my poor son enough for a lifetime this week. Yes, he'd forgotten to set the alarm. Yes, he'd lost his phone. But that was normal life. I needed to ease up and stop acting like every single lapse was lethal. It was stressing me, and all of us, out.

Officer Graham perches on one of the barstools at the counter to sip his tea. He looks comfortable enough and gives me a friendly grin as he raises eyebrows in appreciation. "Good tea, ma'am," he says. "Hot day out in the squad car. I can tell you this goes down well."

"Anytime, and please, call me Gwen. We're neighbors, right? And your sons are Connor's friends?"

I glance at Connor as I say it, but his expression is closed. He is turning his phone over and over in his hands. I think with a stab of guilt that he is probably worried what kind of rant I'll tear off on once the company is gone. It comes to me with ruthless clarity that I've been far too militant with my kids. We've finally settled in a nice place, surrounded by peace. We don't have to act like hunted animals now. There are eight broken trails between the address the troll discovered online and us. *Eight*. It's time to stand down from red alert, before I damage my kids irreparably.

Lancel Graham is looking around the place now with a curious expression. "You've sure done a great job with this house," he says. "I was told it got trashed, right? After the foreclosure?"

"God, it was a total mess," Lanny says, which startles me; she usually isn't one to voluntarily jump into a conversation with a stranger. Especially a uniformed one. "They destroyed everything they could. You should have seen the bathrooms. Utterly gross. We had to wear white plastic suits and face masks to even go in there. I puked for *days*."

"Must have been kids partying here, then," Graham says. "Squatters would have had a little more care for the place, unless they were high all the time. Speaking of that, I should tell you that even out here, we have our own drug problems. Still some meth cooking going on up in the hills, but mainly the big business is heroin these days. And Oxy. So you keep an eye out. Never know who's using or pushing." He pauses in the act of raising his glass to his lips. "You didn't find any drugs in here when you were clearing up?"

"Whatever we found, we tossed," I tell him, which is entirely true. "I didn't open any boxes or bags. Everything went out that wasn't nailed down, and half of that we pried up and replaced. I doubt there's anything hidden around here now."

"Good," he says. "Good. Well, that's most of my job around here in Norton. Drugs and drug-related robberies, some drunk driving. Not a lot of violent crimes, thankfully. You came to a good place, Ms. Proct—Gwen."

Except for the heroin epidemic, I think but don't say. "Well, it's always nice to meet neighbors. Strong ties make the community better, right?"

"Right." He drains his tea, stands, and pulls a card from his pocket, which he lays down on the counter and taps with two fingers, as if nailing it in place. "My numbers are on there. Work and cell. You have any trouble, any of you, don't be afraid to call, okay?"

"We will," Lanny says, before I can, and I see that she's studying Officer Graham with a shine in her eyes. I resist the urge to sigh. She's fourteen. Crushes are inevitable, and he looks like the poster child for what workouts can do. "Thanks, Officer."

"Sure thing, Miss—"

"Atlanta," she tells him, and stands up to offer her hand. He gravely shakes it. *She never calls herself Atlanta,* I think, and nearly choke on my sweet tea.

"Pleased to meet you." Graham turns and shakes Connor's hand, too. "And you're Connor, of course. I'll tell my boys you said hi."

"Okay." Connor, by contrast to his sister, is quiet. Watchful. Reserved. Still holding on to his phone.

Graham puts his hat back on and shakes my hand last of all; then I walk him to the door. He turns, as if he's forgotten something, while I'm disarming the alarm to let him out. "I heard you go to the range, Gwen. You keep your guns here?"

"Mostly," I say. "Don't worry. They're all in gun safes."

"And believe me, we know gun safety," Lanny says, rolling her eyes.

"I'll bet you're both good shots," he says. I don't like the quick brother-sister look Connor and Lanny exchange; the fact that I've not allowed them to touch my guns, or to learn to shoot, is a constant bone of contention between us. It's bad enough that I run panic drills in the middle of the night. I don't want to add loaded weapons to the mix. "I'm there evenings on Thursdays and Saturdays. I'm teaching my boys."

It isn't quite an invitation, but I nod and thank him, and he's on his way in another few seconds. He stops in the open door again and looks at me. "Can I ask you something, Ms. Proctor?"

"Sure," I say. I step out, because I sense he wants it private.

"Rumors say this house had a safe room," he says. "That true?"

"Yes."

"You, ah, been in there?"

"We got a locksmith out to open it up. There wasn't anything inside it. Just some water bottles."

"Huh. I'd always thought someone was stashing something in there, if it even existed. Well." He points back to where he left his card on the counter. "You call me if you need anything."

He leaves without more questions.

Something tight and animal-hot eases up in me as I lock the door again, enter the code, and walk back toward the couch. Having a strange man in my house makes me itch all over. It reminds me of evenings spent on the couch with my kids. With Mel. With the thing that wore

Mel as a disguise. I'd never seen through it. Oh, he could be cold and uninterested and cross, but any human in the world has those flaws.

What Mel really was . . . that was different. Or was it? Would I even know?

"Mom," Lanny says. "He's kinda hot. You should check that out."

"Throwing up in my mouth," Connor says. "Wanna see?"

"Quiet," I tell them, settling in between them on the couch. I reach for the remote, then turn and look at my son. "Connor, about the phone."

He braces for impact and opens his mouth to apologize. I put my hand over his, and the cell he still holds tightly in it, as if it might get away.

"We all make mistakes. It's okay," I tell him, staring right into his eyes to make sure he understands that I'm being honest. "I'm sorry I've been such a terrible mom to you recently. Both of you. I'm sorry about my freak-out over the alarm. You shouldn't have to tiptoe around your own home, afraid of when I might blow up at you. I'm so sorry, honey."

He doesn't know what to say to any of that. He looks helplessly at Lanny, who leans forward, brushing dark hair from her face and hooking it behind one ear. "We know why you're so tense all the time," she tells me, and he looks relieved that she said it for him. "Mom. I saw the letter. You've got a right to be paranoid."

She must have told Connor about the letter, because he doesn't ask, and he doesn't seem curious. On impulse, I reach over and take her hand. I love these kids. I love them so much it steals my breath and squeezes me flat, and at the same time, it makes me feel weightless and exalted.

"I love you both," I say.

Connor comfortably shifts and reaches for the remote control.

"We know that," he says. "Don't go all unicorns pooping rainbows on us."

I have to laugh. He presses the "Play" button, and we sink back into fiction again, warm and comfortable together, and I remember when they were so little I could rock Connor in my arms while Lanny fidgeted and played next to me. I miss those sweet moments, but they're also tainted. Those moments happened back in Wichita, in a home I thought was safe.

While I played family time, Mel had so often been absent. In his garage.

Working on his *projects*. And every once in a while, he made a table, a chair, a bookcase. A toy for the kids.

But in between those things, in that locked workshop, he'd let his monster loose while we were just ten feet away, lost in the wonder of a movie or the shouting fun of a board game. He'd clean up and come out smiling, and *I never knew the difference*. I hadn't even wondered about any of it. It had seemed harmless, just his hobby. He'd always needed alone time, and I'd given it to him. He'd said he kept the outer door padlocked because he had valuable tools.

And I'd swallowed every word of it. Living with Mel was nothing but lies, always lies, no matter how warm and comforting they had seemed.

No, this is better. Better than it's ever been before. My smart, savvy kids, just the way they are. Our home that we've rebuilt with our own hands. Our new, reborn lives.

Nostalgia is for normal people.

And for all we pretend, as hard as we can ever pretend, we will never, ever be normal again.

I pour a glass of scotch and go outside.

◆ ◆ ◆

That's where Connor finds me half an hour later. I love the quiet hush of the lake, the moonlight on the water, the sharp crispness of stars overhead. Soft breezes sway and whisper the pines. The scotch provides a nice counterpoint, a memory of smoke and sunlight. I like finishing the day this way, when I can.

Connor, still in his pants and a T-shirt, slides into the other chair on the porch and sits in silence for a moment before he says, "Mom. I didn't lose my phone."

I turn toward him, surprised. The scotch sloshes a little in the tumbler, and I put it aside. "What do you mean?"

"I mean, I didn't *lose* it. Somebody took it."

"Do you know who?"

"Yeah," he says. "I think Kyle took it."

"Kyle—"

"Graham," he says. "Officer Graham's kid. The taller one, you know? He's thirteen."

"Honey, it's okay if it fell out of your pocket or your backpack. It was an accident. I promise, I'm not going to bust you for it, all right? You don't have to accuse anybody just to—"

"You're not listening, Mom," he says fiercely. *"I didn't lose it!"*

"If Kyle stole it, why would he give it back to you?"

Connor shrugs. He looks pale and tense, old for his age. "Maybe he couldn't get it unlocked. Maybe his dad caught him with it. I don't know." He hesitates. "Or . . . maybe he got what he wanted off it. Like Lanny's number. He was asking me about her."

That's normal, of course. A boy asking about a girl. Maybe I'd misinterpreted her friendliness toward Officer Graham. Maybe I hadn't spotted a sudden infatuation. Maybe she just wanted to get to know his son. *She could do worse,* I thought. *But what if he did steal the phone? How is that okay?*

"You could be wrong, baby," I say. "Not everything has to be a threat, or a conspiracy. We're okay. We'll be okay."

He wants to tell me something else, I can see it in his body language. He's also afraid that I'll be angry at him. I hate that I've made him afraid to tell me things. "Connor? Sweetie? What's bothering you?"

"I—" He bites his lip. "Nothing, Mom. Nothing." My son's worried. I've created a world for him where defaulting to a conspiracy theory makes sense to him. "Is it okay if I just . . . stay away from them, though? Kyle and his brother?"

"If you want to. Of course. But be polite, all right?"

He nods, and after a second I pick up my scotch again. He stares out at the lake. "I don't need friends anyway."

He's too young to say that. Too young to even *think* it. I want to tell him that he should make all the friends he can, that the world is safe and no one will ever hurt him again, that his life can be full of joy and wonder.

And I can't tell him that, because it isn't true. It might be true for other people. Not for us.

Instead, I finish my scotch. We go inside. I set the alarm, and once Connor is in bed, I take all my guns to the kitchen table, lay out the cleaning kit, and make sure that I'm ready for anything. Like practicing my aim, cleaning my weapons feels soothing. Feels like putting things right again.

I need to be ready, just in case.

◆ ◆ ◆

Lanny spends the rest of her suspension acing her homework and reading, headphones blasting, though she does go running with me twice. She even does it voluntarily, though by the end of the run she's swearing she'll never do it again.

On Saturday we call my mother. It's a family ritual, the three of us gathered around my disposable phone. I have an app built in that generates an anonymous Voice over IP number, so that even if anyone is reviewing my mom's call logs, the number won't lead them anywhere close.

I dread Saturdays, but I know the ritual is important for the kids.

"Hello?" My mother's calm, slightly fragile voice reminds me of her advancing years. I always picture her as she was when I was younger . . . Healthy, strong, tanned, lean from all her swimming and boating. She lives in Newport, Rhode Island, now, having left Maine behind. She had to move before my trial, and twice after it, but finally people are leaving her alone. It helps that Newport has that New England closed-in attitude.

"Hi, Mom," I say, feeling the uncomfortable pressure in my chest. "How are you?"

"I'm fine, honey," she says. She never says my name. At sixty-five years old, she's had to learn to be so cautious about talking to her own child. "So glad to hear your voice, sweetheart. Everything okay there?" She doesn't ask where we are, and she never knows.

"Yes, we're fine," I tell her. "I love you, Mom."

"Love you too, sweetheart."

I ask her about her life there, and she talks with false enthusiasm about restaurants and picturesque views and shopping. About taking up a scrapbooking hobby, though what she can scrapbook about *me* I have no idea. The reams of articles about my monstrous ex? My trial? My acquittal? It's almost as bad if she doesn't include any of that, and only has my pictures up to my wedding, pictures of the kids, without any context for our lives.

I wonder what kind of decorations Hobby Lobby sells to ornament the pages dedicated to serial killers in a scrapbook.

Lanny leans over to say, in a bright voice, "Hi, Grandma!" And when my mother responds, I hear the shift in that faraway voice . . . Real warmth. Real love. Real connection. It skips a generation, or at least, it skipped over me. Lanny loves her grandmother, and so does Connor. They remember those dark, awful days after *The Event*, when I was dragged off to jail and the only light left for them was my mom, who'd swept in like an angel. She'd rescued them into something like normalcy, at least for a while. She'd been a lioness in their defense, fending off reporters and the curious and vindictive with sharp words and slammed doors.

I owe her for that.

I almost miss it when she says, "So, kids, what are you studying in school right now?" It seems like a safe question, and it *should* be, but as Connor opens his mouth I realize that one of his classes is Tennessee history, and I quickly interrupt.

"Classes are going well."

She sighs, and I can hear the exasperation in it. She hates this. Hates being so . . . *vague*. "And how about you, dear? Have you got any new hobbies?"

"Not really."

That's the extent of our conversation. We were never quite close, she and I, even when I was a child. She loves me, I know, and I love her, but it isn't the kind of attachment that I see in other people. Other families. There's a kind of polite distance between us, as if we're strangers who happened to end up together. It's odd.

But I owe her everything, even so. She'd never expected to have to keep my children for nearly a year while the prosecution tried to build a case for my guilt. They called me Melvin's Little Helper, and my presumed involvement in Melvin's crimes rested completely on the testimony of one gossipy, vindictive neighbor looking for attention. She claimed she'd seen me help Melvin carry one of his victims from the car into the garage one evening.

I never had. I never would. I hadn't known a thing, *ever*, but it was horrifying and maddening to realize that no one, absolutely no one, believed that. Not even my own mother. Maybe part of the open wound between us stems from that moment when she'd asked me, with such revulsion and horror in her face, *Honey, did you do this? Did he make you do this?*

She'd never insisted it was a lie, never denied I was capable of atrocity. She'd only sought to find a *reason* for it, and that was incredibly hard to understand then, or now. Maybe it was the lack of attachment she'd had to me as a child, and I to her; maybe she could so easily believe the worst because she felt she'd never really known me at all.

I will never, ever do that to my children. I will defend them with complete devotion. None of this is their fault.

My own mother has always blamed *me*. *Well,* she told me at one point, *you wanted to marry that man.*

The reason the trolls are so viciously devoted to my pursuit is that they really believe that I'm guilty. I'm a vicious, predatory killer who managed to evade justice, and now *they're* the ones who can administer the punishment.

On some level I understand it. Mel swept me off my feet with romantic gestures. He took me to beautiful dinners. Bought me roses. Always opened doors for me. Sent me love letters and cards. I really did love him, or at least I thought I did. The proposal was thrilling. The wedding was fairy-tale perfect. In a few months, we were pregnant with Lily, and I thought I was the luckiest woman in the world, someone whose husband earned enough to let her stay home and lavish her children with love and care.

And then, gradually, his hobby had crept in.

Mel's workshop had started small: a workbench in the garage, then more tools, more space, until there wasn't room for even one car, much less two, and he'd built the carport and taken the entire garage as his space. I hadn't loved it, especially in the winter, but by then Mel had taken out the garage door, built a back wall, and added a door that he kept padlocked and dead bolted. Expensive tools.

I'd never noticed anything that had sounded odd, except once. It would have been around the death of his next-to-last victim—he'd told me that a raccoon had gotten into the workshop from the attic and died in the corner, and it would take a while for the smell to air out. He used lots of bleach and cleaners.

I believed every word of it. Why wouldn't I?

But I still think I should have known, and in that, I understand the trolls' anger.

My mother is saying something that, by the tone, is directed again to me. I open my eyes and say, "Sorry, what?"

"I said, are you making sure the kids are getting swimming lessons? I worry that you're not, given the . . . the problems you have." My mother adores the water—lakes, pools, the sea. She's half mermaid. It was especially horrifying to her that Melvin disposed of his victims in water. It's especially horrifying to me, too. My stomach clenches when I even *think* of dipping a toe in the lake that I admire so much from a distance. I can't even take a boat out on that calm surface without thinking of my ex-husband's victims, weighted down and chained to the bottom. A silent, rotting garden, swaying in the slow currents. Even drinking tap water makes me gag.

"The kids aren't really interested in swimming," I tell my mom, without the slightest inflection of dismay that she brought up the subject at all. "We do run pretty often, though."

"Yeah, the path around—" Lanny starts, and lightning-fast, I reach out and hit the mute button. She realizes her mistake in the next instant. She'd been about to say *the lake* . . . And even though there are thousands of lakes in the country, it's a clue. We can't afford even that much. "Sorry."

I unmute.

"I mean, we run outside a lot," Lanny says. "It's nice." It's hard for her not to be able to provide any details—the temperature, the trees, the lake—but she leaves it at that. Generic. My mother knows enough not to push. It's a sad fact of life.

I've wondered before what their life was like without me; my own experience behind bars was hell, constantly burning with fear for my kids. I thought from the glad way they always greeted these phone calls that Grandma represented something peaceful in their lives—a vacation from the awful reality they've been shoved into. At least, I hope that's what it is.

I hope that my kids aren't that good at lying, because that, too, is a Melvin Royal signature trait.

Mom spins tales of Newport and the coming summer, and we can't reciprocate with what the weather will be like near us; she knows that, and the conversation is mostly one-sided. I wonder if she gets anything out of these calls, really, or if it's a duty for her. She might not have bothered if it had only been me, but she truly does love my kids, and they love her back.

The kids' faces dim a little when I end the call and put the phone away until next time. Lanny says, "I wish we could Skype or something, so we could see her."

Connor immediately frowns at her. "You know we can't," he says. "They'd figure stuff out from Skype. I see it on cop shows and things."

"Cop shows aren't reality, dumb-ass," Lanny shoots back. "You think *CSI* is a documentary?"

"Easy, you two," I say. "I wish we could see her, too. But this is good, right? We're good?"

"Yeah," Connor says. "We're good." Lanny says nothing.

◆ ◆ ◆

Sicko Patrol the next day yields nothing much new, but then again, I've grown so accustomed to the general horror of it that I'm not sure if I'd recognize *new* if it bit me. I do some freelance editing work, then some freelance web design work, and I'm deep into an especially demanding piece of coding when a brisk knock strikes the front door. Despite my startled flinch, the sound reminds me of the way Officer Graham knocks, so I am cheerful when I head to answer it. Sure enough, as I check to see who it is, I see Lancel Graham's face.

After the first rush of relief, I hope he hasn't misunderstood my warm welcome the other night, or seen it as an opportunity. I'm not in a place that needs romance. I had enough of that with Mel's letter-perfect seduction, his model-husband performance art. I don't trust myself that way anymore, and I can't bring myself to allow the lowering of barriers that comes with even the most casual of relationships.

I'm busy thinking about that as I disarm the system and open the door, but that train of thought hardly even leaves the station. There's something different about him this time. He's not smiling.

He's also not alone.

"Ma'am." The man standing behind him is the one who speaks first. He's an African American man of medium height who has the build of a former football player, going soggy around the middle. He's got a sharp-edged haircut and heavy-lidded eyes, and the suit looks hard-worn and off the rack on its best day. He's got a tie on, too, a blunt, red thing that just slightly clashes with the gray of the jacket. "I'm Detective Prester. I need to speak to you, please."

It isn't a question.

I freeze in place and involuntarily look back over my shoulder. Connor and Lanny are both in their rooms, and neither of them has come looking. I step out and shut the door behind me. "Detective. Of course. What is it?" Thank God, I don't have to fear for the safety of my children in that moment. I know where they are. I know they're safe. So this, I think, must be about something else.

I wonder if he's dug around and put the trail together to connect Gwen Proctor to Gina Royal. I hope to hell not.

"Can we sit down a moment?"

I indicate the chairs on the porch, instead of letting them inside, and he and I settle into them. Officer Graham lingers at a distance, watching the lake. I follow his gaze, and my heart speeds up with a kick.

The usual fleet of pleasure craft is absent today. Instead, there are two boats out near the middle of the calm surface, both painted in official blue-and-white colors, with light bars on top that strobe slow, red flashes. I see a diver in scuba gear pitch backward over the side of the second one.

"A body was found in the lake early this morning," Detective Prester says. "Was hoping you might have seen something out there last night, heard something? Anything out of the ordinary?"

I scramble to order my thoughts. *Accident,* I think. *Boating accident. Somebody out at night, drunk, tips over the side* . . . "I'm sorry," I say. "Nothing unusual."

"You hear anything after dark last night? Boat engines, maybe?"

"Probably, but that's not really unusual," I say. I'm trying to remember. "Yes. I heard something around nine, I think." Long after dark, which falls early behind the pines. "But there are people here who go out to enjoy the stars. Or do some night fishing."

"Did you happen to look outside at any point? See anyone around the lake or on it?" He looks tired, but there's a sharpness behind that facade, one I wouldn't want to play around trying to avoid. I answer him as honestly as I can.

"No, I didn't. I'm sorry. I was working really late last night on the computer, and my office window looks up the hill, not down. I didn't go outside."

He nods and makes some notes in a book. He's got a quiet sort of confidence, the kind that makes you want to relax around him. I know that's dangerous. I've been lulled into underestimating police before, and I suffered for it. "Anybody else in the house last night, ma'am?"

"My kids," I say. He glances up, and his eyes flash dark amber in the sunlight. Unreadable. Behind that disguise of the tired, slightly frayed, overworked man, he's sharp as a scalpel.

"Can I talk to them, please?"

"I'm sure they don't know anything—"

"Please."

It would seem suspicious not to agree, but I'm tense and anxious as hell. I don't know how Lanny and Connor will react to being questioned again; they'd been subjected to many, many interviews during the course of Mel's trial, and my own, and even though the Wichita police had been careful about it, it left scars. I don't know what kind of traumas it will tear open. I try to keep my voice calm. "I'd rather not have them questioned, Detective. Unless you think it's absolutely necessary."

"I think it is, ma'am."

"For an accidental drowning?"

His amber eyes fix on me, and they seem to glow in the light. I feel them probing into me like searchlights. "No, ma'am," he says. "I never said it was accidental. Or a drowning."

I don't know what that means, but I feel the pit open under me, I feel the drop. Something very bad has just begun.

And I say, in half a whisper, "I'll get them."

3

Connor goes first, and the detective is gentle with him, good with kids. I see the gleam of a wedding ring, and I'm glad that he isn't like the cops back in Kansas. My kids had developed a real fear of police, and for very good reason; they'd seen the anger of the ones who'd arrested Mel, an anger that had only increased as the depth and breadth of his crimes was revealed. Those police had known not to take it out on small children, but some of it had spilled over. Inevitably.

Connor seems tense and nervous, but he gives his answers in short, effective sentences. He hasn't heard anything except—as I'd said—maybe a boat engine out on the water around nine at night. He didn't look out, because it isn't unusual. He doesn't remember anything out of the ordinary at all.

Lanny doesn't want to say anything. She sits silently, head down, and nods or shakes her head but won't speak until the detective finally turns to me in exasperation. I put a hand on her shoulder and say, "Sweetheart, it's okay. He's not here to hurt anybody. Just tell him anything you might know, okay?" I say that, of course, confident that she doesn't know anything, no more than Connor or I do.

Lanny shoots me a doubtful look from a veil of dark hair and says, "I saw a boat last night."

I am rooted to the spot in shock. I shiver a little, even though the day's air is warm, the birds singing. *No,* I think. *No, this can't be happening. My daughter can't be a witness.* A sick abyss opens at my feet, and I imagine her on the stand, testifying. Cameras flashing. Pictures in newspapers, and immediately, the headlines.

SERIAL KILLER'S DAUGHTER WITNESS IN MURDER TRIAL

We'll never get away again.

"What kind of boat?" Detective Prester asks. "How big was it? What color?"

"It wasn't very big. A small fishing boat, like—" She thinks, then points to one that's bobbing at a dock not far away. "Like that one. White, I could see it from my window."

"Can you recognize it if you see it again?"

She's already shaking her head by the time he finishes. "No, no, it was just a boat, like a hundred other ones. I didn't see it real well." She shrugs. "Looked like every other one around here, honestly."

If Prester is disappointed, he doesn't look it. Doesn't look excited, either. "So, you saw the boat. Good. Let's back up. What made you look outside?"

Lanny sits for a moment, thinking, then says, "I guess it was the splash?"

That gets his attention, and mine. My mouth goes dry. Prester leans forward a bit. "Tell me about that."

"Well, I mean, it was a big splash. Big enough that I heard it. But my room faces the lake, you know, at the corner of the house. I had my window open. So I heard a splash when the engine cut out. I thought maybe somebody fell in, or jumped in. People go skinny-dipping out there sometimes."

"And you looked out?"

"Yeah. But all I saw was the boat. It was just sitting there. There was somebody in it, I guess, because after a couple of minutes the engine started up again. I couldn't really see them." She takes in a deep breath. "Did I see somebody dumping a body?"

Prester doesn't answer that. He's busy writing in his notebook, fast scratches of pen on paper. He says, "Did you see where the boat went after the engine started?"

"No. I shut the window; it was getting too windy outside. I pulled the curtain and went back to reading."

"Okay. How long would you say you heard the engine run before it was turned off again?"

"I don't know. I put my earbuds in. I fell asleep and they were still in. My ears were sore this morning. My music played all night."

God. I can't swallow. I stare at Prester, willing him to say something comforting, something like, *It's okay, kid, nothing happened, it's all just a mistake,* but he doesn't. He doesn't confirm or deny. He just clicks his pen, puts it back in his pocket with the notebook, and stands up. "Thank you, Atlanta. That's real helpful. Ms. Proctor."

I can't say anything to him. I just nod, like Lanny does, and we watch as he and Graham rendezvous back at the dust-filmed black sedan parked in our driveway. They talk, but I can't make out a word, and they're positioned so we can't see their faces. I sit down and put my arm around my daughter, and for once, she doesn't shrug it off and move away.

I gently rub my palm back and forth across her shoulder, and she sighs. "This isn't good, Mom. Not good. I should have said I didn't see anything. I thought about lying, I really did."

I think that's probably true; I don't see how what she saw advances the investigation at all. She couldn't identify the boat, hadn't seen anyone to recognize, and telling Prester anything just means that he'll check us out in more detail. I pray that Absalom's work on our new identities will hold up. I can't be absolutely sure of that, and *any* scrutiny, *any* leaks could have dire consequences.

We should get out of here before something happens. I think about that. I vividly imagine the flurry of packing. We have a fair amount of stuff now, and I can't ask my kids to continue to abandon everything they love; we have to take things, and that means more room than the Jeep can provide. We'd need something larger. A van, probably. I can trade for one, but my cash supply isn't unlimited, and my credit is carefully managed under my new identity, with only one card, and only to prop up the illusion. We can't just pull out at a moment's notice, drift away without a trace. It will take a day, at least, to get everything organized. I realize with a shock that for all my paranoia, I haven't considered *this* worst-case scenario: how to pull us safely and quickly out of this home, this place. A day's delay might be nothing to most people, but it could mean the difference between life and death to us.

The Jeep—too small for an immediate evacuation—was a sign I'm putting down roots and getting comfortable, and it's the wrong time for that. *Dammit.*

Lanny, I realize, has been watching me. Watching my face as I think this through. She says nothing until Officer Graham and Detective Prester are in the sedan and backing down the drive in a whisper of pale dust, and then she says in a dead little voice, "So I guess we pack, right? Just what we can carry?"

I hear the damage I've done to them both in her flat intonation. She's become resigned to the terrible, inhuman idea that she can never have friends, or family, or even favorite things, and she's learned to live with that at the tender age of *fourteen*, and I can't. I can't do it to her again.

This time we won't run. This time I will trust Absalom's false identities. This time I will bet on normal life for once, and not rip my children's souls apart to save their physical bodies.

I don't *like* it. But that has to be my decision.

"No, sweetheart," I tell her. "We stay."

Whatever comes, I tell myself, we aren't running away from it.

◆　◆　◆

I avoid any encounters for the next few days, quite successfully. Our runs around the lake are done at a pace that discourages others from chatting, and I don't do any neighborly visiting. I'm not the cookie-baking kind of mother on my best days—not anymore. That was Gina, God rest her soul.

Lanny goes back to school, and though I wait tensely for the phone to ring, she isn't in trouble again in the first few days. Or the next. The police don't return for another chat, and slowly, slowly, my anxiety levels begin to gear down.

It's the following Wednesday that I get a text from Absalom, marked with his standard Å as a signature. It's just a web address, and I type it into the browser on my computer.

It's a newspaper story from Knoxville, quite a bit distant from us, but it's about Stillhouse Lake.

MURDER AT ISOLATED LAKE COMMUNITY STUNS RESIDENTS

My mouth goes dry, and I shut my eyes for a moment. The letters glow randomly against my eyelids, and I can't seem to banish them, so I open and look again. The headline's still there. Beneath, with no reporter byline, sits a story that must have been cribbed from a wire service, and I slowly scroll down past blinking reminders to subscribe, to read the weather, to buy a heating pad and a pair of high-heeled shoes. I finally arrive at the text of the story. It isn't much.

When residents of the small town of Norton, Tennessee, woke to the news of a body in local Stillhouse Lake, no one expected it to be a murder. "We just thought it was a boating accident," said Matt Ryder, manager of the local McDonald's restaurant. "Maybe a swimmer who had a cramp and drowned. I mean, that happens. But this? Just can't believe it. This is a good little town."

"Good little town" describes Norton well. It's typical of the area, a sleepy village struggling to reinvent itself for the modern age, where the Old Tyme Soda Palace occupies space next to SpaceTime, an Internet café and coffee bar. One caters to nostalgia for a time gone by. The other strives for all the conveniences of a much larger town. On the surface, Norton looks successful, but digging deeper reveals a problem facing many rural areas: opioid addiction. Norton, by best estimates of local law enforcement, has a significant addiction problem, and drug trafficking is common. "We do our best to control the spread of it," said Chief of Police Orville Stamps. "Used to be meth cooking was the worst of it, but this Oxy and heroin problem is something else. Harder to find, and harder to stop."

Chief Stamps believes that drugs could have played a factor in the death of the still-unidentified woman, whose body was found floating in Stillhouse Lake last Sunday morning. She is described as a Caucasian with short red hair, between eighteen and twenty-two years of age. She has a small scar that indicates removal of a gall bladder, and a large, colorful tattoo of a butterfly on her left shoulder blade. At press time, there was no official identification, though sources inside the Norton Police Department say there is a strong likelihood the victim is from the area.

Officials are keeping silent on the cause of the woman's death, though they have classified it as homicide and are interviewing residents of the lakeside community—a formerly exclusive, wealthy area fallen, like most of the state, on harder times—to discover who, if anyone, might have information to lead to the identity of the victim or killer. They believe that the body was placed into the water after death and say the killer attempted to weigh it down. "Pure luck it didn't work," said Chief Stamps. "She was roped to a concrete block, but the propeller of the boat must have cut one of the ropes when he started the engine, and up she came in the end."

The Stillhouse Lake area was known as a rustic retreat for locals until the mid-2000s, when a development company sought to reinvent the lake as a high-end refuge for upper-middle-class and upper-class families seeking lakefront second homes. The effort was only partially successful, and the gates to Stillhouse Lake are now open to anyone. Many of the wealthy have fled to more exclusive enclaves, leaving behind retirees, original residents, and empty homes sold at foreclosure auctions. While it's known among residents to be a peaceful place, the influx of new residents—renters and buyers—has made some uneasy.

"I have to believe that somebody up there saw something," Chief Stamps said. "And somebody will come forward to give us what we need to solve this case."

Until then, nights on peaceful Stillhouse Lake will remain as they always have been . . . dark.

I roll my chair back, as if retreating from the article. *It's about us. About Stillhouse Lake.* But even more than that, what strikes me is what likely caught Absalom's attention as well . . . the way the killer weighed down the body. And the age and description of the victim—it rings some kind of bell, something distant, but I can't lay hands on a memory to go with it.

It also sounds eerily like the young women Melvin abducted, raped, tortured, mutilated, and buried in his own watery garden.

Tied to concrete blocks.

I try to get control of myself, my racing mind. It's a coincidence, obviously. Disposing of a body in water is hardly unique, and most smart killers try to weigh them down to delay discovery. Concrete blocks, I remember from Melvin's trial, aren't unusual, either.

But that description . . .

No. Young, vulnerable women are the favorite target of many serial killers. Not definitive in any way. And there's nothing to say it *is* a serial killer. Could have been a suspicious death gone wrong, a panic to hide a body. An inexperienced, unprepared murderer who hadn't planned to kill at all. The story more or less alludes to drugs, and there is a drug problem in Norton; we heard that from Officer Graham. The murder must be, as suggested, tied to that.

Nothing to do with us. Nothing to do with Melvin Royal's crimes. *But murder practically at your front door? Again?*

It's a terrifying prospect, for many reasons. I fear for my kids' personal safety, of course. But I also fear for the torment that we'll go through if we are branded, again, as Royals. I'd made the decision to stay and tough it out, but that is harder now, in the face of this story. The Sicko Patrol will notice. They'll dissect every detail. Look for photos. I can't control pictures others take; no doubt I appear in the background of someone's shot at the park, or the parking lot, or the school. If I don't, then Lanny does, or Connor.

This has just made staying extraordinarily risky.

I text back to Absalom. **Why'd you send?**

Similarities. You saw, right?

I didn't tell Absalom where we'd settled, but I suspect he knows. I had to file paperwork to buy this house under the identity he made for me. It'd be child's play for him to find out my exact address. He was the one who sent me lists of likely destinations when I'd had to flee last time. Still, it helps me to think he doesn't know, or care, where exactly we are. He's never betrayed us. He's only helped us.

But that doesn't mean I can bring myself to trust him completely. **Doesn't seem relevant,** I tell him. **Weird tho. Keep an eye?**

Wilco.

Absalom ends the conversation, and I sit for a long time, staring at the words on the computer screen. I wish I could feel some sympathy for the poor, dead, unknown woman who was found in the lake, but she's just an abstract. A problem. I can only think that her death leads to pain for my kids.

I was wrong to make a knee-jerk decision to stay here. *Never close off escape.* That's been my mantra for years now, and it's pure survival instinct. I'm not reversing my decision, exactly, but this article, the similarities to my ex-husband's crimes . . . it's woken something uneasy in me that I've learned to heed.

I won't uproot my kids on a whim and run, but I damn well need to make plans to do an emergency bugout in case things turn ugly. Yes, I do owe it to my kids to provide them a stable upbringing . . . but even more than that, always, I owe them *safety*.

I no longer feel the safety I did before, in the face of that story. It doesn't mean I'm running.

But it means I need *to prepare*.

I quickly Google vans available for purchase in the area and come up gold: there's a large cargo van for sale or trade just a few miles away, in Norton. I think ahead to packing materials. We have collapsible plastic crates for some things, but I'll need to add a few more from the local Walmart. I try to avoid big-box stores, since it means being recorded on surveillance cameras, but there isn't a whole lot of choice around Norton, unless I want to make the drive into Knoxville for supplies.

I look at the clock and decide there isn't time to be DEFCON One paranoid. I grab a large-billed trucker hat with no logo on it and a pair of large sunglasses. I make sure my clothes are as anonymous as possible. Best I can do as a disguise.

As I'm retrieving cash from the safe, I hear the honk of the post office delivery van down the drive and look out. He's finished filling my box, and I go out to grab the contents, still thinking hard about what has to be done to prep for an emergency. Selling the house wouldn't come into the calculation; it would have to be done post-move anyway. I'd have to pull the kids out of school without warning or explanation, again. But other than those considerations, we don't have a hell of a lot of ties to break, really. I've kept us mobile for so long, keeping things light is still natural for all of us.

I'd thought this would be the place where we'd get to break that cycle. Maybe it still is, but I need to be practical. Escape needs to be a viable option. Always.

Step one is getting the van.

There's an official-type letter in my mess of circulars and junk mail. State of Tennessee. I rip it open and find my license to carry.

Thank God.

I put it in my wallet immediately, dump the rest of the junk mail in the trash, and retrieve my gun and shoulder holster from the safe, too. Feels good, putting it on, feeling the weight—and knowing that unlike other times I've worn it, I actually have the paper to show I'm legally allowed. I've practiced drawing out of this holster many times, so there's nothing odd about it at all. Feels like an old friend at my side.

I add a light jacket to conceal the gun and head out in the Jeep to buy the van. It's a long drive into the country outside Norton, and though I've printed turn-by-turn directions—the downside of refusing to join the smartphone revolution is a reliance on maps and paper—it's still a confusing mess to get to the listed destination. There's a reason, I think, that scary movies are so often set out in the woods; there's a brooding, primitive power out here, a sense of being made so small and vulnerable. The people who thrive here are strong.

It catches me by surprise to find, once I've arrived at the address of the van for sale, that the name on the mailbox of the 1950s-era cabin— small, sturdy, rustic as hell—is ESPARZA. Norton, and Stillhouse Lake, isn't an area that boasts a large Hispanic population, and I realize that it has to be Javier Esparza's home. My range instructor. Former marine. I feel instantly comforted and at the same time strangely guilty. I won't cheat him, of course, but I hate to imagine his disappointment, his anger if he finds out later just who I am. If the worst happens, I bug out, and he wonders if I'm fleeing in the van he sold me for even worse reasons than being married to a serial killer.

I don't want to lose Javi's good opinion. But I will, for the sake of my kids' future and safety. I absolutely will.

I get out and walk to the gate, where I'm greeted by a muscular bristle of brown-and-black fur. The dog comes armed with a fusillade of barks as loud as the gun range. The rottweiler stands waist-high to me, but when he puts his front paws on the top of the fence, he's as tall as I am. He looks like he could rip me to dog food in under ten seconds, and I am very careful to stop where I am and make no threatening moves. I don't make eye contact. Dogs can take it as aggressive.

The barking brings Javier to the door. He's wearing a plain gray T-shirt, soft from years of laundry, equally well-worn jeans, and a pair of heavy boots, which is sensible out here in the country, where timber rattlers and old, forgotten pieces of metal are equal risks to unprotected feet. He's also drying his hands on a red dish towel, and when he sees me, he grins and whistles. At the sound of the whistle, the dog backs off and retreats to the porch, where it lies down, panting happily. "Hey, Ms. Proctor," Javi says, coming to open the gate. "Like my security system?"

"Effective," I say, eyeing the dog carefully. It seems perfectly friendly now. "I'm sorry to bother you at home, but I guess you have a cargo van for sale . . . ?"

"Oh. Oh yeah! Almost forgot, to be honest. Used to belong to my sister, but she dumped it on me when she joined up and shipped out last year. I've got it back here in the garage. Come on back."

He leads me around the side of the cabin, past a chopping block for firewood with an ax still embedded in the stump and an old, weathered outhouse. I cast it a look, and he laughs. "Yeah, not in use for decades. I poured concrete in the hole and floored it and use it for tool storage now. But you know, I like preserving the past."

He must, because *garage* is a generous description. What I actu-ally see is a barn that looks as vintage as the outhouse—original to the property, I think. Horse stalls have been knocked down to fit in a long, blocky cargo van. It's an older model, the paint gone milky and matte instead of shiny, but the tires are in good shape, which is important to me. Spiders have chained the whole thing to the ground in a wispy net. "Shit," Javi says, picking up a broom to scythe through the silky webbing. "Sorry. Haven't checked it in a while. They can't get inside it, though."

That sounds more aspirational than factual, but I don't let it bother me. He retrieves a key from a hook on the wall, opens the door, and starts the van up. It catches almost immediately, and the engine sounds well tuned and smooth. He lets me climb in, and I like what I see. Middling mileage, all the gauges reading clear. He flips the hood to let me take a look, and I check the hoses for any signs of cracking or crumbling.

"Looks great," I say, reaching in my pocket. "Trade me for the Jeep and a thousand cash?"

He blinks, because he knows how much I've put into the Jeep; for a start, I've installed the gun safe in the back, which he helped me source. "No. Seriously?"

"Seriously."

"No offense, but . . . why? That's a sweet trade. Terrain you have around the lake, the Jeep's a better vehicle."

Javi isn't stupid, which is a little unfortunate right now. He knows he's getting the better part of this deal, and there is little to no reason for me to be swapping an environmentally appropriate Jeep for a big, clumsy cargo van . . . Not at Stillhouse Lake.

"Honestly? I don't ever go off-roading, really," I tell him. "And I'm thinking of moving, eventually. If I do, we have way too much stuff for the Jeep. The van makes more sense."

"Moving," he repeats. "Wow. I didn't know you were thinking about that."

I shrug, keeping my eyes on the van and my expression as neutral as I can. "Yeah, well, things happen; you can't always predict what comes next. So. What do you think? Want to take a look at the Jeep?"

He waves that aside. "I know the Jeep. Look, Ms. Proctor, I trust you. I need a thousand to give my sister, and I keep the Jeep. She'll be fine with that."

I take out my wallet and count out the money. It's less than I expected to pay, and I'm relieved. More for us to use when we have to reinvent ourselves, create new names and backgrounds.

Javi accepts, and we sign over titles to each other; I'll have to get the ownership switched officially later, but for now, that'll do. He writes a receipt for me, and I make one for him while sitting at his small kitchen table. He still has the dish towel over his shoulder, and I notice that it matches a red-and-white checked one on a rack over the sink. The place looks clean and orderly, with just a few ornaments and colors among the beiges and dark browns. He still has suds in one side of the dual sink. I caught him washing dishes as I arrived.

It seems like a nice place. Calm. Centered, like Javi himself.

"Thanks for everything," I tell him, and I mean it. He's treated me well since the beginning. It matters, in a life like mine, where I was never treated as just *myself* . . . I was always my father's daughter, then Melvin's wife, then Lily and Brady's mother, and then—to many—a monster who'd escaped justice. Not a person in my own right, ever. It has taken work to get to this point where I feel entirely myself, and I cherish it. I like being Gwen Proctor because real or not, she is a full and strong person, and I can rely on her.

"Thanks for this, Gwen. I'm real happy about the Jeep," Javi says, and I realize that for the first time he's called me by my first name. In his mind we're now equal. I like it. I extend my hand, and we shake, and he holds on just a little longer than is necessary before he says, "Seriously. You in some kind of trouble? Because you can tell me if you are."

"I'm not. And I'm not looking for a knight to come riding to the rescue, Javi."

"Oh, I know. I just want to make sure you know you can always ask me if you need help." He clears his throat. "Some people, for instance, don't want anybody to know where they're going when they leave town. Or what they're driving. And I'm cool with that."

I send him a curious look. "Even if I'm wanted?"

"Why, are you guilty of something? On the run from something?" His tone sharpens just a bit, and I see that it bothers him.

Yes, and yes. But the guilt is nebulous, not actual, and I'm not on the run from the law. Just from the lawless. "Let's just say I might have someone trying to find me when I leave," I say. "Look, you do what you gotta do. I'm not about to ask you to go against your ethics, Javi. I swear. And I promise you, I haven't done anything wrong."

He nods slowly, considering it. He finally realizes he's still got the dish towel, and I like the self-deprecating grin as he flips it toward the sink, where it lands in a heap. I wish he hadn't done it, because suddenly, strikingly, it looks like a disembodied lump of bloody flesh, out of place in this clean kitchen. I let out my breath slowly, hands flat on the table.

"You passed all the background checks to get your carry permit," he says. "Far as I know, you're legal as hell, so I got no problem telling people I don't know where you go when you leave here, and I don't have to tell them about the van. Don't ask, don't tell, you hear me?"

"I hear you."

"Got a few buddies who live off the grid. You know how to do that?"

I nod without telling him how long I've been moving, running, avoiding. Without telling him anything at all, which he likely doesn't deserve. Javi is trustworthy, nothing but, and yet I can't bring myself to disclose things to him about Melvin, about myself. I don't want to see him disappointed.

"We'll be okay," I tell him, and manage to summon up a smile. "This isn't our first rodeo."

"Ah." Javi sits back, dark eyes going even darker. "Abuse?"

He doesn't ask by whom, or whether it's me, the kids, or all of us. He just leaves it there, and I slowly nod, because it's true, in a way. Mel had never conventionally abused me; he'd certainly never hit me. He'd never even verbally abused me. He *had* controlled me, in a lot of ways, but I'd just accepted that as a normal part of married life. Mel had taken care of the finances, always. I'd had money available and credit cards, but he'd kept meticulous records, spent lots of time reviewing receipts and questioning purchases. At the time, I'd just thought he was being detail-oriented, but now I see that it was a subtle form of manipulation, of making me both dependent and hesitant to do anything without consulting him. But still within a normal range of marital behavior, or so I'd believed.

There had been one part of our lives that was strikingly *not* normal, but that was a personal, private hell that I'd been forced to relive under police questioning. Was it abuse? Yes, but sexual abuse between married people is a tangled topic at best. Lines blur.

Mel liked what he called *breath play*. He liked to put a cord around my neck and choke me. He'd been careful about using a soft, padded thing that left no real marks behind, and he'd been an expert at its use. I'd hated it and often talked him out of it, but the one time I'd outright refused, I'd seen a flash of something . . . darker. I never said no again.

He never choked me hard enough to make me pass out, though it had come very close. And I endured it, over and over, never knowing that while he was starving me for oxygen during sex, he was imagining his women in the garage, fighting the noose as he raised and lowered them off the ground.

It might not have been abuse, but there isn't any doubt in my mind that it felt wrong. Looking back, the thought that he was using me to play out his murders, over and over again . . . it's chilling, and sickening.

"We don't want to be found by someone," I say. "Let's leave it at that, okay?"

Javi nods. I can tell this isn't his first rodeo, either. As a range instructor, he's probably seen plenty of frightened women seeking comfort in their own self-defense. He also knows that a gun can't protect you unless you protect yourself mentally, emotionally, and logically. It's the punctuation at the end, not the paragraph.

"I'm just sayin' that if you don't have good paper, I know some people," he says. "People who can be trusted. They help out shelter victims starting new lives."

I thank him, but I don't need his trusted strangers. *I* can't trust them. All I want is the cargo van and the receipts, and I'll be on my way. It's a step toward departing, and I'm sad about it, but I also know it's necessary to be ready. Once I have the van, I have control. We can, if necessary, be long gone before the people hunting us can get organized enough to track us to our doorstep. We'll have warning and a good means of escape. I can sell the van for cash in Knoxville and use another identity to buy something else. Break the trail again.

At least, that's what I tell myself.

I'm getting up from the table when my phone rings. Well, vibrates, since I generally keep it in quiet mode—I've seen too many movies where victims brainlessly forget and their ring tones give them away to their killers. I reach for it and see Lanny's name pop up. Well. I can't say I haven't been expecting it. Lanny's acting out is, I think, only going to get worse. Maybe it's for the best we get moving sooner rather than later. I can homeschool instead, wherever we land.

When I answer, Lanny says, in a tense and unnaturally flat voice, "I can't find Connor, Mom."

I don't understand for a few seconds. My brain refuses to consider the possibilities, the horrible truth of it. Then my breath becomes concrete, heavy in my chest, and I feel like I will never breathe again. I gain control again and say, "What do you mean, you can't find him? He's in class!"

"He skipped," she says. "Mom! He never skips! Where would he go?"

"Where are *you*?"

"I went looking for him to give him his stupid lunch, because he forgot it on the bus again. But his homeroom teacher said he wasn't there and he never showed up for class at all. Mom, what do we do? Is he—" Lanny was starting to panic now, her breath coming too fast, her voice trembling. "I'm at home, I came home because I thought maybe he came back here, but I can't find him . . ."

"Honey. *Honey*. Sit down. Is the alarm on?"

"What? I—what does that matter? Brady's not here!"

In her distress, my daughter is calling her brother by his birth name, something she hasn't done for years. It sends a shock through me, hearing his name from her. I try to stay calm. "*Lanny*. I want you to go turn on the alarm if it isn't on right now and then sit down. Take deep, slow breaths, in through your nose, out through your mouth. I'm on my way."

"Hurry," Lanny whispers. "Please, Mom. I need you."

She's never said that before, and it drives a knife deep into me and cuts out something soft and vulnerable and vital.

I hang up. Javi is already on his feet, watching me. "You need some help?" he asks me. And I nod.

"We'll take the Jeep," he says. "It's faster."

◆ ◆ ◆

Javi drives like the road is a combat zone—fast and aggressive, nothing smooth about it. I don't mind him taking the wheel; I'm not sure I'm in any shape right now to do it. I hang on hard through bumps he doesn't slow down for. The jolts rattling through me are nothing compared to the constant, jittery terror, and I can think of nothing but Connor's face. The vision of him lying bloody and dead in his bed haunts me, even though I know he isn't there. Lanny checked the house, and he *isn't there*—but where is he?

The question goes silent in my mind as Javi pulls the Jeep to a sliding stop in the driveway of our house. I am still now. Ready, the way I'm ready on the range with a target in the distance. I climb out of the Jeep and head for the door, unlock it, and quickly disarm the siren just before Lanny flings herself on me.

I hug my daughter, inhale the scent of strawberry shampoo and clean soap, and think about how far I will go to protect her from anything, anyone, who wants to hurt her.

Javi enters after me, and Lanny breaks free with a gasp, taking a step back in defense. I don't blame her. She doesn't know him. He's just a stranger looming in her doorway.

"Lanny, this is Javier Esparza," I tell her. "Javi is the instructor over at the shooting range. He's a friend."

She raises her black eyebrows a little at that, momentarily amazed because she knows I don't trust people lightly, but she doesn't waste time on it. "I checked the house," she says. "He isn't here, Mom. I can't see he came back at all!"

"Okay, let's take a breath," I say, though I want to scream. I go to the kitchen, where I keep a list of phone numbers pinned to the wall—my son's teachers, and the home and cell numbers of his friends' parents. It's a short list. I start dialing, starting with the friends. My anxiety ramps up with every ring, every answer, every negative. When I put the phone down after the last call, I feel hollow. Lost.

I look up at Lanny, and her eyes are huge and dark. "Mom," she says. "Is it Dad? Is it—"

"No," I say, an instant and unthinking rejection. Out of the corner of my eye, I see Javier noting it. He already believes that I'm running from someone; this just confirms it. But Mel is in prison. He's never getting out, except in a pine box. I'm more worried about *other* people.

Angry people. The Internet trolls, not to mention the justifiably enraged relatives and friends of the women Mel tormented and murdered . . . *but how did they find us?* Still, I flash back to the pictures from just a few days ago, of the faces of my children Photoshopped onto bloody, destroyed bodies, onto suffering, abused bodies.

If they had him, I think, *they would have taunted me by now.* It's the only thing that keeps me sane.

"You were supposed to walk him to class after you got off the bus, Lanny," I say. She flinches and drops her gaze from mine. "Lanny?"

"I—I had things to do," she says defensively. "He went on ahead. It was no big deal—" She stops, because she knows that it *is* a big deal. "I'm sorry. I should have. I got off the bus with him. He was being an asshole, and I yelled at him to go to class, and I went across the street to the convenience store. I know I'm not supposed to."

From the bus, Connor would have walked across the grassy triangle between the schools to the middle building. It would have been more likely for him to run into bullies than abductors, though there would have been plenty of parents dropping off kids outside the guard station entrance. I don't know. I don't know what he did, what happened to him once Lanny turned away.

"Mom? Maybe . . ." She licks her lips. "Maybe he just went somewhere by himself."

I fix her with a long look. "What are you saying?"

"I—" She looks away and seems so uncomfortable that I want to shake it out of her. I'm able to stop myself. Barely. "Sometimes he goes off by himself. He likes to be on his own. You know. Maybe—maybe that's where he went."

"Gwen," Javi says. "This is serious business. You should call the police."

He's right, of course he's right, but we've already drawn the police's attention once. If my son, of all people, has been sneaking away, being on his own . . . that frightens me in a way I can't even explain. *His father liked to be on his own.*

"Lanny," I say, "I need you to think now. Is there some special place he goes to be alone? Anyplace at all? In Norton? Around here?"

She shakes her head, clearly frightened, clearly feeling guilty for having walked away from him this morning. For having failed in her duty as an older sister. "I don't know, Mom. Around here, he likes to go up in the woods. That's all I know."

It's not enough.

Javi says, quietly, "I'll drive around and see what I can spot, if you want."

"Yes," I say. "Please. Please do that." I swallow hard. "I'll call the police."

It's the last thing I want to do. It's a dangerous move, just as dangerous as having Lanny as a potential witness to a body disposal; we need shadows, not spotlights. But every second I waste could be a second that Connor, hurt or (God forbid) taken, stands in real danger.

Javi heads for the exit. I start to dial the phone.

We both pause as a knock sounds on the door.

Javi gives me a look over his shoulder, and when I nod, he swings it open. The alarm chimes but doesn't go off. In the panic, I'd forgotten to reset it.

Standing on the doorstep is my son, with an inadequately wiped bloody nose, and a man I barely recognize.

"Connor!" I rush forward, past Javi, to grab my son in a hug. He makes a gurgling sound of protest, and some of his blood smears on my shirt, but I don't care. I let go and go to one knee to look at his damage. "What *happened?*"

"Got in a fight, I guess," says the man who's brought my son back to me. He's medium height, medium weight, sandy dark-blond hair cut short, but not as short as Javi's. He has an open, interesting face and eyes that lie steady on the two of us. "Hi. Sam Cade. I live up the ridge?" I finally remember him from two different sightings: first, he'd stepped in at the gun range against Carl Getts, and second, I'd seen him walking down the road below our house, earbuds in, waving quietly to us.

He offers a hand. I don't take it. I usher my son inside, where Lanny grabs his arm and drags him off to see that his nose is cleaned up as it drips more dark blood. Javi stands quietly, arms folded, a silent presence that feels very, very comforting right now.

"What are you doing with my son?" It comes out sharp, urgent. I see Cade's Adam's apple bob as he swallows, but he doesn't take a step back.

"I found him sitting on the dock. I walked him home. That's it."

I glare at him, because I'm not sure that I can believe him. Still. He's brought Connor home, and Connor doesn't seem afraid of him. Not in the least. "I remember you, from the gun range. Right?" There's still a sharp edge to my voice.

"Right," he says. My tone has brought a slight flush to his cheeks, but he's working not to sound defensive. "I'm renting the cabin up the hill there, the one up to the east. Just here for six months or so."

"And how do you know my son?"

"I just told you, I don't," he says. "I found him sitting on the dock. He was bleeding, so I cleaned him up and brought him home. The end. I hope he's okay." He's matter-of-fact, but his voice is getting firmer. He wants this to be over.

"How exactly did he get hurt?"

Cade sighs, looks up at the sky as if searching for patience. "Look, lady, I just was trying to be nice. For all I know, *you* hit the kid. Did you?"

I'm taken aback. "No! Of course not!" But he's right, of course. If I'd found a kid sitting with a nosebleed, I'd wonder if he was running from abuse at home. I've come at this all wrong, and too aggressively. "I'm sorry. I should be thanking you, Mr. Cade, not giving you the third degree. Please. Come inside, I'll make you some iced tea." Iced tea, in the South, is the hallmark of hospitality. Shorthand code for making someone welcome, and the all-purpose apology. "Did Connor tell you anything about what happened? Anything at all?"

"He just said it was kids at school," Cade says. He doesn't follow me in. He stands on the outside, looking in. Maybe Javi's silent presence is warning him off, I don't know. I make the glass of tea and bring it to the door. He accepts, though he holds it as if he's not quite sure what it's for. Takes a tentative sip. I can instantly tell this is not a man who's used to the Southern traditions, because the sweetness of it surprises him. He doesn't *quite* make a face. "I'm sorry, I didn't even ask your name . . ."

"I'm Gwen Proctor," I say. "Connor's my son, obviously, and you saw my daughter, Atlanta."

Javi clears his throat. "Gwen, I should probably get going. I'm going to walk to the range; I've got a bike there I can ride home. You bring the Jeep back and pick up the van whenever you want." He puts the keys on the coffee table and nods to Sam Cade. "Mr. Cade."

"Mr. Esparza," Cade says. I can't leave a stranger standing here with my iced tea glass in his hand, obviously, and I'm not ready to run off and leave Lanny and Connor at home alone, either. So I let Javier go, though I hold him back for a moment to look him in the face.

"Javi. Thank you. Thank you so much."

"Glad it worked out," he replies, and then he's gone past Cade, ambling down the drive, then kicking into an easy, loping run toward the gun range on the ridge. *Marine,* I remember. This is just a quick jaunt for him. No effort at all.

I return my attention to Cade, who is looking after Javi with an expression I can't read. "Let's sit out here?" I make it a question. He seems to think about it, then eases down into a chair on the porch. He perches on the edge of it, ready to bounce up and go at any moment. His sips of tea seem more polite than appreciative.

"Okay," I say. "I'm sorry. Let's start over. I'm sorry for accusing you of—well, of anything. That wasn't fair. Thank you for helping Connor. I really appreciate it. I was freaking out."

"Can't imagine," he says. "Well, they wouldn't be kids if they didn't make it a mission to freak out parents, right?"

"Right," I say, but it's a hollow sort of agreement. That might be true of normal kids. Mine are different. They've had to be. "I can't believe he didn't call me, that's all. He should have called me."

"I think—" Cade hesitates, like he's thinking about a line he doesn't want to step across. "I think he was just ashamed. He didn't want his mom to know he lost a fight."

I manage a hollow, shaky laugh. "Is that normal for boys?"

He shrugs, which I take to mean *yes*. "Javier's a marine. You might want to ask him to show the kid a few moves."

I thank him, but inwardly I'm thinking that Sam Cade can also handle himself; he's compact, but not small, and he has a lithe tension in him that makes me think he's had experience at being picked on, and hitting back. Where Javi is so visibly military that someone would have to be blind to miss it, Cade comes across as a normal guy, but with an edge.

On impulse, I say, "Army?"

He glances at me, startled. "Hell, no. Air force. Once upon a time," he says. "Afghanistan. What gave it away?"

"You just leaned a little hard on the word *marine*," I say.

"Yeah, okay, guilty of interforces rivalry." His smile, this time, is unguarded, and I like him better for it. "The advice stands, though. In an ideal world, sure, he wouldn't have to fight back. But the only thing more certain than death and taxes is bullies."

"I'll consider it," I say. His body language is slowly relaxing, one muscle at a time, and he takes a deeper drink of the tea. "So, you said you're only in the cabin for six months, is that right? That's pretty short."

"Writing a book," he says. "Don't worry, I won't bore you to death with the plot or anything. But I was between jobs, and I thought this would be the perfect place to come for peace and quiet before I head off to the next thing."

"What's the next thing?"

He shrugs. "I don't know. Something interesting. And probably far away. I'm not much for being settled. I like . . . experiences."

I would give anything to be settled, and to avoid more *experiences*, but I don't tell him that. Instead, we sit in awkward silence for a moment, and as soon his glass is empty, he stands up to go like he's been released from a trap.

I shake his hand. He has a rough palm, like someone who's done plenty of hard work in his life. "Thanks again for bringing Connor home," I say. He nods, but I realize he isn't looking at me. He's stepped back, and is looking at the outside of the house. "What?"

"Oh, nothing. Just thinking . . . you really should get those roof shingles fixed before the rain comes. You're going to have a hell of a leak."

I hadn't noticed, but he's right; one of the many spring storms has blown a sizable patch of roofing away, leaving fluttering tar paper exposed. "Dammit. Know any good roofers?" I don't mean it. I'm still half out the door, mentally planning our escape for when it's necessary. But he, of course, takes me seriously.

"Not a single one around here. But I've done some roof work in my day. If you just want a repair, I can do it for you cheap."

"I'll think about it," I tell him. "Look, I'm sorry, but I need to see to my son. Thank you for being . . . so kind."

That seems to make him uncomfortable. "Sure," he says. "Okay. Sorry." He rocks back and forth for a moment, as if debating saying something else, then casts me a quick glance. "Let me know."

Then he's gone without a backward look, hands in his pockets, head down and shoulders loose. He doesn't look back. I gather up the glasses and go back inside the house, and just as I'm closing the door I see that Cade has paused a little bit up the hill to look back. I raise my hand silently. He raises his.

And I shut the door.

I wash out the glasses and knock on Connor's door. After a long moment he says, "Come in," and I find him sprawled on his bed, game controller on his chest, all his attention on the screen across the room. He's playing some kind of racing game. I don't interrupt him. I sink down on the edge of his bed, careful not to block his view, and wait until his in-game vehicle crashes. He pauses the game before I reach out to smooth hair back from his forehead.

He's going to have an impressive bruise, I think, but no black eyes or there'd already be darkening from burst capillaries. There's another mark on his left cheek, just where a right-hander would have punched him, and I see raw scrapes on the palms of his hands, where he must have broken his fall. The knees of his blue jeans are abraded and bloodied.

"Does it hurt?" I ask him. He shakes his head mutely. "Okay, sorry, I have to do this." I lean over and touch his nose, pushing and moving it to make sure that I don't feel anything strange. There isn't any break; I'm certain of that. I'll schedule a doctor's appointment in the next few days just to make sure, though.

"Mom, enough!" Connor pushes my hand away and picks up his game controller, but he doesn't start the game again. Just fiddles with it idly.

"Who was it?" I ask him.

He shrugs. Not as if he doesn't know, of course, but he doesn't want to tell. He says nothing, but he doesn't start the new game, either. If he didn't want to talk, I think, he'd have the thing roaring at top volume. Standard avoidance technique these days.

"You'd tell me if you were in trouble, wouldn't you?" I ask him. That draws his focus, just for a moment.

"No, I wouldn't," he says. "Because if I did, you'd just pack us up and move us again, right?"

That hurts. It hurts because it's true. Javi's left me the Jeep, but I still have to go trade it for the van, and the instant I pull that big, white beast into our driveway, my son will be proven right. Worse: now he's going to believe he's caused it to happen, as if his getting hit by bullies is forcing me to uproot the family. I hope Lanny doesn't decide to blame him, too, because there's no viciousness like that of a teen girl deprived of something she wants. And she wants to stay here. I know that, even if she doesn't.

"*If* I decide to move us again, it won't be because of anything you or your sister have done," I tell him. "It'll be because it's the best, safest thing for us all. Okay, kid? We straight?"

"Straight," he says. "Mom? Don't call me kid. I'm not a kid."

"I'm sorry. Young man."

"It's not like this is the first time I got punched. Won't be the last. It's not the end of the world." After another few seconds of fiddling, he puts the controller aside and rolls toward me, head propped up on his hand. "In his letters, does Dad ever say anything about us?"

Lanny must have told him something, but she couldn't have told him all of it—certainly not what she'd read in that vile message. So I choose my words carefully. "He does," I say carefully. "Sometimes."

"And why won't you at least read that part to us?"

"Because that wouldn't be fair. I can't just read you the part where he pretends to be a good dad."

"He *was* a good dad. He didn't pretend about that."

My son says it with perfect calm, and it hurts, hurts like a piece of iron shoved in where my heart should be. And of course he's right, from his perspective. His dad loved him. That's all he ever saw, or knew; his dad was great, and then his dad was a monster. There was never any middle ground, no adjustment period. He saw his dad that morning of

The Event, hugged him, and by that evening his father was a murderer, and he wasn't allowed to mourn him, miss him, or love him, ever again.

I want to cry. But I don't. I say, "It's okay to still love the times you had with your dad. But he was more than just your dad, and that other part . . . that other part was, and is, nothing you should love."

"Yeah," Connor says, thumbing his game back on. He isn't looking at me. "I wish he was dead." That hurts, too, because I wonder if he's just saying it because he knows that I wish it, too.

I wait, but he doesn't pause the game again. I say over the roar of the sound effects, "You're sure you won't tell me who hit you? And why?"

"Bullies, and no reason. Jeez, leave it, Mom. I'm fine."

"Would you like to learn some moves from Javi? Or—" I almost say *Mr. Cade,* but I stop myself. I just met the man. I don't really know how Connor feels about him. I don't know how *I* feel about him.

"I'm not starring in some teen movie," he tells me. "It doesn't work like that in real life. By the time I get any good I'll be graduated."

"Yeah, but think of the epic graduation fight," I tell him. "Middle of the school auditorium? Everybody cheering while you take down your bullies?"

He pauses the game. "More like me ending up bloody and in the hospital, and all of us getting charged with assault. They never show you that part in the movies."

I don't quite know how to phrase it, so I say, "Connor . . . how did you meet Mr. Cade today?"

"Well, Mom, he lured me into a rape van with a puppy."

"Connor!"

"I'm not stupid!" He flings that at me like a knife, and I admit, it startles. I start to speak, but he runs right over me, never taking his eyes off the screen as the image of a car shifts lanes, speeds, jumps, rounds corners. "I got beat up, I walked home, I sat on the dock, and he just asked me if I was okay. Don't make it some freaky Serial Dad creeper thing, all right! He was just *nice*! Not every guy in the world has to be an asshole!"

"I never—" I'm shocked not only by what he says but also by the anger behind it. I haven't realized how much my son has taken his anger and turned it on *me* until this moment. It's understandable, of course; why wouldn't he? I'm here to represent the shitty life he leads, every day.

It begs a larger question. I *do* treat every person I meet with suspicion—and men more than women. I do that out of sheer self-preservation. But I realize now that in doing so, I've appeared unreasonable in my son's eyes. After all, if I distrust those people, especially men, will I eventually look at him the same way? He has to wonder. After all, he's his father's child.

It breaks my heart and shatters the pieces, and I feel tears gather in my eyes. I blink them away.

"I'll get an ice pack for that nose," I tell him, and leave.

I run into Lanny in the kitchen. She's making lunch—enough for all of us, I see, a pasta chicken dish that she's spicing with great abandon. She's a good cook, if a little liberal on flavors. When I open the freezer, she hands me an ice pack already prepared. "Here," she says, rolling her eyes. "Didn't want to interrupt mommy-son time."

"Thanks, honey," I say, and I mean it. "Looks tasty."

"Oh, you'll definitely taste it," she says cheerfully, continuing her stirring while I deliver Connor's ice pack. He's already laser-focused on the game, so I leave it next to him and hope he'll remember to use it before it melts.

"Lanny," I say, as I set the table. "You should go back to school this afternoon. I'll call in an excuse for you."

"Ha. No. I'm staying here."

"Don't you have an English test?"

"Why do you think I'm staying here?"

"Lanny."

"*Okay*, Mom, I get it, fine, whatever." She turns the burner off on the stove with an unnecessarily violent snap of her wrist and bangs the skillet down on a hot pad on the dinner table. "Eat up."

There's no use arguing. "Go get your brother."

She does that without complaint, at least, and lunch is good. Filling. Even Connor seems to like it enough to try to smile, though he winces and probes at his swollen nose afterward. I place phone calls, Connor and I drive Lanny to school, and I think longingly again about the van that waits at Javier's house.

I also think that running almost ensures another stir of interest, and eventual links to our real identities. Maybe we don't need to pull up our tentative roots quite so quickly. Maybe I'm overreacting, the way I did when I pointed a gun at my own son not so long ago.

I'm well aware that my paranoia is part of my huge, overwhelming desire to never give up control, ever again. And I know that same impulse could be hurting my children.

Like Connor, caught between uncomplicated childhood love and adult hate, and nowhere to stand in between. Like Lanny, defiant and furious and ready to take on the world, but far too young to do it.

I need to think of *them*. What *they* need. And as I stand in the hallway and wipe tears from my cheeks, I realize that what they might need right now is for me to stand my ground and trust that we're going to get through this. Not just another hopeless late-night flight, another town, another set of names to memorize until none of them are real anymore. Their childhood has been incinerated. Destroyed. And running is one more log on that fire.

It's ironic that there are protection programs for witnesses, but not for us. Never for us.

But the body in the lake. It nags at me, having this spotlight focused so close to us. There are similarities to my husband's crimes, but I tell myself that it isn't an uncommon way to dispose of a body. I've done that research, obsessively, trying to understand Melvin Royal, trying to understand how *that* killer could be the man I thought I knew and loved.

I can hear Mel's mental whisper again: *The smartest ones are never found out. I never would have been, except for that stupid drunk driver. Our lives would have gone on just the same.*

That is almost certainly true.

It's your fault I'm where I am, though.

That was completely true. Mel would have been convicted of one murder, of course. But it was my fault his true depth of evil had been finally unmasked. Everything in our house had been gone over by the police, of course; they'd missed nothing. But what they hadn't known about, and I hadn't either, was that Mel had taken out a storage locker in the name of my long-dead brother. I only found out about it because the preloaded credit card associated with the account had run out after Mel's arrest, and I'd gotten a call from the storage unit. Apparently— ironically—he'd put the home phone number on the account.

That voice mail had led me to the storage locker, and I'd opened it up to find a bewildering array of folded women's clothing, purses, shoes. Small plastic bins, neatly labeled with victims' names, that contained the contents of their purses and pockets and backpacks.

And the journal.

It was a three-ring notebook, a leather presentation binder. It was filled with lined notebook paper densely covered in his neat, angular writing . . . with printed photographs. Each victim had a section.

I'd only taken one single look before I'd dropped the book on the floor and rushed to call the police. I couldn't bear even what I'd learned from that glance.

Mel's charges went from a single count of abduction, torture, and murder to multiple counts. The clerk's voice had gone hoarse before it was over, or so the newspaper accounts read. By that time, I was back in jail awaiting my own trial. In a rare display of spite, Mel had refused to exonerate me from his crimes, and a zealous, fame-hungry neighbor had claimed she saw me carrying something she *thought* might have been a body . . . though my attorney had picked that apart and gotten me an acquittal. Eventually.

This man will kill again, Mel's voice says in my mind, and I shiver to reject it, reject him. *When he does, you think they won't look at you? Won't investigate? Take your picture? This ain't the old days, Gina. Reverse image search can bring the wolves right to your door.*

I know that voice isn't really Mel, and I also know it's right. The longer we stay here, the more we risk being pulled into Detective Prester's investigation, and that's a sure, slow fuse to blow up our semisettled life.

But taking this home away from Connor now would make his bitterness, his self-protective, guarded anger, that much worse. He's only just begun to relax, to feel part of something. Taking that away because we *might* be found out is cruel.

Still. Having the van ready isn't a bad idea.

I take a deep breath and call Javier. I tell him I'll make time soon to make the swap, Jeep for van, but there's no real hurry. He's okay with that.

It feels like a plan.

But some part of me also knows that it's really not enough.

4

I have learned not to trust anyone. Ever. I spend the night at the computer, turning up everything I can about Sam Cade—who is, indeed, an Afghanistan air force vet. He's not on any sex offender registry, has no criminal record, and even has a good credit rating. I check the popular ancestry sites; often somebody's name pops up in a family tree, and it's a good way to check out their history. But his family isn't enrolled.

Cade's got a couple of social media accounts and a sort of boring dating profile on a match service, though it's several years out of date. I doubt he's even checked it for a long time. His posts are the normal kind of wry observations clever people make, with a support-the-military bent, but in a mostly nonpolitical way, which is a bit of a miracle. He doesn't seem rabidly fanatical about anything.

I'm looking for dirt, and I don't find any.

I could contact Absalom and have him deep-dive it, but the fact is, I rely on him for very specific services, the ones strictly to do with Mel and the stalker posse. If I abuse our fragile, faceless relationship, I could lose a vital resource. Checking out a neighbor probably isn't a good use of Absalom's time. *Probably.* Until I have some better reason to suspect

Cade beyond my normal garden-variety paranoia, I can leave it. As long as he avoids me, I'll avoid him.

Still, it's a little disquieting that when I step outside my front door, I realize that I can see his front porch from here. I've noticed it before, of course, but when we moved in, the cabin was empty, and I'd never found anyone at home when I'd come around the lake on my runs. We're in direct eyeline, though his cabin's modest and tucked in among the trees by the road. I can see the glow of lights in the front windows through red curtains.

Sam Cade, like me, is a night owl.

I sit in the quiet, listening to the owls and distant rustling of the trees. The lake ripples quietly and reflects shattered moonlight. It's beautiful.

It's also very late, and I finish my drink and go to bed.

I take Connor to the doctor to get his x-rays. He has bruises, but nothing's broken, and I'm supremely grateful for that. Lanny goes with us, though she's in silent mutiny the entire time, glowering at me and anyone who gives her a second look with equal displeasure. I ask Connor again if he'll talk about the person who hit him, but he's a well of silence. I let it go. When he's ready to tell me, he will. I think about making the offer to both of them for more self-defense classes; Javier does teach one at the local gym. I make sure, as we pass the gym, to mention it. Neither of them says a word.

So. It's that kind of day.

We eat out at the local diner, which is always a treat for me because of the fluffy meringue pies that they bake fresh daily, and while we're out, I see Javier Esparza, who comes in, slides in at a table not far away, and orders lunch. He sees me and nods, and I nod back.

"Hey, kids? I'm going to have a quick word with Mr. Esparza."

Lanny gives me a glare. Connor frowns and says, "Don't sign me up for anything!"

I promise not to and slide out of the booth. Javier sees me coming, and as the waitress sets down his coffee, he indicates the chair across from him. I slip into it. "Hey," he says, then takes a sip from his cup. "What's up? The kid okay?"

"Connor's fine," I tell him. "Thank you again for jumping to the rescue so quickly."

"*De nada.* Glad he didn't need it."

"Mind if I ask you a question?"

He glances up at me and shrugs. "Shoot—wait, hang on." The waitress is back, delivering a bowl of soup and a piece of coconut meringue. "Okay." He waits for that last until she's out of earshot and clearly minding her own business, and although I don't need the caution, I appreciate it.

"You know Mr. Cade? Sam Cade?"

"Sam? Yeah. Sure. Not a bad shot, for a chair force guy."

"Chair force?"

"I like it better than flyboy. I mean, they do most of their work sitting down." Javier grins to show there's no real ill will. "Cade's all right. Why? He bothering you?"

"No, nothing like that. I just—it was odd, having him show up with Connor. I wanted to be sure . . ."

Javier takes it seriously. He thinks about it for a moment, idly spooning his soup and letting it fall back to splash in the bowl, then finally takes a mouthful as if he's reached a decision. "Everybody I know who knows him, likes him," he says. "Doesn't mean he can't be bad, you know, but my instinct says he's okay. Why, you want me to look into it?"

"If you can."

"Okay. One good thing about being the range master: I know damn near everybody in this town."

Only Sam's new to town, hadn't he said that? He hasn't been here all that long, and he's planning on leaving at the end of a six-month lease. Looking back on it, that seems troubling. Like someone staying a step ahead of trouble.

Or, again, I'm just utterly, hopelessly paranoid. Why do I care? I can avoid him easily enough; I managed not to run into Cade before, and I can duck him going forward.

"He offered to do some work on my house," I say to Javier, as some sort of excuse.

"Yeah, he's good with that," he says. "He put a new roof on my cabin right after he moved in. I think he used to work with his dad in construction, and the price was good. Better than I would have gotten in town, and none of the local guys can nail shingles on straight. And they can't shoot for shit, either."

I wasn't trolling for a testimonial, but I got one. *Well,* some part of me says, quite reasonably, *the roof still has to get fixed.*

"Thanks," I tell Javier. He waves his spoon at me to dismiss that.

"Us outsiders got to look out for each other," he tells me. And I think he believes it . . . that he and I are the same kind of outsiders. We're not, of course. But it's a little comforting to imagine.

I leave him to his pie and go back to mine—chocolate meringue— just in time, because Lanny and Connor have started shaving bits off the side of the slice and hoping I won't notice. They've already finished theirs.

"Do not touch the pie," I tell them sternly, which gets me a shared look and eye roll. Lanny licks her fork. "That's a crime."

Back in the old days, I would use the words *hanging offense.* I wonder if they've ever noticed that I stopped.

I eat my pie, and we head back to Stillhouse Lake.

That afternoon, I take a short walk up the hill to the neat little rustic box of Sam Cade's place and knock. It's 3:00 p.m., which around the lake seems a reasonable time to come calling, and sure enough, I catch him in the cabin.

Sam seems surprised to see me, but he manages to keep it polite. He hasn't shaved, and the golden stubble on his chin glints in the light. He's got on a lightweight denim shirt, old jeans, and waffle-stomper boots, and he waves me inside as he heads back toward the kitchen I can clearly see over a pass-through counter. "Sorry," he says. "Close it, will you? I've got pancakes to turn."

"Pancakes?" I echo. "Seriously? At this hour?"

"Never too late or too early for pancakes. If you don't believe that, you can turn around and go, because we are never going to be friends."

It's a funny, quirky thing to say, and I find myself laughing while I'm closing the door behind me. The laugh dies as I realize I've stepped inside a cabin with a man I hardly know, and the door is closed, and anything can happen now. Anything.

I take a quick look around. It's small, and he doesn't have much: a couch, an armchair, a laptop parked on a small wooden desk that fits in the corner. The laptop's lid is up, and the display shows one of those northern lights wavy screensavers. Sam has no television that I can see, but a nice vinyl stereo setup, with an impressive record collection that must be hell to move with. Bookcases on one wall, crammed full. Not the lifestyle I've developed, where nothing is cherished or necessary. I get a real sense of him having . . . a life. Small, self-contained, but real and vital.

The pancakes smell delicious. I follow him into a small galley kitchen and watch as he teases one loose from the pan and flips it in the air with the showmanship and dexterity of someone who's practiced that move a lot. It's impressive. He puts the pan back on the gas fire and gives me an unguarded smile. "So," he says. "You like blueberry pancakes?"

"Sure," I say, because I do, not because of the smile. I am immune to the smile. "That offer you made about helping me out with the house—is that still on the table?"

"Absolutely. I like working with my hands, and that roof needs replacing. We can negotiate a good price."

"If the blueberry pancakes are your negotiating move, it might not work. I ate pie today."

"I'll take my chances." He watches the pancake that's on the fire and removes it when it's perfectly toasted. It gets added to a pile of three already done, and he hands me the plate.

"No, no, you made those for you!"

"And I'll make some more. Go on, eat. They'll just get cold while I make the next set."

I use the butter and syrup set out on the table, and when he says it's fine, I pour myself a cup of coffee from the pot that's on the warmer. It's strong, and I add a swirl of sugar.

I'm halfway through the pancakes—and *damn* they are warm, fluffy, and tasty, with sweet/tart bursts of flavor from the fresh blueberries—when he pulls up a chair across from me and gets his own coffee. "They're okay?" he asks.

I swallow the bite I've taken and say, "Where the hell did you learn to cook? These are amazing."

He shrugs. "My mom taught me. I was the oldest, and she needed the help." Something comes across his face when he says that, but he's looking down at the pancakes, and I can't tell if it's wistfulness, or a sign that he misses her, or something else entirely.

Then the moment's gone, and he digs in with real appetite.

Works with his hands, loves to cook, decent to look at . . . I start to wonder why he's on his own out here at the lake. But then, not everybody conforms to the love/marriage/baby life path. I don't regret my kids. I only regret the marriage that produced them. Still, I can understand the lonely, solitary life better than most.

And how harshly others can judge it.

We eat in companionable silence for the most part, though he asks me about the budget for the roof and discusses the possibility of putting a nice deck on the back of the house, which is something I've been thinking of in my rich fantasy life. It's a big step—not just repairing the house, but actually improving it. It sounds suspiciously like putting down real roots. We haggle easily over the roof repair pricing, and I balk at the deck.

Commitment is not my strong suit. Nor, I suspect, is it Sam Cade's, because when I ask how long he's going to be around, he says, "Not sure. My lease is up in November. I might be heading on. Depends on how I feel. I like the place, though, so we'll see."

I wonder if he's including me in *the place*. I scan him for signs of flirting, but I don't read any. He seems like a human dealing with a human, not a man sniffing around after a maybe-available woman. Good. I'm not looking for a relationship, and I can't stand pickup artists.

I finish my pancakes before him and, without asking, take my sticky plate and fork and cup to the sink, where I hand-wash them squeaky clean and put them on the drain board. There's no automatic dishwasher. He doesn't say anything until I reach for the cooled pan and the batter bowl.

"No need," he says. "I'll take care of that, but thanks."

I take him at his word and turn to look at him as I dry my hands on a lemon-yellow dishtowel. He seems perfectly at ease, focused on his pancakes, which are on the verge of disappearing.

I say, "What are you really doing here, Sam?"

He arrests the motion of his fork and leaves the pancake bite dripping syrup in the air for a few seconds, then deliberately finishes the journey to his mouth. He chews, swallows, takes a deep swig of coffee, and then puts his fork down to push back in his chair and meet my gaze.

He looks honest. And a little pissed.

"Writing. A. Book. I think the question is, what are *you*?" he asks me. "Because damn if I don't think you've got a hell of a lot of secrets, Ms. Proctor. And maybe I shouldn't get involved, even if it's just climbing all over your roof for money. Your neighbors don't know much about you, you know. Old Mr. Claremont 'round the lake, he says you're skittish. A little standoffish. I can't say I disagree with him, even if you did sit like a good guest and eat my pancakes and make decent conversation."

His response, I think, is a marvel of deflection. I feel defensive, when just an instant ago I was on offense, hoping to score some kind of telling reaction in the event that Sam Cade isn't who he claims to be. Instead, he's turned the mirror on me and put me on my back foot, and I . . . admire that. Don't trust it, per se, but oddly enough I give him points for it.

I'm almost amused as I say, "Oh, I'm standoffish, all right. And as to why I'm here, I guess it's none of your business, Mr. Cade."

"Then let's just keep our mysteries, Ms. Proctor." He scrapes up some syrup and sucks it off the fork, then carries his dishes toward the sink. "Excuse me."

I step aside. He washes things with efficient motions, takes on the batter bowl and the pan and spatula. I let the running water fill the silence, cross my arms, and wait until he shuts the tap off, slots items in the drain board, and picks up the dish towel to dry off. Then I say, "Fair enough. I'll see you tomorrow about the roof. Nine in the morning all right?"

His expression, still calm and mobile and unreadable, doesn't shift much when he smiles. "Sure," he says. "Nine it is. Cash the end of every day until I'm done?"

"Sure."

I nod. He doesn't make an effort to shake my hand, so I don't offer, and I let myself out. I walk down the steps of his cabin and pause on the downhill winding path to take in a slow breath of thick lake air. It's muggy and heavy out here in the slow Tennessee heat. When I let my breath out, I still smell the pancakes.

He really is an amazing cook.

◆　◆　◆

The kids only have another week of school left, which brings with it the stress of last-minute tests. Connor stresses, that is. Lanny doesn't. I see them off on the bus at 8:00 a.m., and by nine I've made some coffee and put out a box of store-bought pastries, since I can't hope to compete with Cade's pancakes. He knocks promptly on the hour, and I let him in for coffee and crullers, and we work out what he'll need to do the repairs. He takes cash up front to get supplies, and heads back up to his cabin; I see him go past fifteen minutes later in an old but powerfully built pickup whose primary color is Bondo gray, with patches of faded green.

I check the Sicko Patrol while he's gone. Nothing new presents itself. I count the number of posts, and it's down again . . . I keep a frequency chart in Excel, tracking the interest our names have online, and I'm pleased to find that as Melvin's atrocities are outdone by others—by lust killers, spree killers, fanatics with a cause, jihadists—some of our stalkers seem to be losing interest. I hate to use the phrase *getting a life*, but it's possible they are. That they're moving on.

Maybe, someday, we can, too. It's a faint hope, but any hope at all is a new feeling for me.

Cade returns just as I'm printing off the slender list of new stuff and filing it away; I have to leave a couple queued to the printer, which always worries me, but there's no choice. I close and lock my office door and go out to meet him.

He's already setting up a ladder against the roof, making sure it's safely anchored in the grass. He's got a load of tar paper, shingles, and a tool belt that he's securing around his waist, dangling tack hammers and bags of nails. He's even got a battered trucker hat on to keep the sun off, and a bandanna trailing out the back to cover his neck.

"Here." I hand him a closed aluminum water bottle with a carabiner clip. "Ice water. You need any help?"

"Nope," he says, looking up at the rise. "I should be able to get this side finished before dark. I'll take a break around one."

"I'll have lunch for you," I tell him. "Then . . . I'll leave you to it?"

"Sounds good." He clips the water bottle to his belt and picks up the first load, which he's fitted with a rope carry that he fits over his shoulders like a bulky backpack. I hold the ladder as he swarms up it, moving as if he's carrying a load of feathers, and step back to make sure he's surefooted up there. He is. The pitch of the roof hardly seems to faze him at all.

Sam waves, and I wave back, and as I turn to go back inside I see a police car cruising by, moving slow with tires crunching gravel. It's driven by Officer Graham, who nods to me when I lift a hand in greeting and speeds up to head up toward the Johansens' cutoff, toward where his place sits farther back. I remember that he sort of half invited me to join him one evening for shooting practice, but I also think about the fact he's going to have his kids with him . . . and I don't want to bring mine. So I make myself a mental promise to drop by with a tin of cookies or something that makes me seem more . . . peaceful. But not *interested*.

By lunchtime, I've completed two client jobs and posted for more work; one pays by the time I've made the spaghetti and meatballs and salad, and Sam Cade comes down to eat with me over the small dinner table; the other client pays by the end of the day, which is a welcome change. I have to chase a lot of payments. The sound of Cade up on the roof is weirdly comforting once I get used to it.

I'm a little surprised when I hear the alarm sound its sharp repeated warning beeps, and the punching of the code to stop it. "We're home!" yells Lanny from down the hall. "Don't shoot!"

"That was mean," Connor tells her, and then I hear an *oof*, as if she's thrown a sharp elbow at him. "It *was!*"

"Shut up, Squirtle. Don't you have nerd things to do?"

I leave the office and head down to greet them; Connor pushes by me without saying a word, face dark, and slams the door of his room firmly. Lanny shrugs when I meet halfway to her room. "Sensitive," she says. "What? It's my fault?"

"*Squirtle?*"

"It's a Pokémon. They're kind of adorable."

"I know it's a Pokémon," I tell her. "Why are you calling him that?"

"Because he reminds me of one, with his hard shell and soft underbelly." It's a nonanswer, and she shrugs, all loose shoulders and rolling eyes. "He's just pissed because he blew his test—"

"I got a B!" Connor shouts through the door. Lanny raises one eyebrow in a sharp arc. I wonder if she's practiced that in front of a mirror.

"See? He got a B. Clearly he's losing his edge."

"Enough," I say sharply, and as if to punctuate it, there are three percussive raps on the wood overhead. Lanny yelps, and I realize that Cade is now working at the back of the house, and she and Connor wouldn't have seen him from the front as they came in.

"It's all right," I tell them, as Connor throws open his door, eyes gone wide and blank with panic. "That's just Mr. Cade. He's on the roof replacing shingles."

Lanny draws in a deep breath and shakes her head. She pushes past me to go into her room.

Connor, on the other hand, blinks and shifts to something quite different: *interest.* "Cool. Can I go help him?"

I consider that. I consider the risk of my son tumbling off the edge of a roof, falling off a ladder . . . and then I weigh that against the hunger I see in him. The need to be around an adult male, one who can show him things I can't. Who can represent something other than the pain, fear, and horror his father does now. Is it smart? Probably not. But it's right.

I swallow all my worry and force a smile as I say, "Sure."

◆ ◆ ◆

I won't lie, I spend the next few hours outside, clearing up all the mess that Cade and Connor are cheerfully throwing down and watching for any sign that my son might get overconfident, overbalance, and get himself hurt—or worse.

But he's fine. Nimble, well balanced, having the time of his life as Cade shows him the science of how to create a solid, overlapping roof pattern. It heals me a little inside to see the fierce, real smiles that Connor flashes, and the genuine pleasure he's taking in doing the work. *This*, I think. *This is a day he will remember: a good day. It's one of those memories that will pave the way to better things for him.*

I hate it, just a little, that I'm not the one to share in it directly. My son doesn't look at me with the same hero worship, and I think he never will. What we have is real love, but real love is messy and complicated. How can it not be, with our history?

It's easy for him to be with Sam Cade, and for that, I'm grateful. I shut up, clean up, and while the heat's a bit much for me, the work's good and healthy.

We eat dinner together around the table, though Cade insists he's not fit for company as is; Lanny has taken over the kitchen and sternly commands him to go home, get cleaned up, and come back, and I can tell he's amused by having this fierce goth child ordering him around while wearing a flowered apron. He leaves and returns, freshly showered. His hair's still damp and clinging to his neck, but he's in a clean shirt and jeans. Deck shoes, this time.

Lanny has made lasagna, and we dig in with real hunger, the four of us; it's delicious, layered with explosions of flavors, all fresh except for the pasta, which she's conceded to buy from the store. Connor is incredibly voluble about all that he's learned today . . . not at school, but how to hammer in a nail straight with one sharp blow, how to line up shingles, how to keep your balance on an incline. Lanny, of course, rolls her eyes, but I can see she's happy to see him in this mood.

"So Connor did okay," I say when my son takes a breath, and Sam, his mouth full of lasagna, nods, chews, and swallows.

"Connor's a natural," he says. "Great work today, pal." He offers a hand, and Connor high-fives it. "Next time, we tackle the other side. Barring wind or rain, we should be done in a few more days."

Connor's face falls a little at that. "But—what about the wood? Mom? The wood on the side of the house where it's rotted?"

"He's right," I say. "We've got some rot. Probably need to replace trim that's gone bad, too."

"Okay. Three days." Sam forks up another healthy mouthful of lasagna, dangling strings of cheese. "Might be a whole week if you want to spring for that deck on the back."

"Yes! Mom, please? Can we do the deck?" Connor's look is so earnest that it hits me like a tide, and washes away any last, lingering disquiet I have. I'll still trade Javi for the van, but if I was looking for a reason to stay, it's here. Here in my son's eyes. I've been worrying about his introspection, his solitary nature, his silent anger. For the first time I'm seeing him open up, and it would be cruel and wrong to cut that off purely for a *what if.*

"A deck would be nice," I say, and Connor raises both arms in a victory pose. "Sam? Would you mind doing the work late, after Connor gets off school?"

Sam shrugs. "I don't mind, but it'll go slower. Might take a month if we only put in half days."

"That's okay," Connor rushes to say. "I only have another week of school. Then we can work all day!"

Sam Cade lifts his eyebrows and sends me an amused look, and I raise my own and take a bite of my food. "Sure," Sam says. "If your mom says it's okay. But only when she's here."

Sam's not a stupid man. He knows how touchy I am, how guarded. And he knows a single dude barging into a family is likely to be suspect of many unpleasant things. I can read it in his face that he's well aware, and has no trouble playing by whatever rules I set up.

I have to admit: it's to his credit.

Dinner's a complete success, and while the kids are happily clearing up the mess, Sam and I take our beers out to the porch. The heat of the day is finally giving way to a cooling breeze coming off the lake, but the humidity's something I might never quite get used to. The beer delivers a crisp, autumnal note, even though we're not even to deep summer yet. A few boats are skimming the lake as the orange sunset fades out—a four-person sculling craft, a fancy cabin cruiser, and two rowboats. Everyone's heading for shore.

Sam says, "You do a background check on me?"

It's a surprise, and I pause, beer bottle halfway to my lips, and shoot him a look. "Why would you say that?"

"Because you seem like a woman who does background checks."

I laugh, because it's true. "Yes."

"How's my credit rating?"

"Pretty solid."

"That's good. I really ought to check that more often."

"You're not angry?"

He takes a pull on his drink. He isn't looking at me at all. His attention seems completely on the boats out in the water. "No," he finally says. "A little disappointed, maybe. I mean, I think of myself as a really trustworthy sort of guy."

"Let's just say I've trusted the wrong people before." I can't help but think of the difference between how Sam Cade just reacted, and how I imagine Melvin would have reacted if he'd been sitting here, having just met me. Mel would be angry. Offended. He'd blame me for not automatically trusting him. Oh, he'd have covered it up, but I'd have felt the stiffness in his manner.

There isn't any in Sam. He's just saying what he means. "Reasonable," he says. "I'm an employee. You have a right to check up on me, especially since I'm going to be around your kids and in your house. Probably the smartest thing you could do, to be honest."

"Did you check up on *me*?" I ask.

That surprises him. He sits back a little and glances my way. Shrugs. "I asked around," he says. "I mean, in the does-she-pay-her-bills kind of way. If you mean did I Google you, no. When women do that to men, I assume it's a precaution. When men do it to women, it looks . . ."

"Stalkery," I finish for him. "Yes. So what was the word about town about me, then?"

"Like I said: standoffish," he says with a laugh. "Same as me, actually."

I offer my beer bottle, and we clink glass. For a moment we just drink. The scullers reach the far dock. The rowboats have already made port. The fancy cabin cruiser is the last one out on the water, and across the still air I can hear laughter. The lights come on in the boat and reveal four people. A snippet of faint music drifts to me. Three of them are dancing as the pilot heads the cruiser in to a private dock on the other side of the lake. Lifestyles of the rich and bored.

"Think they're drinking champagne?" Sam asks me, straight-faced.

"Dom Pérignon. With caviar."

"Savages. I like mine with smoked-salmon toast. But only on days ending with a *y*."

"Mustn't overindulge," I agree, in my best posh New England accent. I have a pretty good one, from Mother. "So common to be intoxicated on good champagne."

"Well, I wouldn't know, because I've never had the good stuff. I think I had a glass of cheap shit at a wedding once." He holds up his beer. "This is my version."

"Hear, hear."

"Your son's pretty great, you know."

"I know." I smile into the growing evening, not quite at him. "I know."

We finish our beer, and I collect the empties. I pay Sam his day's wages and watch as he walks the short distance up the hill to his cabin. I watch the lights come on inside his front room, glowing red through the curtains.

I go back inside to put the glass in the recycling, and I find the kitchen quiet and clean. The kids are off to their neutral corners, as they so often are.

It's a nice, quiet evening, and all I can think of, as I lock up and set the alarms, is that it can't possibly last.

◆ ◆ ◆

But it does. It surprises me more than anything that the next day—Saturday—goes smoothly. Fewer alerts on Sicko Patrol. No visits from the police. I get more work. Sunday, too. Monday the kids are back in school, and at promptly 4:00 p.m., Connor and Sam Cade are up on the roof, hammering away. Lanny gripes that it's driving her crazy, but turning up her headphones solves that minor issue.

A good day slips into another good day, then a week. School lets out, much to the delight of my kids, and Cade becomes a fixture, joining us for breakfast, then taking Connor up to finish the roof. Once that project is complete, they start on replacing the rotten wood trim around the windows and doors. I retire to the office for work and Sicko Patrol, and it feels . . . almost comfortable, having someone around I can trust, at least a little.

By Sunday, there's a new coat of paint on the exterior of the house, and a lot for me to clean up after, but I'm not displeased. Far from it. I'm breathless, paint-spattered, and happier than I've been in a while, because Lanny, Connor, and Cade are just as dirty and tired, and we've accomplished something real together. It feels good.

I find myself smiling in an entirely unguarded way at Sam that day, and when he smiles back, it's just as open and free, and I have a sudden flashback to the first time Mel smiled at me. I realize in this moment that Mel's smiles were never open, never free. For all that he played the good husband, the perfect father, it was Method acting to him. *Never break character.* I can see the difference in the way that Sam talks to the kids, in the way he makes mistakes and corrects them, says goofy things and smart things, and is a real, natural human.

Mel was never those things. I've just never had a good mirror to hold him against to see the differences. My father was mostly absentee, and not very warm; children were there to be seen, not heard. I've come to realize that when Mel found me, he read that thirst in me . . . and the need to fill it. He must have studied for the part. There were times his mask slipped, and I remember every one of them . . . the moment when I got angry at him about missing Brady's third birthday party was the first. He'd turned to me with such sudden, vicious violence that I'd recoiled against the refrigerator. He hadn't hit me, but he'd held me there, hands on either side of my head, and stared at me with a kind of empty blankness that had terrified me then, and still had the power to do it now.

Even when Mel had been perfect in his camouflage, he'd been *shallow.* His calm had felt stretched and unnatural, and so had his affection.

When he'd gone into his workshop, I imagine that was where the real Mel had come out. He must have lived for the closing of that door, the turning of that dead bolt.

As much as I watch Sam, I don't see any of that. I only see a person. A real person.

It makes me ill and sad to realize how little I understood what was right in front of me, right in *bed* with me, the entire nine years of my marriage. It was *my* marriage. Not ours. Because it had never been a marriage to Melvin Royal.

I'd been a tool, like the saws and hammers and knives in his workshop. I'd been his camouflage.

It is terrifying and soothing to understand this, at long last. I never let myself think about it much, but seeing Sam, seeing the kids around him, makes me realize everything that was wrong and artificial in my marriage.

I don't tell Sam this, of course. That would be one hell of a strange conversation, especially since I am in no way going to tell him who I really am. Hell, no. But it means something that the kids like him. They're both so smart, and I know that building this safe place for them to grow and do better—it's important. Risky, but *necessary*. I'm still willing to run if I have to, but not until it's necessary.

So far, all's quiet. Quieter than it's ever been.

By the middle of June, Connor and Sam have the house looking fantastic, and Sam is teaching my son the basics of construction. They're planning on leveling the ground out back. Pouring concrete and putting down posts. Lanny hovers on the outskirts of it, making suggestions, until suddenly she's into it, too, intently watching as Sam draws out plans with an architect's eye.

It's a long-term project. Nobody's in any hurry about it. Least of all me. Work keeps coming in on my freelance businesses, to the point that I'm turning things down. I can afford to be picky, and to charge accordingly, and my reputation is growing. Things are definitely looking up.

I don't depend on the income from my online work, of course, not completely. I don't have to, because Mel did one thing right: in that awful storage locker where he kept his horrific journals, his trophies, he also kept his escape plan.

A duffel bag full of cash.

Nearly two hundred thousand, the inheritance from his parents' estate that he'd told me he'd invested in a mutual fund. It sat for years in his storage shed, waiting for him to sense it was time to bolt. He'd never had the chance to take it. He was arrested at work, and he never spent another day as a free man.

I turned in the contents of that storage locker to the police, of course I did, but before I did that, I picked up that bag and put it in the trunk of my car. I drove far across town to one of those strip mall mailbox stores and opened up a box in a fake name—made up on the spot—and then took the duffel bag to a UPS location far across town to ship it to my new PO box. It was terrifying. I thought I'd get caught, or worse, that someone would open the box and the money would disappear without a trace. I couldn't have complained about it.

But it did arrive. I tracked the progress online, and I paid extra to have the mail center hold it for me until I could pick it up. Good thing I did, because just two days later, despite my cooperation with the police, I was arrested, jailed, and awaiting trial.

The box with the duffel bag inside was still there almost a year later when I was acquitted. Collecting dust in the back corner of the store, which thankfully was still in business. Small miracles.

I'd spent half of it on our safety, shelter, and identities before Stillhouse Lake. This house had come remarkably cheap at auction, but I'd spent twenty thousand buying it and ten thousand more fixing it up. Still, I have enough, with the income I'm pulling in now, to spend a little. I imagine Mel will be furious about the loss of his carefully hoarded fortune, and that makes me very, very happy. It soothes me to think I'm using that money to pay for a new life.

When Cade offers to help me out with the garden, which I've let run wild, I take him up on it, with the provision that he let me pay him for it. Which he does. We spend hours together discussing the plans, choosing the specific varietals, planting them together. Building stone borders and rambling paths. Putting in a small pond and stocking it with little, darting goldfish that shimmer in the sun.

And little by little, I become aware that I trust Sam Cade. It isn't any specific moment I can point to, or anything he says or does. It's *everything* he says, does, is. He is the calmest, easiest man I've been around, and every time I see him smile, or talk to my kids, or talk to me, I realize how poor my choices were before. How barren my life was with Melvin Royal. It had looked full.

It was as lifeless as the moon.

Before I'm even aware of it, two more weeks go by. My garden looks like something a home and garden magazine would feature, and even Lanny seems relatively happy. She moderates her goth to something edgy but cool, and lo and behold, my daughter tells me one day that she's made a friend. Online at first, but she asks, with her usual blend of aggressive reluctance, if I'd drive her to meet Dahlia Brown at the movies. Dahlia Brown, the girl she punched out at school.

I'm dubious about this turn of events, but when I meet Dahlia, she seems to be a nice girl, tall and a little awkward with it, and self-conscious of her braces. The boyfriend, turns out, dumped her over the metal in her mouth. Best thing that could have happened to her.

Connor and I sit in the back of the theater, and Dahlia and Lanny sit together, and by the time Dahlia comes home with us for dinner, she seems to be entirely at ease. So is Lanny.

That becomes a regular thing, the movies, as summer wears on: Lanny and Dahlia together, besties. Dahlia picks up the black nail polish and emphatic layers of eye makeup, and Lanny adopts Dahlia's style of flowing floral scarves.

By mid-July, the girls are thick as thieves, and they've attracted two more friends. I'm on my guard, of course; one young man is full goth, with a pierced septum, but his boyfriend is helplessly preppy, and they seem wonderfully good together. And wonderfully funny, which is a good thing for my daughter, too.

Connor seems much different, too. His D&D buddies are true friends now, and he even—for the first time—tells me he's decided on a career.

My son wants to be an architect. He wants to build things. And as he tells me this, I find tears in my eyes. I have been desperate to believe he would have dreams, have a life beyond running and hiding, and now . . . now that's true.

Sam Cade has given him dreams that I couldn't, and I'm shakily, wonderfully grateful for it. I talk about Connor's new passion to Sam the next night, as we sit together on the porch with our drinks. He listens in silence, says nothing for a long time, and then finally turns toward me. It's a cloudy evening, with the heavy energy of a gathering thunderstorm; we're under a tornado watch in this part of Tennessee, but so far there's no alert.

Sam says, "You don't say much about Connor's dad."

I haven't said anything, in fact. I can't. I won't. So instead, I say, "Nothing much to say. Connor needed someone to look up to. You gave him that, Sam."

I can't see his face in the gloom. I can't tell if I've frightened him or pleased him, or something of both. There's been a guarded tension between us for weeks now, but beyond the occasional, almost accidental brush of fingertips passing tools or a bottle of beer, we haven't so much as touched. I don't know if I *can* feel romantic toward a man again, and there seems to me to be something holding him back, too. A bad relationship, maybe. A lost love. I don't know. I don't ask.

"Glad I could help," he says. His voice sounds odd, but I don't exactly know why. "He's a good kid, Gwen."

"I know."

"Lanny is, too. You're—" He falls silent for a few seconds and takes what sounds like a convulsive swig of his beer. "You're a damn good mom to them."

Thunder mutters off in the distance, though we can't see any lightning. Behind the hills, most likely. But I can feel the weight of the rain coming. The air has an unnatural sticky heat to it, and I want to simultaneously fan myself and shiver. "I've tried to be," I tell him. "And you're right. We don't talk about their dad. But he was . . . he was vile."

Emotion makes me mute when I try to say more, because another letter arrived from Mel this morning. It's back to his normal cycle, because this one is all small talk, all reminiscences and questions about the kids. It's set me on edge, because now, having seen how Sam treats the kids, I can see the difference. Mel was a *good dad* in the stock photo sense: he showed up, smiled, posed for pictures, but it was all surface. I know that whatever he felt, whatever he feels now, it's a shallow shadow of real affection.

I'm thinking about Mel as I sit here next to Sam, and it makes me want to reach out to Sam, to feel the warmth of his fingers on mine, more as a talisman than as any kind of attraction. I need to drive away Mel's ghost and stop *thinking* about him. I realize, with a start, that I am on the verge of telling Sam the truth about Mel. The truth about *me*. If I do, he'll be the first.

It's so startling to me that I find myself staring at Sam, at his profile as he sips his beer and stares out at the lake. A distant blur of lightning illuminates his face, and for a strange instant he looks *familiar*. Not like Sam. Like someone else.

Someone I can't place.

"What?" He turns his head and meets my gaze, and I feel my face grow warmer. That's so odd it unnerves me. I don't blush. I can't imagine why I'm suddenly feeling awkward, out of my depth, while sitting on my own porch with a man who's become so familiar to me. "Gwen?"

I shake my head and turn away, but I'm all too aware of his sudden attention. It feels like a searchlight against my face, both warm and terrifyingly revealing. I'm grateful that the clouds have made it artificially dark tonight. I am conscious of the cold glass of the beer bottle I'm holding, the chilly beads of condensation slipping down the back of my hand.

I want to kiss this man. I want him to kiss me back.

It comes as a shock to me, a genuine and awful shock; I haven't had this impulse in a long, long time. I'd thought it was gone, burned away in the inferno of Melvin's crimes, of the betrayal of trust that reached all the way inside me. Yet here I am, trembling, wanting Sam Cade to press his lips to mine. And I think I know he can feel it, too. It's like an invisible wire pulling tight between us.

It must have scared him as much as it did me, because he suddenly drinks the rest of his beer in quick, thirsty gulps. "I should be going before that storm hits," he says, and his voice sounds off, different, deeper and darker. I don't say anything, because I can't. I can't imagine what I *can* say, really. I just nod, and he stands up and walks past me to the steps.

He's two down when I finally get my voice under control and say, "Sam."

He pauses. I can hear the muttering grumble of thunder again, and another flash of lightning rips the sky, clear as a knife slash.

I roll the bottle between my hands and say, "Coming back tomorrow?"

He almost turns. "Still want me back?"

"Of course," I say. "Yes."

He nods, and then he's gone, walking quickly away. As he does, the security lights we've installed come on, alert to any motion. I watch him as he walks to the gate, to the road, and he's halfway home before the lights click out again.

The rain starts five minutes later. A hesitant patter at first, and then a steady soft knocking on the roof, and then a thick curtain that shimmers off the edges of the porch. I hope Sam made it home before it hit. I hope the downpour doesn't wash the garden away.

I sit in the quiet, listening to the constant roar of the rain, and I finish my beer.

I'm in trouble, I think.

Because I've never felt this vulnerable before. Not since I was Gina Royal.

It takes a while. Slowly, almost imperceptibly over the last of the hot, muggy summer, Sam and I relax our guards, put aside our armor. We allow brushes of hands without flinching, smiles without premeditation. It feels real. It feels solid.

I finally begin to feel fully human.

I don't fool myself that Sam can fix what's broken in me. I don't think he deludes himself about it, either. We're both scarred—I have been able to tell that from the beginning. Maybe only the truly damaged can accept each other in the way we do.

I think about Mel less and less.

I'm glad when the temperature starts to cool on the slippery side of September. School reconvenes, and Connor and Lanny both seem happy. Whoever Connor's bullies were (and he's never confessed to me), his growing pack of friends more than makes up for it. They arrive every Thursday evening for their D&D game, which goes on well into the late hours. I'm delighted by their enthusiasm, their passion, their joy in imagination. Lanny pretends she thinks it's gross, but she doesn't; she starts checking fantasy books out of the library, and she lends them to him when she's done. She stops calling him Squirtle since his friends said they thought it was cool.

At the end of September, Sam and I sit in the late, late evening in the living room, watching an old movie. The kids are long off to bed, and I have a glass of wine in my hand, leaning against his warmth. It's a sweet delight, this quiet peace. I'm not thinking, in that moment, about Mel, or about anything at all. The wine helps ease the constant, vigilant anxiety in me, and it blurs the fear, too.

"Hey," his voice says quietly by my ear. The tickle of his breath is a tease. "You still awake?"

"Very much," I say, then take another drink. He takes the glass from my hand to drain it. "Hey!"

"Sorry," Sam says. "I need a little courage right now. Because I'm going to ask you something."

I freeze. I can't breathe. I can't swallow. I can't *run*. I just sit, waiting for the mask to come off.

He says, "Do you mind if I kiss you, Gwen?"

My mind is blank. A snowfield on a glacier, cold and smooth and empty. I'm stunned by the silence inside, the sudden and violent recession of fear.

And then I feel warm. It happens in an instant, as if the warmth was there, waiting, all the time.

I say, "I'll mind if you don't."

It's a tentative thing at first, until we both get our confidence and our bearings. His lips are soft and strong at once, and I can't help but remember Mel's kisses, always somehow *plastic*. There's none of that studied movement. Sam kisses like someone who means it. He tastes of the rich, dark cherry flavors of the Bordeaux. Everything about that kiss makes me realize how little I know about life, how much I lost in marrying Melvin Royal. How much time I've wasted on him.

Sam is the one to break it, and he pulls back, breathing hard, saying nothing at all. I lean against him. He puts his arms around me, and instead of feeling confined, I feel included. Protected.

"Sam—"

He whispers in my ear, "Shh," and I don't say anything else. It occurs to me that maybe he's as afraid of this as I am.

I walk him outside after the movie. When he kisses me again at the foot of the house steps, it feels like a wonderful promise of better things to come.

◆ ◆ ◆

A letter arrives from the remailing service the next day. I feel my pulse jump, but I'm not as anxious as before. I still take all the usual precautions: I slit the envelope open carefully, wear my blue nitrile gloves, and use utensils to unfold and hold open the paper.

This one is the second kind in the cycle, which I expected. Mel's words are blandly normal, like the mask of humanity. He talks about the books he's reading (he's always been a big reader, generally of obscure philosophy and the sciences); he laments the wretched, tasteless food in the cafeteria. He says he's fortunate to have friends who put money in his commissary account, so he can buy things to make his prison experience more pleasant. He talks about his lawyer.

But then . . . with a quiet curl of disquiet, I realize something is different about this letter. Something new.

When I get to the bottom, I see it. It's a stinger in the tail, and when it strikes me, it plunges its barb in deep.

> *You know, sweetheart, the thing I most regret is that we never got to have that house by the lake that you and I talked about so often. It sounds like paradise, doesn't it? I can almost see it, you sitting on the porch in the moonlight, watching the lake at night. That image gives me peace. I hope you're not sharing it with anyone else but me.*

I think about the nights I've sat out there on my porch, drinking my evening beer and watching the ripples across the lake in the sunset. *That image gives me peace,* he says. *I hope you're not sharing it with anyone else but me.*

He's seen us—a photograph, at least. Seen me and Sam together on the porch.

He knows where we are.

"Mom?"

I flinch and drop the two spoons I'm holding to pin the letter down. When I look up, Connor is standing on the other side of the kitchen counter, staring at me. Behind him are Billy, Trent, Jason, and Daryl, his Thursday-night friends. I've forgotten what night it is. I'd

125

intended to make Rice Krispies marshmallow treats, and I've forgotten that, too.

I quickly fold up the note, slip it back into the envelope, and strip off the gloves to three-point them in the corner trash can. I slip the envelope in my back pocket and say, "Boys, how about some snacks?" And they all cheer.

All except Connor, who's gone still and quiet, watching me. He knows something's wrong. I try a smile to reassure him, but I can tell he isn't fooled. With a sick sense of desperation, I try to order my thoughts while I whip together the marshmallow cream and Rice Krispies into their sticky pan, to the delight of the young men. My mind isn't on it, or on them, or on anything but *what to do.*

Run, all my instincts are screaming at me. *Just get the van. Put the kids in it. Run. Start over. Make him find you again.*

But the cold fact is that we *have* run. We've run and run and run. I've forced my children into an unnatural, damaging life that's cut them off from family, friends, even from themselves. Yes, I've done it to save them, but at what cost? Because looking at where they are *now*, a full year into being settled, I see them blooming. Growing.

Running cuts them off at the roots, again, and sooner or later, everything good in them will turn stunted and stained from it.

I don't want to run anymore. Maybe it's the house, which has become—despite my best efforts—*home.* Maybe it's the lake, or the peace I feel here.

Maybe it's the fragile, breakable, careful attraction I finally feel to a good man.

No. No, I'm not running, goddamn you, Mel. Not again. It's time to trigger a plan that I set in place a long time ago, one I'd hoped never to have to use.

As the boys eat their gooey snacks and roll dice, I step out and call a number that Absalom gave me years ago. I don't know whom it belongs to, and I don't even know if it will work at all. It's a failsafe, a nuclear option. Onetime use, and I paid dearly for it.

It rings, rings, goes straight to voice mail. There's no greeting, just a beep.

"This is Gina Royal," I say. "Absalom says that you'll know what I need done. Do it."

I hang up, feeling sick and dizzy, as if I'm standing on the edge of a very steep drop. That name, *Gina Royal*, it makes me feel like I'm falling backward, into darkness and a time I'd rather never existed. Makes me feel like all the progress I've made has been an illusion, something Melvin could take away from me anytime he wanted.

In the morning, I call the prison where Melvin is being held, and I make an appointment for the next visiting day.

5

I have to get someone to stay with the kids.

I think about it. I agonize about it for hours, staring into space, gnawing the inside of my lip raw. I have a few people I could ask, but few . . . so few. I could put the kids on a plane to their grandmother, I think, but when I check with her I find she's out of town on a trip. I need to make a decision. I can't leave Lanny and Connor alone, and I can't take them where I'm going.

It's an enormous step to take, a *gigantic* step for someone who doesn't trust anymore. I want to ask Sam. I question that very desire, because Mel has taught me I can't trust my own judgment, and the last thing I want, the very last, is to risk my kids.

I wish I knew more women, but the only ones I've become acquainted with in Norton or around the lake so far are chilly and unlikable, or outright hostile toward strangers.

I don't know what to do, and it paralyzes me for a long, long time until finally Lanny throws herself into the chair in my office and stares at me for so long that I have to engage. "What, honey?"

"That was my question, Mom. What the hell?"

"I don't understand."

"Yes, you do," she says, staring harder. Narrows her eyes, in a way I know she got from me. "You're sitting in here chewing your thumbnail off. You hardly slept. What's wrong? And don't tell me I'm too young to know. Flush that noise."

Flush that is her newest phrase, and it makes me laugh. I imagine that will change to something much more direct by the time she's sixteen, but for now, it's a funny, useful phrase. "I need to go out of town," I tell her. "Just for the day. You'll mostly both be in school, but . . . but I need to leave super early, and I'm back very late. I need someone to be here for you." I take a deep breath. "Who would you suggest?"

She blinks, because she probably can't remember the last time I asked. And she won't, because that's not a normal question from me. "Where are you going?"

"Not important. Stay on topic, please."

"Okay, are you going to see Dad?"

I hate to hear her say that, like he's still *Dad*, with that hopeful upward curl in her tone. It makes me shudder, and I know she sees that, too. "No," I lie, with as bland and even a tone as I can. "Just business."

"Uh-huh." I can't tell if my own daughter believes me. "Okay. Well . . . I guess Sam would be okay. I mean, he's over here anyway, fixing stuff. He and Connor are still working on the deck, you know."

Hearing her say Sam's name is a huge relief. And besides, she's right; Sam would normally be here anyway. The deck project has taken on a leisurely pace, a little here, a little there. "I'm just—honey, I won't be here to watch out for you. If you feel *at all* uncomfortable . . ."

"Mom. Please." I get the full eye roll this time. "If I'd thought he was a creeper, wouldn't I have said so *to his face*? And to yours? Loudly?"

She would have. Lily was shy. Lanny is not. Something in me eases, though I know I can't afford to rely on a fourteen-year-old's judgment, however good I think it is.

In this, I can only rely on myself. I have to take a risk, and I flinch at the very idea. I take risks for myself. But with them? With *them*?

"Mom." Lanny is leaning forward now, and I see the earnest stillness in her. I see a ghost of the woman she will become. "Mom, Sam's fine. He's good. We're good. Just do it."

Just do it. I take in a deep, slow breath and sit back and nod. Lanny smiles slowly and crosses her arms. She does love to win.

"I'll watch him like a hawk," she tells me. "And I've got Javier and Officer Graham on speed dial. NBD, Mom."

NBD, I know, stands for *no big deal.* It is. But I need a leap of faith, and this time I take it. I pick up my cell phone and lock eyes with Lanny again as I dial the phone number.

He picks up on the second ring. "Hey, Gwen."

The normality and welcome of it steadies me, and my voice sounds almost normal when I say, "I need a favor."

I hear water running. I hear him shut it off and put something down to give me his full attention. "Tell me," he says. "I'll do it."

It's that simple.

◆　◆　◆

"I'm only going to be gone for about twelve hours," I tell Sam on Sunday night, the night before I have to get on the plane, "but I appreciate you staying over. Lanny's responsible, but—"

"Yeah, but she's fourteen," he says. He takes a drink from the beer I've given him—a pecan porter, which he seems to prefer. Craft beers are a gift from God. I'm sipping a Samuel Adams Organic Chocolate Stout, creamy and smooth. It soothes the jitters in my stomach. "You don't want to come home to a trashed house and a mountain of beer cans, right?"

"Right," I say, though I doubt Lanny would even consider throwing a party. With me gone, she won't feel free, like most girls her age would. She'll feel vulnerable—and she *is* vulnerable. If her father knows where we are, if someone's really watching us on his behalf . . . I try not to think about it. I'm well aware that someone out there could be watching now. There are a couple of watercraft out on the lake in the sunset, making for shore. Maybe one of them has a camera trained on my porch. It makes me itchy. *Mel will destroy this. He destroys everything.*

But that is why I am going to visit him. To be absolutely sure he understands the stakes we are playing for now.

I haven't told Sam where I'm going. I wouldn't know how to even start that conversation. I also don't tell him I've set up wireless cameras. There's one focused on the front door, one on the back, one set back from the property on a tree to give a wide view, and one up high in an air-conditioning grille in the living and kitchen area. I can easily flip from one view to another on the tablet that came with them. In an emergency, I can e-mail the link to the Norton PD.

Not that I don't trust him. Just that I need some kind of reassurance. I do say this: "Sam? Do you have a gun?"

I catch him in midgulp, and he turns to look at me with a curious expression as he coughs. I cock an eyebrow at him, and he turns it into a rueful laugh. "Sorry," he says. "Caught me off guard there. Yeah, I've got a gun, sure. Why?"

"Would you mind making sure you have it with you while you're here? I'm just—"

"Worried about leaving your kids? Yeah. Okay. No problem." Still, he continues to watch me, and his voice drops a little. "Any specific threats I need to know about, Gwen?"

"Specific? No. But—" I hesitate, thinking how to put it. "I feel like we're being watched. Does that sound crazy?"

"Around Killhouse Lake? Nope."

"Killhouse?"

"Don't blame me for that one. Blame your daughter. I think one of her goth buddies came up with it. Catchy, isn't it?"

131

I hated it. *Stillhouse* was plenty creepy enough for me. "Well, just—take care of them, that's all I ask. I'll be gone less than twenty-four hours."

He nods. "I might work on that deck some, if that's all right."

"Sure. Thanks."

On impulse, I reach out to him, and he takes my hand and holds it for a moment. That's all. It isn't a kiss. Isn't even a hug. But it's something strong, and it makes both of us sit for a moment savoring it.

He gets up eventually, draining the last of his pecan porter, and says, "I'll be back early morning before you leave, yeah?"

"Yeah," I agree. "I leave for Knoxville at four a.m. The kids will be off to school by eight, and they can get themselves up and on the bus. You'll have the place to yourself until they're back at three. I'll be in sometime after dark."

"Sounds good. I'll be sure to eat all your food and watch only the highest-dollar pay-per-view. Mind if I buy a bunch of stuff on your account on the shopping channels?"

"You know how to party, Sam."

"Damn right I do."

He gives me a full, sweet smile and leaves to walk up the hill toward his small cabin. I watch him go, hardly aware that I'm smiling, too. It feels normal.

Normal, I think, as the smile finally fades, is so dangerous now. I'd been fooling myself into thinking I could live in that world, but my world is the one beneath, the one in the shadows, the one where nothing is safe or sane or permanent. I'd almost forgotten that with Sam. If I stay here, I am helping my kids, but I'm risking everything, too.

There are no good answers, but this time I'm not just going to be strong. I'm hitting back.

The next day I take an eye-wateringly early morning flight from Knoxville to Wichita, where we once lived, and from there I drive a rental car to El Dorado. It's got a strangely industrial feeling, like a large manufacturing campus surrounded by miles of nothing, but there's no mistaking what it really is once you see the shimmering fences around it in a lace ruff of razor wire. I've never been here before. I don't know how to do this. The air smells different, and it reminds me of my old life, my old house that's long gone. It was foreclosed on by the bank while I was in jail. A month after that, someone had set it on fire and burned it to ruins. There's a memorial park there now.

When I want to punish myself, I look at the spot where I once lived on Google Maps. I try to overlay the house on top of the park from memory. It seems to me that the large stone memorial block sits in the center of what had once been Mel's garage and killing floor. That seems appropriate.

I don't take the detour to look on the way to El Dorado. I can't. I am focused on one thing and one thing only as I follow instructions from the guard on where to park, what I can take inside with me. I've left my Glock locked in my Jeep's gun safe back in Knoxville, and all I have with me now are the clothes on my body, a preloaded cash card for $500, phone and tablet computer, and my old Gina Royal ID.

I endure the sign-in process, where my ID is scrutinized, my fingerprints are taken, and I am subjected to stares and whispers from not just the prison staff but other women coming to see family. I don't meet anyone's gaze. I am an expert at being remote. The guards are certainly interested. I've never been to see Melvin before. They'll be hotly discussing it up and down the corridors.

Next, everything but my clothes is taken and stored in a guard station, and then I'm strip-searched; it's a humiliating, invasive process, but I grit my teeth and get through it without complaint. This is important, I think. Mel likes to play chess. This move, this visit, is my checkmate. I can't afford to flinch at the cost of making it.

Dressed again, I'm shown to another waiting room, where I pass the time reading a dog-eared gossip magazine left by some woman before me. It's an hour before a guard appears to summon me on—he's young and hard-faced, this one, with sharply clinical eyes. African American. A bodybuilder, I think. Nobody I'd want to cross.

He leads me into a small, claustrophobic booth with a stained, worn counter, a chair, a phone fastened to the cubicle wall. Scratched, thick Plexiglas for a barrier. There's a whole row of booths, and desperate people sit hunched in every one of them, searching for some peace, some humanity in a place that offers none of that. I hear whispers of conversation as I go. *Momma's not feeling right . . . brother's been locked up for driving drunk again . . . Can't afford to pay the lawyer this time . . . I wish you could come home, Bobby, we miss you.*

I sink into the chair without feeling it, without thinking, because I'm looking through the cloudy plastic barrier at Melvin Royal. My ex-husband. The father of my children. A man who swept me off my feet with charm and grace, who proposed to me in a swinging bucket on top of a Ferris wheel at the state fairgrounds—and it doesn't escape me now that he'd waited until I was stranded and isolated to do it. I'd thought it wildly romantic at the time. I can guess he found it fun to imagine me plummeting to the ground, or arousing to have me completely at his mercy.

Everything he's done is tainted now to me. Every smile was just mechanics. Every laugh was manufactured. Every public sign of affection was just that: for the public.

And always, always, the monster lay just under the surface of it all.

Not a large man, Mel. Deceptively strong, but we learned at the trial that he still relied on tricks and guile to lure women in close, and stun guns and zip ties to keep them under control once he had them. He's put on weight, a soft, shivering layer of fat over those long muscles, and it's blurred the once-sharp line of his jaw. He was vain about his looks. And about mine. He always wanted me to be trim and neat and reflect well on *him*.

There's not much else I can recognize easily about him right now, because he's been beaten to *shit*. I let myself gaze at the destruction, the ripening bruises, the cuts, his right eye completely closed, his left just barely cracked open. There are ugly red bruises around his throat, and I can see the clear outlines of fingers. His left ear is heavily bandaged. When he reaches for the phone, I see that several of his fingers are broken and taped together for healing.

I can't tell you how happy all this makes me.

I pick up the phone and hold it to my ear, and Mel's voice comes out raspy, but controlled as ever. "Hello, Gina. It took you long enough."

"You look great," I tell him, and to my surprise, my voice sounds entirely normal. I'm shaking inside, and I don't even know if it's from visceral fear or savage joy at seeing him hurt. He says nothing. "No, seriously. That's really a good look on you, Mel."

"Thanks for coming," he says, as if he fucking invited me. As if it's a dinner party. "I see you got my letter."

"I see you got my answer," I tell him, and I lean forward to make sure he can clearly see my eyes. The coldness burning in them like dry ice. He makes me afraid, constantly afraid, but at the same time, I am completely unwilling to let him see that. "This was a warning, Mel. Next time you play with me, *you fucking die*. Is that clear enough? Do we need to have another round of bullshit threats?"

He doesn't seem afraid. He has the same indifference that I remember from the arrest, the trial, the sentencing—though there's that one particular picture of him looking over his shoulder in the courtroom that betrays the monster in his eyes. It's chilling precisely because it's true.

He hardly seems to be listening to me. The noise in his head, the fantasy, must be very strong right now. I wonder if he's imagining taking me apart as I scream. Taking our kids apart, too. I think he probably is, because the pupil that I can see has contracted to a greedy little pinpoint. He's like a black hole: not even light can escape. "You must have bought yourself some friends in here," he says. "That's good. Everybody needs friends, don't they? But you surprise me, Gina. You were never good at making friends."

"I'm not fucking playing with you, asshole. I came to make sure you understand that you need to forget about me and *leave us alone*. We are not connected. Not in any way. *Say it.*" My palms are sweating—one grips the phone, the other is pressed on the stained counter. I can't see his eyes very well. I need to see his eyes to see what's looking out of them.

"I know you didn't mean for me to be hurt like this, Gina. You're not a cruel woman. You never were." His voice. *God.* It's exactly like the one in my head, still. A perfectly calm, reasonable sort of voice, with a hint of compassion. He's practiced it, I'm certain of that. Listened to himself. Adjusted it to hit just the right notes. Predator camouflage. I think about all those nights we sat side by side, his arm around my shoulders as we watched movies or talked. About the nights I curled up to his warmth in our bed, and he said something in that same, soothing tone.

You fucking liar.

"I meant it," I tell him. "Every bruise. Every cut. Get it through your head, Mel, it doesn't work on me anymore."

"What doesn't?"

"This . . . charade."

He's silent for a while. I could almost believe I'd hurt his feelings, if I legitimately thought he had any. He doesn't, none that I'd recognize in any way, and if I managed to bruise them as much as his flesh, I wouldn't care at all.

When he does speak again, his voice is quite different. Same *voice*, I suppose, but the tone, the timbre . . . very different. He's dropped the disguise, the way he drops it every third letter he sends. "You shouldn't make me angry, Gina."

I hate hearing my old name in his mouth. I hate the way he almost purrs it.

I don't respond, because I know not responding throws him off. I just watch him, sitting quietly in my chair, and suddenly he leans forward. The guard stationed on his side of the barrier focuses on him like a laser beam, and his hand hovers near the stun gun he's carrying. I guess they don't want to shoot prisoners in front of their family members.

Mel doesn't seem to notice, or care, that the guard's behind him. He lowers his voice even more to say, "You know, your Internet fans out there are still looking for you. It'd be a shame if they ever found you. I can't imagine what they'd do. Can you?"

I let the silence hiss between us like a live wire, and then I slowly lean forward until I'm an inch away from the Plexiglas. Two inches from him. "The first hint I have that they know where I am, *I will put an end to you.*"

"Tell me how you plan to do that, Gina. Because I have the power here. I've always had the power."

I just stare at him. He has the phone in his right hand, but his left hand is under the level of the tabletop. Blocked by his body from the guard, who is almost directly behind him. The guard is now looking at me, not at Mel.

I realize with a jolt that Melvin is massaging his crotch. It's making him hard, thinking of how he could arrange my murder. I feel sick, but I do *not* feel horrified. I'm past that now. I can't see his eyes, but I know the monster's looking out.

And I'm revolted. I'm *angry.*

I keep my voice low as I say, "Take your hands off your dick, Melvin. Next time you piss me off, you won't have one left. Understand?"

He gives me an untroubled smile. "If I die in here, everything I know goes online. I've made arrangements. Just like you have."

I believe him. It's the kind of thing Mel would do, one last spit from the grave. He wouldn't care that it destroys his children—not anymore. He loved them once, I have no doubt of that, but it was a selfish kind of love. He was proud of them because he was proud of *himself.* He loved them because they loved him, without question or condition.

But in the end, there's only Mel, and walking meat for Mel to use. I've learned that the hard way.

Violence is all he understands, which is why I've called in this favor from Absalom. I want Melvin to clearly *feel* what he risks when he comes after us. Fear of death is the only thing that can possibly persuade him to leave us alone. I don't know if he can fear pain; I know he experiences it, but fear is a tricky thing with him. One thing is certain, though: he won't want to die, or be maimed for life. Not unless it's on his own terms. He takes control to sickeningly perverse levels.

"Here's the deal," I tell him. "You leave us alone and forget about coming after us, and I won't have you fucked with an iron bar and beaten to death in the shower. How's that?"

His lips are split and swollen, but he smiles, and as he does, the purplish skin stretches and a dark crimson split opens, threading a line of fresh blood down his chin. It drools on his broken fingers and wicks into the clean cotton bandage in a spreading red stain. That's the monster, all over him. No longer in hiding at all. He doesn't seem to notice, or care. "Sweetheart," he says. "I never knew you had it in you, all this violence. It's honestly sexy."

"Fuck you."

"Let me tell you how this is going to go, Gina." He likes saying my old name. Rolling it around in his mouth. Tasting it. Fine, let him have it. I'm not Gina anymore. "I know you. You're no more mysterious than a windup toy. You're going to go running back to your rural little patch and pray that I won't follow through on my threat. You'll dither around for a day, maybe two. Then you'll realize you can't count on my goodwill, and you'll grab my children and run away, again. You're destroying them, you know, with all this running and hiding. You think they won't break? Brady's going silently mad, and you don't even see it. But *I* see it. The apple doesn't fall far from the tree. And you're going to run away and rip up their lives and doom them to another slide down the spiral—"

I hang up in the middle of his calm, eerily even diatribe, stand up, and stare at him through the dirty plastic. Other people have leaned against this barrier. I can see the sweaty outlines of handprints and the gauzy impression of lipstick.

I spit.

The saliva hits the glass and rolls down. It makes it look like he's crying, except for the sickening, constant smile on his face. For a moment I'm overcome with it all—the Lysol-and-sweat stink of this place. The sight of fresh blood dripping from his chin. The slick, awful way his voice still worms inside me and sets off tremors of fear and disgust and self-doubt, because I once *trusted this thing*.

He's still talking into the receiver.

I don't pick up the phone again, but I lean both palms on the counter and lock eyes with the monster. The man I married. The father of my children. The murderer of more than twelve young women, whose bodies undulated under the water as they slowly, slowly rotted away. One of them's never been identified. She's not even a *memory*.

I hate him with so much force that it feels like dying. I hate myself, too.

"I'm going to kill you," I tell him, enunciating so clearly I know he can make out the words through the soundproofing. "You filthy fucking monster." I'm well aware that they're recording me through the camera set up high in its protective bubble overhead. I don't give a damn. If I end up on the wrong side of this barrier someday, maybe that's just the price I have to pay to protect my kids. I can live with that just fine.

He laughs. His lips part, his mouth opens, and I can see the raw, dark cavern of his mouth. I remember that he bit his victims with those teeth, chewed off pieces of them. I think that the look in his eyes must have been the same as he gives me now, straining to open up those puffy, bruised lids. It doesn't look human at all.

"Run," I see him say, enunciating it so I can lip-read. "Run away."

I walk instead. Slowly. Calmly.

Because fuck him.

◆　◆　◆

On the way back to the airport, I am shaking so hard from delayed reaction that I have to pull over and buy a sweet, sugary drink to calm my nerves; I drink it parked, then decide to take a detour. I'm wearing a large pair of sunglasses, a blonde wig, and a floppy hat, and it's close to sunset when I park four blocks away and walk to the empty lot that used to be our family home.

It's nice, this little park. Thick green grass, neatly maintained; there's a border of bright flowers and a stark marble square with a fountain bubbling on top of it. I read the inscription, which says nothing about this being a murder scene at all; it only lists the names of Mel's victims and a date, and at the end, Peace Be in This Place.

There's a bench invitingly close. There's another small wrought-iron table and chairs on a concrete patio ten feet farther off, where our living room might have been.

I don't sit down. I don't have the right in this place to make myself at ease. I just look, bow my head a moment, and walk off. If anyone's watching, I don't want them to recognize me or approach me. I just want to be a lady out for a walk on a nice day.

It feels like I'm being watched, but I think that's the weight of guilt on my shoulders. Ghosts must surely still linger here, angry and hungry. I can't blame them for that. I can only blame myself.

I am walking fast by the time I reach my car again, and I pull out a little too quickly, as if something is chasing me. It takes miles for me to feel secure again, and to strip off the suffocating, sweaty weight of the wig and hat. I keep the sunglasses on. The sunset's too bright without them.

I pull over again and take out my tablet computer. The reception isn't great, and I have to wait for the feeds to load, but there it is: my house, viewable from the front door, the back, the long view, the inside. I can see Sam Cade out back, hammering boards on the unfinished deck.

I call Sam, and he tells me all's well there. It all sounds like a normal, placid day. Uneventful.

Normality sounds like heaven, unattainable and forbidden. I'm all too aware how much power Mel still has over us. How he found us, I don't know and probably never will. He's got a source; that's clear enough. Whoever is passing him information might not even be aware of the harm they're doing. He's a good liar. He's always been a master manipulator. He's a virulent virus loose on the world, and I should have used my shot at him to just kill the son of a bitch. If I call Absalom to set up something more final, it'll cost more than I can safely pay. I know that. And when it comes to buying a murder, even the murder of a man on death row . . . there's something in me that balks. Maybe it's just a fear that I'll be caught, and my kids will be left alone in the world. Helpless and unprotected.

I'm extra cautious on the rest of the drive, hyperaware of possible people trailing me, yet desperate to get home now. Every minute I'm gone is another minute I'm not there to protect my children, to act as their shield. I use express drop-off for the rental car. Security seems to take an eternity, and I want to scream at the idiots who don't know how to take their shoes off, or their laptops out, or their phones from their pockets.

It doesn't matter, because once I'm through, I find the flight out to Knoxville has been canceled. I have another two-hour wait for the next flight, and I find myself calculating the distance. I have a frantic impulse to drive it, to be *doing something*, but that would take even longer, of course.

I have to wait, and I do it sitting by a plug, charging my tablet. I watch the feed from the house as the sun starts to set and the picture adjusts to a grainier grayscale image. I flip to the inside camera and find that Sam is sitting on the sofa with a glass in his hand, watching TV. Lanny is making something in the kitchen. I don't see Connor, but he's probably in his room.

I keep watching the outside of the house. In case of . . . anything. I keep the display on even as the flight finally boards, and reluctantly thumb it off when the flight attendant tells me to disable the Internet function. I'm trying not to think about what might happen during the time I'm in the air. It's not a very long flight, but it's long enough. I pull the tablet out as soon as the sign indicates I can, hook it up to the costly airplane Wi-Fi, and check again.

It's all peaceful. Eerily calm. I think about Mel's bloody smile, and I find myself shivering like I'm freezing. Maybe I am. I turn off the overhead air and ask for a blanket, and I watch the tablet's slow, glitching feed throughout the flight, until we're heading in to the airport.

It takes forever to get to the gate and deplane. I am watching the cameras the whole, shuffling way up to the door, and the instant I'm through, I stow the tablet and *run* down the jet bridge tunnel, dodging other passengers, and sprint through the terminal toward the exit. I feel the hot breath on the back of my neck, again. I feel something like the light graze of snapping teeth.

Then I'm outside in the humid darkness and looking frantically for where I parked my Jeep. When I find it, I check the cameras again, and then I leave the tablet up and active on the passenger seat as I speed away from the airport and head toward Stillhouse Lake. I call Sam and tell him I'm on the way.

Whenever it's safe on the drive, I snatch glimpses of the camera feeds, as I reassure myself that my children are all right, that no one has gotten to them . . . All the way, I remember that ghostly, ghastly smile on Mel's broken face.

That smile tells me he's not done.

That we're not done.

6

Darkness already has a firm hold as I make the turn on the road out to Stillhouse Lake. I go too fast, speeding around the inky turns, hoping no one is walking this path tonight, or driving with lights off.

They aren't. It's quiet, and I pull into my driveway with a sense of relief, which is paradoxical because this home, this sanctuary, isn't safe anymore. It's an illusion. It's always been an illusion.

Sam Cade is sitting on the porch drinking a beer as I pull up and shut off the Jeep's headlights. I reach for the tablet to shut it off, only to find that the battery's completely drained. I stow it and take a couple of breaths to compose myself. Somehow, I never expected to arrive and find everything okay.

Even though that was my fondest hope.

I get out and walk up to join Sam on the porch; he silently hands me a cold Samuel Adams, which I twist open and swig gratefully. It tastes wonderfully like coming home.

"That's a hell of a quick trip," he says. "Everything okay?"

I wonder what kind of vibe I'm giving off that he'd ask. "Yeah. I think so. Just some business I needed to take care of. It's done." *No, it isn't. Nothing is done. I thought he'd get the message, but instead he wasn't even worried. He isn't afraid of me.*

That means I'd better be afraid of him. Again.

"Well. We got the deck frame built out. A few more days to put the boards down and waterproof, and it'll be ready to use." He hesitates, then says, "Gwen, the police came around about an hour ago. Said they wanted to reinterview you about, you know, the girl in the lake. I told them you'd call."

My stomach lurches, but I nod and hope that I seem just fine with that. "I guess they're still grasping at straws about the dead woman. I was hoping they'd settle that by now." *Or is this something new? Something courtesy of Mel?*

"Guess nothing's settled, since they haven't caught the killer," he says. He takes another drink. "You're not holding back anything, are you?"

"No. Of course not."

"I only ask because I didn't like the feeling they gave me. Just be careful when you talk to them, okay? Maybe take a lawyer along."

A lawyer? My first impulse is shock and rejection, but then I reconsider. It might be a good idea. I could confess everything about my past to an attorney, and he'd have to keep it under seal. Maybe finally unburdening myself would feel good. And maybe it wouldn't. If I still can't fully trust Sam with all my secrets, trusting some country lawyer out of Norton would be nearly impossible. It's a small town. People talk.

I change the subject. "How are the kids?"

"All fine. Pizza for dinner. They've got homework. Not too happy about it. The homework, I mean. They were really into the food."

"Well, that's normal." I suddenly realize that I'm starving; I've gone without anything more solid than coffee and a soft drink all day. "Any pizza left?"

"With two kids? You're dreaming if you think they didn't finish a large all by themselves." Sam smiles a little. "But I ordered two for that very reason. Just needs a little heating up."

"Sounds like heaven. Join me?"

So we find ourselves sitting at the kitchen table in companionable silence as I eat two slices and think about a third. Lanny breezes in from her bedroom to grab an energy drink and steal a slice. She raises an eyebrow and says, "You're back."

"Don't sound so thrilled."

She rounds her eyes and flutters her hands and pitches her voice into the annoying, saccharine level. *"You're back! Oh, Mom, I missed you so much!"*

I nearly choke on my pizza. She smirks and retreats to her room, slamming the door even though she doesn't need to. That makes Connor stick his head out. He sees me and gives me a quiet grin. "Hi, Mom."

"Hi, honey. You need any help with your homework?"

"Nah, I got it. It's easy. I'm glad you're back."

From him, it sounds sincere, and I smile back with real warmth. The warmth fades as Connor withdraws back into his room, and I'm faced with a stark reality: *Mel knows where we are. He knows. He talked about Brady. Specifically about my son.*

The answer's obvious. Javier has the van ready. All I have to do is drive the Jeep over and pick up the van, load us up, and go. Find a new place to start over. We can use the emergency IDs I have buried in the geocache fifty miles from here; I've also split part of the money there, and I'll leave it for now. I have better than thirty thousand with me, still. I'll have to pay Absalom in Bitcoin to get us new, clean papers and backstories once we burn these identities, and that'll cost us another ten thousand, at the least. From the ease with which he does it, I can only think he works for some shadowy spy agency where false identities are as common as junk mail.

Melvin expects me to run; he said as much. But everyone runs from the monster. *Everyone except the monster slayer,* a voice in my head says. Not Mel's, this time. My own. It sounds calm, and cool, and utterly capable. *Don't do this. You're happy here. Don't let him win. You have the upper hand, and he knows it. He doesn't want to die, and you can always, always pull that trigger.*

I think about it, finishing the pizza and the beer. Sam watches me, but he hasn't broken the silence, hasn't asked. I like that he doesn't.

I finally say, "Sam . . . I have something to tell you. If you walk away, that's okay; I won't blame you at all. But I need to trust someone, and I've decided that it's going to be you."

He looks ever so slightly taken aback, and he says, "Gwen—" I sense he wants to tell me something, and I wait, but it doesn't come. Finally, he shakes his head. "Okay. Hit me."

"Outside," I say. "I don't want the kids overhearing."

We go out into the coolness and settle in the chairs together. There are wisps of cloudy vapor coming off the lake tonight, rendering it eerie and mysterious. The moon's only half, but it rides a clear sky scattered with stars, like a country road sign that's been shotgunned. It's bright enough to see each other.

I don't look at him as I start, though. I don't want to see the moment of realization. "My real name isn't Gwen Proctor," I tell him. "It's Gina Royal."

I wait. His body language, from the corner of my eye, doesn't change. He says, "Okay." And I realize he must not know the name.

"I used to be the wife of Melvin Royal. You might remember him. The Kansas Horror?"

He takes in a sharp breath and sinks back in the chair. Puts his beer to his lips and drains it dry, then sits silently, turning the bottle in his hands. I hear a ripple from the lake. Someone's out in the fog, I guess. No engines. They're rowing. It's a dark night for it, but some people like the dark.

"I was put on trial as an accessory," I tell him. "They called me Melvin's Little Helper. I wasn't. I didn't know anything about what he did, but that hardly mattered; people sure wanted to believe it. I was married to a monster, sleeping in his bed. How could I have not known?"

"It's a good question," Sam says. "How?" There's something hard in his voice. It hurts.

I swallow hard, and I taste metal on the back of my tongue. "I don't know, except . . . he was good at *pretending* to be a human being. A good father. God help me, I didn't see it coming. I just thought he was . . . eccentric. That we'd drifted apart, like married couples do. I only found out when the SUV ran through the wall of the garage, and they discovered the last victim there . . . I saw her, Sam. *I saw her,* and I can never, ever forget what it was like." I stop and look at him. He's not facing me. He's watching the lake ripples, the fog rising. His face is so blank that I can't get any sense at all of what he feels. "I was acquitted, but that doesn't mean much. The people who believe I'm guilty won't let go. They want to punish me. And they have. We've had to move, run, change our names more than once."

"Maybe they have a point," he says. It sounds different. Rigid and harsh, now. "Maybe they still think you're guilty."

"I'm not!" It aches now, this place inside where I'd thought hope might eventually grow. I can feel it dying in real time. "And what about my children? They don't deserve any of this shit. *Ever.*"

He's silent for a long, long time, but he isn't standing up and leaving. He's thinking. I don't know what he's going over in his head, and I think half a dozen times he's going to speak, but then he thinks differently, and the moment's gone.

When he does say something, it isn't what I expect. "You must worry about being tracked down. By the victims' families."

"*Yes.* All the time. It's hard for me to trust anyone, ever. You understand why? We finally have a home here, Sam. I don't want to run away from it. But now—"

"Did you kill her?" he asks me. "The girl in the lake? Is that why you're telling me this now?"

I'm speechless. I stare at his profile, and I can't form words. I feel numb, the way one does after a deep injury. *I've made a terrible mistake,*

I think. *Stupid, stupid woman.* Because I would have never guessed Sam would make that turn, that fast.

"No," I finally say, because what else can I say? "I've never killed anyone. I've never *hurt* anyone." That isn't quite true, I think. I remember Mel's bruises and cuts, the bitter satisfaction I got today from seeing the damage. But it's true except for that one special case. "I don't know how I can convince you of that."

He doesn't answer. We sit in the well of silence for a while. It's not comfortable, but I'm not willing to be the one to end it, either.

Sam finally does. "Gwen, I'm sorry. Should I still call you—"

"Yes," I tell him. "Always. Gina Royal is long dead, as far as I'm concerned."

"And . . . your husband?"

"Ex-husband. Alive, in El Dorado prison," I tell him. "That's where I went today."

"You still *visit him*?" I can't miss the revulsion in it. The betrayal, as if I've shattered some image he's held of me. "God, Gwen . . ."

"I don't," I tell him. "This is the first time I've seen him since he was arrested. I'd rather slit my wrists than look at him, believe me. But he *threatened me*. He threatened *my kids*. That's what I'm trying to tell you: he's found out where we are, God knows how. All he has to do is drop a word to one of the people who've been stalking us. I had to see him to make it very clear that I wouldn't play this game with him."

"And how'd that go?"

"About like I expected," I say. "So I have a big decision to make. Run or stay. I want to stay, Sam. But . . ."

"But it'd be a whole lot smarter to go," he says. "Look, I have no idea what you're going through, but I wouldn't be as worried about an ex in prison as I would . . . relatives of the victims. They lost a family member. Maybe they think if he loses one, that's justice."

I *do* worry about that. I worry about real, righteous grief and anger. I worry about the sterile, uncaring malice of the Sicko Patrol, for whom it's just an exercise in sociopathy. I worry about everyone. "Maybe," I tell him. "God. I can't even say I don't understand that, because I do." I stop and take another pull of my beer, just to rid myself of the bad taste. "Mel's on death row, but it'll be a long time before they ever strap him to a table, and I think he'll kill himself just before that happens. He won't want to give up that control."

"Then maybe you shouldn't run," Sam says. "That's what he expects, to keep you scared and on the move." He pauses and finally puts the bottle down on the floor of the porch. "Are you? Scared?"

"Out of my mind," I tell him. With Mel, I'd have said, *Out of my fucking mind.* It's odd. I cursed like a sailor in Mel's presence, because he'd brought out the rage bottled inside me, but I have no wish to use that language around Sam. I don't feel so defensive. I don't need the shield. "I won't say I don't care what happens to me; of course I do. But my *kids.* They have enough to deal with, just being the children of someone like . . . him. I know it's better for them to stay, but how do I take that risk?"

"Do they know? About their father?"

"Yeah. Most of it. I try to keep the horrible details from them, but . . ." I shrug helplessly. "Age of the Internet. Lanny probably knows almost everything by now. Connor—God, I hope not. It's hard enough for an adult to handle knowing the worst. I can't imagine what it would do to someone his age."

"Kids are stronger than you think. Morbid, too," Sam says. "I was. I poked around dead things. Told gory stories. But there's a difference between imagination and reality. Just never let them see the pictures."

I remember he was in Afghanistan. I wonder what he saw there, to give him that dark tone. More than I had, most likely, even though I'd had to be faced with all the horrible pictures, the horror and rage of the victims' families at my trial. Those who had the stomach to come, which by that time wasn't nearly as many. When I'd been acquitted, there had only been about four of them who'd stayed for the verdict.

Three of them had threatened to kill me.

Most of the families had been there for Mel's trial, or so I'd heard, and they'd been destroyed by it. He'd found it all very boring. He'd yawned, fallen asleep. He'd even laughed when a mother fainted on seeing for the first time a picture of the decaying face of her child floating under the water. I'd read the accounts of it.

He'd thought that woman's pain—that mother's pain—was the *shit*.

"Sam . . ." I don't know what I want to say to him. I know what I want *him* to say: that it'll be all right. That he forgives me. That the peace we'd formed between us, the fragile, unnamed relationship, hasn't just been murdered by my words.

He stands up, still facing toward the lake, and puts his hands in the pockets of his jeans. I don't need to be a psychologist to know that's a withdrawal.

"I know how hard this was for you to talk about. And I'm not saying I don't value your trust, but . . . I have to think about this," he tells me. "Don't worry. I won't tell anybody. Promise you that."

"I'd never have told you if I'd thought you would," I say. The hard part, I realize, isn't letting him know the truth; it's this ripping fear inside now that he'll turn his back on me, that this is the last moment we'll be friends, or even friendly. I never thought that would hurt, but it does. The fragile little roots I'd been putting down, ripping away. Maybe it's for the best, I try to tell myself, but all I feel is grief.

"Good night, Gwen," he says as he starts down the steps . . . but he doesn't go quite all the way. He hesitates, and finally he looks back at me. I can't read his expression well, but it isn't angry, at least. "You going to be okay?"

It sounds, to my mind, like good-bye. I nod and say nothing, because nothing I can say will help. Paranoia bursts out of its shell and starts to wind tendrils around me. *What if he doesn't keep his word? What if he gossips? Goes online and talks about this? What if he posts who we are?*

In a way, I realize, I've made the decision without making any decision. I've closed off options with this conversation. Mel knows where we are. Now Sam Cade knows everything, too. Friend or not, ally or not, I can't trust him. I can't trust anyone. I never could. I've been fooling myself for months now, but the dream is over. It might set my kids back, but I need to protect their bodies first, their minds second.

I watch him walk away into the dark, and then I take out my cell and text Absalom.

Last msg for a while, I send. **Leaving soon. Have to burn idents & phones, will need new packet on the fly. Can use standby docs for now.**

It only takes a few seconds to get a reply. I wonder when Absalom sleeps, if he ever does. **New idents same price in Bitcoin. Might take a while. You know the drill.** He never asks what's happened to make us run. I'm not sure he even actually cares.

I go inside and check the kids. They're fine, living in their own separate worlds; I wish for that peace, that luxury. The savage, black joy in Mel's stare has ripped all that away, and now that Sam's gone, I feel naked to the world in a way I never have before.

I get another beer and sit at the computer. I follow the steps that Absalom has drilled into me to send the Bitcoin payment. It occurs to me that I'm going to have to burn this computer, too; it has too much info buried in it, and I'll need to take it with me, fry the hard drive, smash it to bits, and sink it in a river. Start over with a new machine from the backup drive.

Fresh start, I tell myself, and I try to believe that it isn't just another retreat, another layer of self that I'm stripping away. I'm almost sanded to the bone by now.

I start making a mental list of the things to destroy, the things to pack, the things to leave behind, but before I can get very far, I hear a hard, firm volley of knocks on the front door. It's so loud and forceful that it shocks me out of my chair, and I retrieve my handgun before I go to check the security camera feed and see who's outside.

It's the police. Officer Graham, tall and broad and as sharply creased as ever. I don't like it, but I put the gun back in the safe, lock it, and open the door. He's been a casual visitor, has eaten at my dining table, but now, he doesn't even smile.

"Ma'am," he says. "I need you to come with me, please."

A number of things flash through my mind as I stare at him: first, he must have been surveilling me to know I'd arrived back home. Either that, or Sam has called him, which is equally possible. Second, this late hour is designed to startle me and keep me off my game. Tactics. I know the game as well as he does; I'm almost certain of that.

I wait a few seconds without replying, without moving. I fight the irresistible tide of memory and fear, and finally say, "It's very late. You're welcome to come inside if you have questions to ask me, but I'm not leaving my kids on their own. No way in hell."

"I'll get a colleague to stay with them," he says. "But you need to come with me to the station, Ms. Proctor."

I stare him down. Gina Royal, the poor, stupid weakling, would have fluttered and complained and still gone along passively. She'd been nothing *but* passive. Unfortunately for Officer Graham, I am not Gina Royal. "Warrant," I say, in a flat, businesslike tone. "Got one?"

It takes him back a step. His eyes study me harder, reevaluating his approach of shock and awe. I see him consider and reject a few, before he says, in a far friendlier tone, "Gwen, this will sure go a whole lot easier if you just come voluntarily. There's no need to put yourself through the mess that happens if we end up getting a warrant. And what happens to your kids if this all gets ramped up and you end up with a criminal record? You think you *keep* them?"

I don't blink, but it's a good line of attack. Cunning. "You need a warrant to compel me to come to the station with you. Until you do,

I don't have to answer any questions, and I choose not to. That's my right. Good night, Officer Graham."

I start to close the door. My pulse jumps, and my muscles tense as his palm hits the wood and holds it open. If he puts his weight into it, he can push me off-balance and step inside. I've already considered options. The gun safe is useless now; even the fingerprint lock takes too long, he'll be on me before I can clear it. My best move is to fall back to the kitchen, where I have a small .32 concealed at the back of the junk drawer, not to mention a bristling block full of knives. This calculation is involuntary, drilled in by years of paranoia. I don't honestly expect him to turn violent.

I just know how to react if he does.

Officer Graham stands there, holding the door ajar, looking slightly apologetic. "Ma'am, we've received a tip from someone in the neighborhood that you were seen in a boat out on the water the night that woman's body was put in the lake. As it happens, the description fits the same boat your daughter described. Either you come with me now or the detectives will be here in half an hour, and they're not taking no for an answer. If it takes a warrant to compel your cooperation, they'll bring one. It'd just be so much easier for you, and show better good faith, if you'd come with me right now."

"So what I'm hearing is you've got nothing but an anonymous tip," I say, even while my brain is howling, *Sam, Sam could have done this to you.* But it's more chillingly probable that Mel's behind it, somehow. "Good luck with that warrant. My record's clean. I'm a law-abiding woman with two kids, and I'm not going anywhere with you."

He gives up then and lets me shut the door. I do it quietly, though I want to slam it. My hands are shaking a little as I affix all the locks and bolts back and reactivate the alarm.

I turn to see Connor and Lanny standing in the hall, staring at me. Lanny has moved in front of her brother. In her hand is a kitchen knife. It strikes me in that moment how my paranoia's touched both of them, especially my daughter, who's so obviously ready to kill to protect her brother, even when there's no immediate threat. I'm so glad she didn't get her hands on a gun.

Officer Graham's right. I need to take her to the range and teach her properly, because I know my child, and soon, all my orders not to touch the guns won't be enough. She takes her cues from me, though she doesn't want me to know it. As I look at her standing there, holding the knife, pale and afraid and yet fearless, I love her with an intensity that hurts me. I also fear what I've made her into.

"It's okay," I say, very gently, though of course it isn't true. "Lanny. Please put the knife away."

"Guess it's not a great idea to murder-stab cops," she says, "but Mom, if—"

"If they come back with some official paperwork, I'll go quietly," I tell her. "And *you* will take care of Connor. Connor, you'll do whatever Lanny says. All right?"

"I'm the man of the house, you know," he grumbles, and it chills me, because I hear an echo of his father in it. But unlike his father, it isn't aggressive. It's just a complaint.

Lanny rolls her eyes as she slots the knife back in the block, but she doesn't say anything. Instead, she gently shoves Connor in the direction of his room. He plants his feet and doesn't go. He's too busy looking at me, that knot of concern in between his brows, his eyes fierce with worry. "Mom," he says. "We should get out of here. Now. Just leave."

"What?" Lanny blurts it out before she can stop herself, and I can see that the idea hasn't been far from her mind, either. She's been dreading the news, and expecting it. I've kept my kids balancing on that knife edge for too long. "No. No, we're not. Are we leaving? Do we have to? *Tonight?*"

I can see the unmistakable plea in her. She's only just found friends, something she lost in Wichita in an unimaginable whirlwind of horror.

She's found, however briefly, a little happiness. But she isn't begging. She's just hoping.

I don't need to answer, because she does it for herself. She looks down and says, "Yeah. Yeah, of course we are. We have to, right? If the cops dig deep, they're going to find out . . ."

"If they take my fingerprints, yes. They'll find out who we are. I'm delaying to give us some time." I take a deep breath, so deep it hurts. "Go get what you need. One suitcase, okay?"

"You'll look guilty if we run away now," she tells me. And of course she's right. But I can't stop this train; it's well beyond any control I can exert. If we stay, I risk the storm descending from both sides. Running may make me *look* guilty, but at least I can get them away from this, get my kids safe, and come back to clear myself.

Connor's off like a shot. Lanny looks at me with a mournful silence, then follows.

I say, "I'm so sorry," to her back.

She says nothing at all.

7

It's damn late, but I call Javier and ask him to bring the van as quick as he can; I tell him the Jeep's ready for pickup, and I'll pay him extra for the trouble. He doesn't ask questions but promises to be with us in half an hour. It's cutting things close.

I go to my room, unhook my laptop, and stow it in my go-bag for dismemberment and disposal later. It isn't lost on me that in this I have some common ground with my ex-husband.

It's different this time, isn't it? Mel's haunting voice whispers to me as I stuff extras into the bag, things I want to keep. *You're not just running from stalkers, or even from me. You're running from the police now. How far do you think you'll get once they're really hunting for you? Once everyone is hunting for you?*

I pause in the act of grabbing the photo album I never leave behind. There are no pictures of Mel in it, just me and the kids and friends. Mel might as well have never existed . . . Except that he is right. Mind-Mel, anyway. If I run, and they decide I'm worth chasing, it becomes a whole different paradigm. I doubt Absalom will help me evade the law. He'd be the first one to rat me out.

There's a knock at the door. I shove the photo album in, zip the bag, and leave it on the bed. Everything else I own is cheaply acquired, easily replaced, and disposable.

When I answer the door, Javier is standing there.

"Thanks," I tell him. "I'll get your keys—"

He interrupts me to say regretfully, "Yeah, about that. We never got around to talking about it, but just so you know, I'm a reserve deputy. Heard on the radio that they were looking to question you right about the time you called about the van. You're not going anywhere, Gwen. I had to make the call."

Standing right behind him is Detective Prester. He's wearing a dark suit today, and a blue tie so ineptly knotted I wonder if he just made a square knot and called it good. He seems tired and pissed off, and in his hand is a crisp triple-folded piece of paper with an official seal showing on the front. He says, "I'm disappointed, Ms. Proctor. I thought we had some kind of civil conversation between us. But you were about to go and run away on me, and I have to tell you, that doesn't look good. Not at all."

I feel the trap closing over me. It's not a bear trap, but silk strands weaving together into an unbreakable net. I can scream, I can rage, but I can no longer run from this.

Whatever this is.

I give Javier a smile I don't feel and say, "It's all right." He doesn't smile back. He's studying me with wary intensity. They are all, I think, well aware that I hold a concealed carry permit. They know I'm dangerous. I wonder if they have snipers out in the darkness.

I think about my kids, and I hold up my hands. "I'm not armed. Please. Check me."

Prester does the honors, quick, impersonal sweeps of hands over me, and I flash back to the first time this happened to Gina Royal, bent across the burning hood of the family minivan. Poor, stupid Gina, who'd thought *that* invasive. She hadn't had a clue.

"Clean," Prester says. "All right. Let's make this nice and easy, shall we?"

"I'll come quietly if you let me talk to my kids first."

"All right. Javier, you go in with her."

Javier nods and reaches down to take a black case from his pocket and slot it onto his belt. A gold-washed deputy's star gleams there. He's officially on duty now.

I go inside and find Lanny and Connor sitting tensely, staring at the door; relief melts over them, but then I see the change as Javier comes in, too, and takes up a guard stance at the door. "Mom?" Lanny's voice breaks a little. "Is everything okay?"

I sink down on the sofa and put my arms around them both, holding them close. I kiss them before I say, as gently as I can, "I have to go with Detective Prester for now. Everything's okay. Javier is going to stay here with you until I get back."

I look up at him, and he nods and looks away. Lanny's not crying, but Connor is, very quietly. He wipes his eyes with both hands, and I can tell he's angry with himself. Neither of them says a word.

"I love you both so much," I say, and then I get up. "Please look out for each other until I'm back."

"If you're back," Lanny says. It's almost a whisper. I pretend I didn't hear because if I look at her now, I'll break, and they'll have to drag me away from them.

I manage to walk on my own out of the house, down the steps, and I join Prester at the car. When I look back, I see Javier stepping inside and locking up the house.

"They'll be okay," Prester tells me. He ushers me into the back and ducks in after me. It's like sharing a cab, I think, except the doors don't open from the inside. At least the ride's free. Graham gets in the front seat and drives.

Prester doesn't say anything, and I don't get any kind of vibe from him; it's like sitting next to a piece of sun-warmed granite that smells faintly of dry-cleaning fluid and Old Spice. I don't know what I smell like to him. Fear, probably. The sweaty aroma of a guilty woman. I know how cops think, and they wouldn't have come to get me if I wasn't a—as they like to term it—*person of interest*. Which is a suspect that they haven't quite collected enough evidence on to charge. I worry about Lanny, with so much responsibility landing on her at just the wrong time in her life. Then I realize I'm thinking like I'm *actually guilty.*

Which I'm not. Not of the murder at the lake. Not of *anything* except marrying the wrong man and failing to notice he was the devil wearing human skin.

I take in a slow breath, let it out, and say, "Whatever you think I did, you're wrong."

"I never said you did anything," Prester says. "To borrow a color-ful phrase from the English, you're helping us with our inquiries." He's nearly as bad at British accents as he is at ties.

"I'm a suspect, or you wouldn't have a warrant," I tell him flatly.

For answer, Prester unfolds the paper. It's good, official stock, with the logo of the city on the top, and the word WARRANT printed on it in bold letters, but where the particulars should be, it's just nonsense words graphic designers use to fill space. *Lorem ipsum.* I've used the same text so often, I can't help but let out a soft laugh. "Ain't no way we could get a warrant with the information we have right now, Ms. Proctor, I'll tell you that for free."

"Nice prop. Does it work often?"

"All the damn time. Fools around here take one look at it and think it's in Official State Latin or some such nonsense."

This time I laugh, because I can imagine a drunk, angry guy trying to parse out the words. *Official State Latin.* "So what's really so urgent that you have to come get me in the middle of the night?"

Prester's near-imaginary smile vanishes, and he looks unreadable. "Your name. You've been living a whole pack of lies, and let me tell you, it doesn't exactly sit well with me. We got an anonymous call about your real name today and heard you might be planning to beat it out of town, so I had to make a move fast."

I go a little cold, but I'm not really surprised. It was a logical play for my ex-husband to make, to make my life harder and more miserable. Any little, spiteful thing to hurt. It also locked me here, in Norton, and prevented me from starting the cycle again. Instead of answering, I turn my head.

"You know how strange all this looks," Prester says. "Don't you?"

I don't answer. There's really nothing I can say to make any of it better. I just wait as the cruiser bumps onto the main road leading to Norton, and we speed toward town.

I don't flinch when Prester spreads out the photos in front of me. Why would I? I've been faced with Melvin Royal's gruesome work a hundred times now. I'm fully acclimated to the horror.

There are only two that still wake a flutter in my chest.

The photo of the woman hanging limp from a wire noose in my old garage, naked and yet stripped even further by the removal of pieces of her skin.

The one taken underwater of Mel's garden of women, floating eerily in the dark with their legs chained tight to weights, some hardly more than skeletons.

He'd made a science of body disposal, of exactly how much weight to use. Calculated it, using trial and error with dead animals, until he was sure how much to add to keep the bodies down. That all came out at court.

Mel is worse than a monster. He's a *smart* monster.

I know it doesn't help me that my expression stays calm as I look at all this horror, and my body doesn't flinch, but I know, too, that faking it will be transparent. I look across the array of photos to meet Prester's gaze. "If you're looking to shock me, you'll have to do better than this. Try to imagine how many times I've had to look at these before."

He doesn't answer. Instead, he slides one more photo onto the pile. It was, I realize, taken on the docks of Stillhouse Lake, probably the one not far from my front door. I can see the worn wingtip shoes that Prester's wearing right now peeking in the edge of the shot, and regulation polished black ones that must belong to a uniformed officer, maybe Officer Graham. I am noting the shoes to avoid studying what's in the center of the picture.

The young woman is barely recognizable once I'm forced to focus on her. She is an anatomy lesson of pink muscle and dull yellow ligaments, with the occasional flash of white bone. Sunken, clouded eyes, and a weedy fall of wet dark hair that half hides part of her skinned face. Her lips are intact, which makes the whole obscenity worse. I don't want to think why her lips are still full and perfect.

"She was weighted down some," Prester says. "Rope got cut by the motor, though, and the gut bacteria brought her back up. You know, it wouldn't have taken much to keep her on the bottom since her skin's gone. Lots of places for gases to escape. I suppose you'd know all about that, though. Wasn't that how your husband did it?"

Mel's victims had never floated. He'd have collected another dozen for his silent, drifting garden if *The Event* hadn't happened. That was one thing Mel *wasn't* guilty of: being bad at what he chose to do.

I say only, "Melvin Royal liked to do this kind of thing to women, if that's what you mean."

"And he disposed of his girls in the water, didn't he?"

I nod. Now that I've fixed my gaze on the dead girl, I can't look away. It hurts, like staring into the sun. I know the afterimage will stay burned on my brain for the rest of my life. I swallow, and my throat clicks. I cough, and suddenly, the urge to vomit comes hard; I hold it back, somehow, though sweat breaks out against my suddenly cold skin.

Prester notices. He has a bottle of water, and he pushes it across to me. I uncap and gulp, grateful for the cool, glassy weight that gathers in my stomach. I drain half the bottle before I recap it and set it aside. It's a gambit, of course, for my DNA. I don't care. If he chooses to wait for it, he could request confirmation from the Kansas PD. I'm documented, printed, photographed, and filed, and though the old Gina Royal is dead to me, we still share the same blood and bone and body.

"You see my problem," he tells me in that warm, slow voice. It drones deep, and I think of old-time hanging judges, hoods, ropes, nooses. I think of the girl swaying from the end of a wire. "You were involved in a case like this back in Kansas. Got tried for being an accomplice. It might be hard to see it as some kind of coincidence happening again so close to you, is my point."

"I never knew about what Mel did. *Never*, until the day of the accident."

"Funny that your neighbor said different."

That puts my back up, despite my efforts to stay calm. "Mrs. Millson? She was a vicious gossip, and she saw that as her chance to be some reality-show star. She perjured herself to get on the news. My lawyer destroyed her testimony on the stand. Everyone knows she was lying, and *I had nothing to do with it*. I was acquitted!"

Prester doesn't blink. His expression doesn't shift. "Acquitted or not, doesn't look so good for you. Same kind of crime, same signature. So let's go through this, step by step."

He puts another picture down, covering the first one. In a way, it's almost as upsetting as the first, because I see a fresh-faced young brunette woman with a saucy grin, sitting with her head bent to touch against another woman's. The other woman is the same age, blonde, with a sweetly wistful look. Friends, I think. They're not similar enough to be related.

"This is how she used to look, this girl Rain Harrington we found floating around in our lake. Pretty girl. Well liked around here. Nineteen years old. Wanted to be a veterinarian." He adds another photo, of her cradling an injured, bandaged dog. It's blatant manipulation, sentimentality, but I still feel it move through me like a subtle earthquake. I shift my gaze. "Nice, lovely girl without an enemy in the goddamn world. *Don't you look away!*"

That last comes as a bellow, shockingly loud, and if he expects me to flinch, he will be damn disappointed. If I don't do it at the range, at the kick of the gun in my hand, I fucking well won't show him any weakness *here*. Good tactic, though. The police back in Kansas could have learned something from Detective Prester. He switched so effortlessly, so quickly, that I have no doubt he'd trained somewhere tough . . . From his accent, maybe Baltimore. He's broken real criminals.

His problem now is that I'm not one of those.

I stare steadily at the photos, and my heart aches for her, this poor girl. Not because I've done anything to her, but because I am *human*.

"You took most of her skin off while she was still alive," the detective says, softly, almost like one of the many voices I hear in my head. Like Mel's voice, for instance. "She couldn't even scream, because her vocal cords were cut. That's a hell of a thing. Best we can figure, she was tied down at every possible joint, and her head clamped with some kind of leather band. You started at her feet and worked your way up. We can see the exact point where she died from the process, you know. Living tissue has a reaction. Dead tissue doesn't."

I say nothing. I do not move. I try not to imagine it, her terror, her agony, the utter pointless horror of what happened to her.

"You do it for your husband? For Mel? He make you do it for him?"

"I guess you think that makes some kind of sick sense," I tell him, and I keep my voice just the same pitch, the same volume. Maybe Detective Prester has voices in his head, too. I hope so. "My ex-husband is a monster. Why wouldn't I be, too? What kind of *normal woman* would marry a man like that, much less stay with him?"

He stares through me when I look up. I feel the burn, but I don't move from the gaze. Let him look. Let him *see*. "When I married Melvin Royal, I did it because he *asked*. I wasn't especially pretty. I didn't think I was especially smart. I'd been taught my whole value to the world was making some man a happy little wife and bearing his children. I was *perfect* for him. An innocent, sheltered virgin who'd been sold the fantasy of a knight in shining armor coming to love and protect me, forever."

Prester says nothing. He taps a pen against his notepad, watching me.

"The thing is, yes, I was a fool. I *chose* to be his perfect stay-at-home wife and mother. Mel made a good living, and I gave him two wonderful kids, and we had a happy home. It was *normal*. I know you can't believe that; hell, I can't believe that I did. But I went through all those years of Christmases and birthdays, PTA meetings and dance recitals, drama club and soccer, and *nobody suspected a thing*. That's his gift, Detective. He's really so very good at playing human that even I couldn't see the difference."

Prester lifts his eyebrows. "And here I thought you'd give me the battered-woman defense. Isn't that the go-to explanation?"

"Maybe," I tell him. "And maybe most of those women are victims. But Mel wasn't—" I flash to that one moment in the bedroom when his hands tightened that padded cord around my throat, when I saw the cold, alligator menace behind his eyes and I'd known instinctively that he wasn't right. "Mel is a monster. But that doesn't mean he couldn't be damn good at being everything else, too. How do you think that feels, knowing you *slept with that*? Knowing you *left your kids with it*?"

Silence. Prester doesn't break it this time.

"When I looked into that wrecked garage and saw the truth, something changed. I could *see*. I could *understand*. Looking back on it, I saw the hints, the little things that didn't fit and didn't make sense, but I know there was no way I could see them at the time, coming from where I was, what I believed." I take another swallow of the water, and the plastic cracks like a pistol shot. "After my acquittal, I reinvented myself, and I protected my children. You think I'd ever want to do anything for *Melvin Royal* again? I hate him. I despise him. If he ever shows up in the flesh, I'll put an entire fucking clip of bullets in his head until there's nothing left to recognize."

I mean every word of that, and I know the detective has an instinct for the truth. He doesn't like that, but fuck what he likes, I am fighting for my life. For the fragile safety I've managed to pull together.

Prester says nothing. He just studies me.

"You have no evidence," I tell him finally. "Not because I'm some Hannibal Lecter level of clever, but because I didn't do anything to that poor girl. I've never seen her before. I'm sorry for what happened to her, and no, I can't explain why it happened where I live. I wish to God I could. I mean, Mel has followers who worship every word he says, but even then, I don't know how he convinces someone to do *that* for him. He's not Rasputin. He's not even Manson. I don't know what makes a person that sick. Do you?"

"Nature," he says flatly. "Nurture. Brain injuries. Shit, the worst of them got no excuses at all." He's said *them*, not *you*. I wonder if he recognizes that. "Why don't you tell me what made Melvin like that, since you've had such a close-up view?"

"I have no idea," I say, and I mean it. "His parents were lovely people. I didn't see them often, and they were always so fragile. Looking back on it now, I think they were afraid of him. I never realized that before they died."

"Then what makes *you* rip up young girls like this?"

I let out a sigh. "Detective. I married a monster and I wasn't clever enough to recognize it in time. That's all I did wrong. I didn't do this."

We go around and around for about four hours. I don't ask for a lawyer, though I think about it; the quality of help I'd get in Norton isn't what I'd call promising. No, I'm better off sticking with the truth. For all his skill, Detective Prester can't convince me of a lie. He might have managed it in the old, impressionable Gina Royal days, but this isn't my first go-round, and he knows that. He has nothing. He's got an anonymous call implicating me, and that could be from a troll who's discovered my identity, or another person my ex has paid off to stir the pot. Still, his instincts are right . . . It's no accident, this poor young woman being slaughtered in such a familiar way and dumped in the lake just beyond my home.

Someone's sending a message.

It has to be Mel.

In a strange, uneasy turn, I actually hope it is, because at least I know Mel. I know where he is. *But he has help,* I think. *Help willing to do exactly what Mel asks.* And I won't lie, that frightens me deeply. I don't want to find Lanny dead next. Or Connor, slaughtered in his bed. I don't want to die at the end of a wire noose, burning in unspeakable agony from being flayed alive.

It's the wee hours when Prester sends me home. Norton is a ghost town, not a single other vehicle on the empty streets, and the deep night gets darker and darker as the squad car turns for the lake. It's Officer Lancel Graham driving me—I suppose because that means he can head straight home afterward. He doesn't talk to me. I don't try to start a conversation. I lean my head against the cool glass and wish I could sleep. I won't sleep tonight, or probably tomorrow, either. The photos of that murdered young woman will flare into horrific color against my eyelids, and I won't be able to blink them away.

Mel isn't haunted by his victims. He always slept soundly and woke rested.

I'm the one who has nightmares.

"We're here," says Graham, and I realize that the sedan has stopped, that somehow I closed my eyes and drifted off after all, into an uneasy doze. I thank him as he comes around and opens the door. He even offers me a hand out, which I take for politeness, and then I am unsettled when he doesn't let go immediately. I can see him—no, *feel* him watching me.

"I believe you," he says, which surprises me. "Prester's on a bad trail, Ms. Proctor. I know you have nothing to do with this. Sorry, I realize it's tearing up your life."

I wonder how much Prester has said, and if the news about my other name, about Gina Royal, has started to leak already. I don't think so. Graham doesn't have the look of someone who knows about my ex-husband.

He just seems sorry and a little concerned.

I thank him again, more warmly, and he lets me go. Javier steps out onto the porch as I approach, and he's juggling his car keys in his hand. Impatient to be gone, I think.

"The kids—" I begin.

"They're fine," he says, cutting me off. "Asleep, or at least, pretending to be." He gives me a sharp, merciless look. "He kept you a long time."

"It's not me, Javier. I swear that."

He murmurs something that sounds like *sure* but is hard to hear as Graham fires up his cruiser again in the background. The flare of taillights paints Javier's face crimson. He looks tired, and he rubs his face like a man trying to scrub away the last few hours. I wonder if this will drive him away from being my friend, as surely as it has Sam Cade. As surely as it will Officer Graham, once he knows my past—not that he's truly a friend. Just friendly.

Nobody stays, I should know that by now. Nobody but the kids, who don't have a choice in the matter because they're mired in this bog just as I am, up to the neck.

"Lady, what the hell are you into?" Javier asks me, but I don't think he wants to know. Not really. "Look, I told you, I'm a reserve deputy. I like you, but if it comes down to it . . ."

"You'll do your duty, just like you did tonight." I nod. "I get it. I'm just surprised you agreed to help me leave town in the first place."

"I thought you were running from an abusive ex. I've seen the look plenty of times. I didn't know . . ."

"Didn't know what?" I challenge him directly this time, staring right into his eyes. I can't read him, but I don't think he can read me, either. Not completely.

"That you were involved in something like this," he says.

"I'm *not* involved!"

"Doesn't look like that."

"Javi—"

"Let's keep this real, Ms. Proctor. You get cleared, we're cool. But until you are, let's keep some distance, okay? And if you want my advice, you get the guns out of your house and turn them over to the range for safekeeping. We can hold them for you until this blows over, and I can swear out an affidavit for the PD. I just hate to think—"

"You hate to think about the cops coming and me having a small arsenal in here," I say softly. "About the collateral damage that could cause."

He nods slowly. There's nothing aggressive about his body language, but there's strength underlying it, a kind of calm, masculine strength that makes me want to believe in him. Trust him.

I don't.

"I'll hang on to my weapons until I see a court order telling me to surrender them," I tell him. I don't blink. If he thinks it's aggressive, so be it. In this moment, in *all* moments now, I can't afford to be seen as weak. Not for myself. I have two children in the house, and I'm responsible for their lives—lives that are never safe, never secure. I will do anything I must to defend them.

And I'm not giving up my weapons.

Javier shrugs. The gesture says he doesn't care; the regretful slowness of it says he does. He doesn't say good-bye, just turns and walks to the white van he's driven up in, the one I came so, so close to escaping in. Before I can speak, he rolls down the window and pitches me the title for the Jeep. He doesn't say the trade is off, but then, he hardly has to.

I watch him drive the big cargo van away, title in my hand, and then I turn and go back into the house.

It's dark and quiet, and I silently double-check everything as I reset the alarm. The kids are used to the tones, and I don't think it will wake them . . . but as I walk down to check on Connor, Lanny opens her door. We stare at each other in silence for a moment in the gloom, and then she gestures me in and shuts the door behind me.

My daughter curls up on her bed, knees up, arms circling them. I recognize the posture, though she might not. I remember finding her many times like this in the months after my release from jail after my trial. It's defensive, though she makes it look natural enough.

"So," she says. "They didn't throw you back in."

"I didn't do anything, Lanny."

"You didn't last time, either," she points out, which is flawlessly true. "I hate this. Connor's scared to death, you know."

"I know," I say. I ease down on the bed, and she scoots her toes back so she isn't touching me. It breaks my heart a little, but I'm eased a bit when she doesn't flinch as I put my hand on her knee. "Sweetheart, I won't lie to you. Your father knows where we are. I was planning to get us out of here, but—"

"But now there's this dead girl, and the police know who we are, and we can't go," she says. Smart child. She doesn't blink, but I see something glimmering like tears. "I should never have said anything about it. If I hadn't—"

"Honey, no. You did the right thing, all right? Never think that."

"If I hadn't said anything we'd be gone by now," she continues doggedly, right over me. "We'd be homeless again, but at least we'd be safe and he wouldn't know where we are. Mom, if he knows—"

She stops talking, and the tears glisten harder, fatter, and break free to run down her cheeks. She doesn't wipe them away. I'm not even sure she's aware it's happening.

"He'll hurt you," she says in a faint whisper, and she tilts her head forward to rest her forehead against her knees.

I move up next to her and hold her, my child, and she is a hard knot of muscle and bone and grief. She doesn't relax against me. I tell her it'll be all right, but I know she doesn't believe me.

I finally leave her there, silent, closed into her protective ball, and go to check her brother. He seems asleep, but I don't think he is. He looks pale, and there are dark, delicately lilac smudges under his eyes like the aftermath of bruises. He's so tired.

So am I.

I close the door quietly, go to my own room, and fall into a vast, dreamless sleep with the silence of Stillhouse Lake pressed drowning-deep around me.

◆ ◆ ◆

In the morning, there's another girl floating dead in the lake.

8

I'm woken by a scream. I come bolt upright in bed, scrambling out even before I'm aware of being awake, stepping with the efficiency of a firefighter into my jeans and pulling a T-shirt on as I step into shoes heading to the door. I realize as I come out of my bedroom that it isn't either of my kids screaming; their doors are flying back, too, Lanny looking bleary in her flannel robe, Connor still bare-chested in pajama pants with his hair sticking up on one side.

"Stay here," I shout at them, racing to the front room. I sweep the curtains back and stare out at the lake.

The screaming is coming from a small rowboat drifting about twenty feet from the dock. There are two people inside it, an older man wearing a fisherman's hat and utility vest, and a woman older than me with ash-blonde hair who's recoiled against him. He's holding her, and the boat's violently rocking, as if she's thrown herself backward so suddenly she almost swamped it.

I turn off the alarm and run outside, feet pounding on the gravel and then the wood of the dock, and I slow down when I see the body.

It's come up from the darkness. This one is naked, floating on her stomach, and I can see long hair drifting like seaweed on the surface of the water.

The raw-chicken color of exposed muscles looks nauseating in the dim morning light, but it's unmistakable. Someone has taken off most of the skin from her buttocks and the small of her back, and a broad stripe up to expose the alien white growth of her spine. But not all her skin. Not this time.

The woman suddenly stops screaming and lunges to lean over the side of the craft to vomit. The man hasn't made a sound, and his move to steady the boat is automatic, the reaction of a man who's been on the water most of his life but isn't really *here*. Shock. His expression's blank, and he stares straight ahead, trying to process what he's seeing.

I take out my cell phone and dial 911. There isn't any choice. This is *at my door*.

As I listen to the rings, I think about the inescapable, horrible fact that the body has been down there under the surface, waiting, slowly rising like a lazy, ghostly bubble until it finally breaks the water's smooth hold. It floated there last night while I talked to Javier. It floated there while I slept. It might have been lurking farther below the surface on the night I sat on the porch with Sam Cade and drank beer and talked about Melvin Royal.

The woman in the boat throws up again, weeping.

I finally get an answer on the emergency line. I don't think about what I'm saying, but I describe the scene, the location, give my name. I know I sound too calm, and that will hurt me later when people review the recording. They ask me to stay on the line, but I don't. I hang up and pocket my cell instead as I try to *think*.

One dead, horribly mutilated woman could have been an awful coincidence. Two have to be a plan. The police will be here soon, and when they come, I'll be taken in. This time the questions will come in earnest.

I'm going to be arrested.

I'm going to lose my kids.

A text alert sounds, and I take out my phone to see it's from Absalom's anonymous number. I swipe to read it.

It's just a link. I click it, and watch as the screen fills with the blocky design of a message board. I don't take note of which one, I just blow up the text to read the initial post.

It's about me.

FOUND: ONE MURDERING BITCH! YA BOY, I TRACKED DOWN MELVIN'S LITTLE HELPER! PICTURES AND EVERYTHING. SOLID INTEL. HIS SPAWN ARE WITH HER, SO SHE DIDN'T DROWN THE LITTLE BASTARDS YET. EVEN BETTER: THERE'S A MURDER!!! DEETS LATER.

There is a flood of replies, hundreds of them, but the original poster is teasing the info, giving nonanswers, hints, denying rumors. And then, about five swipes of my finger down the scroll, he drops one deadly piece of solid fact.

BITCH IS HIDING OUT IN THE VOLUNTEER STATE.

That must have sent at least half the readers scrambling for Google, but I know it instantly. He knows I'm in Tennessee. That means he almost certainly knows I'm at Stillhouse Lake. He likely has the same pictures that Melvin has seen, or he's the original source of them.

My chess move didn't work with my murdering ex-husband. He's dropped the hammer, and right now I imagine him lying on his bunk, laughing. Imagining my safety being stripped away, like strips of skin. Masturbating at the thought of it.

The agony of it is breathless.

I feel weightless for a moment. Not quite falling, not quite stable. It's out. *We're out.* All my work, all my running, all the hiding . . . it's done. The Internet is forever.

Trolls never forget.

I hear sirens in the distance. The police are on their way. The dead girl floats in steady dips and bobs, hair twisting and swirling like slow smoke. The rowboat is now moving away, making for the dock; the fisherman must have finally snapped out of his trance. When I look up, I see his face has gone a sickly, pre-heart-attack color, and he's rowing with furious strength. His wife is slumped against him, looking nearly as bad. These are people whose safe, normal world has broken underneath their feet, and they've fallen into a darker place. The place where I live.

I can see the police car lights cresting a distant hill, heading out from Norton.

I text Absalom. **Doesn't matter now. I'm about to be arrested.**

There's an endless space before his reply comes with a sharp vibrating buzz to announce it, like an angry wasp before the sting. **Fuck. Did you do it?**

He has to ask. Everyone has to ask.

I text back **No** and turn off the phone again. As the rowboat bumps hard against the dock—almost a crash—I toss a line to the fisherman. It hits his wife, which I didn't intend, but she doesn't seem to even notice.

I sense someone else watching now, and I turn my head.

Sam Cade is standing on his porch, about two football fields away. He's wearing a red-and-black checked bathrobe and slippers, and he's staring at me. At the traumatized boaters. I sense his attention move to the body in the lake, then back to me.

I don't look away. Neither does he.

He turns and walks back into his cabin.

I help the older woman out of the boat, then her husband, and sit them down on a bench nearby as I run back to the house for warm blankets. I'm pulling those around their shoulders as the first police cruiser scrapes to a halt a few feet away, lights strobing urgently but siren silent now. Behind it comes the boxy sedan, and I'm not surprised to see Detective Prester behind the wheel. He looks like he hasn't slept at all.

I feel dead. Numb. I straighten up as he exits the vehicle. Two other younger uniformed officers get out of the cruiser. Neither one is Officer Graham, but I recognize them from around the Norton beats. There are more on the way, a whole stream of cars heading toward us now. There's a feeling of inevitability about this dawn. I know I should be afraid, but I'm not; somehow, all that fear has gone away after seeing this poor woman in the lake, abandoned and destroyed. As if this has been coming all along, and on some level, I've known it.

I see Prester approach, and I turn to him to say, "Please make sure my kids are all right. Someone's leaked our location to the Internet. They've had death threats. Real ones. I don't care what happens to me right now, but they have to be safe."

His face is set and hard, but he nods quietly. He pauses next to me and looks at the two unfortunates who were in the boat. I turn away as he questions them. I look at Sam Cade's cabin, and before too long, I am rewarded; I see him come out again, dressed in faded jeans and a plain gray T-shirt. He locks his door—both locks, I notice—and slowly descends the steps to walk toward us. The patrol officers haven't managed to set up a cordon yet, and there's not really a need. Sam walks straight across and stops just a few feet from me. We don't speak for a moment, and he puts his hands in his jeans pockets and rocks back and forth, staring not at me, but at the bobbing body in the lake.

"Want me to call anybody?" He asks it of the empty air, as if he's asking the dead girl. I'm not really looking at him, either. It's a conversation in which neither of us is willing to commit. So typical of both of us.

"I think that's a little late," I say, and I mean that for the dead girl and me both. We're both lost and adrift now, exposed to the world without any hope of shelter. I'm instantly ashamed of myself for thinking of us as being in any way alike, though. I didn't spend hours, maybe days, suffering at the hands of a sadist and then experience the horror of dying at his hands. I'd only been married to one. "I told Prester, but if you could just make sure he looks after Connor and Lanny—the word's gotten out, Sam. About where we are. Did you do that?"

He snaps his attention to me with a suddenness that feels completely natural. I can see the pulse of surprise, the shift in the way he feels. "Did I what?"

"Did you dox me out on the Internet?"

"Of course I didn't!" he blurts with a frown, and I believe him. "I wouldn't do that, Gwen. No matter what. I wouldn't put you or the kids at risk like that."

I nod. I don't really think it was him, though he'd be a logical suspect. No, I imagine some bright bulb in the Norton Police Department decided to get some righteous, anonymous justice on. Could even be a clerk. Anyone in the chain of discovery with knowledge of my old identity, ending with Detective Prester. I can't even really blame them. Nobody's forgotten Melvin Royal.

Nobody's forgotten Melvin's Little Helper, either. There's a certain rabid, unhealthy fascination people have with male serial killers, but female accomplices are hated *so* much more. It's a toxic stew of misogyny and self-righteous fury, and the simple, delicious fact that it's *okay* to destroy this woman, where it's not okay to destroy others.

I can never be forgiven for being innocent, because I'll never *be* innocent.

Sam looks away again, and I think, somewhat irrationally, that he wants to tell me something. Confess something. He rocks back and forth some more, says nothing, and then he shakes his head and starts to walk away, toward my house.

Detective Prester says, without turning or shifting his attention, "Mr. Cade. I'll be needing a word with you, too."

"You can find me at Ms. Proctor's house," he says. "I'm going to make sure the kids are okay."

I can see Prester debating whether or not to push it, but he clearly decides it can wait. He's got his big fish on the line. No point in catching more than he can fillet at one time.

I text Lanny quickly that it's okay to let Sam in, and when he gets to the door, she throws it open and flings herself into his hug. So does Connor. It's surprising how easily they welcome him, and I admit I feel a little stab of hurt.

For the first time, I wonder if me continuing to be part of their lives is actively, constantly *damaging them*, and the question is so big, so awful, that it makes my breath catch and swell painfully in my throat. That question might be out of my hands now. My kids might be swept away into the Social Services system, and I might never see them again.

Stop. You're thinking like HE wants you to think. Like a helpless victim. Don't let him take away what you've achieved. Fight for it.

I let my eyes drift close and will myself to let go of the worry, the pain. My breath eases, and when I open my eyes, I find Detective Prester has finished with the two boaters who found the body. He's coming my way.

I don't wait; I turn and head for his sedan. I hear the slight scuffle of his shoes on the deck as he is caught off guard, but he doesn't tell me that I'm wrong. I know that he wants to question me in private.

We get into the back seat, me on the passenger side, him behind the driver's spot, and I sink into the warm, cheap upholstery with a slow sigh. I'm tired suddenly. Still scared, on some deep animal level, but I know that whatever's happening now I can't change.

"You said the information about you is on the Internet," Prester says. "Before we get started, I want you to know that's not my doing. If it was anybody in our shop, I'll find out and tear them a new asshole."

"Thanks," I say. "But that doesn't help now, does it?"

He knows it doesn't and hesitates only a second before he pulls a digital recorder from his pocket and turns it on. "Detective Prester, Norton Police Department. Today's date is—" He checks his watch, which I find funny, until I see he's wearing a vintage one with a calendar built right in. "September twenty-third. The time is seven thirty-two.

I'm interviewing Gwen Proctor, also known as Gina Royal. Ms. Proctor, I'm going to read you your rights; it's just a formality."

It isn't, of course, and I quirk a smile at that. I listen as he lists them with the droning ease of a man who has a lot of practice at Mirandizing, and when he finishes, I tell him that I understand the rights he has explained. We're both pleasant, getting the basics out of the way. Two old hands at this.

Prester's voice changes to a low, quiet rumble. "Would you prefer I call you Gwen?"

"That's my name."

"Gwen, this morning a second body was found floating in the lake within sight of your front door. You have to understand this looks bad, given your—well, your history. Your husband is Melvin Royal, and he has a very specific kind of past. The first girl we found in the lake, that might have been a strange coincidence, I'll allow that. But two of them? Two are a plan."

"Not *my* plan," I say. "Detective, you can ask me a million questions a million ways, but I'm going to tell you everything I know, straight up. I heard the scream. It woke me right out of bed. I came out of my room the same time as my kids; they can vouch for that. I came out here to find out what was going on, and I saw the two people in the boat and the body in the water. That is absolutely everything I know about this situation. I know even less about that first body."

"Gwen." There's so much reproach in Prester's voice that he sounds like a disappointed father. I appreciate his tactics, intellectually. Many detectives would go at me hard, but he instinctively knows that what disarms me, what I don't know how to parry, is kindness. "We both know that isn't going to be the end of it, don't we? Now, let's go back to the beginning."

"That was the beginning."

"Not this morning. I want to go back to the first time you saw a body mutilated like this. I read the trial transcripts, watched all the video I could get. I know what you saw that day in the garage of your house. How'd that feel?"

Cognitive technique. He's trying to lead me back to a traumatic moment, put me back in that feeling of helpless horror. I take a moment, then say, "Like my entire life collapsed under my feet. Like I'd been living in hell and not even knowing it. I was horrified. I'd never seen anything like that. I'd never even imagined it."

"And when you realized that your husband was guilty, not just of that murder but of others?"

I put an edge in my voice. "How do you *think* I felt? And still feel?"

"No idea, Ms. Proctor. Bad enough to change your name, I guess. Or maybe that was just so you could get people to stop harassing you."

I glare at him, but of course he's right, even though he minimizes it. For most people who exist in the normal world, the regular world, the idea of taking some Internet mob's threats seriously is a sign of weakness; Prester is probably no different. I'm suddenly very glad that Sam is with the kids. If the phone starts ringing, he can handle the torrent of abuse. He'll be shocked at the intensity and volume of it. Most men are.

I feel weirdly empty and too tired to care. I think of all the effort, all the money, and I think maybe I should have just stayed put back in Kansas, let the assholes take their best shot. If it all ends the same way, why put all the time and energy into trying to build a new, safe life?

Prester is asking me something, and I've missed it, and I have to ask him to repeat it. He looks patient. Good detectives always look patient, at least at first. "Walk me through your days the last week."

"Starting when?"

"Let's start with last Sunday."

It's an arbitrary place to begin, but I comply. It isn't tough. My life isn't normally a whirlwind of activity. I assume that the second victim disappeared on or around Sunday, given the state of her body. I give a thorough accounting, but as I'm moving forward, I realize that I have a decision to make. The flight I took to visit Melvin in El Dorado falls inside this timeline. Am I going to tell Prester I paid my serial killer ex a call? Am I going to lie about it and hope I don't get caught out? That's really not an option, I realize; he's a good detective. He'll check visitor logs in Kansas, and he'll realize I've been to see Mel. Worse, he'll see I visited him right before the body came up.

No good choices. I get the sense that whatever unseen force is pushing me has designed this moment, too. I look down at my hands, then up, staring out the front window of the sedan. It's warm in here and smells of old, stale coffee. As interrogation rooms go, it could be worse.

I turn and look at Prester and tell him about the visit to El Dorado, about the copies of letters he'll find in my house from Melvin Royal, about the torrent of abuse and threats that keep coming at me. I don't make it dramatic. I don't weep or shake or show him any sign of weakness; I don't think it will matter if I do.

Prester nods as if he already knew all that. Maybe he did. Or maybe he's just a great poker player. "Ms. Proctor, I'm going to have to take you in to the station now. You understand that?"

I nod. He takes handcuffs out from behind him; they're in a worn old case on the back of his belt, and I turn without complaint and let him lock them on. As he does, he tells me I'm under arrest for suspicion of murder.

I can't say I'm surprised.

I can't say I'm even angry.

◆ ◆ ◆

The questioning is a blur. It goes on for hours; I drink bad coffee, water, eat a cold sandwich of turkey and cheese sometime in there. I nearly fall asleep, because I'm so tired and—finally—the numbness is gone, and I can be afraid, so afraid it feels like a constant, cold storm inside. I know that if the news hasn't gotten out yet, it will in a matter of hours, and in less than a day it'll be around the world. The twenty-four-hour news cycle feeding an endless appetite for violence and spawning thousands of new, eager recruits to punish me.

My children are exposed, fragile, and it's *my fault*.

I stick to my story, which is all the truth at this point. I'm told there are witnesses to swear that I was seen in town the day the first girl disappeared; turns out she was also eating at the bakery where Lanny and I stopped to gorge ourselves after her suspension from school. I barely remember her—the girl in the corner, with the iPad and tattoo. I wasn't focused on anyone but my daughter, and all my petty problems.

It prickles needles all up and down my spine to think that no one saw that girl *after* the bakery. That someone abducted her out of that parking lot, maybe while we were still inside, maybe just after we'd gone.

Whoever was doing this, I think, watched us the entire time. Even worse, they must have been following us, following *me*, waiting until there was proximity to a victim who matched the profile that they could safely grab. Even then, it was a huge risk, not something for amateurs; even in a small town, *especially* in a small town, people notice anything out of the ordinary. Abducting a woman in broad daylight . . .

Something slips across my mind, something important, but I'm too tired to make sense of it. Prester wants to start at the beginning again. I go through my life since fleeing Wichita. I describe in detail my movements, from the time the first girl disappeared to the time the second surfaced in the lake. I tell him everything I can remember of my conversation with my ex-husband. None of it helps him at all, but I'm *trying*, and I know he can tell.

A knock comes at the door, and another detective offers another sandwich and a soda, and I accept. So does Prester. We eat together, and he tries casual chat; I'm not in the mood, and besides, I recognize it as technique, not interest. We finish our food in silence, and we're just getting back to the questions when the knock comes again.

Prester sits back in his chair, frowning, as the other officer leans in. I don't know him—he's also African American but far younger than Prester. Barely old enough to be out of college, I think. He glances at me, then turns his attention to the detective. "Sorry, sir," he says. "There's been a development. You should probably hear this."

Prester looks irritated, but he shoves back from the table and follows.

Before the door is closed, I see someone being led down the hall past the door. It's only a glimpse, but I take in that it's a white man, in handcuffs, and I have an instant impression of *recognition* well before I can think who it is.

When I do, I sit back hard in my chair, clutching the half-empty can of Coke so hard it crackles with pressure.

Why the *hell* is Sam Cade here in handcuffs?

And where the hell are my kids?

9

The interrogation room door is locked, of course, and though I batter at it and yell, I get no response at all . . . not until my voice has grown hoarse and my knuckles red from knocking.

It's Prester who finally unlocks the door and shoves himself in the way to keep me from charging out. I don't *quite* make contact with him. I back off a step, breathing hard, and say in the harsh, growling voice I've developed, "Where are *my kids*?"

"They're fine," he tells me in that low, soothing tone as he closes the door behind him. "Come on, now, Ms. Proctor, you sit down. Sit. You're tired, and I'll tell you everything you need to know."

I find myself sinking into the chair again, wary and tense, hands fisted on my thighs. He stares at me for a second before he sits and leans forward on his elbows. "Now then. You must have seen Mr. Cade being brought in a while ago."

I nod. My gaze is fixed on his. I wish desperately that I could read him. "Did—did Sam do something to my kids?"

Prester's face goes a little slack and then tightens, and he shakes his head. "No, Gwen, not at all. They're just fine. Nothing's happened to them. I expect they're a little scared about what's going on and where they are right now."

"Then *why do you have Sam*?"

Prester stares at me for a long while this time, reading me. He has a file in his hand, I realize. Not the same one he had before. This one has a new buff-colored exterior. Hasn't even gotten a label on it yet.

He puts it on the table but doesn't open it. He says, "What exactly do you know about Sam Cade?"

"I—" I want to scream at him to *just tell me*, but I know I have to play the game. So I control my voice and say, "I ran a background check on him. Credit check. All that kind of stuff. I do it for anyone who comes around me or my kids. He was clean. A veteran who served in Afghanistan, just like he said."

"That's all true," he tells me. He opens the folder and takes out a formal military photo: Sam Cade, a little younger, a little less ragged, in a sharply creased blue air force uniform. "Decorated helicopter pilot. Four tours, Iraq and Afghanistan. Came home to find out his beloved sister was dead." He opens *my* folder now. Takes out the picture of the nightmare, the dead woman dangling from her steel noose. Suddenly I am there again, standing in the sun on the ruined lawn, staring into the shattered sanctum of Mel's garage. I smell the stench of dead flesh, and it takes everything I have not to shut my eyes, hide myself from it.

"This," Prester says, tapping the photo with one thick fingernail, one time, "is his sister, Callie. No surprise you missed his relationship to her; they got orphaned in a car wreck when he was eight and she was just four. Sent to separate foster homes. He kept his birth parents' name, but she didn't. She got a full adoption and grew up not even knowing him. They started corresponding when he was deployed. I guess he was really looking forward to reconnecting with her when he got home. And he comes back from serving his country to find *this*."

My mouth has gone dry. I think about how close I came to discovering the connection. I think about the searches that turned up nothing.

He must have gone to some lengths to keep his name off the web. Or he hired someone to clean it off.

Sam Cade has been stalking me. I have no question about it now; he moved in after I had, into that cabin, though he made a point of not encountering me until much later on. He made it seem natural. He worked his way in the door, into my life, into the lives of my kids, and *I hadn't seen a thing.*

I wanted to throw up. Gwen Proctor wasn't a new person. She was just Gina Royal 2.0, ready to fall for anything sold to her by a man with a nice face and an easy smile. *I'd left him with my kids. Jesus. God forgive me.*

I can't get my breath. I realize I'm sucking in air too fast, and I duck my head and try to control my breathing. I feel light-headed, and I hear the scrape of the chair as Prester gets up and comes around to rest his hand gently on my back. "Easy," he tells me. "Easy, slow down now. Deep breaths. In, out. Good."

I pant the question out, ignoring his advice. "What did he do?" Anger is what I need. Anger steadies me, grounds me, gives me a purpose and forces the panic right out. I straighten up, blinking away the spots, and he takes a step back. I wonder what he's just seen in my face. "Is it him? Is Sam the one who killed those girls?" Because wouldn't *that* just be perfect. Gina Royal falls for a serial killer, *twice.* Can't say I don't have a type.

"We're looking into that," Prester says. "Point is, Mr. Cade is a person of interest, and we're questioning him. Sorry about springing it on you that fast, but I wanted to know . . ."

"You wanted to see if I already knew who he was," I snap back. "Of course I fucking didn't *know.* I'd never have left my kids with him, would I?"

I can see him taking the idea out for a spin. No way I'd willingly allow a victim's relative into my life, into my house, if I had known better. Prester's trying to fit some scenario together where Sam Cade and

I have done this together, but not only do the edges not fit, they're not even from the same damn puzzle. Either I killed these girls or Sam Cade did, in some crazy attempt to implicate me and earn me the prison sentence he thought I'd cheated . . . or neither of us did it. But we didn't do it together. Not by the facts he's got before him.

Prester doesn't like this at all. I can see him working at it, and I don't blame him for looking like he needs a bottle of bourbon and a day off.

"If Cade did this," I tell him, "then you nail his ass to the wall. For God's sake, *do it.*"

He sighs. He's in for another long day, and I can tell he knows it. He reads the file folder again, flipping pages, and I let him think about it.

When he finally stands up, he gathers his files and pictures. I can see he's made a decision, and sure enough, he holds the door open for me and says, "Your kids are down the hall to the right, in the break room. Sam drove them here in your Jeep. Take 'em home. But don't leave town. If you do, I'll make it my personal mission to set the FBI on your trail, and I *will* ruin whatever life you've got left. Understand me?"

I nod. I don't thank him, because he's not really doing me any favors. He realizes that he's got precious little to hold me on, if anything, and a good defense attorney—like, say, one from Knoxville—would knock his case into the trash without even breaking a sweat, especially with Sam Cade right there hiding in plain sight. Christ, I even feel a little sorry for Prester in that moment.

But not enough to hesitate. I am out the door in a second, rushing past the small bullpen room of the Norton Police Department. I see Officer Graham filling in some paperwork, and he looks up as he sees me pass. I don't nod or smile, because I'm too fixed on the break room door. It's clear glass with miniblinds hanging at a cockeyed angle, and through the gap I see Lanny and Connor sitting together at a square white table, dispiritedly picking at a bag of popcorn sitting open between them. I take a breath, because seeing them alive and fine and unharmed feels so good it physically hurts.

I open the door and step in, and Lanny stands up so fast her chair skids backward across the tile and nearly tips over. She rushes to me and remembers that she's the oldest just in time to *not* throw herself into my arms. Connor blasts past her and flings himself at me instead, and I hug him fiercely and open one arm to her, and she grudgingly accepts. I feel the stabbing relief start to melt, replaced with something sweeter, warmer, kinder.

"They arrested you," Lanny says. Her voice is muffled against me, but she pulls away to look directly at me on the last word. "Why did they do that?"

"They think I might be responsible for—"

I don't finish the thought, but she does. "For the murders," she says. "Sure. Because of Dad." She says it like it's the most logical conclusion in the world. Maybe it is. "But you didn't do it."

She says it with casual conviction, and I feel a swell of love for her, for that unthinking trust. She's usually so suspicious of my motives that having her grant me this one thing means more than I can begin to comprehend.

Connor pulls away, then, and says, "Mom, they came and got us! I said we shouldn't go, but Lanny said—"

"Lanny said we're not getting into a stupid fight with the cops," Lanny supplies. "Which we didn't. Besides, they didn't come for us, exactly. They just couldn't leave us there alone. I made them bring the Jeep. So we'd have a way home." She hesitates for a moment and tries to make the next question look casual. "Um . . . so did they tell you why they want to talk to Sam? Was it something you told them?"

I don't want to open up the subject of what their father did, how many people he destroyed, how many families he shattered, including his own . . . but at the same time, I know I have to explain. They're not little children now, and things—I know this instinctively—are about to get a whole lot worse for all of us.

But I'm reluctant to destroy Sam Cade in their eyes. They like him. And as far as I could tell, he liked them, too. But then again, I thought he liked *me*.

Maybe he *is* part of the murder plot that has cost those two girls their lives. I still can't see Sam killing them, even now, and yet . . . yet I can easily understand how grief and rage and pain pushes someone past limits they never think they'd cross. I destroyed the old Gina Royal and rebuilt myself from her ashes. He's focused his anger outward, at *me*—at his imaginary enemy. Maybe the young women were, to him, collateral damage, cold military math to reach an objective. I can almost, *almost* believe that.

"Mom?"

I blink. Connor's looking at me with real worry, and I wonder how long I've wandered off in my thoughts. I'm so tired. Despite the sandwich, I find I'm starving, and I need to pee so badly I wonder if my bladder will burst before I can make it to the bathroom. Funny. All these were unimportant details until I knew the kids were safe.

"We'll talk on the way home," I tell him. "Quick pit stop and then we'll go. Okay?"

He nods, a little doubtfully. He's worried about Sam, I think, and I hate to break his heart, again. But this one isn't my fault.

I make it to the toilet in time and shiver and cry silently as I sit there. By the time I've washed my face and hands and taken some deep breaths, the face staring back at me from the mirror almost looks normal. Almost. I realize that I need to get a haircut and renew my hair color; a few gray hairs are starting to make an unwelcome appearance. *Funny. I always thought I'd die before I got old.* That's a whisper from the old Gina, who'd seen the day of *The Event* as the end of her entire life. I hate the old Gina, who'd somehow naively believed in the power of true love and the smug certainty that she was a good woman, and her husband was a good man, and that it was something she deserved without putting out any effort at all.

I hate her even more now that I realize I'm still, even after all this, very much like her.

◆ ◆ ◆

The drive home starts in silence, but I can tell it's weighted. The kids want to know. I want to tell them. I just don't quite know how to find the words, so I reach out and fiddle with the Jeep's radio knobs, jumping from new country to southern-fried rock to old country to what sounds like tinny folk music, until Lanny reaches forward and switches it off with a decisive punch of her finger. "Enough," she says. "Come on. Spill. What's the deal with Sam?"

Dear God, I don't want to start this, but I swallow that impulse of cowardice and say, "Sam's sister—it turns out that Sam isn't who he said he was. Well, he is, but he didn't tell us the whole truth."

"You're not making any sense," Connor tells me. He's probably right. "Wait, is Sam's sister in the lake? Did he kill his sister?"

"Hey!" Lanny says sharply. "Let's not jump right to killing sisters, okay? Sam didn't kill anybody!"

I wonder why I didn't see it before, because right now, with a single glance over at her face, I can see that she's irate, agitated, and truly defensive. She'd had an instacrush on Officer Graham, but this is different. This I read not as a crush, but as a *need*. Sam, who's been quietly in her life, being strong and kind and steady? He's the next-best thing she has to a father.

"No," I tell her, and reach out to squeeze her hand just for a second. I feel her tense up as I do. "Of course he didn't. Connor, they took him to the police station because they found out he has a connection to us. From before."

Lanny draws away to press against the vehicle's door. I see Connor sit back, too. "Before?" my son asks quietly. His voice trembles slightly. "You mean, like, when we used to be other people?"

"Yes." I'm guiltily relieved I don't have to lead them to it. "When we lived in Kansas. His sister . . . his sister was one of the people your father killed."

I don't tell them his sister was the last one. Somehow that makes it even worse.

"Oh," Lanny says in a small voice. It sounds empty. "So. He followed us here. Didn't he? He was never really our friend. He wanted to watch us. Hurt us because he was angry about what Daddy did."

Oh God. She called him Daddy. It cuts deep and leaves me feeling frantic with anguish. "Honey—"

"She's right," Connor says from the back. When I glance in the rearview mirror, I see him staring out the window, and in that moment he looks quite chillingly like his father. So much that I stare for too long and have to correct a little sharply back into my lane as we drive up the winding road to the lake. "He wasn't our friend. We don't have any friends. It was stupid to think we did."

"Hey, that's not true," Lanny says. "You've got the Geek Squad playing nerd games with you. And what about Kyle and Lee, those Graham kids? They're always asking you to do things . . ."

"I said I don't have any friends. Just people I play games with is all," Connor says. There's an edge to his voice I haven't heard before, and I don't like it. At all. "I don't like the Graham kids, either. I just pretend I do so they don't beat me up again."

From the look on my daughter's face, she didn't know that until this moment, either. I think that Connor must have confided in Sam, and that with Sam's betrayal, Connor has no more use for his secret. I feel frozen. I remember the stiff way Connor held himself when he was around the Graham boys. I remember his warning, that first time, about how he hadn't lost his phone, that one of them must have taken it. I hate myself for not questioning that. In the rush of events, in my worry about what Mel was doing and the murder, I'd forgotten. I'd let my son down.

When Sam found him with the bloody nose, the bruises, that was the work of the Graham brothers.

I grit my teeth and don't say anything for the rest of the drive. Lanny and Connor don't seem to want to talk, either. I pause at the entrance to the driveway, put the Jeep in park, and turn to face them. "I can't fix what's gone wrong for us. It's just happened. I don't know whose fault it is, and I don't really care anymore. But I promise you one thing: I'm going to take care of you. Both of you. And if anybody tries to hurt you, they're going to have to come through me first. Understand?"

They do, but I can see it doesn't soothe something in them that's still wire-tense. Lanny says, "You're not always here, Mom. I know you want to be, but sometimes we have to look out for each other, and it'd be better if you'd let me have the code to the . . ."

"Lanny. No."

"But—"

I know what she wants: access to the gun safe. And I'm not willing to do it. I never wanted this. I never wanted to raise my kids to have to be gunslingers, warriors, child soldiers.

As long as I have the power to protect them, I won't allow it.

I put the Jeep in gear in the fraught silence and crunch up the gravel road to our house.

As the headlights hit it, I see blood. That's all I see in the first rush of recognition: a vivid red splash over the garage door, splatters and whorls and drips. I brake hard, throwing us all against restraints. The halogens pick it out, and I realize the red probably isn't blood at all; it's too red, too thick. It's still wet and glimmering in the lights, though, and as I watch I see one of the drips is still lengthening its descent.

It hasn't been long since this happened.

"Mom," Connor whispers. I don't look at him. I'm staring now at the words scrawled on our windows, across the brick, on the front door of our house.

MURDERER
BITCH
SCUM
KILLER
WHORE
FUCK YOU
DIE

"Mom!" Connor's hand grips my shoulder, and I hear the panic in my son's voice, the very real fear. "Mom!"

I jam the Jeep in reverse and spray gravel, rocketing down the driveway toward the road. I have to brake suddenly, because there are vehicles in the way. Two of them. A mint-condition, dust-free Mercedes SUV and a dirty jacked-up truck that might be red under the mud coating. They've blocked us in.

The Johansens, the nice, quiet couple from up the hill, the ones I introduced myself to when I moved in . . . they're in their SUV, not looking at me. Staring at the road, as if blocking my fucking driveway is an *accident*. As if they're not involved.

The asshole in the muddy red truck and his friends have no such scruples. They're *happy* to be noticed. There are three of them getting out of the extended cab, and another three sloppily crawling out of the bed of the truck. Drunk, from the lack of coordination, and pretty thrilled about it, too. I recognize one of them. He's the jackass from the range, Carl Getts, the one Javier blackballed for bad behavior.

They start walking toward us, and I realize with a chill that I have my kids with me and *I am unarmed*, and *Jesus*, the cops haven't even bothered to leave a cruiser in the neighborhood to watch out for harassment. So much for Prester's good intentions, if he ever had any. Less than a day out from being hauled in and we're already in fear of our lives.

This is why I drive the Jeep.

I slam it into low gear, go uphill a bit, and then take it on a bouncing course down the steep slope, over wild grassland littered with buried, jutting stones. I steer around the worst of it, but I have to speed up as I realize that the truck's driver and crew are piling back in. He's got four-wheel drive, too. He'll be coming after us, fast as he can. I need to put distance between us.

I need my gun, I think desperately. I don't have a weapon in the safe at the back right now. I'd taken it out in preparation for trading the Jeep to Javier. *Doesn't matter,* I tell myself. Depending on anything or anyone else is bad. I have to rely on myself, first, last, and always. That's the lesson Mel taught me.

First, I have to get us to safety. Second, regroup. Third, get my kids away from this place, however that has to happen.

I almost, *almost,* make it to the safety of the road.

It happens like this: I have to twist the wheel sharply to avoid a jutting boulder that's hidden by a clump of thick weeds, and in doing so, I run the right wheel into a wide, unseen gully. The whole Jeep tips, and for a heart-stopping moment I think about the high incidence of rollover crashes, and then we bounce up and back out even before Lanny's sudden yelp hits my ears, and I think, *We're okay.*

We're not okay.

The left wheel hits and glances off a half-buried rock, and we veer over it. I hear the metallic crunch of collision, and the whole steering assembly shudders out of my hands, jumping wildly. I grab hold again, heart thudding in a steady staccato race, and realize that the axle's broken. I've lost control of the front wheels and the steering.

I can't go around the next rock, which is big enough to smash us right in the center of the Jeep's hood and send us all flying forward into the restraints, hard enough to leave bruises, and I know the airbags deploy because I feel the puff of it against my face, the impact, the burning smell of the propellant. My face hurts and feels hot from the rush of blood and friction. I'm more aware of surprise than pain, but my first instinct is not for myself. I twist in my seat to look frantically at Lanny, at Connor. They both seem dazed but okay. Lanny makes a little whimpering sound and probes at her nose. It's bleeding. I realize I'm bleating questions at them—*are you all right, are you okay*—but I'm not even listening for answers. I'm grabbing up handfuls of tissues to press to the flow of blood from her nose even as I'm looking anxiously at Connor. He seems okay, better than Lanny, though he has a red mark on his forehead. The flaccid white silk of a deflated airbag is draped over his shoulder. *Side curtain airbags*, I remember. Lanny's deployed, too, which is why her nose is bleeding.

Mine might be, too. I don't care.

I compose myself enough to remember that we didn't just accidentally get into a car wreck, that there's a truck full of drunken men rambling over this same hillside, hunting us. I've screwed up. I've put my children in mortal danger.

And I have to *fix it*.

I scramble out of the Jeep and almost fall. I catch myself on the door and realize I'm trailing fat drops of blood in a ragged line down the front of my white shirt. Doesn't matter. I shake my head, sending red drops flying, and fumble my way to the back of the Jeep. I do have two things: a tire iron and an emergency flashlight that strobes disorienting white and red with a flick of a switch. It even has a built-in piercing alert signal. The batteries are fresh, because I changed them out just last week. I grab it and the heavy iron curve of the toolbar, and before I slam the driver's-side door again, I find my cell phone and pitch it to Connor, who seems more together. "Call 911," I tell him. "Tell them we're being attacked. Lock these doors."

"Mom, don't stay out there!" he says, and I worry that he won't lock the doors after all. That he'll hesitate and get dragged out. So I open the door and trigger the locks, which thunk down solidly. Then I roll up the windows to leave him, Lanny, and the keys inside.

I turn with the tire iron in my right hand, the multipurpose flash in my left, to wait for the pickup truck to get closer.

It doesn't make it. Halfway down the hill they hit something, skid sideways, and I watch as the men in the back throw themselves out, yelling, as the truck overbalances on the downhill side. One screams in a way that makes me think he's broken something, or bent it pretty badly, but the other two bounce up the boneless way drunks have. The truck rolls over in a long screech of metal and a cymbal crash of shattering glass, but it doesn't keep going down the hill. It stops on its side, tires spinning, engine still roaring like the driver hasn't the good sense to take his foot off the gas. The three inside start yelling for help, and the two still upright from the truck bed scramble to help them. They nearly overbalance the whole thing and send it tumbling farther downhill. It's a bit of a comedy.

I see the Johansens' SUV suddenly start up and peel out hastily on the road, as if they just remembered they are late to their own party. I'm assuming they faint at the sight of blood. Even mine. I know they won't be calling the police, but it hardly matters. Connor's already done it. All I need to do, I tell myself, is to keep anyone hostile occupied until the lights and sirens show up. I haven't done anything wrong.

Not yet, anyway.

One of the drunk guys peels off and heads my direction, and I find myself tremendously not surprised that it's the one from the range, Carl. The one who insulted Javi. He's yelling something at me, but I'm not really listening. I'm just trying to see if he has a gun. If he does, I'm sunk; not only can he kill me from where he stands, but he can claim I attacked him with my handy tire iron and it was self-defense. I know Norton well enough to guess how that will go. They'll hardly pause for five minutes before they acquit the bastard, even if my kids give testimony. *I was in fear for my life,* he'll say. The standard defense of murderous cowards. Problem is, it's also the defense for legitimately frightened people. Like me.

A relief: he doesn't seem to have a gun, at least, not that I can see, and he's hardly the type to be coy about it. He'd be waving it around if he had it, which makes my tire iron into a real threat.

He pauses, and I realize that Connor is hammering at the window of the Jeep, trying to make me look at him. I risk a glance. His face looks desperately pale. I hear him yell, "I called the cops, Mom. They're coming!"

I know you did, sweetie. I give him a smile, a real smile, because this might be the last time I get to do that.

Then I turn on the drunk guy, whose other friend is heading toward us now, and I say, "Back the fuck off."

They both laugh. The one who's just arrived is a little broader and a little taller, but he's also even more drunk and has to hang on to the first guy as rocks turn under his feet. Keystone Kops, but deadly serious about the violence they'd like to do.

"You fucked up our truck," he says. "Gonna have to pay for that, you murdering bitch."

Back at the overturned truck, the passenger-side door is creaking up like the hatch in a tank, but unlike a tank—and I could have told these idiots this—car doors aren't designed to flip back and lie flat. The attempt to throw the door up and out of the way causes it to hit the hinge point and rebound at the man pushing it with vicious speed.

He yelps and lets go of the sides of the truck just before his fingers are crushed. It'd be funny if I weren't scared shitless and responsible for two innocent children, whereas these jackasses aren't even responsible for their own selves.

When the two facing me decide to rush me, I flip the stun function switch on the flashlight and keep it pointed away from me as I activate it. It's still like a brick to the face; the strobing, asymmetric, incredibly bright lights and the ear-shattering shriek are bad enough behind the thing, much less ahead of it.

It knocks Carl and his friend flat on their asses, mouths open in frantic yells I can't hear over the din. I feel a bitter, fantastic rush of adrenaline that makes me want to smash the hell out of them with the tire iron and make sure, absolutely sure, that these assholes never threaten my children again.

But I don't. I'm on the thin, shivering edge of it, but what stops me is the idea that I'll just prove Prester right. Prove myself a murderer. Local blood on my hands. As quickly as they'd acquit someone else for shooting me, they'd strap me down for the needle if I hit these guys when they're down. It's really all that keeps me standing there, holding the strobe and siren on them instead of finishing this for good.

Even though I'm blinded by the strobes, I know the police are coming when Connor rolls the window down next to me and grabs my arm. He's pointing down at the road, and when I look that way, I see a cruiser pulling up with its light bar slashing the night. I see two figures get out and start toiling up the hill toward me, flashlights bobbing and illuminating startling patches of green brush and bone-pale rocks.

I shut the flashlight's defense mode down and keep the halogen beam fixed on the two drunks, who are now struggling up to their knees, spitting mad. They're still holding hands to their ears. One of them leans over and throws up a gush of pale beer, but the other—Carl—keeps his gaze fixed hard on me. I see the hate in it. There's no reasoning with him. And no way to feel safe.

"Police are coming," I tell him. He looks over, like he didn't notice—and he probably hadn't—and a flash of pure rage makes me tighten up my grip on the tire iron again. He wants to hurt me. Maybe kill me. And maybe he wants to take his fury out on the kids.

"You fucking whore," he says. I think about what a satisfying crunch the tire iron would make coming in contact with his teeth.

He's five foot eight of bad breath and shitty posture, and I can't think I'm taking a light out of the world if I end him. But I suppose he has people who love him.

Even I have that much.

Officer Graham is the first to make it to my side. I'm glad to see him; he's bigger and taller, and he looks like he could intimidate the spine out of just about anyone if he wanted to give it a try. He takes in the situation, frowns, and says, "What the *hell* is going on?"

It's in my best interest to get my story in first, and I'm quick off the mark. "These idiots decided to pay me a not-so-friendly visit," I say. "They blocked us into the driveway. Somebody—probably them—vandalized the house. I tried to go cross-country, but a rock took out my steering. I didn't have a choice. I had to try to keep them away from my kids."

"Lying *bitch*—"

Graham extends a hand toward the drunk without taking his gaze off me. "Officer Claremont will be taking your statement," he tells him. "Kez?"

Graham's partner tonight is a tall, lean, African American woman with close-cropped hair and a no-nonsense briskness. She leads the two drunks over to the wrecked pickup and calls for rescue and an ambulance to get the three from the cab and the one broken farther up the hill. They're babbling at her in high-pitched, urgent, slurring voices. I don't imagine she's enjoying herself.

"So all this came with no provocation at all, is what you're saying," Graham says.

I turn back to look at him, then lean into Connor's open window to kiss his forehead. "Lanny? You all right, sweetheart?"

She gives me a thumbs-up and tilts her head back to help slow down the bloody nose.

"Mind putting down the tire iron?" Graham says in a dry voice, and I realize I'm clutching it tightly, as if I'm still facing threats. My thumb is resting on the stun function button of the flashlight, too. I ease myself back from that invisible cliff and lay both things down next to the Jeep, then take a couple of steps away. "Okay. Good start. Now, you said these boys blocked you in. You had words with them?"

"I don't even know them," I say. "But I guess the information is out about my ex. I'm assuming you know."

He doesn't betray much, but I see something stir down in the depths of his gaze, and his mouth goes tight. He deliberately loosens it. "As I understand it, your husband is a convicted murderer."

"Ex-husband."

"Uh-huh. A serial killer, if I got it right."

"You know you do," I say. "Word's traveling fast. Guess it would in a small town like this. I asked Detective Prester for some kind of protective detail for my kids—"

"We were on the way to take that up," he tells me. "We'd have been parked out front tonight."

"I guess the paint would have probably dried by then."

"Paint?"

"Feel free to go look once you're done here. Can't miss it," I tell him. I'm flat exhausted. The aches from the crash are starting to make themselves felt. I have tenderness in my left shoulder, where I probably wrenched it against the restraints. My neck's stiff, and now my nose has a dull ache around the bridge. My nosebleed has stopped, at least, so I must not have broken anything, and when I touch it I don't feel anything shifting. I'm fine, I think. Better than I deserve to be. "This is just Round One. That's why I said we needed *protection*."

"Ms. Proctor, maybe you should consider that of the six guys who came after you, at least four of them have some kind of injuries," Graham says, not unkindly. "I think we can call this round for you, if you're keeping score."

"I'm not," I say, but that's a lie. I'm glad that shitty pickup is lying on its side leaking radiator fluid into the ground. I'm glad four of them get a chance to nurse wounds while thinking about never coming back at me. I'm just sorry they aren't hurt badly enough to keep them from ever doing it again. "You're not arresting me."

"You didn't even make that a question."

"Any decent defense attorney would make dog food out of you. A mother with her kids, attacked by six drunk jerks? *Really?* I'll be the trending hero on Twitter in half an hour."

He sighs. It's a long, slow sound that mingles with the lapping of the lake's waves below. Mist is beginning to rise from the water as the air cools just enough to start the cycle, like a thousand wisps of ghosts escaping. *Lake of the dead,* I think, and try not to look at it. Stillhouse Lake's beauty is ruined for me. "No," Graham finally says. "I'm not arresting you. I'm arresting them for criminal mischief and good old Bobby over there for driving under the influence. Good enough?"

It isn't. I want them all arrested for assault, and that word hadn't even crossed his lips.

He must have seen the argument coming up in me, because he holds up a hand to forestall it. "Look, they didn't lay a hand on you. At least one of 'em is sober enough to figure out he can claim they saw you wreck and came down here to help, and you got paranoid and fired off that—whatever the hell it is—at them. Unless we find paint or evidence of it on them or in the truck, they can claim they have no idea your house got tagged—"

"*Tagged?* It's not Banksy art!"

"All right then, vandalized. But the point is, they've got good deniability for everything to do with any stalking or assault. And you're the one who had the tire iron. Far as I can tell, these men were unarmed."

Six on one don't need weapons, and he knows that, but he's right, of course. Defense attorneys cut both ways.

I lean against the broken wreck of my Jeep, out of strength. "We'll need a wrecker," I tell him. "My Jeep's not going anywhere without one."

"I'll arrange for it," he says. "Meanwhile, let's get your kids and go back to your house. Make sure nobody's gotten inside."

I know they hadn't. I have mobile notification for my alarm system, and if it goes off I can immediately look at the tablet and rerun the footage to see who's been in there. Nobody broke any windows or kicked in any doors, but even so, the last place I want to take my kids right now is back to the house, with that red paint still dripping. I suppose they picked the garage for that particular splash pattern on purpose. Reminding me where Melvin liked to do his gruesome work.

But there really isn't a choice. I know just from Graham's expression that he's not taking us to any Norton motel for the night, and I strongly suspect that any calls to Detective Prester will go unanswered. With the Jeep destroyed, my only option would be to rely on the kindness of strangers, and . . . I'm far too paranoid to even consider it. My nearest neighbors, the Johansens, helped block my driveway. Sam Cade lied to me from the beginning. Javier's a reserve deputy and probably won't return my calls, either.

I reach into the open Jeep window and hit the unlock button, retrieve my keys, and help Lanny out. Her nose has mostly stopped bleeding now, and it doesn't seem broken, but she might have bruises. We all might. My fault.

I hold on to her as the three of us slowly follow Officer Graham up the hill, to a house that no longer feels like home.

10

Officer Graham takes diligent pictures of the damage. The red isn't blood; it's still vividly red, and blood would have oxidized to brown by now. Paint. Most of the words are spray-painted, the exception being *Killer*, which has extra-gothic drip from the vandal's liberal dip of the paintbrush. I unlock the door and disarm the alarm, and Graham checks the whole place thoroughly. He finds nothing, but then again, I knew he wouldn't.

"All right," he says, settling his sidearm in its holster as he comes back to us in the living room. "I'm going to need your guns, Ms. Proctor."

"You have a warrant for them?" I ask. He stares back at me. "That's a no, then. I decline to cooperate. Get a warrant."

His expression hasn't changed, but his body language has; it's shifted a little forward, become a touch more aggressive. I sense it more than see it. I remember what Connor said on the drive back: Graham's boys were the ones who beat up my son. I wonder exactly what they learned from their father. I *want* to trust the man; he's wearing a badge, he's the only thing truly standing between me and the angry people coming at me right now. But looking at him, I'm not sure I can make the leap.

Maybe I can't trust anyone anymore. My judgment's been so *off*.

"Okay," Graham says, though clearly he doesn't think it is. "Keep the doors locked, alarm on. Does it ring at the station?"

Why, so you can ignore it? "It rings directly there," I tell him. "If the power gets cut, it also goes off."

"And what about the panic room . . . ?" I say nothing to that, just look at him. He shrugs. "Want to make sure you've got a way to get help if you're inside there. Can't help if we don't know you're in there."

"It has a separate phone line," I tell him. "We'll be just fine."

He can tell I've gone as far down this road as I'm going, and Graham finally nods and heads for the door. I open it and see him off, and try not to look at the damage to our front door. Once it's shut, I can pretend, a little, that everything's normal. I enter the alarm code, and the soft beep of the "Stay" signal soothes something inside me I didn't know was trembling. I put all the locks on and turn to put my back to the door.

Lanny is sitting on the couch with her knees up, her arms circling them. Defensive again. Connor leans against her. There are smears of blood on my daughter's chin, and I go into the kitchen, wet a hand towel, and come back to gently clean her off. Once I have, she takes the cloth and silently does the same for me. I haven't even realized that I have so much on me; the white hand towel comes away with vivid red smears. Connor's the only one who doesn't need the cleanup, so I put the towel aside and sit with my kids, holding them and rocking with them slowly. None of us has anything to say.

None of us needs to.

Finally, I pick up the soiled towel and rinse it in cold water in the sink, and Lanny comes in to grab the orange juice carton and swig it down thirstily. Connor takes it when she's done. I don't even have the energy to tell them to use glasses. I just shake my head and have water, lots of it. "Do you want anything to eat?" I ask them. Both kids murmur no. "Okay. Go and get some sleep. If you need me, I'll be in the shower, and I'm going to sleep out here tonight in the living room, okay?"

They're not surprised. I think they must remember how, after my acquittal and before we left Kansas, I slept every night on the old sofa in the bare living room of the rented house with a gun right at my side. We had bricks smashed through the windows, and once a flaming bottle that guttered out without starting a fire. Vandalism was a constant fact of life before we'd moved for the second time.

And I'd known then, like now, that I couldn't rely on the neighbors for help. Or the police.

The shower feels like heaven, like a sweet, normal, warm respite from the hell of the day. I towel-dry my hair and put on a fresh sports bra and underwear; then I find the softest pair of sweatpants I have, plus a microfiber shirt and socks. I want to be as fully dressed as possible, except for my running shoes, which I've rigged up with elastic ties so I can slip them on in an emergency. The couch is comfortable enough, and I keep my gun tucked just where I can reach it, pointed away from me. Too many paranoid people have failed to practice trigger safety.

To my surprise, I fall asleep, and I don't even dream. Maybe I'm too tired. I wake up to the soft beep of the automatic coffeemaker as it brews the morning pot, and I make a groggy mental note to tell Lanny that if I get arrested again, to turn the damn thing off. It's still dark outside. I find my shoulder holster and put it on over my shirt, tuck the gun inside, and go to pour my coffee. I'm in my stocking feet and very quiet, but even so, I hear the creak of a door opening down the hall.

It's Lanny. I know at a glance she didn't sleep much, because she's already dressed in black cargo pants and a half-ripped gray T-shirt with a skull on it and a black tank showing through the gaps. Two years from now, I think, I'll have to fight with her to keep the tank top on under it. She's brushed out her hair but not straightened it, and the faint natural wave in it catches the light as she moves. The reddened bruising under her eyes has turned a rich crimson, verging on brown, and her nose is a little swollen but not as much as I'd feared.

Even with the damage, she's beautiful, so beautiful, and I catch my breath on an unexpected pain and have to busy myself stirring sugar into my coffee so I don't show her the emotion. I don't even know why I'm feeling it. It comes as an overwhelming, warm wave that makes me want to destroy the world before it can hurt her again.

"Move," Lanny says, annoyed, and I edge out of the way as she yanks a cup from the shelf. She checks it—an automatic thing for her, from the time she was twelve and found a cockroach in a cup in a rental house—and then splashes coffee in. She drinks hers black, not because she likes it but because she thinks she should. "So. We're still alive."

"Still alive," I agree.

"You check the Sicko Patrol?"

I dread doing it, but she's right. That's the next step. "I will in a bit."

She lets out a bitter laugh. "I guess I won't be going to school."

She isn't dressed for it, I think, and of course she's right. "No school. Maybe it's time for homeschool."

"Oh, yeah, that's great. We'll never get to leave the house ever again. Federal background checks on the UPS guy before we let him deliver a package."

She's in a foul mood, spoiling for a fight, and I raise my eyebrows. "Please don't," I tell her, which makes her glare. "I'm going to need your help, Lanny."

That merits an eye roll on top of the glare, which is a neat trick I suspect only a teen girl can truly master. "Let me guess. You want me to take care of *Connor*. As per, Warden. Maybe you should give me a badge and you know . . ." She gestures at my shoulder holster, vaguely but significantly.

"No," I tell her. "I want you to come with me and help me go through the e-mails. Get your laptop. I'll show you what to do. And when we're done with that, we'll talk about next steps."

She's momentarily at a loss for words, which is a new thing, and then she puts her cup down, swallows, and says, "About time."

"Yes," I agree. "It is. But believe me, I wish I could keep it away from you forever."

It's a tough morning's work, slowly acclimating her to the levels of depravity she'll encounter, and showing her how to sort and categorize them. I prequalify what I send her; no rape porn or Photoshops of our faces onto murder victims. I can't do that to her. She might see it soon enough, but only because I can't help it, not because I allow it.

There's a tsunami of hatred this morning, and even with two of us culling through it and reporting it back to the various abuse agencies, it takes a long, long time. Most of it's fairly regular stuff—death threats. One finally makes her stop and roll her chair away from her laptop, hands coming away as if she's touched something dead. She looks at me wordlessly, and I see something flame out inside her. A little bit of hope. A little bit of faith that the world could still be kind, even to us.

"They're just words," I tell her. "From small men who are brave on the other side of a keyboard and an Internet handle. But I know how you feel."

"It's awful," she says in a voice that sounds more like a little girl than the adult she's trying to be. She clears her throat and tries again. "These people are vile."

"Yes," I say in agreement, putting my hand on her shoulder. "They'll never care whether or not you were hurt by what they said, or even if you read it; it was all about *writing* it for them. It's natural to feel afraid and violated by all this. I feel that way all the time."

"But?" My daughter knows there's a *but*.

"But you have the power," I tell her. "You can turn off this computer and walk away anytime. They're pixels on a screen. They're assholes who might be halfway around the world, or on the other side of the country, and even if they're not, the odds are astronomically on your side that they'll never do anything that doesn't involve shouting at a computer screen. Okay?"

That seems to steady her. "Okay," she says. "And . . . if they beat the odds?"

"Then that's why you have me, and I have this." I touch the shoulder holster. "I don't like guns. I'm not a crusader. I wish guns were *harder* to get, and I could rely on a cattle prod and a baseball bat. But that's not the world we live in, baby. So if you want to start learning to shoot, we'll do that. And if you don't, that's good, too. I'd rather you didn't, believe me, because your chances of getting shot are a hell of a lot better if you're armed. I do this as much to draw fire *away from you* as I do to return it. Understand?"

She does, I can see that. For the first time, she sees the weapon I'm carrying as much a danger as a shield. Good. It's the hardest lesson for someone who's been taught guns are the answer . . . that they're only the answer to a pure, simple, direct set of problems: killing someone.

I never want her to have to do it. *I* don't want to have to do it.

I get her laptop back online, and we're both silently working when Connor appears in the doorway, yawning, still in his pajama pants. He has a wide, blackening bruise on his shoulder, but other than that, he seems fine. He blinks at us and tries to finger-comb his hair straighter. "You're both up," he says. "Why isn't there breakfast?"

"Shut up," Lanny says, but it's a reflex. "Such a boy. Learn to make pancakes, not like it's rocket science."

He yawns and gives me a mournful look. "Mom." I see he wants to be treated, today, like a child, to be coddled and pampered and made to feel safe. It's the opposite of Lanny, who wants to face things head-on. And that's fine, too. He's younger, and it's his choice. And hers, too.

I take a break from the torrential acid bath of hate and go whip up pancakes from a mix, add fresh pecans that I need to use up anyway, and we're in the middle of what feels like a startlingly normal breakfast when there's a decisive sort of knock on our disfigured front door.

I get up. Lanny has already put her fork down and half risen out of her chair, but I motion her down. Connor stops chewing and stares at me, and my mind is racing with the possibilities. Today, of all days, we face a whole new set of risks. It could be the mailman. It could be a guy with a shotgun ready to blow my face off the second he sees it. It could be someone's left me a mutilated pet on the doorstep. There's no way to tell without looking, and I get my tablet and try to boot it up, then remember that it's dead. Battery's drained. *Damn technology.*

"It's okay," I tell them, though there's no way I can possibly know that. I go to the door and check the peephole, carefully, and see a tired-looking African American woman standing there. She looks familiar, but I have trouble placing her for a few seconds because the last time I saw her, it was a fleeting glimpse and she was wearing a police uniform.

It's the cop who was with Graham last night, who handled the drunks while he talked to us.

I disarm and unlock, and she freezes a second as her eyes fix on the shoulder holster. "Yes?" I ask, neither inviting nor rejecting. Her dark-brown eyes move up to fix on mine, and she very carefully shows me she has nothing in her hands.

"My name's Claremont," she says.

"Officer Claremont. I remember you from last night."

"Yeah," she says. "My father lives on the other side of the lake. He says he met you and your daughter when you were out on a run."

The old man, Ezekiel Claremont. Easy. I hesitate, then extend my hand, and we shake. She has a firm, dry, businesslike grip. Up close, in casual clothes, she has an elegant style to her, something not only in the drape of her clothes but in the cut of her hair, her perfectly shaped fingernails. Not what I would have expected from the Norton PD. "Can I come in?" she asks. "I want to help."

Just like that. She keeps her gaze steady, and there's something quiet and strong about the way she says it.

But I step outside and close the door behind me. "Sorry," I tell her, "but I don't know you. I don't even know your first name."

If she's taken aback by my lack of warmth and courtesy, she doesn't show it; she narrows her eyes just a bit, just for a second, and then smiles over it to say, "Kezia. Kez, for short."

"Nice to meet you," I tell her, which is empty politeness. I'm wondering why the hell she's *really* here.

"My father wanted me to come check on you," she says. "He heard about the trouble you were in. Not much a fan of the Norton PD, my pa."

"Must make things awkward over Sunday dinners."

"You have *no* idea."

I gesture to the porch chairs, and she settles into the one that I realize, with a sharp, glancing sort of pain, Sam Cade has always taken. It hits me with an unwelcome weight that I miss the son of a bitch. *No, I don't. I miss someone who never existed in the first place, the same way my Mel never existed.* The real Sam Cade is a stalker and a liar, at the very least.

"Pretty over on this side," she says, scanning the view to the lake. I'm sure she's also thinking, just as everyone else has, of how good a view I would have had of a body being dumped right out there. "His side's a little more blocked by the trees. Cheaper, though. I keep trying to get him to move down the hill so he doesn't have to climb that trail, but—"

"I'd love to make small talk, but my pancakes are getting cold," I tell her. "What is it you want to know?"

She shakes her head just a little, gaze still fixed on the lake. "You know, you don't make it easy to help you out. In the position you're in, you might want to put a rein on that attitude. You're going to need some friends."

"This *attitude* keeps me alive. Thanks for stopping by."

I start to get up again. She puts out a perfectly manicured hand to stop me and finally turns her gaze to lock on mine. "I think I might be able to help you find out who's doing this to you," she says. "Because we both know it's somebody close. Somebody local. And somebody who's got a reason."

"Sam Cade has a reason."

"I helped confirm his alibi, both times the girls went missing," she says. "He is absolutely not the guy. They've already let him go."

"*Let him go?*" I look at the paint slopped on my garage, the words sprayed on the brick in a red fury of anger. "Great. I guess that explains this."

"I don't think—"

"Look, *Kez*, thanks for trying, but you are not helping me at all if your point is to convince me Sam Cade isn't a bad guy. He *stalked me*."

"He did," she says. "He's admitted to that. Said he was angry and wanted revenge, but you weren't what he thought. If he'd meant you harm, he had plenty of opportunities to do something, wouldn't you say? I think this is somebody else altogether, and I've been working on a lead. Now, do you want to know what I think, or not?"

It's so tempting to say no, shove out of the chair, and stalk away . . . but I can't make myself do it. Kezia Claremont may have ulterior motives, but her offer seems pretty sincere. And I do need a friend, even if it's someone I can't trust any farther than I can jump. No more than I can trust Sam.

"I'm listening," I finally say.

"Okay. So, Stillhouse Lake's always been a pretty closed-in community up here," she says. "Mostly white. Mostly well-off if not wealthy."

"Not since the downturn, when all these houses went into foreclosure."

"True, about a third of the properties ended up getting sold or rented out in a rush last year. If we eliminate the residents who are original to the lake, that leaves about thirty houses to look at. We take yours away, that's twenty-nine. Hope you don't mind if I take my father out. Twenty-eight."

I'm not willing to grant much, but I'm willing, for argument's sake, to eliminate Easy Claremont. He hadn't looked up to scaling the hill to his house, much less abducting, killing, and disposing of two healthy, strong young women. I can exempt myself. *Twenty-eight houses.* That includes Sam Cade, whom the police already eliminated and I suppose, grudgingly, I might have to as well. Twenty-seven, then. That's a small number.

"Do you have names?" I ask her. She nods, and from her pocket she produces a folded piece of paper that she hands over. It's plain copy paper, standard from any office printer, and on it is a list of the names and addresses and phone numbers. She's been thorough. Some have asterisks, and I see that those notate criminal records. I'm not particularly suspicious of the two guys with the conviction for cooking meth who share a cabin way up the slope, but it's certainly good information to know. There's a sex offender, too, but Kezia's bold handwritten notation shows he's already been thoroughly questioned and, though not eliminated, mostly discounted as a suspect.

Kezia says, "I would have done more on my own, but I figured you might need something to do to take your mind off things. This is all my own time, nothing on the books."

I look at her. She's not smiling. There's something unyielding in her, something that bends but doesn't break, and I recognize it. I feel it in myself, too. "You know who I am," I say. "Why do you want to help me?"

"Because you need it, and Easy asked. But also . . ." She shakes her head and looks away. "I know what it's like to be judged for something you never got to control."

I swallow hard, taste the fleeting ghost of my cooling pancakes and syrup. I'm thirsty for coffee. "You want to come inside?" I ask her. "We're having pancakes. I've got enough to stretch to another plate."

She gives me a slow, quiet smile. "I wouldn't mind."

11

Kezia Claremont, it turns out, is a hit with my kids, who start off quiet and wary, but she has a way with them, a natural charm that teases out conversations from silence. She, I think, will make a great investigator someday. She's wasted in uniform, handling rowdy drunks—though she was flawless at that, too. I warm up my breakfast as I make hers, and we eat together as the kids clean their plates and wander off to their separate areas. I think Lanny wants to stay, but I give her the quiet shake of the head, and she retreats.

"I have some contacts," Kezia tells me quietly, once we're alone. "I can start them on background work, off books. Listen, my father said you were in trouble, and no shit, those vandals hit you fast. You're going to need some on-site protection."

"I know," I tell her. "I'm armed, but—"

"But offense isn't defense. Listen, you know Javier. He's the other reason I'm here. He likes you. Not willing to believe you're all the way innocent just yet, but he's willing to help keep the wolves off you if you'll agree."

I think about how things might have been different if only I'd loaded up the van and departed that first time I had the impulse, headed

Stillhouse Lake

hellbound and out of town instead of lingering like some fool who couldn't see it coming. I had good reasons, but those reasons seem useless now. They seem like illusions. I can't trade for that van now that I've wrecked the Jeep, and anyway, Javier would never give it to me. Neither of us will want paper trails.

"If he's willing to keep an eye out for us, I'm good," I say. "I'd feel better if I had the rest of his regiment along with him."

Kez raises a sharply arched eyebrow. "You'd better take what you get. Allies are going to be thin on the ground for you right now."

She's right, and I shut up and nod. "I'll take half the list," I say. "I have someone who might be willing to help do the research." Absalom won't be free, but trying to avoid paying for help would be cutting my own throat right now. I can't run. I might as well put my money to use cutting myself out of this net that Mel (because it has to be Mel) has thrown around me. Can't start a new life with it if I'm behind bars. Can't save my family if my kids are taken from me and sent to foster care.

Kezia's right; at this moment I need to take every ally I can get.

So when we finish breakfast, I thank her and get her phone number in return. I realize that if I've read her wrong, everything we've discussed could be recorded, documented, part of the official Norton police record . . . but I don't think Prester would go that route.

I text Absalom, who replies with a simple WHAT, as if I've caught him in the middle of something important, and I tell him in simple terms what I need. His reply is blunt and to the point: thot u in jail. I text back not guilty and get silence for a full minute before he types one single question mark, which I know means *what do you need* in his particular, peculiar shorthand.

So I take a picture of the piece of paper, with Kezia's neat, precise handwriting, and I tell him which names I want him to research. He texts back a price in Bitcoin that makes me wince, but he knows I'll pay it, and I do, from my computer. I don't check e-mail. It's time to

213

destroy the account again; even if there are clues in there, I can't swim in the toxic flood without corrupting my soul along with it. I leave it for now, transfer the money to him, and send an e-mail with the same picture of the list, names marked, to the private investigator I've used before, along with her standard fee.

I'm in the bathroom peeing when my burner phone rings, and I grab it and look at the number. I don't recognize it, but it could be Absalom.

I quickly wipe and flush before I hit the "Answer" button and say, "Hello?"

"Hello, Gina."

The voice takes my breath away. It's the voice from my head, the voice I can never exorcise no matter how much I pray. My fingers go numb, and I lean against the sink, staring at my horrified, stark face in the mirror.

Melvin Royal is on the phone with me. *How is this happening?*

"Gina? Still there?"

I want to hang up. Keeping an open connection is like holding a bag full of spiders. But somehow, I manage to say, "Yes. I'm here." Melvin likes to brag. Likes to savor his victories. If he's orchestrated this, he'll say so, and maybe, just maybe, he'll say something that I can use.

He has my number. How did he get my number? How could he?

Kez. She was new in my life . . . but I hadn't given her my number. *Sam.* No, not Sam. Please, not Sam.

Wait.

I'd taken my phone to the prison. I'd had to surrender it on the way in, pick it up on the way out. Someone inside there is responsible for passing along his mail. Not impossible they hacked my phone, too. They'd have had enough time. I'm ill that I didn't think of it before.

Mel's still talking. His voice holds that artificial warmth now. "Sweetheart. You're having a real bad week. Is it true there's another body?"

"Yes. I saw her."

"What color was she?"

I'd expected a lot of responses from him. Not that one. "Sorry?" I say blankly.

"I made a color chart once, of how they look at different stages without skin. Was she more of a raw-chicken color, or was it more of a slimy brown?"

"Shut up."

"Make me, Gina. Hang up on me. But wait, if you do, *if you do,* you'll never find out who's coming for you."

"I'm going to kill you."

"Absolutely, you should do that. But you won't have time. I promise you that."

I'm colder than I think I've ever been. His voice still sounds so *like him* . . . reasonable, calm, measured. Rational. Except nothing he's saying is rational at all. "Then tell me. You're wasting time."

"I guess you found out about your new friend Sam. You just can't catch a break with men, can you? I'll bet he was thinking about all the things he was going to do to you. Got him off every night, that anticipation."

"Is that what gets you off, Mel? Because it's all you'll ever get. You're never seeing me again. Never touching me. And I'm going to get through this."

"You don't even know what's happening. You can't *see* it."

"Then tell me," I say. "Tell me what I'm missing. I know you're dying to tell me how stupid I am!"

"I will," he says, and suddenly his tone shifts. The mask shreds loose, and I hear the monster talking. It's very, very different. It doesn't even sound human. "I want you to know that when it comes, when it all falls down, it's *your fault,* you worthless, stupid bitch. I should have started with you. But I'll finish with you, one of these days. You think I won't touch you? *I will.* From the inside out."

It raises my skin into goose bumps, makes me back into a corner, as if somehow he can reach out and grab me even through the phone. *He isn't here. He won't be here.* But that voice . . .

"You're never leaving that cell," I manage to say. I know I no longer sound like Gwen. I sound like Gina now. I *am* Gina now.

"Oh, didn't you hear? My new lawyer thinks I have a rights violation case. Might get some evidence thrown out. Might be a new trial, Gina. What do you think, you want to go through it all again? Do you want to *testify* this time?"

The idea makes me physically sick, and I feel acid scorch the back of my throat in a bitter wave. I don't answer him. *Hang up.* I'm screaming it at myself, as if I'm standing outside of my body. *Hang up hang up hang up!* It's like being trapped in a nightmare, and I can't seem to move . . . and then I take a breath and the paralysis breaks, and I move my thumb to the "Disconnect" button.

"I've changed my mind," he says, but I'm already pressing. "I'll tell you—"

Click. I did it. He's gone. It feels like I won a point . . . did I? Or did I just run away?

Oh God. If they got into my phone, they might have more from it. The kids' numbers. Absalom's. What else did I have in there?

I sink down to a crouch with my back wedged in the corner between the sink and the hinges of the door, and I put the phone carefully on the floor and stare at it as if it might change into rotting meat, or burst into a flood of scorpions. I reach up and take down the hand towel and I bite into it hard, so hard my jaw muscles ache, and I scream into the muffling comfort of it.

I do that until my mind is clear again. It takes a couple of minutes. Finally, I start to close in on the questions. *How?* Someone at the prison must have ganked my number from the phone while I was there. *But how did he call?* Melvin's phone privileges are strictly reserved for his lawyer; he's not allowed contact with anyone else, and I am specifically on his do-not-call list. But even on death row, I imagine it's possible to buy time with a smuggled cell phone.

I hope it cost him plenty, the bastard.

I can't stay in the house. I feel suffocated, desperate, *angry*. I pace the living room for a while, and then I call Kezia Claremont at the number she's left to ask her to please, for the love of God, keep an eye on my kids.

"Look out your window," she says. I do, pulling the living room curtain aside, and I see her car is still sitting in the driveway. She waves. "What's up?"

I tell her about Mel's call, and she gets cool, all business, noting down the number as I read it off—he didn't bother to block it—and saying she'll check into it. I have no doubt it'll be a dead end. Even if they find the phone, it doesn't matter. He's proven he can reach out from behind those bars whenever he wants. Next time it won't be him. It'll be someone else doing his bidding.

"Kezia . . ." I'm vibrating with tension, sick with it. "Can you stay here and watch the house for about an hour?"

"Sure," she says. "It's my free time. Nice day and all. Why? He give you some specific threat?"

"No. But—I need to go. Just for a little while." I feel trapped in here. I'm on the verge of a meltdown, and I know it. I need to get some space, enforce some control. "Hour at the most." I need to flush the confrontation with Mel out of my system before it turns toxic.

"No problem," she tells me. "I'm making phone calls anyway. I'll be right here."

I tell the kids I'll be back and that Kezia is right outside, and I make them swear they won't open the door while I'm gone. We go over emergency procedures. The kids are quiet and watchful; they know something's wrong with me, and it scares them. I can see that.

"It'll be okay," I tell them. I kiss Lanny on the head, then Connor, and they both let me without wiggling out of the embrace. That's how I know they're worried.

I grab a plastic locking gun case and put my weapon in, clip removed and chamber cleared. I leave the shoulder holster on, but empty. I put a zip-up hoodie on to cover it and stash the case in a small backpack.

"Mom?" It's Lanny. I pause with my hand on the alarm pad, ready to deactivate. "I love you." She says it quietly, but it hits me like a tsunami, and I'm knocked down inside, drowned in a storm of emotion so violent I can't even breathe. My fingers tremble on the buttons of the keypad, and for a second I'm blinded with tears.

I blink them away, turn, and manage to smile at her. "I love you, too, honey."

"Come back soon," she says. I watch as she goes to the knife block and takes one. She turns and goes back to her room.

I want to scream. I know I can't do it here. I punch in the code, get it wrong, try again, and deactivate. The door's open almost before it's safe, but I've timed it right, just barely, and I reset the alarm as I exit, then lock the door. *There.* My kids are secure. Protected. Kezia is on the phone as I pass, and she nods to me as she makes notes in a spiral book.

I kick it into a run. Not a jog, a flat-out sprint down the drive, every step just on the edge of balance, the edge of control. One wrong move will send me sprawling, probably break a bone, but I don't care, *I don't care*, I need to drive the poison of Melvin Royal out of my system.

I run like I'm on fire.

I hit the road and keep running clockwise, up the incline. With the hood up, I'm just another anonymous runner at the lake. I pass a few other people, some walking, some at the docks, and I get a few glances for my speed, but nothing else. I pass Sam Cade's cabin on the right but I don't pause; I pour more energy into my muscles, grinding off the tension, and make it all the way to the top of the ridge, where the range parking lot provides a welcome, flat, easy surface. I slow down and walk to let my muscles slow their burn. I walk in circles. My hoodie is soaked with sweat, heavy with it, and I still feel the rage screaming inside me.

I'm not letting Mel win. Not ever.

I pull my hood down before I open the range door—simple courtesy, as well as caution—and nearly run into Javier, who's standing in the way, back to the door as he pins something up on the bulletin board. This is the store area, where they sell ammunition, hunting gear, bow hunting supplies . . . even camouflage-colored popcorn. The young woman manning the counter is named Sophie, and she's a seventh-generation Norton native. I know because she told me, at length, the day I signed up here. Talkative and friendly.

She takes one look at me, and her face closes up shop. No small talk here, not anymore. She has the tense, glassy look of someone willing to grab an under-the-counter weapon and blast away at a second's notice.

I say, "Mr. Esparza," and Javier finishes putting the last thumbtack into a poster and turns to look at me. He's not surprised. I'm sure, with his excellent spatial awareness, he knew exactly who I was the second I opened the door.

"Ms. Proctor." He doesn't look unfriendly, like Sophie, just politely blank. "Better not be anything in that holster. You know the rules."

I unzip the hoodie to show him that it's empty, and sling the backpack off to show him the gun case. I can see him hesitate. He could refuse to allow me on the premises—it's his right, as range instructor, to do that for any reason, anytime. But he just nods and says, "Bay eight at the end is open. You know the drill."

I do. I grab hearing protection from the rack and move quickly past the turned backs of other shooters, all the way to the end. Perhaps not so coincidentally, bay eight's overhead light seems darker than the rest. I usually shoot in the bays closer toward the door; this, I remember, is the spot Carl Getts was using that day Javi busted him for improper range procedure. Maybe it's where he puts the pariahs.

I lay out my gun and clips and put on the heavy earmuffs; the relief from the steady, percussive explosions is visceral, and I finish loading with smooth, calm motions. This, for me, has become like meditation, a space to let emotions trickle away until nothing exists but me, the gun, and the target.

And Mel, who stands like a ghost in front of the target. When I'm shooting, I know exactly who I'm killing.

I destroy six targets before I feel clean and empty again, and then I lower the gun, clear the clip and chamber, and put the weapon down, ejection port up, pointed downrange. Exactly as I should do.

As I do, I realize the shooting has stopped. It's silent in the range, which is shocking and weird, and I quickly strip off the earmuffs.

I'm alone. There's not a single person left in the bays. There's just Javier at the end by the door, watching me. Because of where he's standing, I can't see his face that clearly; he's right under one of the spots, which glares bright on the top of his head, shimmering on close-cropped brown hair, and casts his expression into shadow.

"Guess I'm not that great for business," I say.

"No, you're fantastic for business," he replies. "Sold so much ammo the past few days I had to restock twice. Too bad I don't own a gun store. I could retire just on this week. Paranoia sells."

He sounds normal, but something about this feels strange. I load everything into my gun case and lock it, and I'm shoving it back into the backpack when Javier takes a step forward. His eyes are . . . dead. It's unsettling. He's not armed, but that doesn't make him any less alarming. "Got a question for you," he says. "It's pretty basic. Did you know?"

"Know what," I say, though there's really only one question he could be asking.

"What your husband was doing."

"No." I tell him the absolute truth, but I have zero hope that he'll believe me. "Mel didn't need or want my help. I'm a woman. Women are never *people* to someone like him." I zip up the backpack. "If you're going to do some vigilante justice here, get on with it. I'm not armed now. I couldn't take you even if I was, and we both know it."

He doesn't move. Doesn't speak. He's just regarding me, assessing me, and I remember that like Mel, Javier knows what it means to take a life. Unlike Mel, the reason for his anger right now doesn't come from selfishness and narcissism; Javier sees himself as a protector, as a man who fights for right.

It doesn't mean I'm in any less danger.

When he does finally speak, it comes out soft, almost a whisper. "How come you didn't tell me?"

"About Mel? Why do you *think*? I left all that behind me. I wanted to. Wouldn't you?" I let out a sigh. "Come on, Javi. Please. I need to get back to my kids."

"They're all right. Kez is watching them." There's something about the way he says her name that clears things up for me. Kezia Claremont didn't come *just* because of her father's concern; her father had met me exactly once, and while he seemed a nice old guy, that hadn't quite rung true for me. She'd mentioned Javier in a businesslike way. But the way Javier refers to her is more revealing. I can see the connection immediately; Javier likes strong ladies, and Kez is definitely that. "Thing is, I almost *helped* you get out of town right after that first murder. Doesn't sit right with me, Gwen. Not at all. You sat in my kitchen and drank my beer, and I think, what if you *did* know? What if you sat in your own kitchen back in Kansas and listened to those women scream in the garage while your husband did his thing? You think I wouldn't care about that?"

"I know you would," I tell him, and slip the backpack over my shoulder. "They never screamed, Javier. They couldn't. The first thing Mel did was cut their vocal cords when he abducted them. He had a special knife for it; the police showed it to me. I never heard them screaming *because they couldn't scream.* So yes. I fixed lunch in my kitchen, I made meals for my children, I ate breakfast and lunch and dinner, and *there were women dying on the other side of that fucking wall and don't you think I hate that I didn't stop it?*" I lost control at the end of that, and the echoes of my shout come back like bullets, striking me hard. I close my eyes and breathe, smelling burned powder and gun oil and my own sudden sweat. My mouth tastes sour, all the breakfast sweetness curdled. I see her in a flash again, that skinless girl dangling, and I have to bend over and put my hands on my knees. The gun case slides forward and knocks me in the back of the head, but I don't care. I just need to breathe.

When Javier touches me, I flinch, but he just helps me stand up and braces me until I nod and pull away. I'm ashamed of myself. Of my weakness. I want to scream. Again.

Instead, I say, "I used all the ammo I brought. Can I buy a couple of boxes?"

He silently leaves and comes back to set two boxes on the ledge of bay eight. Turns to go. I slide the backpack off and sit it at my feet, braced against the wall of the bay, and say, "Thank you."

He doesn't answer. He just leaves.

I go through most of the two boxes, shredding target after target—center mass, head, center mass, head, targeting extremities for variety—until my ears are ringing even with the hearing protection, and the noise inside me is finally still. Then I pack up and leave.

Javier's not in the store. I pay for the ammunition; Sophie conducts the transaction in mutinous silence, thrusting me my change across the counter rather than handing it to me. God forbid she might accidentally touch the ex-wife of a killer. That shit might be contagious.

I exit, still looking for Javier, but his truck is gone, and the parking lot is pretty much deserted, except for Sophie's conventional blue Ford parked in the shady spot.

I reverse my run to head home, but as I pass Sam Cade's house, I see that he's sitting on the front porch, drinking a cup of coffee, and against my conscious decision I slow down to look at him. He looks back, sets the coffee down, and stands up.

"Hey," he says. It's not much, but it's more than I got at the range. He looks uncomfortable, a little flushed, but also determined. "So. We should probably talk."

I stare at him for a second. I think about kicking up my run and taking off, fast and hard. Retreating. But two things that Kezia said keep echoing in my head: First, Sam Cade has alibis for the girls' abductions. Second, I need allies.

I look down at the house. Kez's car is still there.

"Sure," I tell him, walking over to mount the steps of the porch. He gets a little more tense, and so do I, and for a second there's silence as deep as back in the shooting range. "So. Talk."

He looks down at his coffee cup, and from where I stand I can see it's empty. He shrugs, throws open the front door of the cabin, and walks inside.

I pause on the doorstep for one second, two, and then follow.

It's dark inside, and I have to blink a couple of times as he turns on some dim overheads and skims back one of the checkered curtains covering the windows. He goes straight to a coffeepot, fills his cup, takes down another, and splashes it full. He hands it to me, along with the sugar, without a word.

It should feel comfortable, but it feels like effort, like a steel bar between us that we're struggling to get around. I sip the coffee and remember that he likes hazelnut blend. So do I. "Thanks," I say.

"You smell like gunpowder," he tells me. "Been up shooting at the range?"

"Until they tell me I can't, I will," I say. "Cops let you go, then."

"Seems like." He studies me over the top of the cup, cautious, dark eyes guarded. "You too."

"Because I'm not fucking guilty, Sam."

"Yeah." He drinks. "So you said. *Gwen.*"

I nearly throw the coffee in his face for that, but I manage not to, mainly because I know it would only get me arrested for assault, and besides, it's not hot enough to scald. Then I wonder why I'm so damn angry. He has the right to hate me. I don't have the right to hate him back. I can resent his deception, sure, but in the end, there's only one of us with a real grudge. Real pain.

I sink down in a chair, suddenly very tired, and am only aware of drinking the coffee in a peripheral sense kind of way. I'm consumed with watching him, with wondering, suddenly, who he really is. Who *I* really am. How we can possibly rebuild any kind of ease between us.

"Why did you come here?" I ask him. "The truth this time."

Sam doesn't vary his focus at all. "I wasn't lying. I'm writing a book. It's about my sister's murder. Yeah, I tracked you down. It took a friend in military intelligence to do it, and by the way, he was *very* impressed with how you kept disappearing. I missed you four times in a row. I took a chance you'd stay here, since you bought the place this time."

So. The stalking isn't in my imagination. Not at all. "That's how. Not why."

"I wanted you to confess what you did," he says. He blinks, as if he's surprised he said it out loud. "It was all I thought about. I'd built you up into . . . Look, I believed you were part of it. Knew everything. I thought you—"

"Were guilty," I finish for him. "You're hardly alone. You're not even in the minority." I swallow some coffee without tasting it. "I don't blame you for that. I don't. In your position, I'd have—" *I'd have done anything to get justice.*

I'd have killed me.

"Yeah." He draws that out into a sigh. "Problem is, once I met you, talked to you, got to know you . . . I couldn't see it. I saw somebody who barely survived what she'd gone through and just wanted to keep her family safe. You just weren't . . . *her.*"

"Gina wasn't guilty, either," I tell him. "She was just naive. And she wanted to be happy. He knew how to take advantage of that." Silence falls. I find myself breaking it by saying, "I saw your sister. She was—she was the last one. I saw her the day the car crashed into the garage."

Sam freezes, holds for just a bare second, then smoothly puts down his coffee. The mug hits the table surface a little hard. There's a matte, polished expanse of wood between us, not an invisible barrier, and maybe that's better. I could reach across it. So could he.

Neither of us does.

"I saw the photos," he says, and I remember how he told me never to let my kids see pictures. Now I know why. It wasn't a vague sympathy after all, and it hadn't been about what he'd seen in Afghanistan. "I don't suppose you can forget it, either."

"No." I swallow coffee, but my mouth feels dry anyway. I've taken the seat nearest the open window, and the buttery light illuminates him in ways that are both kind and unkind. It reveals the fine lines around his eyes, bracketing his mouth, a peculiar little indention near his left eyebrow. A pale, almost invisible spiderweb of scarring that runs from under his hairline onto his right cheek. It sparks color flecks in his eyes that make them mesmerizing. "I see her all the time. In flashes. Whenever I close my eyes, she's there."

"Her name was Callie," he tells me. I already know that, but somehow it's been so much easier to think of her as *the body* and *the woman* and *the victim*. Putting a name on her, hearing him say it with that mixture of sorrow and love—it hurts. "I lost track of her when we got separated in the foster system, but I found her—no, she found me. She wrote to me when I was deployed."

"I can't begin to understand how you feel," I tell him. I mean it, but he hardly seems to hear me. He's thinking about the living girl, not the dead one I remember.

"She Skyped with me when she could. She'd just started at Wichita State. No major yet, because she couldn't decide between computer science and art, and I told her—I told her to be practical, to pick computers. I probably should have told her to do what made her happy. But you know. I thought—"

"You thought she'd have time," I finish for him in the silence. "I can't imagine, Sam, I'm so sorry. I'm so—" My voice, to my horror, breaks right in two, cracks on the word, and inside, I begin to shatter. I hadn't realized I was made of glass until now, when it all gives way and the tears come, tears like nothing I've felt before, a tsunami of grief and rage and fury and betrayal and horror, of *guilt*, and I put my coffee cup aside and sob openly into my hands, as if my heart is broken along with everything else inside me.

He doesn't speak. Doesn't move, except to push a roll of paper towels across the table. I grab handfuls and use them to muffle my grief, my guilt, the keening awful pain that I've felt at a distance for so long and never quite faced head-on.

How long we sit there, I don't know. Long enough that the handful of paper towels is soaked with tears, and when I drop it to the wood it makes a soft, wet *plop*. I murmur a shaky apology and clean up after myself, carry everything away to the trash, and when I get back, Sam says, "I was stuck in country during your husband's trial, but I followed it every day. I thought it was your fault. And then when you were acquitted . . . I thought—I thought you'd gotten away with it. I thought you *helped*."

He doesn't believe that now; I hear it in the pain in his voice. I don't say anything. I know why he thought it; I know why everyone did. What kind of idiot did you have to be to have that going on in your house, your bed, your marriage, and *not* be part of it? I'm still dimly surprised anyone ever acquitted me at all. I haven't begun to forgive Gina Royal.

So I say, "I should have known it. If I'd stopped him—"

"You'd have been dead. Your kids, too, maybe," he says, without any sign of doubt. "I went to see him, you know. Melvin. I had to look him in the eyes. I had to know—"

That takes my breath away, the idea that he sat in that same prison chair, looking into Melvin's face. I think about the corrosive horror Mel wakes in me. I can't imagine how it felt for Sam.

So I reach impulsively for his hand, and he lets me take it. Our fingers lie loose together, not demanding anything except the lightest possible contact. Either his or mine are trembling slightly, but I can't tell which. I only feel the motion.

I see something in the window behind him. It's just a shape, a shadow, and when my brain finally identifies it as *human*, that no longer matters, because *human* isn't as important as the thing the shape is carrying, raising, *aiming*.

It's a shotgun, and it's aimed at the back of Sam's head.

I don't think. I grab Sam's hand hard and haul sideways, knocking him off-balance and down, and at the same time I throw myself down out of my own chair. I keep pulling. Sam is yanked out of his chair and sprawls halfway across the table, and then the chair spins out from under him and he falls heavily sideways on the floor just as I hear an incredibly loud *boom*. I dimly register the feeling of the coffee cup falling from the table and striking my thigh. It spills heat and liquid over me, warm as blood, and then a shower of glass shards hits me, and I shield my face against the cuts.

If I hadn't seen, if I hadn't reacted, the back of Sam's head would have been jam. He'd have been dead in a second.

Sam's on the ground next to me, and he lets go and rolls across the glass to crab-crawl with shocking speed to a corner, where a shotgun of his own leans, half-concealed by shadows. He grabs it on the roll, comes to a stop with his elbows braced on the floor, shotgun raised, and sights the window before he pistons his knees forward and levers up to a crouch. I don't move. He comes slowly up, ready to dodge or drop, but he clearly sees nothing, and he quickly swivels to the front door. He's right; that could be the next threat to appear.

I take the opportunity to crawl over to my backpack, unzip, unlock the box. I assemble my weapon with fast, practiced motions, rack one into the chamber, and roll on my elbows on the floor. We have an unspoken agreement: he shoots high, I shoot low.

But there's nothing. Someone's shouting out on the lake, a distant smear of sound, and I think, *It came from the side of the house by the trees,* the one hardest to see from the road or the lake. All anyone will know is that someone shot a gun. *They'll know it came from this direction. And I'm covered with gunpowder residue,* I think, and wonder if that, too, was part of a plan. Wouldn't be surprised. Not at all. Still, the forensics are blindingly obvious: we were in here, at the table. Someone shot in at us.

I hear more shouts from around the lake area, the dimly heard cry of "police," as in *call the,* and Sam rises from his crouch. He doesn't lower the shotgun; he advances toward the door with military caution, checks the window, throws open the door, and waits. I can see the view of the lake beyond, the boats hastily making for docks. Peaceful. Distant. Utterly out of sync with the adrenaline racing through my body, sending hot and cold flashes through me that mask any actual injuries I might have.

Nothing happens. Nobody fires. Sam flashes me a wordless look, and I scramble up and hug the wall beside him, and as he eases out, I go behind him, watching the other angles as he focuses forward.

We circle the entire house.

There's nobody there. Sam points out some scuffed footprints—waffle-soled boots, but the prints are indistinct and incomplete. But it's clear that someone stood here, took aim, and fired right at the back of his head—and I saved his life.

The shakes set in. I make damn sure I'm careful as I clear the round from the chamber, then snug the gun back into the shoulder holster. The familiar weight feels good, even as it digs into the curve of my breast. I crouch to take a closer look at the footprints. I'm no expert. There isn't anything obvious to learn.

"You'd better put that Sig back in the case," Sam tells me, as he rests his shotgun against his shoulder. "Come on. Cops will be on the way, again."

Sam's right. I haven't fired my gun, and I damn sure don't want to be shot accidentally-on-purpose for carrying a legal gun, either.

Inside the cabin, I break the weapon down and lock it up; just as I put the box back in my backpack, Sam leans his own shotgun in the corner and opens the door to afford me a fine view of a car burning rubber up the road toward us.

It isn't Officer Graham. It's Kezia Claremont, who steps out of the car with her weapon drawn and at her side. "Mr. Cade. Got a report of shots fired here."

I look down the road at my house, which sits quietly down the slope. *She just left them. It'll be okay.* The only thing even slightly different is what looks like an SUV disappearing over the hill on the other side. The Johansens, maybe.

"Yep," he says, as calmly as if the whole thing is just a hunter's poor aim. "Take a look. It took out the window. There's buckshot inside, too."

"Lucky as hell," Kezia says, looking at Sam. "Guess you saw it coming?"

"No. My back was to it." He jerks his chin at me. "*She* saw it coming."

I'm staring at my house. Willing for no one to approach it while I'm gone. Nobody's in sight. *They're okay. It'll be okay.* "I didn't see enough," I say. "Just a blur. He—I think it was a white guy, but I can't swear to it—popped up from under the window. I'll be honest, mostly I just paid attention to the muzzle sighting in and to getting us out of the way."

Kezia nods. "All right. You two, sit down where you were."

"I need to go home," I say.

"In a sec. Just sit down. I need to see this." There's a ring of command in her voice. I back up, never looking away from the house, and slip into my seat at the table.

After a beat, Sam turns his chair back upright and sits. I can tell, from the way his fists are clenched on the table, that sitting with his back to the window is *not* comfortable for him right now. Coffee drips from the table's edge and soaks into the fabric of my running pants.

I hate this. I can see the road from here. I can't see the house. "Make it fast!" I tell Kezia, but she's already outside, going around to the window.

Sam and I stare at each other in silence. He's pale, and beads of sweat have started on his forehead.

"You're keeping an eye on my back, right?" he says. I nod. He shifts a little, and I wonder what kind of discipline it takes to stay where he is, with a virtual target on his head. What kind of trauma it might bring back up inside. "Thanks, Gwen. I mean it. I'd have never seen that coming."

"He's gone," I tell Sam. "We're okay now." I'm sore, scratched in bleeding red ribbons from shattered window glass, and I think I've torn something in my left shoulder. And I need to go. *Now.*

Kezia appears in the shattered window behind him, and Sam's sixth sense kicks in; I can see the shudder that goes through him. Effort holds him in place. "It's okay," I tell him. "It's Officer Claremont. You're all right." He's gone very pale now. A bead of sweat runs down the side of his face, but he doesn't move.

Behind him, Kezia extends her arms, miming a shotgun. "Had to be my height or taller," she says. "He got up close and personal about it. I'm standing where I'd pick, but his footprints are maybe another foot closer up. Gun had to be damn near against the window glass." She lowers her imaginary gun. "Bold son of a bitch. You're lucky either one of you is alive."

She's right. I'd seen the embedded buckshot in the wall across the way, behind where I'm currently sitting. Sam's brains would have ended up there, and for a second I can see the wall painted red, pale pink, sharp shards of bone. I'd have been drenched in his blood. His skull would have been shrapnel.

"Coming in," Kezia says as she disappears from view. I see Sam relax a little, and he gets up and moves his chair around to the side of the table, out of line from the window. I don't move. I figure it's best I keep my eyes on it where I am, because some of Sam's paranoia has replaced some of mine, momentarily.

"Christ," Sam says, reaching for the roll of paper towels that is still, miraculously, on the table. It has a few holes punched through it. He unrolls some sheets and mops up the spilled coffee. "Bastard killed my favorite cup."

It's so random that I almost laugh, but I know if I start, it'll spiral out of control, so I don't. I start cleaning up the fragments of coffee cup near me, but then I realize what I'm doing. What *he's* doing. "Sam." I put a hand on his arm, and he flinches a little. "Stop. It's a crime scene."

"Shit." He leaves the paper towel, soaked now with brown liquid, limp in the middle of the table. "Right."

Kezia comes back inside. She's making notes in a Moleskine notebook, and as she does, she says, "Okay, I'm going to ask the two of you to please move outside now. As soon as another unit arrives, I'll get the crime scene secured. Detectives are on the way."

I stand up and move to the door, where I have a sight line of the house again. Nothing's changed. I pull the phone from my pocket. "You just left the house to come here, right?"

"No," Kez says. "I had to respond to an officer down, up on the main road. All hands. I was just coming back when I got this call. Sorry. But I knocked and told them I was going before I left. Your daughter said they'd be fine."

It hits me in a rush, and I see Sam's eyes widen, too. He says, "*Was* there an officer down?" He beats me to it by just a breath.

Kez's face goes blank, then hard. "No. Couldn't find anything."

It strikes all of us that the report and even the shooting here . . . those were *diversions*.

Sam is on his feet in the next second and grabs his shotgun and my backpack. He tosses the backpack to me, still on the move, and I am already running, running as if the monster is chasing me.

"Wait!" Kezia yells after me. I don't. I run faster, faster, I can't stop. I hear the roar of engine behind me and swerve to the side, and Kezia slows while Sam throws the door open and beckons. I dive in and narrowly miss slamming the door on my legs. She's right. This is faster.

I watch the road slide under us. Kezia Claremont drives like a fucking lunatic, but there's no one blocking the road, and it's a short haul; she takes the turn onto my drive and fishtails on the gravel, then hits the gas to drive us up with a lurch toward the house. The red paint glares from the garage, growing larger like a fresh wound, still bleeding.

And then I'm out. I'm running for the front door. It's locked, and as I unlock it and open it, the alarm starts its frantic, warning beeps. I punch in the code and pull in a deep breath. *Thank God.* The alarm's still on. The kids haven't gone anywhere. *It's okay, they're safe.*

I drop the backpack on the couch and head down the hall. "Lanny! Connor! Where are you?"

No answer. No sound at all. I'm still moving at the same pace, but time seems to slow down. The hallway grows darker. The closed doors on either side loom larger. I want to turn back, to wait for the others, but I don't. I *can't.*

I throw open Lanny's door and see that the covers are in a tangle on the floor, pulled off; one side of the fitted sheet has slipped free, and the other dangles loosely. Her laptop is on the floor, open and upside-down at an acute angle. I grab it and look. A screensaver of a colorful Day of the Dead skull bounces gleefully from corner to corner. Her screensaver only lasts a short while before the computer sleeps. *More than five minutes, less than fifteen.* This isn't her. She'd never treat her laptop like this.

I put the computer on the mattress and look around, open the closet though I'm dreading what I might find. I check under the bed.

"Gwen—" That's Sam's voice from behind me. I look over my shoulder. He's facing into my son's room. There's something still and quiet about his voice, and when he glances at me, the pupils of his eyes are pinpoints, as if he's staring into a bright, white light. I move toward him, and he stops me with his free hand outstretched, a guardian trying to keep me from a fatal drop, but he can't really stop me without using that shotgun in his other hand.

I slip past him and grab the door frame to keep him from pulling me physically back.

I see the blood.

It's straight out of my nightmare. There's blood smeared on the twisted fabric of Connor's light-blue sheets. There's blood on the floor, in dark strings. There's a long, clean tear in a pillow leaking puffs of blood-flecked feathers.

My son is not there.

My children are gone.

I feel my knees start to buckle, and I hold myself up with a grip on both sides of the door frame. Sam's talking to me, touching my shoulder, but I can't hear him; as I get my legs under me again and start to lunge forward, though, it's Kezia Claremont who wraps one strong arm around my waist and spins me away, where she holds me with my back to the wall. Her gun's back in her holster, and her brown eyes study me with commanding intensity.

"You need to *think*, Gwen," she says to me. "You cannot go in there." She takes her phone from her pocket and speed-dials, gets an almost immediate answer. "Detective? Gonna need you here fast at Gwen Proctor's place. We have a possible child abduction. Multiple victims. All hands." She hangs up, still holding me in place. "We good? Gwen? Gwen!"

I manage to nod. I'm not good, I can't be, but there's no point in arguing, and besides, that isn't what she's asking. She's asking if I can control myself, and I can. At least, I can try.

Sam's looming there, too, and it isn't until I look at his face, at the sick focus there, the *doubt*, that I realize this scene could mean *two different things*.

One, the truth: my children have been abducted.

Two, the very plausible lie: I did something to my own kids before I left this house. Someone's going to think that. Kezia can't; she was out there, watching, and she talked to Lanny through the door. But I'll be their first suspect. Maybe their only one, despite what she says.

"No," I say. "Kezia, you know *I didn't do this!*"

"I know. But let's not get any evidence in there that confuses the issue," she tells me, and moves me with professional ease toward the living room, the couch. Game controllers are in the way, and I pick them up and move them with numb care. Bad habit that Connor has, leaving those where he drops them. It occurs to me then that his hands were last on these controls, and I hold on to one gently, as if it might break, might vanish, as if my son might never have even existed except in my imagination.

"Gwen." Sam's crouching next to me, staring into my face. "If what you're saying is right, then someone *knew* you'd be gone from this house. Who did you tell?"

"Nobody," I say numbly. "You. And the kids. I told the kids I'd be back. They were fine." This is my fault. I never should have left. *Never. "You were supposed to be watching!"* I throw that last at Kezia.

She doesn't react to that, though she braces, and I have the sense that it hurts. That she knows she's failed, and the price . . . the price may be higher than either of us wants to face.

"Who would they let in?"

"Nobody!" I half cry that, but I realize it isn't true almost instantly. They'd probably let Sam Cade in, but Sam . . . would Sam have had

time to do this? *Yes.* He'd have seen me heading up the hill. That would have given him at least an hour to come here and . . . do what? Talk his way in, somehow abduct my kids without getting a mark on him? And take them *where?* No. No, I can't believe it was Sam. It didn't make sense, not emotionally. Not even logistically. My kids would have fought like *hell.* He hadn't had a drop of blood on him when I stopped at his house. And Kezia would have seen him.

Unless they're in it together?

Meanwhile, I can sense he was thinking the same thing about *me.* Trying to work out how I could have done it to my own kids. Each of us mistrusting the other again, which might have been exactly the point.

Who else? Who else besides Sam? I don't think my kids would have let Kezia Claremont in, despite the fact they'd liked her and she had a badge. Detective Prester? Maybe.

And then it comes to me in a cold, horrible, skin-tightening rush. I've forgotten someone. Someone they trusted. Someone they would let in without a second thought because he'd been trusted *by me* to stay with them before. Javier Esparza. Javier, who'd disappeared after delivering my ammo.

His truck had been gone from the range's parking lot when I'd left. *He might know the code to the alarm system.* He would have seen me arm and disarm, and seen the kids do it, too. Javier Esparza was a trained soldier. He'd know how to abduct people, and do it quietly.

I try to say that, and I can't. I can't get sound to my mouth. My lungs hurt, and I pull in air in a rush to soothe them, and the plastic of Connor's game controller feels warm in my hands, like skin, and I think, *Connor's skin might be cold now, he might be . . .* but my brain protects itself, it won't tell me the rest of it. Javier, who would have had easy access to a shotgun from the range, or from the back window of his truck. Javier, whom I trusted enough to watch my kids. Who was trusted enough by them to be allowed inside, have the alarm turned off for him. Who could have easily gotten the code from the kids and reset it on the way out.

You're forgetting something, Mel's voice whispers to me. I flinch, because I don't want it, don't want his voice in my head, I don't, but he's right, too. I am forgetting something . . .

"I'm going to call the security company," Kez says. "Going to need you to give them clearance to talk to me, okay? They should have records of when the alarm went off and came on—"

"Cameras!" I blurt. I lunge away, to where I'd left the tablet plugged in to charge. The cameras are streaming to the device. I can see exactly what happened.

But the tablet is gone. The cord is still there, dangling limp.

I take the end of it, as if I can't believe it's not connected, and I look wordlessly at Kezia, as if she can somehow solve this for me. She's frowning. "You have cameras? Are they built into the security system?"

"No," I say. "No, separate, there was a tablet—" I don't know what makes my brain jump from one idea to the next; it happens so fast it's a blur of thought, something about watching my kids to keeping them safe to *safe*, and then I realize what I've *really* forgotten.

The safe room.

I come bolt upright and charge around the kitchen bar toward the wall, while the other two look at me in baffled surprise.

The safe room of this house, the one that the old, wealthy owners built in, is hidden behind a piece of hinged paneling in the corner of the kitchen area, near the breakfast table. I shove the table hard, nearly sending it crashing into Kezia as she approaches, and push frantically at the paneling. It's supposed to spring free, but it stays put. I have a strange out-of-body feeling, as if I've imagined the very existence of the room, as if reality has shifted around me into an insane funhouse version of my life and the safe room has vanished along with my children. I push again, again, *again*, and finally, the far corner springs up with a click. I grab it and yank it open. Beyond it is a heavy steel door, and a keypad inset beside it.

There's blood smeared on the numbers. I stop breathing when I see that, but at the same time it means they're inside, they're *okay*. There's no other option.

I type in the password, but my fingers are trembling hard, and I get it wrong. I take a breath and force myself to slow down. Six digits. I get it right this time, and the tone trills and a green light flashes. I turn the handle, and I'm shouting "Connor! Lanny!" even before the seal breaks.

Inside, the panic room is wrecked. Bottled water is scattered across the floor, knocked from a shelf, and a box of emergency high-protein supplies has been knocked over and spilled packages across the floor. Some are crushed from a struggle.

There's blood. Drops. Long strings that show motion. A small pool of it near the corner, under a yellow sign that reads CAUTION: ZOMBIES HERE. Connor's sign.

There's still a crossbow broken on the floor. Also my son's, because he adores the guy who carries one on that zombie show. The phone, with its hard line, has been ripped out of the wall and thrown broken in the opposite direction.

I keep looking at the blood. It's fresh. Fresh and red.

My kids are not here.

I am so certain that I stand there for a moment, staring without comprehending; they *have* to be here, nothing else makes sense. This is their sanctuary, their safe place. Their escape. No one could get to them here.

But someone has. They were in here. They fought here. They bled here.

And they're gone.

I lunge forward to the only possible cover in the room, the small toilet closet. It's only got a frosted-glass door, and I can already see that nobody's in it, but I yank it open anyway and gag on my own terror when I see the clean, empty stall.

I stand there, totally still, and the silence of the room soaks into me like cold. The absence of my children is an open wound, and the blood is so red, fresh, so bright it's blinding.

Kezia puts her hand on my shoulder. The warmth of it feels shocking, radiating against my face. I've gotten very chilled, I realize. Shock. I'm shivering without really feeling it. "Come on," she tells me. "They're not here. Come on out."

I don't want to. I feel that leaving this strange, chilly sanctuary is admitting something huge. Something I want to hide from, like a child pulling covers over my head.

Irrationally, *insanely*, I suddenly *want Mel*. It horrifies me, but I want someone to turn to, someone who might share this feeling of emptiness. Maybe I don't want Mel. Maybe I want the idea of him. Someone who shares my grief, my fear, our *children. I want his arms around me.* I want Mel to tell me it'll be all right, even though that Mel is a lie, was always a lie. Even then.

Kezia pulls me out. We leave the secret room open, and I sink down in one of the kitchen chairs—the one Lanny sat in at breakfast. Everything has a memory attached to it—the fingerprints on the wood of the table, the mostly empty salt shaker that I asked Connor to refill but he forgot.

One of Lanny's skull-themed hair clips lies discarded on the floor under the chair, a single, silky strand still caught in the hinge. I pick it up and hold it loose in my hand, and when I lift it to my nose, I can smell the scent of her hair. It brings tears to my eyes.

Sam's sitting next to me now, and his hand is lying limply close to mine. I don't know when he sat down; it's as if he's just appeared, like time jumped. Reality collapsing again. Everything feels distant now, but the warmth of his skin radiates into me like sunlight, even half an inch away.

"Gwen," he says. After a short delay to process that yes, that's my name, I've taught myself to *believe* it's my name, I raise my head and meet his gaze. Something in it steadies me. Brings me an inch or two up from the darkness, into something that's at least faintly hopeful. "Gwen, we're going to find them, okay? We're going to find the kids. Do you have any idea—"

He's interrupted by the ringing of my cell phone. I grab for it with frantic, clawing hands, slap it down on the table, and answer the call on speakerphone without even glancing at the caller ID. "Lanny? Connor?"

I don't recognize the voice that answers. It's a man's voice, I think, but it's been run through a synth program to disguise it. "You think you got away with your crimes, you sick bitch? You can run but you can't hide, and when we get to you, you're going to wish your fucking husband had strung *you* up and skinned you alive!"

It catches me off guard and knocks the breath out of me, and I can't move for a second, can't *think*. Sam sits back as if he's been physically punched. Kezia, leaning over, draws away. The venomous glee in the words, even with the processed flatness of the voice, is shocking.

It feels like half an hour before I can find words, but it can't be more than a heartbeat, and then I scream, *"Give me back my kids, you bastard!"*

There's silence on the other end of the phone. As if I've caught him out. As if I'm not following some kind of script. Then the synthesized voice says, any surprise stripped from the words by the algorithms that change it, "What the fuck?"

"Are they all right? If you've hurt my kids, you son of a bitch, I will find you, I will rip you apart—" I'm standing up now, leaning over the phone on stiffened arms, and my voice is sharp enough to cut, loud enough to shatter.

"I didn't—uh—fuck. Shit." The call disconnects with a crackle, and the calm musical beeps of the phone telling me it lost the signal. I sink down in the chair, grab the phone, and swipe to the caller ID. It was a blocked number, of course.

"He didn't know," I say. "He didn't even know they were gone." I should have seen this coming; my address was out in the open. Someone who got close to me leaked it, took pictures. Mel must have distributed my number, too. I can expect a torrent of calls like this: death threats, rape threats, threats to kill my children and pets, torch my house, torture my parents. I've been through it before. There isn't much that shocks me anymore, in the Sicko Patrol world. I also know, as the police remind me every time I report it, that most of these sad, sick little men will never follow through on their vicious promises. Their enjoyment comes from psychological damage.

The troll didn't hang up because he felt guilty for doing this to me. He was caught by surprise and was afraid of being swept up in a kidnapping investigation. The upside is, he won't call back.

But there will be a thousand others in line behind him.

Kezia interrupts my thoughts by taking the phone out of my hand. She says, "I'll answer for you until we decide how to handle this, okay?" And I nod, even if I know it's a ploy to grab my phone as evidence. Sam averts his gaze as if he's ashamed. I wonder if he left a few angry messages on my voice mail, back in the day. Sent me a few rage-filled e-mails from an anonymous account. He wouldn't have done the truly sociopathic ones; his would have been stuffed with pain and real loss and justified anger.

I wish now that he'd put his name on them, that we'd been honest with each other, understood each other, *seen* each other from the beginning.

It doesn't take long for the police to arrive. Things get busy. We're ushered outside as the police thoroughly check the house and start the process of investigation. Prester arrives with another, younger detective— apart from him, they all seem too young to have any experience—and shakes his head when he sees me standing there with Kezia and Sam. The fact that Sam's with us raises his eyebrows, and I see him recalculating things, revising all his earlier judgments and assumptions. I wonder if this puts me and Sam back in a box together as conspirators.

If it does, that would have an ugly ring of authenticity to it. We *do* have a past, even if I hadn't known it. We *do* know each other. We *do* like each other now, on some level. It makes my head hurt, trying to think like Prester, but I have a notion that he's already seeing us in a very different light.

"Tell me everything," Prester says.

Once I start, I can't stop.

12

I don't want to leave the house, though I don't want to be here, either . . . It no longer feels like our safe space, our haven. It feels spoiled, cracked open like that house back in Wichita to reveal something ugly at its center. Not Mel's evil this time. The house is no longer a home because of the cold absence . . . the absence of the one thing that makes any kind of home for me.

I sit outside on the porch with Prester, who quizzes me and Sam in great detail, with Kezia nearby to add her confirmations as needed. I imagine the timeline he's sketching out in his notebook. I wonder where the red star goes on it, the moment someone came into my home and ripped my heart out. He must also believe that I could have done it, but I no longer care about that. They have to be *found*.

I have to believe they're okay—scared, but okay. That the blood is stage blood, or animal blood, put there to terrify me. That a ransom call will come. That *anything, anything* is true but what I instinctively, horribly believe.

I give Prester the cell phone numbers for my kids, and he gives them to Kezia; she comes back half an hour later to say, "The phones are off and not pinging on GPS."

"No surprise," he says. "Any TV-watching moron knows to ditch the damn phones these days." He shakes his head a little and closes his notebook. "I've got every cop in the county out looking, Ms. Proctor, but meanwhile, I need you to tell me what happened this morning after Officer Claremont ate breakfast with you."

"I already told you."

"Tell me again." His eyes are cool and remorseless, and I hate him with a clear, pointed fury in that moment, as if he's the one holding my children, hiding them from me. "Because I need to understand exactly how this happened. After seeing the officer off, what did you do?"

"Locked the door. Reset alarms. Washed dishes. Got the call from Mel. Grabbed my shoulder holster, my gun from the safe, the box to put it in. My hoodie."

"And did you knock on the kids' doors? Tell them where you were going?"

"I told Lanny. I told her I'd be gone about an hour. Then I asked Kezia to keep an eye on the house."

He nods, and I think, *He's judging me for leaving them*, but I left them in a locked, fortified house with a safe room, with clear plans for what to do if anything, *anything* went wrong. With a police car right in front. *It was an hour!* It had ended up being more, by twenty minutes, because I'd stopped off at Sam's, and someone had tried to kill him. An hour and twenty minutes. That's how long it took for my life to fall apart.

"So you'd say about, what, half an hour between when Kezia left your house after breakfast, and when you went out to go up the hill?"

"I saw her pass my house," Sam says without being asked. "Seems right. It was almost exactly an hour from the time she went up to the gun range to when she came down, and I invited her inside."

Prester gives him a slitted look, and Sam holds up his hands and sits back. But he's right. "Half an hour at the very most before I left the house," I tell Prester. "And Sam sees me on the road then. Look, none of this matters. Talk to Kezia. She spoke with my daughter."

"I'm not concerned with what she says right now. So. There's half an hour between when Officer Claremont last sees your kids and when you are next seen heading up to the gun range, alone. Does that sound right?"

"You think in half an hour I somehow slaughtered my kids and spirited them away, and went for a run without a single speck of blood on me?"

"I didn't say that."

"You don't need to say it!" I sit forward, hands on my knees, and stare at him with all the intensity that I have. I know it has to be a lot, but Prester doesn't back off. "I. Would. Never. Hurt. My. *Kids*." My voice breaks on that word, and my eyes blur, but I don't let it stop me. "I am not Melvin Royal. I'm not even Gina Royal. I am the person I had to be to save my kids from the people who wanted to hurt them *and still do*. If you want suspects, I'll give you the files. Maybe you can do something useful with them for a change!" I'd love to be able to throw the files at him, the vile pictures, the reams of paper full of deadly, violent words designed to kill my hope and peace. "It's all in my office. And talk to Melvin. He knows something about this. He has to know!"

"You think he's broken out of death row and somehow made his way all the way to Stillhouse Lake without a soul seeing him?"

"No. I think that Melvin has *people*. For all I know, he might have had a partner after all. They tried to put that on me, but it wasn't me. Maybe his real partner—" I stop, because I sound like I'm losing it, even to my own ears. Melvin Royal hadn't had a partner. He hadn't needed one. He was the king of his particular little, horrible kingdom, and I can't imagine him sharing it with anyone else. But followers? Yes. He would love to have followers. He thought of himself as charismatic, as influential as a cult leader. If he couldn't torment me on his own, he'd love to have someone else act as his puppet.

But Prester's already shaking his head. "Been checking out your ex," he tells me. "Man's on a real tight leash. No computer time at all. He gets a few books a month, some time with his lawyer, some letters but they all get checked ahead of time by prison officials. He gets some . . . I guess you could say fan mail from women, of the *he's not bad, he's just misunderstood* variety. One of them wants to marry him. He says he's thinking about it since—his words, not mine—his wife abandoned him."

"Can you check—"

"I already did," he heads me off. "Royal Wife Wannabe never left her home, which is in rural Alaska, of all places. She'd be almost as noticeable as Melvin if she made a move. Local cops say she's deranged but harmless about it. Kansas staties are already looking into the entire list of correspondents he has, and it's short."

"They're not catching it all. I don't know how he's getting his letters to me out, but he's doing it somehow."

"And we're looking into that. And the shooting at Mr. Cade's cabin. And the false officer down report. And the phone call you said you got. We've got a lot to sort right now, and we're doing it as fast as we can." He leans forward on his elbows. "I've got people looking into all your kids' friends, too. Couldn't find much in the way of social media—"

"You know why!"

"Yeah, I guess. But if you can think of anybody we need to talk to, you say it now. We need to get on every possible track, right now."

What he's not saying, I realize, are the odds. The harsh truth is that if my kids are alive, they probably won't be for long, especially not if they've been taken by someone with a grudge against me, or against Mel. Probably even less time if they were taken by the Stillhouse Lake killer. I flash back to the blood, and I feel suffocated again by the possibility of failure.

I'm still forgetting something. I can't grasp what it is. It's something I've seen, something that didn't make any difference, and now I can't slow my mind down enough to find that nagging, whispering, elusive *thing*. It's about Connor. Something about Connor. I close my eyes and see him, just as he was this morning: my serious kid, quiet, self-contained, charmingly nerdy.

Nerdy.

I try to chase that thought, but I can't; it shatters as Prester says, "I'm going to need for you to come down to the station. Lots to do here, and you can't be in the way. Mr. Cade, I'd like you to join us, too. Need some more information about this shooting situation."

I say something meaningless, an agreement of some kind, but I am not agreed. My mind is working fast, too fast, spinning out in a thousand different directions, and nothing makes sense anymore. But there is something I can do, I realize. Just one thing.

I ask for my phone back, and I text Absalom to say, **Someone has my kids. I don't know who. Please help.**

I hit "Send," not knowing if that is going out as a prayer into the darkness or a cry of despair. I can't be angry if he doesn't want to get involved; Absalom is a bottle thrown into the vast, dark ocean of the Internet, and the Internet, as I have good reason to know, is not a friendly place.

No reply comes. I ask Prester to wait, which he does, impatiently, for a solid five minutes, and then he takes the phone away and seals it into an evidence bag.

If it chimes again, I don't hear it, because it goes into a brown cardboard box, part of an inventory of evidence that will be taken back to Norton from the house. Not my home, not anymore. Just bricks and wood and steel, with a not-quite-finished deck. I regret not finishing it and sitting out there, at least one time, with Sam and the kids. Maybe I'd have one last happy memory of this place.

Sam offers his hand to me, and I stare at it without much understanding until I realize that Prester's waiting by the sedan. It's time to go.

I won't be back here, I think.

One way or another, it's not home.

◆ ◆ ◆

The interrogation room at the police department is wearily familiar, even down to the chipped corner. I work at it with a fingernail restlessly, waiting. Sam's been taken to another room—separate interviews, of course—and Kezia left us to go put on her uniform and join the rest of the force out on patrol, tracking down my children. I don't put much faith in the police, even though Prester's given me calm, logical talk about roadblocks and local knowledge and hiring up some of the finest tracking dogs around to get the scent out of Connor's bedroom.

I imagine all it will do is lead them to a place where a car once sat, or a truck, or a van. If parked at the right angles, I think, the van that Javier tried to sell me would be perfect for the purpose . . . angled in toward the front of the house, a sliding side door behind the passenger seat. Perfect cover to carry unconscious young bodies from the house out to the van, load them in, lock them down.

The dogs wouldn't take us to them. They'd only take us to where they'd been last, maybe to the road.

I hadn't noticed it until the car ride, but the heavy, humid air has finally turned dark overhead, clouds wisping and clumping and layering, and as I wait in the interrogation room, I hear the faint drumming of the beginning of rainfall. Rain, to wash away the scent tracks.

Rain, to wash away tracks and evidence and wipe it all clean, until the bodies of my children float slowly to the surface, breaking like pallid bubbles of flesh.

I put my face in my hands and try not to scream. At least I muffle it, but someone outside the door opens it and looks in, frowning, then closes it when they see I'm not bleeding or unconscious. I don't know how they'd have treated the parent of two other missing children, but Gina Royal? Gina Royal is a suspect first, last, always.

Prester takes his good time getting to me. When he finally does, the rain has intensified into a hissing storm on the roof, and although there are no windows, I can hear the distant booms of thunder rolling through the hills. It's distinctly cooler in here. Damp.

He's been out in the storm, that much is clear, because he's using a hand towel that has probably last been on a rack in their break room to wipe his face and hair, and dab the worst of the rain off his suit jacket. It patters down to make dark stars on the floor, and I think of the drops, the smears in Connor's room. Brown smears, brown drops now, surely. It no longer looks like what people expect when they think of blood.

Connor's blood is hours old, and I am sitting in this room, cold and shivering and desperate, and Prester is telling me that he hasn't found them yet. "We haven't found Javier Esparza, either," he tells me. "Sophie up at the range tells me he took a fishing trip."

"That's convenient."

"Not a crime, not up here. About ten percent of Norton's out camping, fishing, or hunting any given week. But we're looking hard. Got Fish and Game on it, checking campsites; we've asked Knoxville for a helicopter. Have to wait a bit for it to get free, but it's coming." He walks me through a map of the area around Stillhouse Lake, of the search parties, roadblocks, checks of every Stillhouse resident. I tell him about the Johansens in their shiny SUV, looking the other way while offering us up for a beating, or worse. My fists clench hard and press down, and I realize that where the edge of the wood is chipped, the hardened top surface is a little curled up, a little sharp. With work, someone could cut a wrist here.

"Can I leave?" I ask him quietly. He studies me over the top of the reading glasses he's put on to look at the map. He looks like a dry college professor, like the horrific abduction of my kids is some kind of academic puzzle. "I want to look for my children. Please."

"Rough conditions out there," he tells me. "Mud. Rain's coming down in buckets, makes it hard to see in those trees. Easy for someone to get turned around and lost, fall and break something, you name it. Right now it's best left to experts. Tomorrow maybe it'll be better. Easier going, and we'll have the chopper to help."

I can't honestly tell if he thinks he's being kind to me, or if he's just intent on holding me here as long as possible, in case any evidence comes back. I'm sitting now in different clothes; Kezia has retrieved a pair of jeans from my closet and a shirt, and with uncanny precision has chosen my least favorite things to wear. My other clothes—the hoodie, the shirt, the sweatpants, the running shoes and socks—all have been sent off to the lab for testing for, presumably, the blood of my children.

I want to scream again, but I don't think Prester would understand. And it won't do any good. If anything, it will let him keep me here even longer.

I just stare back, wanting to blink and somehow managing not to, and Prester finally sighs and sits back. He removes his glasses, dropping them on top of the map, and rubs his eyes. They're tired. He looks wrecked, his skin loose and drooping, as if the last few days have taken pounds and years off him. I'd feel sorry for him if I didn't feel worse.

"You can go," he tells me. "I can't keep you here. There's no evidence of anything except you being the victim of not one but two crimes today. I'm sorry, Ms. Proctor. I know that isn't much, but I really am. Don't know what I'd do if my girls were gone like this." I'm already out of my chair. "Wait a second. *Wait.*"

I don't want to. I stand there, vibrating, ready to leave, but Prester heaves himself up and leaves the room. He locks the door; I hear it engage. *Son of a bitch!* I'm ready to batter it down, but he isn't gone long. He comes back carrying . . . my backpack. And the evidence bag with my phone in it.

"Here," he says. "We already checked your gun and test-fired it. Sophie confirmed your timeline, and Officer Claremont's statement clears you as well. We cloned your phone."

He shouldn't have given me these things, I think; police don't release evidence, not so easily as all that. But I can see in his tired eyes that he's worried about my kids, and about me. He has good reason for both.

I take the backpack and sling it over my shoulder, then slip my phone out of the evidence bag and turn it on. I've still got decent battery on it, which is lucky, because I can't go back home for my charger. I slip it into the side pocket of the backpack.

"Thank you," I tell him, twisting the door handle. It opens without resistance, and though there's a police officer passing, he just gives me a look and moves on. Nobody steps in to block my path.

I turn and look back at Prester. He looks defeated. Frustrated.

"Get them to sand down that edge on the table," I tell him. "Somebody could open a vein with that thing."

He looks where I point and reaches over to run a finger across it.

Before he can say anything, if he intends to, I'm heading out through the bullpen. I grab the first detective I see—the young one who was holding Prester's coffee this morning—and ask where Sam Cade is. He tells me that Cade's out with one of the search teams, and I tell him I need a ride to join them. I can see by the look on his face that he's not here to be my taxi service.

"I'll take her," says a voice from behind me, and I turn to see Lancel Graham. He's not in his uniform; he's in a light flannel shirt, worn old jeans, hiking boots. He has at least a day's growth of heavy, blond beard. He looks like a Nordic travel poster. "I'm headed out there to join them. Gwen, sorry. I'd taken my boys out camping up on the mountain. Came back as soon as I heard about your kids. You okay?"

I swallow and nod, suddenly feeling wrecked by his sympathy, the steady way he's looking at me. Kindness is hard. The detective, who's not looking at me at all, as if I might infect him with Serial Killer Relative disease, seems relieved. "Yeah," he says to Graham. "You do that." They, I sense, are neither friends nor friendly. Graham doesn't spare the other man a glance, though. He leads the way out through the doors under the awning, and the sudden chill in the air surprises me. My breath puffs faintly white.

Rain falls in a shimmering silver curtain, kept at bay only by the roof above us that extends out in a blunt square. I can see red and green stoplights in the distance, and the glow of streetlights over the parking lot, but the details are watercolored. "Wait here," Graham says. He takes off into the rain at a jog. In about a minute he's back at the helm of a massive SUV, one that's seen rough road that even the current monsoon can't completely wash off. A dark gray or black. The orange-tinted streetlights make it difficult to judge.

He pops the front passenger door and I scramble in fast—not fast enough to avoid a torrent of cold water that slicks my hair and runs chilly fingers down my neck and back. My backpack slips to the floor and blends in with the darkness in the foot well. He's got the heater on, and I warm my hands in front of it, grateful for the consideration. "Where are we going?" I ask him. He puts the SUV in gear and as he does, the automatic feature pops the locks down with a harsh *snap*. I put my seat belt on. This vehicle rides far higher up than my Jeep; I feel like I'm on a double-decker bus. But I admit that the ride's smooth as he pulls out of the parking lot, into the rain-clogged, nearly deserted streets of Norton.

"You wanted to find Sam Cade, right?" Graham says. "I gave him a ride into the back country, up the hill from my house. Rough out there, though. He was joining up with a party that was going to work their way up. Might not be easy to catch up to him now; you sure you want to do that?"

I don't have anywhere else to go, and I certainly can't go back to that house, disfigured, broken, empty of those I love. I'm not dressed for the outdoors, especially not with the rain and cold, but I'm not going home. I think about calling Sam, but if he's out on the search, he might not hear his phone in this mess.

My backpack vibrates against my foot, and for a second I can't think why, until I remember I put the phone in there for protection against the rain. I lean forward and slip it out. The number's blocked, but I can't take the chance, so I answer. It's another troll. This one's masturbating while he tells me he's going to tear my skin off. I hang up on him. As I do, I see that I have two texts. Both from blocked numbers.

"Anything useful?" Graham asks me.

"No. That was a pervert getting off on tormenting me," I tell him. "That's what it's like, being the ex-wife of Melvin Royal. I'm not a person. I'm just a target."

"Rough," he says. "I've got to admit, you've got a lot of guts, the way you kept your family together and tried to move on. Couldn't have been easy."

"No," I tell him. My family isn't together. The ache of that hurts so badly it's hard to take the next breath against it. "Not easy."

"I'm a little surprised Prester let you keep that phone," Graham says. "Usually they want to keep it, monitor the calls at the station. Must have some kind of trace on it, I suppose."

"He said they cloned it. Maybe they can catch the assholes calling me."

While I'm saying that, I check the first text. It's from Absalom, because it has his peculiar little symbol at the end of it. It says U have a cop living close. I checked. Good resource.

That is a shock. Absalom's standard advice is *never trust a badge*.

I delete it. I was hoping desperately he had good intel on my kids, but instead, it's nothing I don't already know. It feels like he's checking out of our problems.

"This weather's too hard to be out there tonight," Graham tells me. "I'm going to turn around and go back to my house. You can stay on the couch tonight, join the search at first light. How's that?"

"No, I need—I need to be looking, if the search party's still out there. I'll manage."

Graham eyes me with a trace of a frown. "Not wearing that you won't. Those boots are all right, but you'll get hypothermic up there in an hour with what you have on, wet as it is. There's a coat behind your seat. You can wear that."

I put the phone down. I feel behind me on the floorboards and come across the silky fabric of a down jacket, one with a fur-edged hood. I pull it toward me, and as I do, the back of my hand skims over something smeared on the leather surface of the seat behind me—low, near the bottom. It feels tacky and slightly damp. I pull the coat free and dump it in my lap, and as I do, I see that my knuckles are smudged with what looks like grease. I reach for a tissue from the holder that sits in between us and wipe it off, and as I do, I think, *This doesn't feel like grease.*

As my hand comes closer, I catch a dark copper scent that is utterly unmistakable. That smear on the back of my hand is not grease at all.

We're out of Norton now, and Graham has his foot firmly on the gas, speeding faster than we should on these wet roads. The incline up to Stillhouse Lake is just a black screen with the lights firing raindrops and a gray, indistinct wash of road.

There is blood on the back of my hand.

The realization wipes me clear inside, light and clear and empty, and I think for a second or two that I might pass out from the enormity of it. Lancel Graham has blood in his SUV. And everything, *everything*, begins to make sense. I don't dare let that show.

I finish wiping my hand and ball up the tissue and stick it in my jeans pocket as I say, "You sure Kyle won't mind my taking this for a while?" It probably is his son's jacket. It has that peculiar adolescent boy smell. "I think he spilled something back there, by the way."

"Yeah, meant to clean that up; we hit a deer and I loaded the car- cass. Dumped it off at my house on the way to the station. Sorry,"

Graham says. "Listen, Kyle won't care about the coat. Keep it as long as you need it. He's got plenty."

He has such a nice voice. Layered, nuanced, friendly. He's got a ready explanation for the blood, but I don't feel anything either way now. I'm numb inside. I'm not really here anymore. I'm just a mind, putting together puzzle pieces, all the emotion blocked the way a blood vessel will clamp down to slow the blood loss. That's shock, I realize. I'm in shock. *Fine.* I can use it.

I remember him visiting the house, what seems an age ago, to return my son's phone . . . or a phone that looked just like it. Another burner could have been programmed with everything my son's phone contained—easy enough, since all he had in it were phone numbers and texts. It could have been cloned, just as Prester had demonstrated. The history copied over. Even the number replicated.

And what came back into our house could have been a *different phone*. A phone that could listen to us. A camera that could *see us* when left out. I thought about that phone sitting next to Connor's bed, learning about our habits, our patterns, what time Connor got up and went to bed. It might have been able to record the tones and figure out our passcode.

Though maybe that one had been the easiest of all. Maybe Officer Graham had simply watched me enter it that night when he first came over.

Something cracks inside me, just a little. I feel the first, violent pulse of panic as the shock begins to let go, as the bleeding starts. I close my eyes and try to keep thinking, because this?

This is the most important moment of my life.

The silence is heavy in the SUV; the excellent noise canceling dims the roar of the rain to a dull, monotonous hiss, like the screaming of distant stars. There are no other cars behind us on the road, no friendly, glaring headlights approaching. We might be the only two people alive in the world.

My phone buzzes again. I position the coat so it covers my phone, and read the second text. **We are at NPD where r u.**

It's from Sam Cade. He's not on the mountain, searching. This whole trip has been a lie.

My phone is on silent, so it makes no noise as I carefully, slowly, type my reply. **Graham has me.**

I am hitting "Send" when the truck lurches wildly sideways, and next thing I know, I'm being knocked hard against the passenger door. My phone goes flying, and from the last glimpse I have, I can't tell if the text sent or not. I grab for it.

Graham reaches for it at the same time, and as he does, he deliberately—I think—smashes it hard against one of the metal struts under the seat. The glass stars, obscuring the screen. The power sputters out.

"Shit!" he says, holding it up. Shakes it, as if he can magically reset it. It's excellent theater. He even looks concerned, and if I wasn't so terrified now, so *angry*, I'd have believed that, too. I try to slow the pounding of adrenaline into my bloodstream, because I don't need it now; I need to *think*. I need to plan before I can act. Let him think he's got me.

I have to kill this man. But first, I have to find out where he's taken my kids. So slowly, very slowly, I pull the weight of my backpack up. The hiss of the rain and road noise may disguise the sound of the zipper pulling. My hands are shaking badly from the terror and the rapid-fire pulse of my heart. I feel around inside the opening and touch fingers to the pebbled plastic of the gun case.

It's turned the wrong way. I need to move it to get access to the lock.

Lancel Graham is looking mournfully at the broken phone. "Goddamn it, I'm sorry about that. Look, they probably are getting copies of the calls at the station. Want me to check?" He doesn't wait for a response. He takes out his own cell phone and seems to make a call; the screen lights up. It looks legitimate, but for all I know, he's talking to a recording. "Hey, Kez—I just fucked up Ms. Proctor's cell phone.

Yeah, I know. Dropped it like an idiot, it's busted all to hell. Listen, are her calls being intercepted? Recorded?" He glances at me and smiles in what looks like real relief. "Good. That's good. Thanks, Kez." He thumbs it off. "No worries. They're monitoring the calls. Kez will call me if there's any news about your kids, okay?"

It's all pure theater. He damn sure hasn't called the police station.

The gun case is heavy inside the backpack. If I make too obvious a move, he'll punch me, and one solid hit from a man this size in close quarters might put me down. I have to control my fear. I *have to.*

I work to inch the case up and turn it sideways. It seems to take forever. I'm praying that Graham can't tell what I'm doing; the gloom's heavy in the car, and we're on a very dark road. But I can see him glancing over.

I've managed to turn the case, but this side is the hinges. I need two more turns to get to the lock, and I want to cry, I want to scream, I want to take the backpack and slam it into the side of his head, but there's no advantage to this, not now. Not here, on this deserted road, on this rainy night. I'm sure he's armed.

I'm sure his gun is far easier to reach than mine. If I don't keep control, if I react with pure emotion, *I will lose.*

I have to be better at this than a psychopath.

We make the turn for Stillhouse Lake. There are no boats out tonight; lights blaze in almost every house to keep away the dark, the monsters, as we pass. At the turnoff that leads to the Johansens' house, he takes a left up the hill. We pass their driveway, and I see the couple standing in their kitchen, glasses of red wine in their hands, talking as they carry plates to a dinner table. The cozy life of total strangers. That eerie postcard of normality is gone in the next instant.

We keep driving. I see Graham's house off to the right. It's genuinely country, a sprawling ranch house with no pretensions to elegance like the Johansens' modern, sharp-cornered glass monstrosity down the way. It's something generations have built onto, and you can see the differences in brick colors.

There's another SUV parked up front and a couple of trail bikes and one ATV. A medium-size boat on a tow, ready to be taken down to the lake. All the necessary trappings for a man living the lakefront dream.

We keep going past his house. Now the trail gets rough, the suspension bouncing and sloughing in mud as the gravel begins to run out. I've missed my shot. Somehow, I really thought he'd stop at his house, and my plans were to bail out, lose myself in the dark, and fire a shot or two into the Johansens' plate-glass windows. That would damn sure get them to call 911, even if they wouldn't let me in.

But he isn't stopping, and I turn the gun case again. Faster. Another blank side to my searching fingers.

"I dropped Sam off top of this ridge," he tells me. *Liar.* "The road goes that far, but then it's just game trails from there on. You wanted to catch up to them, right? This is the only way to do it. Sorry about the rough ride."

I'm well aware that this man is playing a game with me. His voice is warm and quiet and ever-so-slightly pleased. I can't tell in the ghostly glow of the dashboard light, but I think he's a bit flushed from his success. Enjoying himself, but trying not to show it. This is the part he likes, the part where he has control, where he's in charge and his prey doesn't even know how badly things have gone yet.

But I know.

I'm turning the gun case the last bit when suddenly we hit a huge bump, and the backpack jumps and I lose my grip entirely. *God. Oh God no.* This is going wrong. Very wrong.

Lancel Graham reaches down for the backpack, which has become wedged between us. He heaves it up and tosses it in the back seat without any comment at all. I can tell the game's starting to wear thin. I'm out of time. I'm out of time, *and I don't have a gun,* and my God, he's going to kill me and my children, and *he's going to get away with it.*

I need to act. Now.

"Does the search team have radios?" I ask him, reaching for his police band, which is tucked into the space between us. "We should probably find out exactly where—"

He grabs my hand, and for a second I think, *This is it,* and I start finding options. I calculate things in fractions of a second: he has one hand on the wheel, one holding my left hand. If I lean across, I can punch him as hard as I possibly can in the balls; his legs are relaxed and open, and it'll give me at least a minute or two. But then what? He's big, and I suspect he's fast. I don't know his pain tolerance, but I know mine. If he wants to stop me, he's going to be in the fight of his life. I need to disable him long enough to get my gun out of the backpack, put it together, and shoot until he *tells me where my kids are.* Then shoot him again until he is gone from the face of this earth.

There's a shotgun in the rack behind me. I see it from the corner of my eye, like a long metal exclamation point. I can also see the padlock shivering as the truck bounces. The shotgun is firmly locked in place. No help.

I'm ready to move, to let loose with everything I have, when Graham lets go of my hand and says, "Sorry, Gwen. It's just that the thing is police property. Can't let you use it on your own like that." It's just enough to stop me. He enters some code with his thumb and switches the radio on; the screen glows an unearthly blue, and he changes to a channel I don't see. "NPD search party two, do you read me? NPD search party two, looking for a location. Relay your coordinates."

It startles me that he's actually playing this out, and the fear inside me doesn't go away, but it's crowded by doubt. I don't know what the hell he's doing. I blink and draw back, adrenaline bubbling uselessly in my veins, shaking in my muscles. He lets the button go, and listens. Static like rain. The SUV hits a deep muddy patch, and he gives me an apologetic grin as he has to drop the radio to straighten the steering out.

"Weather sometimes plays hell with these things. Plus, the mountains aren't great for signals. You want to try? Go ahead."

I keep my eyes on him as I take the radio, press the switch, and repeat the words. "NPD search party two, do you read me? Relay coordinates of your location." I know what he's doing. He's playing with me, the way Mel played with his victims in that workshop. Testing me. Little cuts, to see me bleed. It's exciting to him.

There's no reply, of course. Only static. I glance at the glowing screen, then out the front window. The rain is obscuring everything, but I can tell that we're approaching the end of the road. Once we reach the ridge, we'll be far, far from anyone. Out here in the rain and the mud, nobody's going to come looking.

Just as he's planned.

I can't diagnose what's wrong with the radio. Could be that it's on the wrong channel, or that he's done something to the antenna. It's probably useless to me, useless to even try to—

My thought is derailed by a changing frequency of static, and a weak voice says, "NPD search party two, roger. Our coordinates are . . ." It fades out in a renewed wash of noise before I can catch more than two of the numbers. I forget my plans. I press the button.

"Say again, NPD search party two. Say again!" Is it possible, *somehow*, that I've misread all of this? That somehow, Graham is really telling the truth? It seems impossible, but I've been wrong, so wrong, so often these days.

Another burst of static. No discernible voice this time. I try again, and again, and when I look up the tilt of the vehicle is changing, and we are on the ridge at the end of the road.

Graham brings the truck to a stop under the overhanging branches of a giant tree; the drops that fall from the branches are thicker and more emphatic than the rain beyond, like sharp taps of a hammer. I hear them clearly as he shuts off the engine, pulls the parking brake, and turns toward me. I press the radio button again, but he takes the radio from my hand and turns it off. He puts it in the well between us. "No use," he says. "Like I said. Hard to get a signal."

He sounds amused, and I wasn't wrong, I was never wrong at all. Not about the blood. Not about his actions.

Not wrong about Lancel Graham.

I was never talking to a Norton Police Department search team.

"We're on our own here, Gina," he says. It sounds obscenely like a come-on. I want to scream. I want to punch him in the balls, but he's ready, I can tell he's ready, and *I'm not.*

"My name isn't Gina. It's Gwen," I say. "Which way did Sam go? I saw the map from Prester, was he taking the northeast route?" I try my door. As I feared, it won't open. Useless. Something dies inside me, that last hope of retreat. I have no choice now. I fight. And I'm scared out of my mind, alone, unarmed, against a much larger man.

I can't lose. Not for an instant.

"You don't want to do that," he tells me. "You'll just get lost out there, probably break your neck falling down a hill. Hey, I know. I'll call Sam direct. Maybe we can get through." He's still playing the game.

I'm not.

I pick up the radio and smash it into his temple with as much force as I can manage in the small space, and I can hear the scream that rips out of me. It's shatteringly loud in the cabin. My first hit rips a gash in his skin, and blood gushes out, and Lancel Graham screams and flails at the radio as I bash him again, and *again*, no control now, nothing but pure, glorious rage that makes me want to destroy him. The plastic casing splinters. I leave a thick fragment of it embedded in his cheek. He's dazed. I lunge past him to the door control on his side, the one I've been staring straight at, and I hear the heavy *thunk* as the locks disengage. As I draw back, I slam my fist straight down into his balls, and I see him go still as the pain rockets through him. His eyes fix on mine for the second I'm there, and then I'm moving on before I hear his howl.

I grab my backpack from the back seat.

I throw my door open and roll out, backpack and coat held tight.

His hand closes over the trailing end of the coat and yanks, and the cold mud under my feet gives, and I slide, off-balance, and panic bolts through me in painful sparks. I can't let him get his hands on me. I let go of the coat, catch myself on the door frame, and I *run*.

Because this time, I really will feel the monster's breath against my neck.

13

Once I'm in the open, the rain hits me like a cold knife, cutting straight through me, but I don't slow down. I'm panting, nearly blind with terror, but I push that back. I have to *think*.

I've hurt Graham, but I haven't stopped him. I don't know what weapons he has with him—a shotgun, probably a handgun, no doubt knives. I have my Sig Sauer and the scant remains of the ammunition I bought from the gun range. The loss of the coat, I realize, is deadly. The cold front that's pushing through has pulled the temperature down into the fifties, maybe the forties, and with the damp I can already feel the chill biting, though my fear and rage are coating me in their own special warmth. The mud leaves the ground slippery and uncertain, and I don't know these woods. I'm not native. I'm not military trained, like Sam, like Javier. I don't have a prayer.

I don't damn well care. *I will not lose.*

I make it to the thick line of undergrowth and thrash through it as fast as I can. I'm collecting cuts and bruises, and I know that running in the dark is a terribly stupid idea. I slow down, feel my way, and avoid impaling myself on a sharply broken branch. I touch it, and then I crouch down and open the backpack. I pull out my gun case and open it. I assemble my gun blind and check the mag. It's empty. I look for the extra rounds in the backpack and realize that the bastards at the NPD must have test-fired nearly everything I had.

I load everything into the clip. Seven bullets left. Just seven.

It only takes one, I tell myself. It's a lie, of course. I know it is. Adrenaline keeps people moving, keeps them dangerous, even when they ought to fall down.

But that works on my side, too. I am not going to lie down. I am not going to quit.

My fear is making me strong now. Alert. Weirdly steady.

A startling flash of white light blares, and I feel an electric hiss across the hair on my body, and then I hear the ear-shattering *boom* of the lightning strike. It's on the next hill, and instantly, a pine tree is aflame. Half of it topples away, trailing fire.

In the light of the flash, I see the dark shape of Graham coming through the undergrowth. He's only about ten feet away.

I have to move. He'll have seen me, too.

It's a nightmare lit by the distant, flaming tree: underbrush, tree trunks, rain, thick mud sliding underfoot and clinging hard to my boots and the legs of my jeans. I'm freezing, but I hardly feel it; my entire focus is on moving fast, as safely as possible. I don't know where Graham is. I can't risk a shot until I have a clear, unbroken line of sight. Panic shooting is stupid shooting.

And I can't kill him by accident. I need him alive. I need to know where my children are.

My job is harder than his, and weirdly, in this moment, I imagine Mel whispering to me, *You can do this. I made you stronger.*

I hate it, but he's right.

I'm halfway up a sloping, slippery trail when I feel the sting of buckshot. It's a hot spray across my left arm, like being hit by boiling water from a fire hose. The shock clamps down quick and sends me dodging, slipping, grabbing for tree trunks to hold myself upright. The sharp, bright smell of burned gunpowder cuts through the rain, and I think, in a kind of genuine surprise, *He hit me*. The logical part of my mind tells me it isn't bad; it was a glancing blow, not the full power of the shotgun. That would have torn my arm to ribbons. This is . . . inconvenience. I can still move my arm, still grip things. Everything else has to wait. The terror inside me threatens to make me swerve off the path, find a hiding spot and curl up and *die*, and I can't let it get control.

I hear something through the roar of the rain and the distant rumble of thunder.

Graham's laughing.

I slip behind a thick tree trunk and catch my breath, and as I look back I catch a lucky bolt of lightning that lights up the trail. He's not far behind me, and he throws up a hand to shield his eyes from the bright flash—and I realize he's wearing night vision.

He can see me running through the darkness.

I feel a wave of despair. I have seven bullets to his shotgun, no way to accurately sight my shots in this dark, soaking hell, and he has *night vision*. I feel it all slipping away from me. I'll never find my children. I'll die out here and rot on this mountain, and no one will ever know who killed me.

What steadies me again is a vision of what the Sicko Patrol will make of that fate. *Served her right, the bitch. Justice at last.*

I will never be their victory.

I wait while Graham closes the distance. If I'm going to shoot, I'm going to make it good. I can do this. Wait for the lightning flash to blind him again, step out, open up. He's a paper target on the range, *and I can do this*.

It all happens perfectly. The hot, blue-white flash of the lightning lights Graham perfectly, and I aim, smooth and calm now, and just before I squeeze the trigger, I feel the barrel of a shotgun press hard against my neck and hear Kyle Graham, the older son, yell, "I got her, Dad!" Surprise dulls the flush of panic, but I don't think. I just act.

I spin to my left, graceful and fast in the mud—finally, it's working for me—and sweep the barrel away with the edge of my hand, reversing as I go to take a good grip on the metal and twist. While that's in motion, I kick hard into Kyle's groin. I pull it at the last moment, remembering that I'm not fighting a man. He's a boy, just a boy about my daughter's age, and it's not his fault his father's a world-class psychopath any more than it's Lanny's fault she is Mel's child.

All this is still enough to shock Kyle. He chokes and staggers back, letting go of the shotgun. The weight of it drags at my wounded left arm. I jam the pistol into my jeans pocket, hoping to hell I don't shoot myself, and shove Kyle hard in the flat of his back. "Run or I'll kill you!" I scream at him, and the next flash shows him flailing through the underbrush, heading *up* the hill, not down. I wonder why, but I don't have time to think. I bring the shotgun up and spin toward where his father must be, and I pull the trigger.

The weapon's kick nearly knocks me on my ass in the slippery footing, but I manage to catch myself against the thick, moist bark of a pine. The photo-flash of the gun igniting showed me that I'd missed him. Not by much, though. Maybe I'd given him a couple of pellet kisses to remember me by.

"Bitch!" Graham yells. "Kyle! *Kyle!*"

"I let him go!" I shout back. "Where are my kids? What did you do to them?" I duck behind a tree in the darkness.

"You'll be with them soon, you fucking—" Though thunder mutes the sound of the gunshot, I feel the tree shiver slightly as it absorbs the pellets. I wonder how well armed he is. If I can get him to run out of ammunition . . . but no. Lancel Graham would have planned this as meticulously as everything else. I can't count on something so simple.

I realize in the flash of another lightning strike that I'm standing not far from another trail, one that branches off to the west. It seems to wander that way, and I think it slopes down. The lightning has picked up now, and I think it might be enough to lessen the effectiveness of

Graham's night vision equipment. He'll have trouble picking me out in all the flashes.

I go low, hoping that even if he spots me he'll think I'm a deer, and I make it to the point where the trail begins to curve down. If I can make it to the ridge, it's possible that Graham's one of those hide-a-key fools, and I can find a magnetic box in the wheel well that will let me steal the thing and get out of here, find help, *find my children*. He must have GPS. Maybe a record of where he's been.

I fall halfway down the trail, slide, and my head slams hard into a jutting boulder. Sparks and stars, and a wave of icy, tingling pain that makes everything strangely soft. I lie for a moment in the cold rain, gasping, spitting out water like a drowning victim. I'm cold. I'm *so cold*, and I wonder, suddenly, if I'm going to be able to get up. My head feels strange, *wrong*, and I know it's bleeding badly. I can feel the warmth running out of me.

No. I'm not dying here. I'm not. I don't know if Graham is still tracking me; I don't know anything except that I have to get up, cold or not, hurt or not. I have to get to the ridge and find a way to get help. Somehow. I will fucking shoot one of the Johansens' prize paintings if I need to, to make my point.

I slip and slide my way to my hands and knees, and I remember that I had a shotgun, but I can't find it now. It's gone, pitched into the darkness by my fall, and there's no way for me to find it now. I still have the pistol, which miraculously hasn't blown a big, devastating hole in my thigh. I take it out of my pocket and hold it tight as I get up and rest against the boulder. Blood is sheeting down the side of my face in a warm torrent that the rain dilutes almost instantly.

I slither down the trail, grabbing for handholds.

It's a nightmare that I can't escape, this descent, and I form the idea that Graham is right behind me, grinning and taunting me. Then Graham morphs into Mel, the Mel behind the Plexiglas at the prison, grinning at me with bloody teeth. It feels eerily true, but when I finally, breathlessly twist around, I find that the next flash of lightning shows me there's no one on the trail at all.

I'm alone.

And I'm nearly to the ridge.

As I get to the thick undergrowth that marks the place where the forest clears, something makes me stop and crouch down as I stare through the leaves. I'm aware of my heart beating fast, but it also feels sluggish, weary, as if it might take a nap at any moment. I must have lost more blood than I thought, and the cold is making my body work harder and harder. I'm shaking convulsively. It is, I know, the last step before false warmth sets in, and the urge to sleep. I don't have much time left. I need to get to the truck and get Kyle's coat. It'll help me for the next part: the run down the hill. Like it or not, I am going to have to depend on the Johansens for help.

A little flicker of movement by the truck freezes me in place. The rain is lessening a little, though the thick mutter of thunder overhead rolls almost continuously. The easing downpour lets me see a fraction of a curve that shouldn't be there, braced on the far side of the truck and protected by the solid wall of the engine block. It's a head, and it's too big to be Kyle's. Kyle ran up the hill, not down.

Lancel Graham is lying in wait. He's taken a classic ambush predator approach. Watching him, I remember the calm, offhand way that Melvin talked about his *process* in an interview a few years back: he'd crouch in just that spot by a car and wait for the woman to approach, then attack like a praying mantis in an overwhelming rush. It almost always worked.

Graham is a real fanboy. He knows my ex-husband's habits, his moves, his strategies.

But he doesn't know me. I survived Melvin.

I'm going to survive this asshole, too.

I'm not far from the original trail we took up the hill, and I work my way carefully around to it. I position myself exactly right.

I hit my mark, and then I hesitate. I'm cold. I'm slow. I'm confused from the head wound. *What if this doesn't work? What if he just shoots me?*

No. He's been hunting me to capture me, not just dispose of a problem. With the night vision he was wearing, he could have cut me in half already. He wants me.

He likes games.

All right, Lance. Let's play a game.

I come around a tree, limping, moving slowly; I make sure I look just as miserable and ill as I feel, and as I come into the opening right at the trail head, I brace myself and slide down to my knees. Weak. Beaten.

In just the right place.

I don't look up to see where he is. I just wait, breathing heavily. I try to get up, but not very hard, and then I let myself fall over, left side down in the mud. The pistol's beneath me, concealed where I've rolled forward enough to shade it. It looks like I'm trying to find the strength to rise.

I wait.

I can't hear him coming over the steady, slowing drum of the rain, but I sense him, almost like a heat source on the edge of my awareness. He's careful. He circles at a distance. I can dimly see him through my eyelashes, smeared by the rain. He's got the shotgun. He circles closer. Closer.

And then he's there.

I see the muddy toes of his boots edge in closer and the hem of his mud-caked jeans. The barrel of the shotgun is aimed not at me but at the ground between the two of us. He can still kill me. It's a small movement to bring the muzzle up and fire, but he's enjoying this. He likes seeing me beaten.

"Stupid, stupid woman," he tells me. "He said you'd fall for this shit." Graham's voice hardens. Sharpens. "Get your worthless ass up, and I'll take you to your kids."

Random thought: I wonder where Graham's wife is. I feel an overwhelming surge of pity for his sons, raised by this man. But it's all fleeting, because underneath that, I feel as cold and hard as the barrel of that shotgun. As much of a weapon.

Because I'm not dying here.

I'm not.

I don't move much, and I make myself look weak, flailing, like I'm trying to obey him. I move my right hand and lift myself up to my knees, and as I come up I smoothly, calmly raise the gun.

He sees his mistake just before I fire.

It's precise, where I put the bullet. I don't go for the head shot, or even for center mass. I go for the nerve plexus in Graham's right shoulder. He's a right-hander, like me.

The bullet—a hollow point—goes in exactly where I want it. I can almost see the way it opens up on impact into a flesh-cutting scythe of destruction. It'll destroy his shoulder, sever nerves, break bones. A shoulder wound isn't the clean, simple thing they show in the movies and on television; you don't walk it off. Done right, a shoulder wound can take away use of that arm forever.

And I've done it right.

Graham's cry is short and sharp. He staggers back and tries to bring up the shotgun, and shock would have allowed for that except that I'd destroyed nerve and muscle necessary to make the physics work. He drops it instead and blindly fumbles for it with fingers that are no longer capable of picking it up. He's hurt, and hurt bad, but one thing about shoulder wounds that the silver screen gets right: it's probably not fatal.

Not immediately, anyway.

I roll to my feet. I feel warm now. Loose and calm, the way I do at the range. Graham keeps trying to pick up the shotgun until I pull it away, and then he gives me a weird, tired grin. "You fucking bitch," he says. "You were supposed to be easy."

"Gina Royal was easy," I tell him. "Tell me where they are."

"Fuck you."

"I let your boy go. I could have killed him."

That registers a little. I see something move in his expression. It's just a twitch, but it's real.

"I'll let you live if you tell me where my kids are. I don't want you dead."

"*Fuck. You.* They aren't yours. They're *his*. And he wants them back. He needs them. This isn't about you, *Gina*."

"Okay," I tell him. I take a step to my right, and he takes a wary step the same direction, keeping in front of me. I do it again, and again, until I'm the one with my back to the ridge, and he's got his back to the trail. "We do this the hard way."

He doesn't expect it when I step forward and push him, and he's clumsy with shock, slow to react. I'd never have tried it if he weren't already wounded, but it works perfectly. Graham staggers backward, and he screams. His feet go out from under him, and his weight falls back, and I see the bloody, sharp point of the branch I'd nearly impaled myself on earlier punch through him, at just about the level of his liver. Not an immediately fatal wound, but serious. Very serious. He flails and breaks the branch off. The mud doesn't do him any favors. He falls. He tries to grab the wood and pull it out, but there isn't much that's sticking out, and his right hand won't work properly.

"Get it out! Get it out!" His voice has gone high and desperate. "Jesus *Christ!*"

The rain's almost stopped now. He's writhing in the mud, fingers brushing that ugly, sharp point that's soaked with his blood, and I crouch down and put my gun to his head.

"Jesus doesn't like it when you take his name in vain," I tell him. "And that didn't sound like a prayer. Tell me where my children are, and I'll get you help. If you don't, I'll leave you here. These woods have black bear, cougars, wild hogs. Won't take them long to find you."

My arm hurts so bad now. It feels like it's been set on fire. I keep it steady despite that, because I must. Any show of weakness will be fatal.

His face has gone starkly pale, luminous in the dark. I take the truck keys from his pocket. He has a hunting knife in a case, and I take it, too. I search in his pockets for his phone. It needs a thumbprint to unlock, and I take his wildly shaking right hand to press it in place. It doesn't work the first two tries as he tries to jerk away, but finally it's ready to use.

"Last chance," I tell him as I pick up the shotgun. "Tell me where they are and I'll save your life."

His mouth opens, and I think for a second that he *is* going to tell me. He's scared, suddenly. Vulnerable. But he closes it again without speaking and just looks at me, and I wonder what has made him so afraid. Me? No.

Melvin.

"Mel doesn't care if you live or die," I tell him. I mean it almost compassionately. "Tell me. I can save you."

I see the moment he breaks. The moment his fantasy disappears and the cold truth of his situation really hits him. Melvin Royal won't be coming for him. No one will. If I leave him here, he'll die of blood loss, and the animals will tear him apart—or, if he's not lucky, the order of that could be reversed. Nature's brutal.

So am I, when I have to be.

"There's a hunting cabin," he tells me. "Up mountain. Belonged to my grandfather. They're in it." He licks very pale lips. "My boys are watching them."

"You son of a bitch. They're all just *children*."

He doesn't answer that. I feel a surge of rage and weariness, and I just want this to be done. I turn away and make my way through the clinging mud toward the truck. He tries to get up, of course, but between the shoulder wound and that stab through the liver, he isn't going anywhere. The cold will help keep him alive for now; it'll slow blood loss. But as I climb into the truck and start it up, I scroll through the call list, looking for Kezia Claremont's number.

I stop on the *A* list of names, because right there at the top is one I recognize. It isn't common. I've never seen it before, except in the Bible.

Absalom.

It sinks in on me, then, the magnitude of the deception. The game. Absalom, the troll who'd become my constant ally. Absalom, who took my money and made my new identities. Who could locate me at a moment's notice, anywhere I ran. Could *direct me where he wanted me to go.*

It explained why we'd been looking the wrong way. Lancel Graham's family had been here for generations. His Stillhouse Lake home was a family heirloom, and Kezia and I had marked him off the list immediately as not a suspect. *Hell.* I'd even sent Absalom names to check out. He must have found it hilarious.

He's never been helping me. He's been helping Melvin all this time, moving me like a chess piece, setting me up, knocking me down.

Putting me in the backyard of his copycat fanboy.

I have to close my eyes for a moment to contain the incandescent rage that burns through me, but then I keep scrolling. I find Kezia's phone number, and I dial.

There are only two bars of connection, but the call completes. She's in a car. I can hear the engine noise just before she says, carefully, "Lance? Lance, *I know*. You need to let that woman go, right now, and tell me where you are. Lance, listen to me, okay? We can make this right. You know that needs to happen. Talk to me."

I'd been afraid that she was part of it, too, but I hear the tense anger in her voice, though she's trying to hold it back. She's trying to talk him down.

She's trying to save me.

"It's me," I say. "It's Gwen."

"Jesus!" I hear a confusion of noise, like she's nearly dropped the phone. I also hear another voice, male, but I can't make out what he's saying. "Jesus, Gwen, where are you? Where the hell are you?"

"Up on the ridge past Graham's house. We need an ambulance up here," I tell her. "He's shot, and he has a stab wound in his side. I need police. He told me my kids are up in his grandfather's cabin. Do you know where it is?"

I'm shivering so hard my teeth are clacking together. The truck's engine has warmed a little, and the blast of the heater feels fantastic. I drag Kyle's down jacket over and put it over my shoulders. My left arm still burns, but when I look at it in the overhead light, I find the pellets haven't gone deep enough to do real damage. The wound to my head, though . . . I feel sick and weak and dizzy. The bleeding hasn't stopped. I reach up and feel the pulse of warm, watery blood coming from the slash in my scalp, and fumble for tissues to press against it. I almost miss Kezia's reply.

No, it isn't Kezia. It's Sam. He's in the car with her. "Gwen, are you all right? Gwen?"

"I'm okay," I lie. "My kids. Graham's boys are at that cabin, too. I don't know if they're armed, but—"

"Don't you worry about that. We're coming to you right now, okay?"

"Graham needs an ambulance."

"Fuck Graham," he says, and I hear the vicious edge in his voice. "What about you?"

The tissues I've pressed to my wound are already a sodden mess. "I might need stitches," I say. "Sam?"

"I'm here."

"Please. Please help me get the kids."

"They're going to be okay. We'll get them. You just stay there. Hang on. Kez has the location of the cabin. We're coming to you. It's all coming straight to you."

Kezia's driving, and I've been in the car with her; she's using police tactics, driving with controlled wildness and tremendous speed. I look in the rearview mirror. I can see the headlights of a police cruiser swerving and speeding down the main road. I see them turn at the Johansens' cutoff.

Sam's still talking, but I'm tired. The phone rests on my leg, though I'm not sure when I put it down. My aching, pulsing head is leaning against the window glass. I'm not shivering anymore.

I say, *Get my kids*, or at least I think it, before everything goes very, very dark.

14

"Gwen? My God."

I open my eyes. Sam is crouched beside me, and he looks . . . odd. He turns and says, "I need that first-aid kit!"

Kezia is right behind him, and she dumps a large red bag beside him. He rips open the Velcro top and searches inside.

"What are you doing?" I ask him. I'm not clear. I'm definitely not, but I've stopped hurting, mostly. Amazing what a little sleep will do. "I'm okay."

"No, you're not. Quiet." He takes a thick pad of bandages and presses them tight to my head, and the pain comes back in a sullen roar. "Can you hold that for me? Hold it." He presses my hand to the pad, and I manage to do as he says while he breaks out more bandages and wraps everything in place. "How much blood did you lose?"

"Lots," I tell him. "Doesn't matter. Where's the cabin?"

"You are not going to the cabin." I fumble for my gun. He effortlessly takes it away, empties the chamber and strips the mag in one move, then tosses the pieces in the back seat of the SUV. "You are not going anywhere but to the hospital. You need x-rays on that skull. I don't like the look of that. You could have a depressed fracture."

"I don't care. I'm going." And I will, in a minute. It seems a monumental effort to get out of the truck right now. "Did you get my text?"

He gives me an odd look. "When?"

"Never mind." Graham was successful in that. He'd managed to break my phone before the text got sent. "How did you figure out he was bad?"

"He didn't show up for the search," Sam tells me. He's busy checking my eyes with a penlight, which is annoying and painful, and I try to bat him away. "Kez did a little digging. Turns out he'd been gone a full day off work during the time of each abduction, and again on the days we figure he disposed of the bodies. She'd been having a feeling about him for a while. When we found out he showed up at the station and gave you a ride—"

"Thanks," I tell him. He looks set and grimly angry.

"Yeah, not like we got here in time to do much good rescuing you."

I still one of his hands that's probing my neck for injuries and hang on to it. "Sam. Thank you."

We look at each other for a few seconds, and then he nods and continues his evaluation.

Kezia's gone to check on Graham. She comes back and takes the first-aid kit, and soon after that I see the flashing signals of the ambulance. Out here in the sticks, the ambulance comes with four-wheel drive, which allows it to pull up past the truck and toward the trail head, where I see Kezia tending to Graham in the wash of the headlights.

"Do you know where the cabin is?" I ask Sam. He's found the pellets in my left arm. "Please. I need to know. I'm fine, Sam, leave it."

"You're not."

"Sam!"

He sighs and sits back, hands on his thighs. "It's a long hike up, and you aren't up to it."

"I told you. I'm all right. Look." I force myself into high gear, and I step out of the truck. I'm steady. I hold my hands out. No shakes. "See?"

I'm a little shocked when he pulls me into a hug, but it feels good. It feels safe. I've trusted all the wrong people, and I've pushed away all the right ones, and this upends everything I thought I knew about myself.

"You're not okay, but I know you have to do this," he says. "I know you'll do it without me."

"Damn right I will," I tell him. "Give me back my gun."

He doesn't like it. He kisses me on the forehead, just below where the bandages are wrapped, and checks to make sure they're secure. Then he ducks in the back, puts the spare bullet in the mag, slaps my Sig together, and hands it to me. I slide it in the pocket.

The paramedics are working on Lancel Graham, but Kezia has left them to it, and she comes back to us. She has on her uniform under a thick coat, and her gun strapped to her hip. She passes us and heads to her cruiser, where she opens up the trunk and takes out two bulletproof vests. She puts one over her head and carries the other over to us. She hands it to Sam.

Sam puts it on me. When I start to protest, he shakes his head. "No. Just no." I let it pass. He and Kez get shotguns from the cruiser, and she has a supply kit that she slings over her head bandolier-style. Stuffed, I would bet, with survival supplies and ammunition.

Kezia goes back to talk to the paramedics, then takes out her phone and makes a call. When she returns to us, she says, "Prester's got backup coming, but it'll be a while for all the search parties to come back in and get over to us."

"He said to go ahead?" Sam asks.

She gives him arched eyebrows. "Hell no, he didn't. He said wait. You want to wait?"

He shakes his head.

I say, "Which way is it?"

◆ ◆ ◆

Sam's right, I'm not up to it, but that doesn't matter. I don't let my increasing dizziness slow me down, though Sam keeps a watchful eye on me. I feel smothered under the weight of the bulletproof vest strapped on under the down jacket; it's hot, and I'm sweating freely now. The night is still cold. My body's running at redline levels just to keep me moving up the hill.

Kezia is as surefooted as a cougar as she leads us up the trail—not the one I'd taken earlier, but the one I'd come slipping down. We pass the rock where I hit my head, and her flashlight shines on the wet, red glisten of my blood. There's a lot of it. She doesn't say anything. Neither does Sam, but he moves a step closer as we hike up.

The trail breaks off to the northwest, still wandering upward. The lightning has stopped now, and the rain, too, but there's a wind kicking up through the trees that sways the pines overhead in a whispering dance. I find myself wanting to look behind me, in case Lancel Graham is creeping up. *Graham's in the hospital. He'll be lucky if they can save his damn liver.* But that doesn't stop me from imagining the horror show. Once, I see him.

I'm starting to hallucinate. I can hear someone crying. Lanny. I can hear my daughter crying, and it makes me thin and raw inside, and I turn to Sam. The question is almost on my lips, *do you hear that*, but I know he doesn't.

I'm losing control.

We come out half an hour later on a thin, slender shelf clear of trees. There's a tiny shack of a cabin squatting in the overhang of a rock ridge. It'd be almost invisible from overhead. You had to know this thing was here to find it at all, and it's old. Repairs have been made, but there's something old-time country about the construction.

Kezia lights it up with her flashlight in a blue-white glare. "Kyle and Lee Graham! Come on out right now! This is Officer Claremont!" She has a commanding voice, like a teacher calling out students for bad behavior, and I think it would have worked on me at that age.

There's a flutter of movement at a curtained window, and then the door cracks and a boy yells, "Where's my dad?"

Kezia steps forward and motions the two of us to stay back. "Lee? Lee, you know me. Your dad's okay. He's on the way to the hospital. You come on out now. Look, I'm putting my gun away, okay? You come on out."

The younger Graham boy slips out. He's wearing a coat too big for him, and he looks pale and scared. "I didn't want to," he says in a rush. "I didn't! I don't want to get in trouble!"

"You won't, honey, you won't. You come on here." Kezia motions him forward, and once he's to her, she gestures to Sam, who comes forward, takes the boy by the elbow, and half drags him to where I stand. Lee opens his mouth to protest. I put a hand on his shoulder and crouch down to look him in the eye.

"Are my kids in there?" I ask him.

He finally nods. "It wasn't my fault," he tells me. "I told Kyle we shouldn't have. But—"

"But you can't say no to your dad," I say, and I see the relief spread over his face. The trauma. And even though he stood between me and my own children, I want to hug him. I don't, but I feel how lost he is. "I understand. It'll be okay. You just stay right here. Sit down and don't move."

Kezia's moved a little closer. "Kyle! Kyle, you need to *come out*. Can you hear me? Kyle?"

I turn to Lee, who's hunched in on himself now, not looking at the cabin or anybody. "Lee. Is your brother armed?"

"He has a rifle," he says. "Don't hurt him! He's just doing what Dad told him!"

I think that it's more than that. Lance Graham had trusted Kyle to sneak up on me in the dark. I wonder if Kyle has helped his father with anything else. He's big for his age, and handsome. He could have been a real asset in distracting a young woman before an abduction. I picture him going up to that girl in the parking lot of the bakery. Leading her off to his dad's SUV.

It makes me feel a spasm of disgust so strong it's like nausea.

I tell Kezia that Kyle has a rifle, and she nods grimly. She's already eased her gun out of its holster. "Get Sam to go around back. I don't want Kyle having another way out of this. You stay here with the boy."

Sam's already on it, I see. He moves around the cabin, between it and the rock face; I hope there aren't sleeping snakes back there, or worse. He doesn't come back, so I assume there is a door. I assume he's covering it.

I tell Kezia, "I'm going in."

"No, you're not!" she says. She reaches out, but I'm already gone, walking straight for the door. I can see the curtain move. Kyle's watching me. I wonder academically if a rifle bullet will go through this vest; it might, at this range. Depends on the caliber and the grain.

I have my Sig out of my pocket, and I hold it down, finger off the trigger, as I try the door. It opens. Kyle hasn't thought to lock it after his brother left.

Inside, it's very dark except for a single, guttering candle that sits on a rough table at the back of the room. The bitter, uncertain light flickers over Kyle, sitting on a bunk near the window. He has his rifle aimed straight at me.

There's no one else in the cabin. *No one.* This is straight up a trap.

I turn and yell, dodging out the door, and Kyle's shot misses me by fractions. I am moving toward Kezia, and behind her, I see Lee has moved from where I left him at the tree line. He's now standing in a perfectly learned shooting stance. He has a handgun that he's pulled from his pocket because *I didn't search him, he was just a boy*, and he's pointing it at Kezia's back.

"Lee!" I scream, bringing my gun up. "Don't do it!"

He's startled, and his shot goes wide. Just barely wide. It shatters the window of the cabin, and Kezia turns low and fast. She advances on him with a stunning volley of shouts to *drop the gun drop the gun* and he does, convulsively throwing it away, and I spin back toward the cabin because Kyle is still in there, armed, and *where are my children, God, please . . .*

Kyle throws open the door and aims the rifle straight at my face. I have time to react, to shoot, but I don't. I can't. He's a child. He's a stunted, twisted child, but *I can't.*

Sam tackles him from behind and drives him facedown into the mud. The rifle slides away, and Kyle fights, screaming, to get to it. Kezia has snapped handcuffs around his brother Lee's wrists, and she sits the boy down hard and takes out another pair. She lets out a shrill whistle, and Sam looks up. She pitches, and he plucks them out of the air and restrains him. He hauls the boy up and makes him kneel with his face against the cabin's wall.

I can't breathe for the terror pounding through me. Not from the near-miss. Not from Kyle and Lee.

My kids have to be here. *They have to be here.*

I run back into the cabin. It's tiny, barely big enough for a cot, a small table, a thick fleece rug, the open back door . . .

I kick the rug away and uncover a trapdoor.

I take the candle from the table and pull the handle on the trapdoor, and the cold, moist air that glides out makes the flame shiver uneasily. I wish for Kezia's powerful little flashlight, but only for a second. There's a wooden ladder leading down.

I go.

My arm doesn't like the strain, but I hardly notice the pain now. I still feel sick and dizzy, but it's not important, nothing is important but what I will find here, under the earth.

What I find is hell.

◆　◆　◆

I step into the past.

There, ahead of me as I turn from the ladder, is a metal stand with a winch attachment. The thick cable hanging from it ends in a loop.

A noose.

It's the same as the one in Melvin's garage. But it isn't just that. I recognize the tool shelves to the right, filled with parts, drills, vises. I recognize the red tool drawers that form a line across the top of a workbench.

As I turn back toward the ladder, I recognize the pegboard that's been set up behind it, heavy with saws, knives, screwdrivers, hammers. There's a tray to the side with medical equipment. Another that has a hunter's tools to flay the skin.

And my gaze falls on the last, perfect addition: the rug. It's the same style of rug that Melvin kept right below his victims, an incongruous little middle-class detail in a torture chamber.

Graham has re-created Melvin's killing floor down to the last, obsessive detail.

The smell of this place makes me reel and put my shoulders against the ladder, because *I know this smell.* It had rolled out of my Wichita garage, spoiled meat and old blood and the metallic stench of terror, and it is here, in this place. Exactly the same.

I can't help it. I scream. I scream the names of my children as my heart breaks and my mind snaps and all I want to do is die.

Graham never meant for them to live. He only meant for me to see *this*.

I'm still holding the Sig, and for a terrible, beautiful moment of clarity, I think how perfect it is that I'm going to die here, in the same way that Gina Royal withered away and perished. Looking at the same horrors. Feeling the same sense of complete loss.

And then I hear my son say, "Mom?"

It's a whisper, but it is as loud as a shout, and I drop the gun, drop it like it's on fire, and I scramble on all fours across the floor, the rug, around the hulking horror of that winch, and behind it, *behind it*, I see the barred grate set into the false wall. It's padlocked. I stumble back to the tools and rip a crowbar out of the pegboard with such force I send things flying and clattering, and I run back to the door. I jam the forked end under the hasp and yank. Wood splinters. Gives. The hasp tears free.

I use the crowbar to lever the door, and inside I see Connor, I see Lanny. They are alive, *alive*, and all the strength leaves me in that moment and I crash to my knees as they rush toward me and throw themselves on me as if they want to disappear inside me.

Oh God, it's so beautiful. The relief hurts, but it's the hurt of a wound being cauterized, all the bleeding stopped.

I am still rocking my children back and forth on the floor of this hell when Kezia and Sam find me. Both are breathless, braced for the worst. I see Sam's face and I think, *My God,* because he has just walked through a shrine to the place where his sister suffered and died, and I can only imagine how hard this has been, to take these steps past that winch and reach us.

But we're alive.

We're all alive.

15

The blood in my house, I find, was from Kyle. And it was Lanny's doing.

"I heard them fighting," she tells me, once we're outside again in the clean night air. Kyle and Lee Graham are both tightly handcuffed, and Kezia has fastened them to a hook set into the cabin's wall. I can't imagine what it's for. I don't want to. "I grabbed the knife and I came in and I cut him. Kyle, I mean. I would have got him, too, if his damn dad hadn't been with him. I got us to the panic room just like you taught us, but he knew the code. I'm sorry, Mom. I let you down—"

"No, I did." Connor's voice is a bare whisper, almost pulled away by the wind. "The code was in my phone. I should have said so. You could have changed it."

It all fits together now. Connor's phone, taken from him by Graham's kids. I remember my son's hesitance the night Graham brought the phone back, how Connor had *almost* told me something important. He hadn't wanted to make me mad, because I'd told him over and over again not to write the codes down.

I can't let him believe this is his fault. Ever.

"No, baby," I tell him. I kiss his forehead. "It doesn't matter. I'm so proud of you both. You stayed alive. Right now, that's what matters, okay? We're alive."

Kezia's got foil blankets in her survival kit, and I wrap the kids up to preserve their body heat. They're bruised. They took a beating in the fight. I ask if there's anything they want to tell me about what happened at the cabin. Lanny says nothing happened. Connor says nothing at all.

I wonder if my daughter is lying to me.

We sit in the clearing. Backup finally arrives in a swarm of NPD uniforms, and I see Javier Esparza's there, too. He nods to me, and I nod back. I doubted him. I never should have.

Detective Prester himself has made the climb; he's still got a suit that's never going to survive this mud, but he's thrown on a heavy pea jacket. He comes immediately to us, and I see something new in his face.

Respect.

"I owe you one hell of an apology, Ms. Proctor," he says. "They okay?"

"Time will tell," I say. "I think so." I don't know, but I have to believe they will be. It's going to be hard. They'll have questions. I can't imagine what Lancel Graham told them about their father. I think that, more than any other trauma, is what keeps my son mute.

Prester nods and sighs. He doesn't look like he wants to go down into that basement, but I imagine he's seen worse. "Kezia says you have Graham's phone. I'll need that for evidence, and anything else you took."

"I left most of that stuff in his truck," I say. "The gun's mine." I've retrieved it from the floor of the basement; I don't need more complications. "Here." I dig the phone out of my pocket.

The screen is on. I pushed the button accidentally. It's just the lock screen, and without Graham's thumbprint or code I can't unlock it, but what freezes me is the text message that's appeared on the screen.

It's from Absalom, and it says, **He wants an update.**

I show it to Prester. He doesn't seem surprised. "Who's Absalom?"

I tell him about my hacker benefactor. My ally, who's been selling me out the entire time. I don't know how to find Absalom, and I tell him that, too. I hold out the phone and say, "My turn. Who do you think Absalom is talking about?"

Prester takes an evidence bag from his pocket, and I slip it in. He seals it before he answers. "I think you can guess."

I don't want to say his name, either. It's almost like saying the name of the devil. I'm afraid he will appear.

Prester's expression has turned darker now, and I don't like the way he keeps watching me, tentative and thoughtful. Like he's trying to decide if I'm strong enough to stand what he's got in mind.

So I say, "You have something to tell me." I'm not afraid of anything anymore. My children are with me. Safe. Lancel Graham isn't going anywhere. It's possible his sons can be saved, unless his particular psychopathy is inherited.

Prester gestures me off to the side. I don't want to let go of Lanny and Connor, but I do take a few steps away and position myself to watch them. I know this is something he doesn't want them to hear.

But I'm still not afraid.

"There was a well-coordinated breakout from El Dorado. Seventeen prisoners. Nine of them are already in custody. But—"

He doesn't even have to say it. I know, with the sick inevitability of fate, what he's going to tell me. "But Melvin Royal is loose," I say.

He looks away. I don't know what I'm feeling, or what he's seeing in me. But I do know one thing.

I'm not afraid of Mel anymore.

I'm going to kill him. One way or the other, it ends the way it began so long ago: with the two of us.

The Royals.

SOUNDTRACK

I choose music for each book I write, to help guide me through the intense process, and *Stillhouse Lake* presented an interesting exercise in finding just the right groove to help propel Gwen through this tense story.

I hope you enjoy the musical experience as much as I did, and please remember: piracy hurts musicians, and music aggregation services don't provide a living. Buying the song or album direct is still the best way to show your love, and to help artists create new work.

- "I Don't Care Anymore," Hellyeah
- "Ballad of a Prodigal Son," Lincoln Durham
- "Battleflag," Lo Fidelity Allstars
- "How You Like Me Now (Raffertie Remix)," The Heavy
- "Black Honey," Thrice
- "Bourbon Street," Jeff Tuohy
- "Cellophane," Sara Jackson-Holman
- "Drive," Joe Bonamassa
- "Fake It," Bastille
- "Heathens," twenty one pilots
- "Jekyll and Hyde," Five Finger Death Punch

- "Lovers End," The Birthday Massacre
- "Meth Lab Zoso Sticker," 7Horse
- "Bad Reputation," Joan Jett
- "Peace," Apocalyptica
- "Send Them Off!," Bastille
- "Tainted Love," Marilyn Manson
- "Take It All," Pop Evil

ACKNOWLEDGMENTS

As usual, this book wouldn't have been written without the support of my husband, R. Cat Conrad; my wonderful assistant and sanity reader, Sarah Weiss-Simpson; and my long-suffering, awesome editors, Tiffany Martin and Liz Pearsons.

Special shout-out to my friend Kelley and the rest of the Time Turners for constant encouragement and support.

ABOUT THE AUTHOR

Photo © 2014 Robert Hart

Rachel Caine is the #1 internationally bestselling author of more than fifty novels, including the *New York Times* bestselling Morganville Vampires and The Great Library young adult series. She's written suspense, mystery, paranormal suspense, urban fantasy, science fiction, and paranormal young adult fiction. Caine and her husband, award-winning artist, comic historian, and actor R. Cat Conrad, live in Fort Worth, Texas.